PRIZE STORIES 1977
The O. Henry Awards

PRIZE STORIES 1977

The O. Henry Awards

EDITED AND WITH AN INTRODUCTION BY

WILLIAM ABRAHAMS

DOUBLEDAY & COMPANY, INC., GARDEN CITY, NEW YORK, 1977

THE LIBRARY OF CONGRESS CATALOGED THE FIRST ISSUE OF THIS TITLE AS
FOLLOWS: PRIZE STORIES. THE O. HENRY AWARDS, 1919–   GARDEN CITY,
N.Y., DOUBLEDAY [ETC.] V. 21 CM. TITLE VARIES: 1919–46, O. HENRY
MEMORIAL AWARD PRIZE STORIES. STORIES FOR 1919–27 WERE "CHOSEN BY
THE SOCIETY OF ARTS AND SCIENCES." EDITORS: 1919–32, B. C. WILLIAMS.—
1933–40, HARRY HANSEN.—1941– HERSCHEL BRICKELL (WITH MURIEL
FULLER, 19 –46). 1. SHORT STORIES. I. WILLIAMS, BLANCHE COLTON,
1879–1944, ED. II. HANSEN, HARRY, 1884– ED. III. BRICKELL, HERSCHEL,
1889– ED. IV. SOCIETY OF ARTS AND SCIENCES, NEW YORK. PZ1.O11
813.5082   21–9372 REV 3*

ISBN: 0-385-11673-x
Library of Congress Catalog Card Number 21–9372

Contents

PUBLISHER'S NOTE

THIS VOLUME is the fifty-seventh in the O. Henry Memorial Award series.

In 1918, the Society of Arts and Sciences met to vote upon a monument to the master of the short story, O. Henry. They decided that this memorial should be in the form of two prizes for the best short stories published by American authors in American magazines during the year 1919. From this beginning, the memorial developed into an annual anthology of outstanding short stories by American authors, published, with the exception of the years 1952 and 1953, by Doubleday & Company, Inc.

Blanche Colton Williams, one of the founders of the awards, was editor from 1919 to 1932; Harry Hansen from 1933 to 1940; Herschel Brickell from 1941 to 1951. The annual collection did not appear in 1952 and 1953, when the continuity of the series was interrupted by the death of Herschel Brickell. Paul Engle was editor from 1954 to 1959 with Hanson Martin coeditor in the years 1954 to 1960; Mary Stegner in 1960; Richard Poirier from 1961 to 1966, with assistance from and coeditorship with William Abrahams from 1964 to 1966. William Abrahams became editor of the series in 1967.

Doubleday also publishes *First-Prize Stories from the O. Henry Memorial Awards* in editions that are brought up to date at intervals. In 1970 Doubleday also published under Mr. Abrahams' editorship *Fifty Years of the American Short Story*, a collection of stories selected from the series.

The stories chosen for this volume were published in the period from the summer of 1975 to the summer of 1976. A list of the magazines consulted appears at the back of the book. The choice of stories and the selection of prize winners are exclusively the responsibility of the editor. Biographical material is based on information provided by the contributors and obtained from standard works of reference.

INTRODUCTION

THIS IS the fifty-seventh collection of O. Henry Prize Stories, and the eleventh for which I have had sole responsibility. When I first assumed my tenure as editor of the series, I may have been a little too responsive—or so it seems to me now, in retrospect—a little too ready to accept the "crisis" of the short story as it arose in the 1960s, and so perhaps a little too eager to defend a position that was never quite as embattled as it may have seemed at the time. That a crisis did exist, however, was undeniable, and it took many forms. There were the triumphant achievements of the new journalists and the photojournalists, closing off whole areas of contemporary life from writers of stories who could not catch up with or rival their sense of immediacy: the click of the camera preserving the look of things-as-they-are; the clack of typewriter memorializing the action of the moment. Concurrently, there was the withering away of a clearly defined, accessible and lucrative market, fewer magazines that were prepared to give even token space to fiction, still fewer that were eager to encourage it. This was the "crisis" facing the story from without; while from within, there was a kind of "identity crisis," an attempt at redefining and reshaping the form itself on the part of an increasing number of younger writers who were determined to break with the older story—if realism had been pre-empted by the new journalists, then goodbye and good riddance to it!—and to jettison it in favor of something new, different and better: the perennial objectives of the avant-garde. One might have predicted for the short story then, embattled as it was from within and without, a fate not unlike that of the verse play: a mortal illness, a salon or camp "last gasp," and then a dwindling into oblivion.

But, as we know, this has not happened. The short story has not merely survived, it has gone from strength to strength, contrary to the bleak expectations of a decade ago. The crisis from without seems to have abated: the story is no longer a form editors shy away from; magazines which a few years back had virtually given up on fiction are opening their pages to it with unwanted generosity, from *Harper's* to *McCall's* to *The Kansas Quarterly*. Pervasively, unobtrusively, sometimes formidably, the story seems to be having its way. More than one of the second generation of new journalists have come round 180 degrees, drawing upon techniques specifically associated with the short story, preferring the subjective and impressionistic to "the judgmental and objective"—those stances peculiar to the older journalism—with the result that the line of demarcation between story and article blurs at times almost to invisibility. One foresees the moment when braver, dissatisfied spirits, fictionists in spite of themselves, will shamelessly cross over, and even *New York Magazine* will admit the occasional story to its pages—its sibling, *New West*, has already in effect done so, with a remarkable article-in-the-form-of-a-story, "A California Woman," by Judith Rascoe.

So much for the crisis from without, and while I do not wish to appear unduly optimistic, I think it is true that the story has survived the crisis from within also, indeed has profited from it, absorbing much that was innovative and is already becoming traditional—as has always been the case, for the story is the most eclectic and adaptable of forms. That quest for the new—a preoccupation of the avant-garde of the later 1960s, ranging from typographical experiment to a philosophical reconsideration of the nature of fiction itself—has made its most important contribution not in its particular innovations in technique, but in its generally liberating effect. Reacting against the notion of telling a story from the point of view of one of its characters—the way of Henry James, which had gained rather too much primacy in approved circles, advancing from a "notion" to a "law"—the new writers opted instead for omniscience, the intrusion of the author into the story, dispelling the semblance of fiction, a denial that the story need be a mirror image of reality. Beyond this was an implicit conviction that a story could be whatever its author wanted it to be, and while in practice the theory was sometimes carried to ludicrous extremes, it has put an end to or suggested alternatives to conventionalized and hence depersonalized ways of telling a story. The story, certainly, is a form allowing a wider range of performance than seemed permissible in the heyday of the Jamesian revival; the many different kinds of story in the present collection will be evident and, I hope, impressive to any serious reader, which is not to say that such a reader will find all of them equally congenial. The risk of individuality is to give offense, and it is a risk that the authentic writer takes on gladly enough, not out of bravado, but in response to the needs of the story he or she has chosen to tell.

It is something of a paradox that the story here that most closely approximates the notions of the new as I have set them forth should come not from a new writer, but from one who for some thirty years now has been the master of an ever-changing, deeply personal art. John Cheever's "The President of the Argentine" wittily and very seriously takes advantage of the new non-conventions to tell what is ostensibly an artless, haphazard non-story, but is, in fact, as artful and purposive as any story in the tradition he pretends to break away from. Deadpan, he begins with a sentence straight out of the tradition: "Coldness falls from the air, she thought, as she carried the white roses up the stairs to the paneled library." One more such sentence, and then: "Zap Blam, Pow. Here endeth my stab at yesterday's fiction. No one's been reading it for forty years. It went out with easel painting. . . . Painting has cast off its frames, and yet one deeply misses these massive and golden celebrations—fruit and angels—for their element of ultimate risk. By framing a painting the artist, of course, declared it to be a distillate of his deepest feelings about love and death. . . . The woman climbing the stairs with her white roses is in a sense a frame, a declaration, and my account of putting a hat on a statue [the non-event, literally so, around which the non-story revolves] is frameless and may indeed not deserve a frame at all."

So the narrator of the story begins his account of a stroll past the commemorative statues on the mall in Commonwealth Avenue in Boston, and when he is at an end—of his stroll and the story—he is at pains to identify the young man and afterward the girl he has encountered en route. We are not to mistake them, or himself, for invented characters: her "real name is Alice-Mae Plumber"; the young man is "Lemuel Howe and he will be arrested three days later. . . . The man who wanted to put his hat on the statue of the President is I." This is very much in the vein of the new non- or anti-story, which asks us not to believe in it and to believe in it both together; or to put it another way, the device of the author is to alienate us from the story even as he is involving us in it. But Mr. Cheever's aim in "The President of the Argentine" is more complex than he pretends. The beginning and the end, breaking with the conventions of the traditional story, nonetheless serve as a frame for the other, the true story that is being revealed to us—not that lighthearted stroll among statues of the illustrious and forgotten dead, but a sense of an ending, of the fabric of society being stretched and tearing, a contrast between the Boston the narrator knew as a young man forty years earlier and the city of the present, and parallel to it, a contrast between the man he was and the man he has become: ". . . my life is impetuous and unorthodox and I cannot distinguish persiflage from profundity." Unlike the "I" of his story, whom he would have us believe/disbelieve is himself, Mr. Cheever can indeed distinguish one from the other: the manner is joking, the matter is profound.

We know from Wallace Stevens that there is more than one way of looking at a blackbird, and we know from Mr. Cheever's own career that there is more than one way of telling a story—I would urge readers interested in the point to look up his very beautiful and traditional "The Embarkment for Cythera," for which he was awarded First Prize in this series in 1964. The ways of telling a story that are available to the contemporary writer are so numerous and so various as to suggest not only the privileges but also the perplexities inherent in the freedom to write as one pleases. Clearly, it is a problem to any writer to estimate to what degree he will figure in his story: I am not thinking now of the shaped memoir, where the author is his own subject, and an invented veneer is imposed upon actual experience, but of the author as a felt presence in the story being told. Consider, as contrasting examples, the two remarkable stories which this year have been jointly awarded First Prize, each very different from the other and both very different from "The President of the Argentine," "A Long Story Short" by Shirley Hazzard and "Last Courtesies" by Ella Leffland.

"A Long Story Short" begins:

> It was in the late nineteen-sixties that something terrible, or at least highly regrettable, happened to Christian Thrale. This came about while his wife, Grace, was at Winchester with the children; which will suggest the nature of the occurrence. Grace had hardly been gone long enough to be properly, let alone acutely, missed; and certainly not long enough for Christian to have telephoned, for he was frugal in these and other matters.

What we hear in this paragraph is an ironic voice, the author's, and it is the author who, unobtrusively (as a kind of shadowy presence), will lead us through the intricacies of the affair, "the occurrence," between Christian Thrale and Cordelia Ware. It is by the author that judgments will be made—not by Christian, the limits of whose sympathies and feelings, even whose discriminations, are evident from the start, "for he was frugal in these and other matters," not even by Cordelia, whose point of view is not presented to us at all: she remains a figure of beauty, enigma and pathos. No, it is the author who speaks, observes, judges and restores to the etiolated phrases of "civilized discourse" a weight of significant meaning. "Something terrible, or at least highly regrettable . . ." And Miss Hazzard, placing the event in the late 1960s, when something terrible was indeed happening in the world—beyond Christian's "highly regrettable" summer adultery —exercises her right as an ironist to be heard: her voice belongs to a tradition that extends from Jane Austen to E. M. Forster, that of the unconcealed author at work. One has to keep in mind Miss Hazzard's intention: she is not writing simply a story of an affair that will end badly—for that, to have told it all from Cordelia's point of view would have been enough to wring the heart. As it is, Christian, the civil servant, is the focus of Miss Hazzard's ironic attention: to what degree can this civil servant be expected to understand the damage of which he is capable, indeed has inflicted, since he can draw around himself the protective, delusive, ever so polite phrases and forms of "civilized" society? Irony thrives in the wide-ranging point of view that plays over this superb story: to write strictly from within Christian himself would be virtually to write from within a void.

In "Last Courtesies" Miss Leffland begins:

> "Lillian, you're too polite," Vladimir kept telling her.
>
> She did not think so. Perhaps she was not one to return shoves in the bus line, but she did fire off censorious glares; and, true, she never yelled at the paper boy who daily flung her *Chronicle* to a rain-soaked fate, but she did beckon him to her door and remind him of his responsibilities. If she was always the last to board the bus, if she continued to dry out the paper on the stove, that was the price she must pay for observing the minimal courtesy the world owed itself if it was not to go under. Civilized she was. Excessively polite, no.

This is very different from the method of "A Long Story Short." As meticulous and intelligent a writer as Miss Hazzard, Miss Leffland has aimed for intensity, not irony, and she has rediscovered in the unfashionable device of the single, undeviating point of view—that of its central character—how best to achieve the intensity, passion, inevitability and surprise essential to the story she wishes to tell. For all the skill and subtlety of the writing, the story is given to us without, as it were, interventions by the author. Here, horrifyingly, the fabric of society tears: violence enters into Lillian's life not in the absence of minimal courtesy, but as its consequence. I do not wish to particularize further for fear of blunting the appalling impact of the story's ruthless but inevitable conclusion. "Last Courtesies" seems to me amazing in its power, and heartening in its repudiation of fashion. Miss Leffland has even been resolute enough, going her own way, to allow into her complex and artfully constructed story a pattern of events that might once have been called a plot. Rooted in a tradition that, contrary to the shibboleths of its detractors, proves sturdily viable, she signals a possible new direction waiting to be explored all over again.

William Abrahams

Last Courtesies

ELLA LEFFLAND

ELLA LEFFLAND was born in Martinez, California, and graduated from San Jose State College. She has published stories in *Harper's, Quarterly Review of Literature, The New Yorker, Epoch* and *Cosmopolitan*, as well as two novels, *Mrs. Munck* and *Love Out of Season*.

L ILLIAN, you're too polite," Vladimir kept telling her.

She did not think so. Perhaps she was not one to return shoves in the bus line, but she did fire off censorious glares; and, true, she never yelled at the paper boy who daily flung her *Chronicle* to a rain-soaked fate, but she did beckon him to her door and remind him of his responsibilities. If she was always the last to board the bus, if she continued to dry out the paper on the stove, that was the price she must pay for observing the minimal courtesy the world owed itself if it was not to go under. Civilized she was. Excessively polite, no.

In any case, even if she had wanted to, she could not change at this stage of life. Nor had Aunt Bedelia ever changed in any manner. Not that she really compared herself to her phenomenal

aunt, who, when she had died four months ago at the age of
ninety-one, was still a captivating woman; no faded great beauty
(the family ran to horse faces), but elegant, serenely vivid. Any
other old lady who dressed herself in long gowns circa 1910
would have appeared a mere oddity; but under Bedelia's antiquated hairdo sat a brain; in her gnarled, almond-scented fingers
lay direction. She spoke of Bach, of the Russian novelists, of her
garden and the consolations of nature; never of her arthritis, the
fallen ranks of her friends, or the metamorphosis of the neighborhood, which now featured motorcycles roaring alongside tin
cans and blackened banana peels. At rare moments a sigh escaped her lips, but who knew if it was for her crippled fingers
(she had been a consummate pianist) or a repercussion from the
street? It was bad form, ungallant, to put too fine a point on life's
discomfitures.

Since Bedelia's death the flat was lonely; lonely yet no longer
private, since a supremely kinetic young woman, herself a music
lover, had moved in upstairs. With no one to talk to, with thuds
and acid rock resounding from above, Lillian drifted (too often,
she knew) into the past, fingering its high points. The day, for
instance, that Vladimir had entered their lives by way of the
Steinway grand (great gleaming relic of better times) which he
came to tune. He had burst in, dressed not in a customary suit
but in garage mechanic's overalls and rubber thong sandals, a
short square man with the large disheveled head of a furious
gnome, who embellished his labors with glorious run-throughs of
Bach and Scarlatti, but whose speech, though a dark bog of
Slavic intonations, was distinctly, undeniably obscene. Aunt
Bedelia promptly invited him to dinner the following week.
Lillian stood astonished, but reminded herself that her aunt was
a sheltered soul unfamiliar with scabrous language, whereas she,
Lillian, lived more in the great world, riding the bus every day
to the Opera House, where she held the position of switchboard
operator (Italian and German required). The following morning
at work, in fact, she inquired about Vladimir.

Several people there knew of him. A White Russian, he had
fled to Prague with his parents in 1917, then fled again twenty
years later, eventually settling in San Francisco, where he
quickly earned the reputation of an excellent craftsman and a vi-

olent crackpot. He abused clients who had no knowledge of their pianos' intestines, and had once been taken to court by an acquaintance whom he had knocked down during a conversation about Wagner. He wrote scorching letters of general advice to the newspapers; with arms like a windmill he confronted mothers who allowed their children to drop potato chips on the sidewalk; he kept a bucket of accumulated urine to throw on dog-walkers who were unwary enough to linger with their squatting beasts beneath his window. He had been institutionalized several times.

That night Lillian informed her aunt that Vladimir was brilliant but unsound.

The old woman raised an eyebrow at this.

"For instance," Lillian pursued, "he is actually known to have struck someone down."

"Why?" Her aunt's voice was clear and melodious, with a faint ring of iron.

"It was during a conversation about Wagner. Apparently he disapproves of Wagner."

Her aunt gave a nod of endorsement.

"The man has even had himself committed, aunt. Several times, when he felt he was getting out of hand."

The old woman pondered this. "It shows foresight," she said at length, "and a sense of social responsibility."

Lillian was silent for a moment. Then she pointed out: "He said unspeakable things here."

"They are mutually exclusive terms."

"Let us call them obscenities, then. You may not have caught them."

The old woman rose from her chair and arranged the long skirt of her dove-gray ensemble, "Lillian, one must know when to turn a deaf ear."

"I am apparently not in the know," Lillian said dryly.

"Perhaps it is an instinct." And suddenly she gave her unique smile, which was quite yellow (for she retained her own ancient teeth) but completely beguiling, and added: "In any case, he is of my own generation, Lillian. That counts for a great deal."

"He can't be more than sixty, aunt."

"It is close enough. Anyway, he is quite wrinkled. Also, he is a man of integrity."

"How can you possibly know that?"

"It is my instinct." And gently touching her niece's cheek, she said goodnight and went to her room, which peacefully overlooked the back garden, away from the street noises.

Undressing in her own smaller room, Lillian reflected, not for the first time, that though it was Bedelia who had remained unwed—Lillian herself having been married and widowed during the war—it was she, Lillian, who felt more the old maid, who seemed more dated, in a stale, fusty way, with her tight 1950s hairdo, her plain wool suits and practical support stockings . . . but then, she led a practical life . . . it was she who was trampled in the bus queue and who sat down to a hectic switchboard, who swept the increasingly filthy sidewalk and dealt with the sullen butcher and careless paper boy—or tried to . . . it seemed she was a middlewoman, a hybrid, too worldly to partake of aunt's immense calm, too seclusive to sharpen herself on the changing ways . . . aunt had sealed herself off in a lofty, gracious world; she lived for it, she would have died for it if it came to that . . . but what could she, Lillian, die for? . . . she fit in nowhere, she thought, climbing into bed, and thirty years from now she would not have aged into the rare creature aunt was—last survivor of a fair, legendary breed, her own crimped hairdo as original as the Edwardian pouf, her boxy suits as awesome as the floor-sweeping gowns—no, she would just be a peculiar old leftover in a room somewhere. For aunt was grande dame, bluestocking, and virgin in one, and they didn't make that kind anymore; they didn't make those eyes anymore, large, hooded, a deep glowing violet. It was a hue that had passed. . . . And she closed her own eyes, of candid, serviceable gray, said the Lord's Prayer, and prepared to act as buffer between her elite relative and the foul-mouthed old refugee.

AUNT BEDELIA PREPARED the dinner herself, taking great pains; then she creaked into her wet garden with an umbrella and picked her finest blooms for a centerpiece; and finally, over the knobbed, arthritic joint of her ring finger, she twisted a magnificent amethyst usually reserved for Christmas, Easter, and Bach's birthday. These touches Lillian expected to be lost on their wild-eyed guest, but Vladimir kissed the festive hand with a cavalier click of his sandals, acknowledged the flowers with a noisy inhalation of his large, hairy nostrils, and ate his food with admirable if strained refinement. During coffee he capsized his cup, but this was only because he and Bedelia were flying from Bavarian spas and Italian sea resorts to music theory, Turgenev, and God knew what else—Lillian could hardly follow—and then, urged by aunt, he jumped from the table, rolled up the sleeves of his overalls, and flung himself into Bach, while aunt, her fingers stiffly moving up and down on her knee, threw back her head and entered some region of flawless joy. At eleven o'clock Vladimir wrestled into his red lumber jacket, expressed his delight with the evening, and slapped down the steps to his infirm 1938 Buick. Not one vulgar word had escaped his lips.

Nor in the seven following years of his friendship with Bedelia was this precedent ever broken. Even the night when some drunk sent an empty pint of muscatel crashing through the window, Vladimir's respect for his hostess was so great that all scurrility was plucked from his wrath. However, when he and Lillian happened to be alone together he slipped right back into the belching, offensive mannerisms for which he was known. She did not mention this to her aunt, who cherished the idea that he was very fond of Lillian.

"You know how he detests opera," the old lady would assure her, "and yet he has never alluded to the fact that you work at the Opera House and hold the form in esteem."

"A magnanimous gesture," Lillian said, smiling.

"For Vladimir, yes."

And after a moment's thought, Lillian had to agree. Her aunt apparently understood Vladimir perfectly, and he her. She wondered if this insight was due to their shared social origins, their bond of elevated interests, or their more baroque twinhood of eccentricity. Whatever it was, the couple thrived, sometimes sitting up till midnight with their sherry and sheet music, sometimes, when the Buick was well, motoring (Bedelia's term) into the countryside and then winding homeward along the darkening sea, in a union of perfect silence, as the old lady put it.

Bedelia died suddenly, with aplomb, under Toscanini's direction. Beethoven's Ninth was on the phonograph; the chorus had just scaled the great peak before its heart-bursting cascade into the finale; aunt threw her head back to savor the moment, and was gone.

The next morning Lillian called Vladimir. He shrieked, he wept, he banged the receiver on the table; and for ten days, helpless and broken, he spent every evening at the home of his departed love while Lillian, herself desolated, tried to soothe him. She felt certain he would never regain the strength to insult his clients again, much less strike anyone to the ground, but gradually he mended, and the coarseness, the irascibility flooded back, much worse than in the past.

For Bedelia's sake—of that Lillian was sure—he forced himself to take an interest in her welfare, which he would express in eruptions of advice whenever he telephoned. "You want to lead a decent life, Lillian, you give them hell! They sell you a bad cut of meat, throw it in the butcher's face! You get shortchanged, make a stink! You're too soft! Give them the finger, Lillian!"

"Yes, of course," she would murmur.

"For your aunt I was a gentleman, but now she's gone, who appreciates? A gentleman is a fool, a gentleman's balls are cut off! I know how to take care of myself, I am in an armored tank! And you should be too. Or find a protector. Get married!"

"Pardon?" she asked.

"Marry!"

"I have no desire to marry, Vladimir."

"Desire! Desire! It's a world for your desires? Think of your scalp! You need a protector, now Bedelia's gone!"

"Aunt was not my protector," she said patiently.

"Of course she was! And mine too!"

Lillian shifted her weight from one foot to the other and hoped he would soon run down.

"You want to get off the phone, don't you? Why don't you say, Vladimir get the shit off the phone, I'm busy! Don't be a doormat! Practice on me or you'll come to grief! What about that sow upstairs, have you given her hell yet? No, no, of course not! Jesus bleeding Christ, I give up!" And he slammed the receiver down.

LILLIAN HAD in fact complained. Allowing her new neighbor time to settle in, she had at first endured—through apparently rugless floorboards—the girl's music, her door slams, her crashing footfall which was a strange combination of scurry and thud, her deep hollow brays of laughter and shrieks of "You're *kidding!*" and "Fan*tastic!*"—all this usually accompanied by a masculine voice and tread (varying from night to night, Lillian could not help but notice) until finally, in the small hours, directly above Bedelia's room, where Lillian now slept, ears stuffed with cotton, the night was crowned by a wild creaking of bedsprings and the racketing of the headboard against the wall. At last, chancing to meet her tormentor on the front steps (she was not the Amazon her noise indicated, but a small, thin creature nervously chewing gum with staccato snaps), Lillian decided to speak; but before she could, the girl cried: "Hi! I'm Jody—from upstairs?" with a quick, radiant smile that heartened the older woman in a way that the hair and hemline did not. Clad in a tiny, childish dress that barely reached her hip sockets, she might have been a prematurely worn twenty or an adolescent thirty—dark circles hung beneath the eyes and a deep line was etched between them, but the mouth was babyish, sweet, and the cheeks a glowing pink against the unfortunate mane of brassy hair, dark along its uneven part.

Having responded with her own name (the formal first *and* last) Lillian paused a courteous moment, then began: "I'm glad to have this opportunity of meeting you; I've lived in this flat for twenty-four years, you see . . ." But the eyes opposite, heavily outlined with blue pencil, were already wandering under this gratuitous information. Brevity was clearly the password. "The point *is*"—restoring attention—"I would appreciate it if you turned down your music after ten P.M. There is a ruling."

"It bugs you?" the girl asked, beginning to dig turbulently through a fringed bag, her gum snaps accelerating with the search.

"Well, it's an old building, and of course if you don't have carpets . . ." She waited to be corroborated in this assumption, but now the girl pulled out her house key with fingers whose nails, bitten to the quick, were painted jet black. Fascinated, Lillian tried not to stare. "Not to worry," the girl assured her with the brief, brilliant smile, plunging the key into the door and bounding inside, "I'll cool it."

"There's something else, I'm afraid. When that door is slammed—"

But the finely arched brows rose with preoccupation; the phone was ringing down from the top of the stairs. "I dig, I dig. Look, hon, my phone's ringing." And closing the door softly, she thundered up the stairs.

After that the phonograph was lowered a little before midnight, but nothing else was changed. Lillian finally called the landlord, a paunchy, sweating man whom she rarely saw, and though she subsequently observed him disappearing into his unruly tenant's flat several evenings a week, the visits were apparently useless. And every time she met the girl, she was greeted with an insufferable "Hi! Have a nice day!"

Unfortunately, Lillian had shared some of her vexation with Vladimir, and whenever he dropped by—less to see her, she knew, than to replenish his memories of Bedelia—his wrath grew terrible under the commotion. On his last visit his behavior had frightened her. "Shut up!" he had screamed, shaking his fist at the ceiling. "Shut up, bitch! Whore!"

"Vladimir, please—this language, just because Bedelia's not here."

"Ah, Bedelia, Bedelia," he groaned.

"She wouldn't have tolerated it."

"She wouldn't have tolerated *that!* Hear the laugh—hee haw, hee haw! Braying ass! Bedelia would have pulverized her with a glance! None of this farting around you go in for!" His large head had suffused with red, his hands were shaking at his sides. "Your aunt was a genius at judging people—they should have lined up the whole fucking rotten city for her to judge!"

"It seems to me that you have always appointed yourself as judge," Lillian said, forcing a smile.

"Yah, but Vladimir is demented, you don't forget? He has it down in black and white! Ah, you think I'm unique, Lillian, but I am one of the many! I am in the swim!" He came over to her side and put his flushed head close, his small intense eyes piercing hers.

"You read yesterday about the girl they found in an alley not far from here, cut to small bits? Slash! Rip! Finito! And you ask why? Because the world, it is demented! A murder of such blood not even in the headlines and you ask why? Because it is commonplace! Who walks safe on his own street? It is why you need a husband!"

Lillian dropped her eyes, wondering for an embarrassed moment if Vladimir of all people could possibly be hinting at a marital alliance. Suddenly silent, he pulled a wadded handkerchief from his pocket with trembling fingers and wiped his brow. He flicked her a suspicious glance. "Don't look so coy. I'm not in the running. I loathe women—sticky! Full of rubbishy talk!" And once more he threw his head back and began bellowing obscenities at the ceiling.

"It's too much, Vladimir—please! You're not yourself!"

"I *am* myself!"

"Well then, I'm not. I'm tired, I have a splitting headache—"

"You want me to go! Be rude, good! I have better things to do anyway!" And his face still aflame, he struggled into his lumber jacket and flung out the door.

THAT NIGHT her sleep was not only disturbed by the noise, but by her worry over the violence of Vladimir's emotions. At work the next day she reluctantly inquired about her friend, whose antics were usually circulated around the staff but seldom reached her cubicle. For the first time in years, she learned, the weird little Russian had gone right over the edge, flapping newspapers in strangers' faces and ranting about the end of civilization; storming out on tuning jobs and leaving his tools behind, then furiously accusing his clients of stealing them. The opinion was that if he did not commit himself soon, someone else would do it for him.

On the clamorous bus home that night, shoved as usual into the rear, Lillian felt an overwhelming need for Bedelia, for the sound of that clear, well-modulated voice that had always set the world to rights. But she opened her door on silence. She removed her raincoat and sat down in the living room with the damp newspaper. People at work told her she should buy a television set—such a good companion when you lived alone—but she had too long scorned that philistine invention to change now. For that matter, she seldom turned on the radio, and even the newspaper—she ran her eyes over the soggy turmoil of the front page—even the newspaper distressed her. Vladimir was extreme, but he was right: everything was coming apart. Sitting there, she thought she could hear the world's madness——its rudeness, its litter, its murders—beat against the house with the rain. And suddenly she closed her eyes under an intolerable longing for the past: for the peaceful years she had spent in these rooms with Bedelia; and before that, for the face of her young husband, thirty years gone now; and for even earlier days . . . odd, but it never seemed to rain in her youth, the green campus filled the air with dizzying sweetness, she remembered running across the lawns for no reason but that she was twenty and the sun would shine forever. . . .

She gave way to two large tears. Shaken, yet somehow consoled, and at the same time ashamed of her self-indulgence, she went into the kitchen to make dinner. But as she cooked her chop she knew that even this small measure of comfort would be destroyed as soon as her neighbor came banging through the door. Already her neck was tightening against the sound.

But there was no noise at all that night, not until 1 A.M. when the steady ring of the telephone pulled her groggily from bed.

"Listen, you'll kill me—it's Jody, I'm across the bay, and I just flashed on maybe I left the stove burners going."

"Who?" Lillian said, rubbing her eyes, "Jody? How did you get my number?"

"The phone book, why? Listen, the whole dump could catch fire, be a doll and check it out? The back door's unlocked."

Lillian felt a strange little rush of gratitude—that her name given to such seemingly indifferent ears on the steps that day, had been remembered. Then the feeling was replaced by anger; but before she could speak, the girl said, "Listen, hon, thanks a million," and hung up.

Clutching her raincoat around her shoulders, beaming a flashlight before her, Lillian nervously climbed the dark back stairs to her neighbor's door and let herself into the kitchen. Turning on the light, she stood aghast at what she saw: not flames licking the wall, for the burners were off, but grimed linoleum, spilled garbage, a sink of stagnant water. On the puddled table, decorated with a jar of blackened, long-dead daisies, sat a greasy portable television set and a pile of dirty laundry in a litter of cigarette butts, sodden pieces of paper, and the congealed remains of spare ribs. Hesitating, ashamed of her snoopiness, she peered down at the pieces of paper: bills from department stores, including Saks and Magnin's; scattered food stamps; handwritten notes on binder paper, one of which read "Jamie hony theres a piza in the frezzer I love U"—then several big hearts—"Jody." A long brown bug—a cockroach? was crawling across the note, and now she noticed another one climbing over a spare rib. As she stood cringing, she heard rain blowing through an open window somewhere, lashing a shade into frenzies. Going to the bedroom door, which stood ajar, she beamed her flashlight in and switched on the light. Under the window a large puddle was forming on the floor, which was rugless as she had suspected, though half carpeted by strewn clothes. The room was furnished only with a bed whose convulsed, mummy-brown sheets put her in mind of a pesthouse, and a deluxe television set in a rosewood cabinet; but the built-in bookcase was well stocked, and, having shut the window, she ran her eyes over the spines, curious. Many were cheap paperback thrillers, but there was an abundance of great authors: Dostoevsky, Dickens, Balzac, Melville. It was odd, she puzzled, that the girl had this taste in literature, yet could not spell the simplest word and had never heard of a comma. As she turned away, her eardrums were shattered by her own scream. A man stood in the doorway.

A BOY, ACTUALLY, she realized through her fright; one of Jody's more outstanding visitors, always dressed in one of those Mexican shawl affairs and a battered derby hat, from under which butter-yellow locks flowed in profusion, everything at the moment dripping with rain. More embarrassed now than frightened —she had never screamed in her life, or stood before a stranger in her nightgown, and neither had Bedelia—she began pulsating with dignity. "I didn't hear anyone come up the stairs," she indicted him.

"Little cat feet, man," he said with a cavernous yawn, "Where's Jody? Who're you?"

She explained her presence, pulling the raincoat more firmly together across her bosom, but unable to do anything about the expanse of flowered flannel below.

"Jody, she'd forget her ass if it wasn't screwed on," the boy said with a second yawn. His eyes were watery and red, and his nose ran. "If you'll excuse me," she said, going past him. He followed her back into the kitchen and suddenly, with a hostlike warmth that greatly surprised her, he asked, "You want some coffee?"

She declined, saying that she must be going.

At this he heaved a deep, disappointed sigh, which again surprised her, and sank like an invalid into a chair. He was a slight youth with neat little features crowded into the center of his face, giving him, despite his woebegone expression, a pert, fledgling look. In Lillian's day he would have been called a "pretty boy." He would not have been her type at all; she had always preferred the lean profile.

"My name's Jamie," he announced suddenly, with a childlike spontaneity beneath the film of langour; and he proffered his hand.

Gingerly, she shook the cold small fingers.

"Hey, really," he entreated, "Stay and rap awhile."

"Rap?"

"Talk, man. Talk to me." And he looked, all at once, so lonely, so forlorn, that even though she was very tired, she felt she must stay a moment longer. Pulling out a chair, she took a temporary, edge-of-the-seat position across the hideous table from him.

He seemed to be gathering his thoughts together. "So what's your bag?" he asked.

She looked at him hopelessly. "My bag?"

"You a housewife? You work?"

"Oh—yes, I work," she said, offended by his bold curiosity, yet grateful against her will to have inspired it.

"What's your name?" he asked.

He was speaking to her as a contemporary; and again, she was both pleased by this and offended by his lack of deference. "Lillian . . . Cronin," she said uncertainly.

"I'm Jamie," he laughed.

"So you mentioned." And thought—Jamie, Jody, the kinds of names you would give pet rabbits. Where were the solid, straightforward names of yesteryear—the Georges and Harolds, the Dorothys and Margarets? What did she have to say to a

Jamie in a Mexican shawl and threadbare derby who was now scratching himself all over with little fidgety movements? But she said, breaking the long silence, which he seemed not to notice: "And what is *your* bag, if I may ask?"

He took several moments to answer. "I don't know, man . . . I'm a student of human nature."

"Oh? And where do you study?"

"Not me, man, that's Jody's scene . . . into yoga, alpha waves, the whole bit . . . even studies macramé and World Lit at jay cee . . ."

"Indeed? How interesting. I noticed her books."

"She's a towering intellect." He yawned, his eyes glassy with fatigue. He was scratching himself more slowly now.

"And does she work, as well?" Lillian asked, once more ashamed of her nosiness.

"Work?" he smiled. "Maybe you could call it that. . . ." But his attention was drifting away like smoke. Fumbling with a breadknife, he picked it up and languidly, distantly, speared a cockroach with the point. Then, with the side of the knife, he slowly, methodically, squashed the other one.

Averting her eyes from the massacre, Lillian leaned forward. "I don't mean to sound familiar, but you seem a quiet person. Do you think you might ask Jody to be a little less noisy up here? I've spoken to the landlord, but—" She saw the boy smile again, an odd, rueful smile that made her feel, for some reason, much younger than he. "You see—" she continued, but he was fading from her presence, slowly mashing his bugs to pulp and now dropping the knife to reach over and click on the food-spattered television set. Slouched, his eyes bored by what the screen offered, he nevertheless began following an old movie. The conversation appeared to be over.

Lillian rose. She was not accustomed, nor would Bedelia have been, to a chat ending without some mutual amenity. She felt awkward, dismissed. With a cool nod she left him and descended the splashing stairs to her own flat. Such a contrast the youth was of warmth and rudeness . . . and Jody, an illiterate studying Dostoevsky at college . . . food stamps lying hugger-mugger with bills from Saks . . . it was impossible to bring it all into focus; she felt rudderless, malfunctioning . . . how peculiar life

had become . . . everything mixed up . . . a generation of fragments. . . .

Climbing heavily back into bed, she wondered what Bedelia
would have thought of Jody and Jamie. And she remembered
how unkempt and disconcerting Vladimir had been, yet how her
aunt had quickly penetrated to the valuable core while she,
Lillian, fussed on about his bad language. No doubt Bedelia
would have been scandalized by the filth upstairs, but she would
not have been so narrow-souled as to find fault with spelling mistakes, first names, taste in clothing. . . . Bedelia might not have
pulverized Jody with a glance, as Vladimir suggested, but instead seen some delicate tragedy in the worn cherubic features,
or been charmed by the girl's invincible buoyancy . . . it was
hard to tell with Bedelia, which facet she might consider the
significant one . . . she often surprised you . . . it had to do with
largeness of spirit. . . .

Whereas she, Lillian, had always to guard against stuffi-
ness. . . . Still, she tried to hold high the torch of goodwill
. . . too pompous a simile, of course, but she knew clearly and
deeply what she meant . . . so *let* Vladimir rave on at her for re-
fusing to shrink into a knot of hostility; what was Vladimir, after
all? Insane. Her eyes opened in the dark as she faced what she
had tried to avoid all day: that Vladimir had been wrenched off
the tracks by Bedelia's death, and that this time he felt no need
to commit himself. Without question it was Lillian's duty to en-
lighten him. But she winced at the thought . . . such a terrible
thing to have to tell someone . . . if only she could turn to
Bedelia . . . how sorely she missed her . . . how sorely she
missed George's lean young face under his Army cap . . . youth
. . . sunlight . . . outside the rain still fell . . . she had only herself, and the dark, unending rain. . . .

"Stop this brooding," she said aloud; if she had only herself,
she had better be decent company. And closing her eyes she
tried to sleep. But not until a gray watery dawn was breaking
did she drop off.

THE OPERA HOUSE telephoned at three minutes past nine. Leaden,
taut-nerved, sourly questioning the rewards of her long, exquisite
punctuality, she pulled on her clothes, and, with burning eyes

and empty stomach, hurried out of the house. At work, though the board was busy, the hours moved with monumental torpor. She felt increasingly unlike herself, hotly brimming over with impatience for all this switchboard blather: calls from New York, Milan; Sutherland with her sore throat, Pavarotti with his tight schedule—did they really think that, if another *Rigoletto* were never given, anyone would notice? She felt an urge to slur this fact into the headphone, as befitted a truant traipsing in at a quarter to ten, as befitted someone with minimally combed hair and crooked seams and, even worse, with the same underwear on that she had worn the day before. As if a slatternly, cynical Lillian whom she didn't recognize had squeezed slyly into prominence, a Lillian who half-considered walking out on the whole tiresome business and indulging in a lavish two-hour lunch downtown—let someone else serve, let someone else be polite.

Sandwiched into the bus aisle that night, she almost smacked an old gentleman who crunched her right instep under his groping heel; and as she creaked into the house with her wet newspaper and saw that a motorcyclist had been picked off on the freeway by a sniper, she had to fight down a lip curl of satisfaction. Then, reflectively, still in her raincoat, she walked to the end of the hall where an oval mirror hung, and studied her face. It was haggard, flinty, stripped of faith, scraped down to the cold, atavistic bones of retaliation. She had almost walked off her job, almost struck an old man, almost smiled at murder. A feeling of panic shot through her; what were values if they could collapse at the touch of a sleepless night? And she sank the terrible face into her hands; but a ray of rational thought lifted it again. "Almost." Never mind the querulous inner tremble, at each decisive moment her principles had stood fast. Wasn't a person entitled to an occasional fit of petulance? There is such a thing as perspective, she told herself, and in the meantime a great lust for steam and soap had spread through her. She would scrub out the day in a hot bath and in perfect silence, for apparently Jody had not yet returned from across the bay. God willing, the creature would remain away a week.

Afterward, boiled pink, wrapped in her quilted robe, she felt restored to grace. A fine appetite raced through her, along with visions of a tuna casserole which she hurried into the kitchen to

prepare, hurrying out again at the summons of the telephone. It
was Vladimir, very excited, wanting to drop by. Her first response was one of blushing discomfort: entertain Vladimir in her
quilted bathrobe? Her second she articulated: she was bone-
tired, she was going to bed right after dinner. But even as she
spoke she heard the remorseless door slam of Jody's return, and a
violent spasm twisted her features. "Please—next week," she told
Vladimir and hung up, clutching her head as tears of rage and
exhaustion burst from her eyes. Weeping, she made a tuna sandwich, chewed it without heart, and sank onto her unmade bed.
The next morning, still exhausted, she made an emergency appointment with her doctor, and came home that night with a
bottle of sleeping pills.

By the end of the week she was sick with artificial sleep, there
was an ugly rubber taste in her mouth, her eye sockets felt caked
with rust. And it was not only the noise and pills that plagued
her: a second neighborhood woman had been slashed to death
by the rain man (the newspapers, in their cozy fashion, had thus
baptized the slayer). She had taken to beaming her flashlight
under the bed before saying the Lord's Prayer; her medicinal
sleep crackled with surreal visions; at the sullen butcher's her
eyes were morbidly drawn to the meat cleaver; and at work not
only had she upset coffee all over her lap, but she disconnected
Rudolf Bing himself in the middle of a sentence.

And never any respite from above. She had called the landlord
again, without audible results, and informed the Board of Health
about the cockroaches; their reply was that they had no juris-
diction over cockroaches. She had stuck several notes under
Jody's door pleading with her to quiet down, and had stopped
her twice on the steps, receiving the first time some capricious
remark, and the second a sigh of "Christ, Lilly, I'm trying. What
d'you want?" Lilly! The gall! But she was gratified to see that the
gum-snapping face was almost as sallow as her own, the circles
under the eyes darker than ever, new lines around the mouth. So
youth could crumble, too. Good! Perhaps the girl's insanely late
hours were boomeranging, and would soon mash her down in a
heap of deathlike stillness (would that Lillian could implement
this vision). Or perhaps it was her affair with Jamie that was
running her ragged. Ah, the costly trauma of love! Jealousy,

misunderstanding—so damaging to the poor nervous system! Or
so she had heard . . . she and George had been blessed with rap-
port . . . but try not to dwell on the past . . . yes, possibly it was
Jamie who was lining the girl's face . . . Lillian had seen him a
few times since their first meeting, once on the steps—he smiled,
was pleasant, remembered her, but had not remembered to zip
his fly, and she had hurried on, embarrassed—and twice in the
back garden, where on the less drenching days she tended
Bedelia's flowers, but without her aunt's emerald-green thumb
. . . a rare sunny afternoon, she had been breaking off geraniums; Jody and Jamie lay on the grass in skimpy bathing suits,
their thin bodies white, somehow poignant in their delicacy . . .
she felt like a great stuffed mattress in her sleeveless dress, soiled
hands masculine with age, a stevedore's drop of sweat hanging
from her nose . . . could they imagine her once young and tender on her own bed of love? or now, with a man friend? As if everything closed down at fifty-seven, like a bankrupt hotel!—tearing off the head of a geranium—brash presumption of youth! But
she saw that they weren't even aware of her, no, they were kissing and rolling about . . . in Bedelia's garden! "Here, what are
you doing!" she cried, but in the space of a moment a hostile little flurry had taken place, and now they broke away and lay separately in charged silence, still taking no notice of her as she
stood there, heart thumping, fist clenched. She might have been
air. Suddenly, sick from the heat, she had plodded inside.

The next time she saw Jamie in the garden was this afternoon
when, arriving home from work and changing into a fresh dress
for Vladimir's visit, she happened to glance out her bedroom
window. Rain sifted down, but the boy was standing still, a melancholy sight, wrapped in a theatrical black cloak, the derby and
Mexican shawl apparently having outlived their effectiveness as
eyecatchers . . . youth's eternal and imbecile need to shock . . .
Jody with her ebony fingernails and silly prepubescent hemlines;
and this little would-be Dracula with his golden sausage curls,
tragically posed in the fragile mist, though she noticed his hands
were untragically busy under the cloak, scratching as usual . . .
or . . . the thought was so monstrous that she clutched the curtain . . . he could not be standing in the garden abusing himself;
she must be deranged, suffering prurient delusions—she, Lillian

Cronin, a decent, clean-minded woman . . . ah God, what was happening, what was happening? It was her raw nerves, her drugged and hanging head, the perpetual din . . . even as she stood there, her persecutor was trying on clothes, dropping shoes, pounding from closet to mirror (for Lillian could by now divine the activity behind each noise) while simultaneously braying into the telephone receiver stuck between chin and shoulder, and sketchily attending the deluxe television set, which blared a hysterical melodrama . . .

Outside, the youth sank onto a tree stump, from which he cast the upstairs window a long bleak look . . . they must have had a lovers' quarrel, and the girl had shut him out; now he brooded in the rain, an exile; or rather a kicked puppy, shivering and staring up with ponderous woe . . . then, eyes dropping, he caught sight of Lillian, and a broad, sunny, candid smile flashed from the dismal countenance . . . odd, jarring, she thought, giving a polite nod and dropping the curtain, especially after his rude imperviousness that hot day on the grass . . . a generation of fragments, she had said so before, though God knew she never objected to a smile (with the exception of Jody's grimace) . . . and walking down the hall away from the noise, she was stopped woodenly by the sound of the girl's doorbell. It was one of the gentlemen callers, who tore up the stairs booming felicitations which were returned with the inevitable shrieks, this commingled din moving into the front room and turning Lillian around in her tracks. With the door closed, the kitchen was comparatively bearable, and it was time to eat anyway. She bought television dinners now, lacking the vigor to cook. She had lost seven pounds, but was not growing svelte, only drawn. Even to turn on the waiting oven was a chore. But slowly she got herself into motion, and at length, pouring out a glass of burgundy to brace herself for Vladimir's visit, she sat down to the steaming, neatly sectioned pap. Afterward, dutifully washing her glass and fork in the sink, she glanced out the window into the rain, falling in sheets now; the garden was dark and she could not be sure, but she thought she saw the youth still sitting on the stump. It was beyond her, why anyone would sit still in a downpour . . . but everything was beyond her, insurmountable . . . and soon Vladimir would arrive . . . the thought was more than she could bear, but she could not defer his visit again, it would be too rude. . . .

HE BURST in like a cannonball, tearing off his wet lumber jacket, an acrid smell of sweat blooming from his armpits; his jaws were stubbled with white, great bushes sprouted from his nostrils.

"You look terrible!" he roared.

Even though she had at the last moment rubbed lipstick into her pallid cheeks. She gave a deflated nod and gestured toward the relatively quiet kitchen, but he wanted the Bedelia-redolent front room, where he rushed over to the Steinway and lovingly dashed off an arpeggio, only to stagger back with his finger knifed up at the ceiling. "Still the chaos!" he cried.

"Please—" she said raggedly. "No advice, I beg of you."

"No advice? Into your grave they'll drive you, Lillian!" And she watched his finger drop, compassionately it seemed, to point at her slumped bosom with its heart beating so wearily inside. It was a small hand, yet blunt, virile, its back covered with coarse dark hair . . . what if it reached farther, touched her? . . . But spittle already flying, Vladimir was plunging into a maelstrom of words, obviously saved up for a week. "I wanted to come sooner, why didn't you let me? Look at you, a wreck! Vladimir knew a second one would be cut—he smells blood on the wind! He wants to come and pound on your door, to be with you, but no, he respects your wish for privacy, so he sits every night out front in his auto, watching!" Here he broke off to wipe his lips, while Lillian, pressing hard the swollen, rusty lids of her eyes, accepted the immense duty of guiding him to confinement. "And every night," he roared on, "While Vladimir sits, Bedelia plays 'Komm, Jesu, Komm,' it floats into the street, it is beautiful, beautiful—"

"Ah, Vladimir," broke pityingly from her lips.

Silence. With a clap of restored lucidity his fist struck his forehead. It remained tightly glued there for some time. When it fell away he seemed quite composed.

"I have always regretted," he said crisply, "that you resemble the wrong side of your family. All you have of Bedelia is a most

vague hint of her cheekbones." Which he was scrutinizing with
his small glittering eyes. Again, nervously, she sensed that he
would touch her; but instead, a look of revulsion passed over his
features as he stared first at one cheek, then the other. "You've
got fucking gunk on! Rouge!"

With effort, she produced a neutral tone. "I'm not used to
being stared at, Vladimir."

"Hah, I should think not," he snapped abstractedly, eyes still
riveted.

Beast! Vile wretch! But at once she was shamed by her
viciousness. From where inside her did it come? And she remembered that terrible day at work when a malign and foreign Lillian had pressed into ascendancy, almost as frightening a character change as the one she was seeing before her now, for
Vladimir's peering eyes seemed actually black with hatred.
"Stinking whore-rouge," he breathed; then with real pain, he
cried: "Have you no thought for Bedelia? You have the blessing
of her cheekbones! Respect them! Don't drag them through the
gutter! My God, Lillian! My God!"

She said nothing. It seemed the only thing to do.

But now he burst forth again, cheerfully, rubbing his hands together. "Listen to Vladimir. You want a husband, forget the war
paint, use what you have. Some intelligence. A good bearing—
straighten the shoulders—and cooking talent. Not like Bedelia's,
but not bad. Now, Vladimir has been looking around for you—"

"Vladimir," she said through her teeth.

"—and he has found a strong, healthy widower of fifty-two
years, a great enjoyer of the opera. He has been advised of your
virtues—"

"Vladimir!"

"Of course you understand Vladimir himself is out, Vladimir is
a monolith—" A particularly loud thump shuddered the ceiling,
and he jumped back yelling, "Shove it, you swine! Lice!"

"Vladimir, I do not want a man!" Lillian snapped.

"Not so! I sense sex boiling around in you!"

Her lips parted; blood rushed into her cheeks to darken the
artificial blush. For certain, with the short, potent word, *sex*, his
hands would leap on her.

"But you look a thousand years old," he went on, "It hangs in folds, your face. You must get rid of this madhouse upstairs! What have you done so far—not even told the landlord!"

"I *have!*" she cried; and suddenly the thought of confiding in someone loosened a stinging flood of tears from her eyes, and she sank into a chair. "He has come to speak to her . . . time and time again . . . he seems always to be there . . . but nothing changes. . . ."

"Ah, so," said Vladimir, pulling out his gray handkerchief and handing it to her. "The sow screws him."

She grimaced both at the words and the reprehensible cloth, with which she nevertheless dabbed her eyes. "I don't believe that," she said nasally.

"Why not? She's a prostitute. Only to look at her."

"You've seen her?" she asked, slowly raising her eyes. But of course, if he sat outside in his car every night . . .

"I have seen her," he said, revulsion hardening his eyes. "I have seen much. Even a bat-man with the face of a sorrowful kewpie doll. He pines this minute on the front steps."

"That's her boyfriend," Lillian murmured, increasingly chilled by the thought of Vladimir sitting outside all night, spying.

"Boyfriend! A hundred boyfriends she has, each with a roll of bills in his pocket!"

Tensely, she smoothed the hair at her temples. "Forgive me, Vladimir," she said gently, "But you exaggerate. You exaggerate everything, I'm afraid. I must point this out to you, because I think it does you no good. I really—"

"Don't change the subject! We're talking about her, upstairs!"

She was silent for a moment. "The girl is—too free, I suppose, in our eyes. But I'm certain that she isn't what you call her."

"And how do you come to this idiot conclusion?" he asked scornfully.

She lifted her hands in explanation, but they hung helplessly suspended. "Well," she said at last, "I know she reads Dostoevsky . . . she takes courses . . . and she cares for that boy in the cape, even if they do have their quarrels . . . and there's a quality of anguish in her face . . ."

"Anguish! I call it the knocked-out look of a female cretin who uses her ass every night to pay the rent. And that pea-brain boyfriend outside, in his secondhand ghoul costume to show how interesting he is! Probably he pops pills and lives off his washer-woman mother, if he hasn't slit her throat in a fit of irritation! It's the type, Lillian! Weak, no vision, no guts! The sewers are vomiting them up by the thousands to mix with us! They surround us! Slop! Shit! Chaos! Listen to that up there! Hee-haw! Call that anguish? Even pleasure? No, I tell you what it is! Empty, hollow noise—like a wheel spun into motion and never stopped again! It's madness! The madness of our times!"

But as he whipped himself on, Lillian felt herself growing diametrically clear and calm, as if the outburst were guiding her blurred character back into focus. When he stopped, she said firmly, "Yes, I understand what you mean about the wheel spinning. There is something pointless about them, something pitiful. But they're not from a sewer. They're people, Vladimir, human beings like ourselves . . ."

"Ah, blanket democracy! What else would you practice but that piss-fart abomination?"

"I practice what Bedelia herself practiced," she replied tartly.

"Ah," he sighed, "The difference between instinct and application. Between a state of grace and a condition of effort. Dear friend Lillian, tolerance is dangerous without insight. And the last generation with insight has passed, with the things it understood. Like the last generation of cobblers and glass stainers. It is fatal to try to carry on a dead art—the world has no use for it! The world will trample you down! Don't think of the past, think of your scalp!"

"No," she stated, rising and swaying with the lightheadedness that so frequently visited her now. "To live each moment as if you were in danger—it's demeaning. I will not creep around snarling like some four-legged beast. I am a civilized human being. Your attitude shows a lack of proportion, Vladimir; I feel that you really—"

A flash of sinewy hands; her wrists were seized and crushed together with a stab of pain through whose shock she felt a marginal heat of embarrassment, a tingling dismay of abrupt intimacy. Then the very center of her skull was pierced by his shriek. "You *are* in danger! Can't you *see!*" and he thrust his face at hers, disclosing the red veins of his eyes, bits of sleep matted in the lashes, and the immobile, overwhelmed look of someone who has seen the abyss and is seeing it again. Her heart gave the chop of an axe; with a wail she strained back.

His fixed look broke; his eyes grew flaring, kinetic. "One minute the blood is nice and cozy in its veins—the next, slice! and slice! and slice! Red fountains go up—a festival! Worthy of Handel! Oh marvelous, marvelous! The rain man—" Here he broke off to renew his grip as she struggled frantically to pull away. "The rain man, he's in ecstasies! Such founts and spouts, such excitement! Then at last it's all played out, nothing but puddles, and off he trots, he's big success! And it's big city—many many fountains to be had, all red as—as—red as—"

Her laboring wrists were flung aside; his hands slammed against her face and pressed fiercely into the cheeks.

"Vladimir!" she screamed, "It's Lillian—Lillian!"

The flared eyes contracted. He stepped back and stood immobile. Then a self-admonishing hand rose shakily to his face, which had gone the color of pewter. After a long moment he turned and walked out of the house.

SHE BLUNDERED to the door and locked it behind him, then ran heavily back into the front room where she came to a blank stop, both hands pressed to her chest. Hearing the sound of an engine starting, she wheeled around to the window and pinched back the edge of the shade. Through the rain she saw the big square car jerk and shudder, while its motor rose to a crescendo of whines and abruptly stopped. Vladimir climbed out and started back across the pavement. Her brain finally clicked: the telephone, the police.

With long strides she gained the hall where the telephone stood, and where she now heard the anticipated knock—but mild, rueful, a diminished sound that soon fell away. She moved on haltingly; she would call the police, yes—or a friend from work—or her doctor—someone, anyone, she must talk to someone, and suddenly she stumbled with a cry: it was Vladimir's lumber jacket she had tripped over, still lying on the floor where he had dropped it, his wallet sticking out from the pocket. Outside, the Buick began coughing once more, then it fell silent. A few moments later the shallow, timid knock began again. Without his wallet he could not call a garage, a taxi. It was a fifteen-block walk to his house in the rain. If only she could feel Bedelia's presence beside her, look to the expression in the intelligent eyes. Gradually, concentrating on those eyes, she felt an unclenching inside her. She gazed at the door. Behind it Vladimir was Vladimir still. He had spoken with horrifying morbidity, and even hurt her wrists and face, but he was not the rain man. Bedelia would have seen such seeds. He had been trying to warn her tonight of the world's dangers, and in his passion had set off one of his numerous obsessions—with her fingertip she touched the rouged and aching oval of her cheek. Strange, tortured soul who had stationed himself out in the cold, night after night, to keep her from harm. Bending down, she gathered up the rough, homely jacket; but the knocking had stopped. She went back into the front room and again tweaked aside the shade. He was going away, a small decelerated figure, already drenched. Now he turned the corner and was lost from sight. Depleted, she leaned against the wall.

It might have been a long while that she stood there, that the noise from above masked the sound, but by degrees she became aware of knocking. He must have turned around in the deluge and was now, with what small hope, tapping on the door again. She hesitated, once more summoning the fine violet eyes, the tall brow under its archaic coiffure, which dipped in an affirmative nod. The jacket under her arm, Lillian went into the hall, turned on the porch light, and unlocked the door.

It was not Vladimir who stood there, but Jamie, as wet as if he had crawled from the ocean, his long curls limply clinging to the foolish cape, his neat little features stamped with despair, yet warmed, saved, by the light of greeting in his eyes. Weary, unequal to any visit, she shook her head.

"Jody?" she thought she heard him say, or more likely it was something else—the rain muffled his voice; though she caught an eerie, unnatural tone she now sensed was reflected in the luminous stare. With a sudden feeling of panic she started to slam the door in his face. But she braked herself, knowing that she was overwrought; it was unseemly to use such brusqueness on this lost creature because of her jangled nerves.

So she paused for one haggard, courteous moment to say, "I'm sorry, Jamie, it's late—some other time." And in that moment the shrouded figure crouched, and instantaneously, spasmlike, rushed up against her. She felt a huge but painless blow, followed by a dullness, a stillness deep inside her, and staggering back as he kicked the door shut behind them, she clung to the jamb of the front-room entrance and slowly sank to her knees.

She dimly comprehended the wet cloak brushing her side, but it was the room that held her attention, that filled her whole being. It had grown immense, lofty, and was suffused with violet, overwhelmingly beautiful. But even as she watched, it underwent a rapid wasting, paled to the faint, dead-leaf hue of an old tintype; and now it vanished behind a sheet of black as the knife was wrenched from her body.

A Long Story Short

SHIRLEY HAZZARD

SHIRLEY HAZZARD was born in Sydney, Australia, and lived in the Far East, New Zealand, and Europe before settling in the United States in the 1950s. She has published many short stories, and three novels. She now lives in New York City and in Italy and is completing a fourth novel.

I T WAS in the late nineteen-sixties that something terrible, or at least highly regrettable, happened to Christian Thrale. This came about while his wife, Grace, was at Winchester with the children; which will suggest the nature of the occurrence. Grace had hardly been gone long enough to be properly, let alone acutely, missed; and certainly not long enough for Christian to have telephoned, for he was frugal in these and other matters.

It was early evening on a Tuesday, and Christian was standing at his window in a government office observing the bloom of silky light extending in great reconcilement over London: looking at forests of leaves spread like open hands, and white colonnades and porticoes, and roads that shone like rivers. In the park could be seen a streak of turf, a dab of water, the blue tilting steeples of delphinium. The evening bore the cachet of a huge success magnificently consummated after many botched attempts.

Christian was enjoying not only the manageable rapture of sundown but the novelty of his own high pleasure in it: he had merely glanced out, not expecting anything but weather. Though traffic rumbled, the mnemonic light had a quality of silence; yet seemed no simple fact of nature—for one scarcely felt such a radiance could exist without such a city to encompass. There was human engagement in it, as at some momentous passage of human greeting, or leave-taking, with the world.

Christian, moreover, was aware of himself looking: a sandy man of more than average height and above-average intelligence —yet always keeping at hand the bolt hole of the average; the yardstick, rather, by which departures and excesses might be measured.

A door opened at his back. He did not turn, being pleased to be discovered in the very act of survey and reflection: a sandy man with narrow shoulders who had retained perspective. In childhood Christian had, like many children, defined himself as sensitive; and had made no reassessment in the light of later promptings. In office affairs he had frequently cautioned, "If we lose our humanity we are done for." Although at other times he had said, "We have to draw the line somewhere," and "It's not for me to say."

A crisis had blown up, and what luck, Thrale, you are still here. A meeting was being called, since the cables must be sent that evening. What luck, as Talbot-Sims had just gone down in the lift.

Christian could not feel what luck, thinking of Talbot-Sims spurting for home, for dear life, flying free across London in what he visualized as an open car, although Talbot-Sims was known to travel exclusively by Tube. Drooped over the willow pattern of his blotter, Christian assembled papers, begrudging what, by curious reversal, he felt to be an interruption. He assumed with reluctance the willing expression he normally wore with ease.

Christian Thrale was rising in his profession. Those peering into the oven of his career would report, "Christian is rising," as if he were a cake or loaf of bread. They did not say, "He will go far," which would have suggested temperament; but from time to time remarked his gradual ascent: "Christian has risen."

The conference room looked toward the park. Only the room did so, the men present being focussed on a table, on papers, on one another: on themselves. They stared into the glossy grain of that table as if into a tank. Revived by a fresh draught of importance, they rustled, they murmured, they struck matches and matched watches; because there was a delay. The first rank of the stenographers having got clear, having somehow packed themselves along with Talbot-Sims into that escape hatch of the downward lift—and the doyenne, Miss Ratchitt, being home today bilious—they were waiting for a girl to take the minutes.

This was an aggravation when every moment was precious.

IT WAS like the delphiniums, when she came. For this emergency she had been called back from the ladies' room, where she was preparing to go home—perhaps, who knows, to go out. In those preparations she had literally let down her hair, which was yellow like ripe corn; and had been given no time to redress it. Merely combed back, it fell over her slim blue shoulders and streaked down her spine; and even the worst man there, of whom there were several, yearned for it. Christian could not recall having seen her before in the zones of exercise and encounter, lift or corridor; but perhaps with the hair down it was different.

When she came, it was like the delphiniums.

She sat in a heavy chair—that no one, to put it mildly, pulled out for her. Never having pulled it out for Ratchitt, the contrast would in any case have exposed them. Behind the arras of his expression, Christian watched entranced. The movements, deliberate, shy, with which she laid her lined notebook on the table and folded it, and restrained an extra pencil from rolling; the elbow poised on the table, the head inclined long-lashed to the page, evoking the schoolgirl she had lately been.

Around the tank the flickering intensified before falling ceremoniously away. It was a ritual moment, as if the soloist flung

back coattails over the piano bench or fixed the protective pad
between Stradivarius and jowl. Gentlemen, shall we begin. A
note of reproof from the soloist—even of self-reproof perhaps, of,
Gentlemen, let us now be serious. I need not stress that these
proceedings take place in the utmost confidence, I trust that was
made clear also to Miss—I'm afraid I don't know your—

Cordelia Ware.

Miss Ware. Very good. The Cabinet will conclude its deliber-
ations within the hour and we are informed that.

It fell forward, the flag of hair. An arm came up to pass it
uselessly back over the shoulder. A page hastily turned. A ga-
zelle in the room. China in the bull shop. Everything frail and
fair, cheek, ear, wrist, and the earnest curve blue from waist to
shoulder. It was courting disaster to have closed the creature in
here.

In view of the events of the past week the significance of such
a decision can hardly be overestimated, the far-reaching conse-
quences. Would you make a heading of this, Miss—I'm afraid I
don't recall your—Gentlemen, time is not on our side.

She was taking the minutes. The minutes flew; it was she who
took them; every moment was precious and time not on our side.

Christian remembered lines:

> How can I, that girl standing there,
> My attention fix
> On Roman or on Russian
> Or on Spanish politics?

The verse ended, "O that I were young again, and held her in
my arms!" He remembered that, too. If you learnt the stuff
young, you never lost it. Thirty-eight is not old. You're as old as
you feel. I feel old. Another page flicked, the wrist arching anxiously. There was the same gesture casting back the hair. Time
was on her side. She wore a round watch, inexpensive, with a
band of ribbed black ribbon—grosgrain, they called it in the ads.
She was sinking him, he was listing like a ship. O Christ, it is the
Inchcape Rock. This is ridiculous, and how very unjust. Nine
years of happy marriage decidedly not foundering in any such
rut or reef as is here implied. A wide variety of interests. Spain

this year and the Swan's tour in '65. It is true the office. . . . But not to the extent this girl's effect appears to insinuate.

So Christian tacked, zigzagging on a course of yellow hair and blue flowers. His shipmates might have been bound to the mast, their ears stopped with wax. They seethed, they droned. They plied the ropes. They knew the ropes. As to the humanitarian aspect, deep concern will be voiced; however, this will be done confidentially in order not to exacerbate an already delicate. They were at the stage of leaning back, ties askew. A sensible precaution, Bickerstaff; a good point, Barger. Pertinacity commended as at school; with Christian on this occasion not among the bright boys.

There was no following her when at last she was sent away to type in some room where lights were now switched on and cleaners would have to be excluded. The contents of the wastepaper basket would be burnt. The captains melted away, the kingpins departed.

Roaming a grey corridor, Christian was accosted by a bleached colleague, Armand Elphinstone by name. Christian had sometimes said, "I don't hit it off with Elphinstone." Always adding, "I'm sure it's my fault."

Elphinstone churned loose change in the pockets of unpressed trousers. He shrugged shoulders tweedy with dandruff, pinstriped by fallen hairs.

"And why, may I ask, are we always disorganized. We had no preparation. That meeting could have been called at least an hour earlier. I must say. I don't know how we can look the standing committee in the face." In Elphinstone's pockets invisible sixpences percussed, with a bunch of keys forming the brass. He looked away. "And sending that girl in half dressed."

So he too. Even the blanched Armand.

There was no use hanging about. Elphinstone had rather spoiled things.

THE FOLLOWING DAY there was something else. Christian's own secretary was leaving for her summer holiday.

"And what have they got in mind for me?" As he asked her this, he knew.

"They're giving you a girl from the pool. I'll show her the main things. A Miss Waring. Or Ware. Of course there'll be chaos by the time I get back."

The first day, she had on a dress of worn brown velvet, her hair smoothly coiled. Christian was a man of few words all that morning, thumping down this or that for three copies; this has priority, do that in draft. He could only keep it up till lunchtime; by afternoon he was wanting to sound her and needing her good opinion. She sat taking his dictation, and he could hardly believe he had her there at his tender mercy: he felt tender but not merciful. When she closed her book he said, "I hope you weren't kept too late the other evening."

She lifted her eyes, blank.

He felt he had given himself away. "The evening of the Cabinet announcement."

"I missed the train. We live at Dulwich." Hesitant, as if she trespassed on his interest even by so much as a reply. "One of the girls let me stay at her place."

"You did not have to cancel anything, I hope."

"It was my father's birthday."

What lives we give them, Christian reflected—not without gratification: Well, that's what you're there for. He could recognize a pleasure in displacing her father, with whom he must necessarily stand—one was aware of such things—in rival status. Her eyes were so clear, upward, almost circular, washed like grey glass. He saw that she wished to please him: I hope to give satisfaction, sir. Her voice, like her dress, was doeskin, an excellent thing in woman. The father had called this child Cordelia.

When he heard her typing he made a pretext to stand awhile by her desk. There was something nearly sexual in this, like the relation of tenor to accompanist, he standing and commanding, she seated and subsidiary. She faintly sweetly smelt of talcum or shampoo. Her fingers, grubby from carbon, unnerved by his proximity, turned six copies to scrub at an error. He saw also that pages were spread to be sorted. A "Style Manual"—what style could there conceivably be in all this?—was open to instructions of inane and infinite tedium. I have the honour to be, Sir, Your Excellency's humble and obedient. On the surface of the desk there was a dusting of molted rubber over the clawings and droppings of a score of previous, vanished secretary-birds.

Excellence and honor. With less satisfaction, he wondered, Why do they put up with this?

He all but placed his hand on her brown velvet shoulder, bidding her depart in peace. He could very nearly feel the smooth life curve into his palm—and at that instant would have let her off, wished her safe from all his harm, while she was so anxiously, innocently bent to her rubbishy task.

"That one is of prime importance," he said. "The rest can wait."

From his room he heard her storming the keys, the rip of the roller, arpeggios of sentences, the andante of an indented passage. A distraught exclamation for a false note. It was curious that a machine could reproduce the anxiety of the person operating it. The imagined globe of her velour shoulder stayed, tremulous, in his hand still cupped to its contour. If he had touched her, it would not have resulted in her departure or her peace.

Evening rose like dawn. *Aux uns portant la paix, aux autres le souci.* The city inhaled it like a breath of immense relief. A wave of excitement lifted Christian from desk to window—where the metropolis once more lay helpless and expectant under a dusk phenomenal as an eclipse. A cautious man would have looked through special glasses, or a hole cut in cardboard. With the naked eye Christian gazed; and yet again knew himself to be gazing. He was one who could still see the sky. Who knew his Yeats. His Baudelaire. His Freud.

Not for nothing were these names prefaced by the possessive pronoun.

He was tempted to ask her outright to go to dinner with him. But no, not outright; and not the first evening. Let a decent interval elapse, and hope the weather would hold. There was prodigality in this—they had so little time. In thought he said "they"; and could not think unjustified this newly possessive pronoun.

The following day was hot. The city opened all its windows as Christian rode to work in his car. Down to tower'd Camelot. As if by assignation, she wore the dress of the cornflowers—was it? —and her hair down. He had heard that girls were ironing their hair that year, in order to wear it long and flat; but did not think that would apply to her. It would not be possible to do this

oneself—perhaps their mothers did it for them. He tried to picture the little kitchen at Dulwich, neat as a new pin, the mother
shapeless in flowered apron, and she with her head laid on the
ironing board. It was like an execution.

It was a simple matter to detain her after work. There was no
difficulty in manufacturing a crisis—most crises in that place
being manufactured ones—by retarding some memorandum into
the afternoon. When she came back at two from her hasty sandwich (he assumed the sandwich, noted the haste), he struck. At
six they were alone, he attentively reading over, she pounding.
He got up, went to the gents to spruce. He ran water, ran a
comb, ran a critical eye. Smiled into a square of quicksilver that
was cracked from side to side. Walking back along the inert grey
arteries, he could hear the machine still racing, like a heart.

He had plumped for the magisterial assertion: "I am going to
drive you home." Had, of course, hoped she wouldn't look quite
so bowled over. "Let's face it"—with this interpolation Christian
habitually reproved a widespread tendency to shirk—"we're
going to be another half hour here, at least. Might as well"—
foregone conclusion—"have a bite of dinner somewhere, then I'll
drive you."

He thought he detected slight equivocation—he would not call
it suspicion—mingling with her astonishment. She must be
pleased, however; even thrilled. A girl who passed her days turning carbons would welcome any diversion. Your Excellency's
humble and obedient.

Not that he regarded himself as any diversion.

"You are kind," she said, without causing him a qualm.

She was in the car at his side. They were crossing a river, the
river, after Chablis and Dover sole. It was by no means dark.
Ahead, the smooth common was an innocence of late cricket
balls and unleashed terriers and elderly couples safely benched.
(The hanky-panky would come later, with nightfall.) The trees,
though; he had never felt it before—such trees, like clouds, like
screens, like great bouquets. She was doing this: first cornflowers,
now trees. Light-winged Dryad, beechen green, Rima the bird-
girl that was her type, the constant nymph what was her name
Tess of the—no, not that: Tessa. All this at Clapham.

He would have liked to stop the car, there and then, just to look at the trees; and would have taken her in his arms almost incidentally. But the decent interval must elapse. She had said so little, everything correct and nothing foolish. She was quite still, and looked at the evening and the trees, her head tipped toward the seat back though not reclining. They drove on, along suburban avenues for which he felt the kindliness one summons for a boyhood friend who has not prospered.

"You turn left at the College."

He turned.

"It's along here on the right. This one."

He had been confident of a row of demoralized asters, three front steps, a porch of frosted glass glumly bulging from brick. And could not have been more irritated if she had deliberately deceived him. Not that the house was grand: a pretty house, white but eighteenth century, banked with fuchsia along a brief crescent of raked gravel. But it was a house, precisely, of the sort he and Grace had looked at and decided they could not afford.

Every window was lit. It was like a party house described in a novel: "ablaze." (Christian himself preferred to switch lights off when not in use.) Or it was like a ship, festive and stately with all her canvas up and pennants fluttering. On the ground floor a silk curtain belled through French windows, like a spinnaker.

He pulled up at the door. The car turned shabby in the glow from the house. He remembered plastic toys on the rear seat.

"You'll come in." She was almost social on her own territory.

"I'll be getting back. It's late." He was being rude, but the house was a menace. He could feel the father's eye on him, see himself blinking in the lights, shown up as if at a police station. I must warn you that anything you say will be.

Even so, heard himself announce, "Another time." And boldly leant across her lap to manage the door, laying his hand over her own ineffectual grip as if sealing a contract.

"Up and push," he said. Then, "Give it a good bang."

A Scots terrier scrambled down the steps to her, all muzzle and paws and little sprout of tail. He heard her say, "Here, Hoots. Here, Hootsie," in a kind of ecstasy.

He withdrew to town in confusion. Definitely a reversal. He had been prepared for his role, genial but restrained, master of the situation in the modest house of the begonias and new-pin kitchen; helping them over their natural diffidence. Had even been ready for a possible Socialist brother whose surly challenges could be gracefully debunked. But distinctly not prepared for the equalizing properties of Lowestoft, Regency, bound editions, a faded but valuable Samarkand; and, perhaps, attributed-to-Hoppner over the original fireplace.

Was there not, in fact, a recognized condition called the Cophetua Complex? Or had he made that up?

He disliked, moreover, the sensation of the narrow squeak.

Reaching home, he put in a call to Grace. This, which should have been a help, was not. A neighbor had dropped in, it was too late to bring the children to the phone, just one second I have to turn something off. Jeremy had been disappointed in the authentic Round Table, which they had paid to see that morning; and had cried.

"Anything going on at the office?"

"This dustup in Africa's got us jumping. Then there's always the Secretary of State. And we're short-handed as usual. They've given me a temporary."

"Miss Mellish got away, then?"

"There'll be chaos by the time she gets back."

He put the phone down and took off his shoes. He could see the House of Ware, its white sails crowding. The girl bending, in that doorway lit like a stage: her face and hands active with love as she reached to the dog scrabbling in a ferment at her ankles, her knees. He could hear her speaking, in her voice of an articulate doe; but could feel the very burr in the animal's coarse coat. He could scarcely wait for tomorrow.

NEXT MORNING he stowed the toys away in the boot of the car. The weather was holding, the decent interval elapsing. A Friday sense of near-abandon enlivened the department, as if something other than an English weekend lay ahead. There was a lull even in Africa, where crocodiles idled on sluggish waters between walls of motionless bamboos.

The sight of Cordelia Ware in pink printed flowers dispelled the defeat of Dulwich; exorcising the spectre, even, of Detective-Inspector Father.

Only Elphinstone had a cold. Elphinstone was flying to an important conference in Brussels that evening, and was concerned about effects of cabin pressure on the ears.

Christian stood by Elphinstone's desk. "All set?"

Elphinstone coughed. At first phlegmlessly, like faulty ignition, the engine turning over and over till it caught. He pulled a handkerchief from his pocket in a flurry of lint.

Christian turned away and looked at two framed photographs hung beside the map on the wall: Elphinstone's grandfather in diplomatic dress; and a weeding party of British residents once organized by Elphinstone at the English cemetery on Capri.

The map was so old that India was pink.

At last Elphinstone replied. "I have no problem." He said the word "problem" with sardonic emphasis, to make clear he knew it for an Americanism.

"You know I'm on call tomorrow." Christian was duty officer for the weekend. "If anything blows up."

Elphinstone was all sympathy. "You're not having much of a summer. I must say. Losing your weekend." He raised the clotted handkerchief to his face and looked at Christian over it, like a bandit. "And working late."

Christian took his eyes off the trowels, grins, and brandished dandelions of the English cemetery, and stared Elphinstone down. "Not to worry."

When Christian went out, Elphinstone hawked once more into his handkerchief, and spread it to dry on the ventilator with malodorous result.

In innocence of this, in all innocence, Cordelia Ware glanced up from her scruffy papers as Christian came through—her look a refreshing contrast to Elphinstone's. Christian sat at his desk signing papers and vengefully slinging them into boxes. He felt rage, and triumph. Elphinstone's eyes above the bandanna had been something to see. Old Gandolf envied me, so fair she was. An incompetent, an intolerable fool imposed on us, let's face it, because his grandfather negotiated a disastrous treaty in 1908. God, if the public only knew.

The afternoon wore on, wore out. Steadily relieved of the ballast of early departures, the entire floor became airy, buoyant. Miss Ware—Cordelia—brought him the incoming. The lull persisted, extending over continents, taking the wind out of

Africa's sails. The official boom swung ineffectually to and fro in the global Doldrums. There were copies for information, and the text of a ministerial speech which would not now be delivered owing to altered circumstances. There were papers marked PUS, for the Permanent Under Secretary of State, on which action was neither contemplated nor required. There was a postcard of the rocks at Étretat from Miss Mellish: Hope all goes well.

"Mellish is in Monet country."

"She sent me one too." She handed it to him. The same rocks: I forgot to mention, just leave the filing for my return.

They stood, each holding a card, ticket of leave, with time running out.

He could not be mistaken in its stillness. The phone rang.

It was an opposite number in a parallel department. "Look here, Thrale. We're not getting the picture on the Brussels meeting."

"What more do you want? We're sending one of our best people."

"No reflection on your nest, old boy. Merely a matter of communication." The word "communication" was given the arch inflection Elphinstone had conferred on "problem."

Grimacing to the girl, Christian waved the receiver in a show of exasperation. He had never committed improprieties with Miss Mellish. He was in a fever for the day to end: or begin. The voice twanged on, irresistibly drawn to jargon but unwilling to take the blame.

With impatient ball-point Christian scored, on the blotter, the outline of the colored postcard, his *carnet de bal*.

All at once she was saying, "If there's nothing more," and holding her handbag. She had a scarlet cardigan over her arm and was mouthing Goodbye, Mr. Thrale. It had never occurred to him that she would of her own accord leave promptly. Before he could get the phone down she was gone; and in the corridor nowhere to be seen.

He lost his head completely and strode out to stop the lift.

Only Elphinstone was poised between the lift doors, ready to plunge. Elphinstone grinned at Christian over his shoulder, and raised his fingers in a Victory sign. He might have been taking a parachute jump. As he disappeared his hand went to his heart as if fumbling for the rip cord.

Back in his office, Christian stood at the window where it had all begun. Disappointed as a child confronted with the original Round Table. He was unsure of what he had intended, but definitely not this prospect of brooding through a failed evening. On a last clangor of filing cabinets and desk drawers, the office fell silent. All across London, girls were gliding in and out of cars, and younger men were leaning over saying, "Up and push." Couples were lifting trays and saying, "You bring the ice," and the garden furniture from Harrods was outdoors at last.

Only Christian stood disconsolate by his office casement.

Had it not been for the crimson sweater, he would scarcely have credited what came next. She was crossing the street below, walking slow and heading for the park. Or, it could be, for the Underground; but one does not walk that way toward a train, lifting one's head to the sky and hitching one's woolly casually over a shoulder. She had slim legs and little flat shoes; and, like all her movements, her walk was charming.

He left the web, he left the loom. In three paces was at his desk slamming drawers and snatching pen and spectacles. He retained enough presence of mind to grab up an envelope of weekend documents as a prop.

When, in the street, he had her in view, he held back in imaginary relish of the sweetness of it. Stalking her, he knew an assurance of happiness such as he had never felt as an adult and which was incompatible with childhood. Christian had been in love as a lad, and as a young man ready to take a wife. But not as now when, quite out of any context, representing no forces other than those beyond his control, he watched Cordelia Ware in a frenzy of tenderness, confused between worship and condescension.

He overtook her as she was turning into the park. He was the soul of amiable surprise: No Dulwich? She explained, the evening was so beautiful, and the park. They passed through the gateway together. They were drifting past banks of iridescent flowers and among cornelian trees. They crossed a bridge and sat on a bench alone. The office envelope, whose wadded warm sensation had grown repugnantly alive in Christian's hand, was stationed on his other side like an overzealous accomplice.

Here there was a vast repose, the earth all grass and the sky all heaven; although waterfowl were squabbling over the flung crusts and a newspaper was carried past with an atrocious headline. Somewhere overhead, Elphinstone was safely airborne, swallowing hard to protect his ears and taking an extra mint from the proffered dish to be on the safe side.

She sat straight, not in a gym-class way, with her fingers intertwined on her crossed knee; and, with the evening on her hair and her pale skin, was all light. She was looking at him, grave and listening. Like the Muse: patient, but accessible only to those acting in good faith.

"Will you dine with me?" It was his most humble speech to her yet.

Pink flowers rose on her printed breast. "If that is all right," she said.

He did not know how to treat that appeal to his authority, and let it pass. Anything now seemed possible. The whole world, like the weekend, lay before them. He had not forgotten how she had once spent the night in town with a friend; even at the time he had filed that info for possible future use.

"Won't they expect you at home?"

"I'll telephone."

He did not wish to learn what she would say. To hell with Inspector Father. They would sit between grass and sky while the light lasted, and later he would take her to dinner at a little place off Duke of York Street where one went on red-letter days.

He had cashed a check that morning.

The immeasurable expansion of likelihood shed new tolerance on every mortal thing: the subdued honkings of human enterprise that reached them from the road, the screech of an intemperate fowl almost at their feet, the couple on the nearby grass whose undulations beneath a spread mackintosh were like some lewd wink in their own direction; the iron dukes and stone admirals fixed atop pedestals and columns. All were appropriate to this earth, even the Guardsmen in their vermilion Mao jackets and Afro busbies, and the distant reticulation of a rising skyscraper against whose erection Christian had recently signed a petition.

Christian was removed from pettiness, as one is only by immeasurable happiness or grief. His preoccupation with importance had unfitted him for greatness: he was a man of vicarious consequence only; but in those moments understood the large hearts of heroes.

In this mood the evening passed. Christian took her arm at the first green light and did not release it until they reached the restaurant. Over dinner he talked of Spain, where she had never been—"Let's face it, Madrid *is* the Prado"—and the Hebrides, where she had. He discovered that the house at Dulwich had belonged to her grandfather; that she had three brothers, and an uncle deafened by too much quinine during a decade in Bengal. In addition to the Scottie there was a fringed cat called Ruffles.

All this—the Grecos, the Cuillins, the uncle, and the ruffled cat —paraded glittering through space in one narrow room.

They walked back toward the car through the broad streets and capacious squares laid out in narrower times. Scarcely a vehicle passed them; not a soul ascended the steps of the right clubs or issued from the little petuniaed porticoes of the great corporations. You could hear a footfall, or peal of laughter, all the length of that noble and unearthly promenade.

Christian unlocked the car door for her, and stood holding it but blocking her entry.

"I must see you."

"I know," she said.

He let go of the door, which lurched slowly open like a shutter on a derelict house. Into the back seat, from which that morning he had put away childish things, he hurled his envelope of bogus papers. He drew Cordelia Ware into his arms.

THEY—they—had almost three weeks before Miss Mellish returned. As luck would have it, luck held. The weather also. Africa continued quiescent, Cordelia's parents left for the Dordogne, and Grace felt the extra fortnight would do the boys a world of good.

Even Elphinstone, though back from Brussels, was having extensive work done on his teeth.

Christian Thrale took Cordelia Ware by her perfect little elbow in vacant evening streets, and drew her to him in silent rooms. He leant his cheek on her smooth coiled head, and took her golden tresses—there was no other word for them—loose in incredulous hands. She in turn slipped her arms about his neck, or lifted his palm to her face and kissed it. In his Hillman Minx they crossed and recrossed the Rubicon at Battersea Bridge. *Iacta alea est.* They sat, as he had dreamed of doing, beneath the elegiac trees.

As far as Christian was concerned, these delicious proceedings nevertheless left, quite literally, something to be desired. While the virginal aspect of this girl had first attracted him, Time, gentlemen, was not on our side—what with Grace consulting timetables and Miss Mellish pushing the boat out from the Normandy beachhead.

She said, "I am happy just being with you." Her hand along his arm in one of her precise and fragile gestures. "You cannot decently complain of that."

He laughed. "Then indecently I complain." It was hard to make her see that her wishes were not the only thing to be—rather, that she herself did not know them.

It would be unusual if she turned out to be—girls these days were not; at least, not by the time one met up with them.

It is hard to say which of her limned attitudes most delighted him, the intently curved, or slimly upright; or which of her movements, chaste and extravagant as those of a ballerina. She had this way of looking—you would not have said "trustful" exactly, but "believing." She applied to one's judgment. She put simple questions with genuine inquiry, as if wishing to discover how the world turned. The look, the appeals, the inquiries had the effect of assigning responsibility. Christian enjoyed being the framer of constitutions, the dispenser of unalterable law.

"Your Socratic Method," he told her, taking her upturned face between his hands and smiling down from the stature she conferred. She did not ask what this was, but maintained unde-

flected her unfathomable openness. It was hard to see how a look
could be both level and uplifted.

Never in any circumstances did she use his name, his Christian
name. His remarking on this led to a small misunderstanding: "I
thought," she said, "you would not like that in the office."

He had assumed as a matter of course she would not use it
there. Some things went without saying.

One day she asked him, "Do you mind the deception?"

He said, "Somewhat to my surprise, no." He could not leave
himself there, and went on, "I just don't want people's feelings to
get hurt."

He did not mean hers.

It was not until the end of the final week that he had, as the
old saying goes, his way with her. Christian lived in a crescent of
Victorian dwellings that had once been ivory, robust, slightly ir-
regular, like a mouthful of sturdy teeth; but were now pared,
drilled, recapped, and made uniform. It was here that, locking
doors and drawing curtains, he finally lay down in his matrimo-
nial bed with Cordelia Ware.

The question of beds, indeed, could not be gracefully resolved.
It was either the children's or his own. She made, in this regard,
one of her inquiries: "Do you mind it?"

"Not in the least." He added, "This is my side anyway."

It was curious how abandon begot precaution. It was that very
evening he began to make himself clear. "I shall never forget
this. Any of it." Surely she could not, to employ her own phrase,
decently complain of that. He told her, "I shall be wildly jealous
of the man you marry. I hate him already."

She lay looking at the ceiling, eyes wide as if she could not
close them. After a while she asked, "How shall we go on now?"

"My dear, I don't know." After all, he was not an oracle. She
was staring up as if scanning the heavens. "We'll have to play it
by ear." He delivered this Americanism with the Elphinstone
intonation.

The following day, he telephoned to Winchester. Grace had
seen Jane Austen's grave: "I wish you had been here, Chris."

"The only one I like is 'Pride and Prejudice.'"

"I mean here this summer. It will never be so beautiful again."

Their days apart, and nights, their divided pleasures pained him. She was speaking of the Close, the roses, the labyrinth of streams, and the meadows beyond the school; all of which perturbed him. He broke in: "I can't hang on forever. This is costing the earth."

FOR THREE WEEKS Christian had felt himself an explorer in his native city. Not because he had taken Cordelia Ware much about, unless you count once to Chiswick, once to Greenwich, and the Wallace Collection, where they did not get upstairs. But because the visibility had cleared for him as for a smogbound pilot, disclosing roofs and spires and gardens and the congested flow of roads at thrilling and dangerous proximity; revealing birds in flight and cats walking on walls. The curves of earth and water had become landmarks not to be taken for granted. Above all, he had perceived in the human form the sweet glory of the elms and oaks of Battersea: he saw men as trees walking.

How, on a Monday filled with normality, a morning of wives ringing the butcher or going through trouser pockets before sending to the cleaner, Christian travelled once again by Underground. And Miss Mellish was in early, sorting the backlog and murmuring, "I don't know I'm sure."

"We managed." Loyally. "And not badly, considering."

Miss Mellish, who had been unlucky with the *fruits de mer* and whose back had gone out at Château Gaillard, was forbearing: "She's willing. Which is saying a lot these days."

Christian agreed. "Of course it's not like having you."

"That's experience, Mr. Thrale," Mellish told him. "I was just as green as that girl myself, in the beginning. The very same. We all have to begin somewhere."

Christian could have cried out for the pain of it.

Later they brought him a form to fill out, on the performance of Cordelia Ware. He wrote that she was willing; that she could take responsibility; and that her work looked neat on the page.

Grace came home, carrying a heavy suitcase and a crock of lavender honey. The children rampaged through the house: "Where's Bimbo? I can't find Bimbo."

"Bimbo's in the boot of the car."

All things were being brought to light, set to rights. Except Cordelia Ware. Limitless vertiginous space was contracting to a decent acreage. A place for everything and everything in its place.

Cordelia Ware was back in the pool.

Christian's situation had rather abruptly become a predicament. To feel for his isolation in it, one must understand that Cordelia Ware had been, as she was to remain, the most impetuous episode of Christian's life. By far. Other precipitate action, in combat, office, or home, having been sanctioned or demanded by the social order and—even when carried out single-handed— performed in mighty concert. Only in the Cordelia Ware undertaking had he ventured out on his own—rushing out-of-doors, literally, without looking. It was a mutation as of fish to land; and Christian, gasping on the bleak shingle, knew himself a creature of the ocean and the shoal.

In his solitude he said, "I blame myself." An accusation that seldom rings entirely true. If Christian placed blame elsewhere, then it was, curiously enough, on literature. He blamed—but that was not the word—the promptings and colorings of language, that put sights in his eyes and sentiments in his heart. He felt himself importuned by echoes that preceded utterance, betrayed by metaphors and exaltations that, acquired young, could never be eradicated.

Literature was a good servant but a bad master.

In the pool, Cordelia Ware sat straight at her long-carriage Underwood, though not in a gym-class way. Budgetary figures were being prepared: the machines hurtled violently from point to tabulated point like shuttles in a textile factory. She no longer bent intently to the page, and, relieved of that anxiety, had grown proficient. The supervisor told her, "There you are. The experience has done you good."

There was no window. She looked at the wall where a window might have been.

All of this Christian somehow and reluctantly knew. His time was not his own. Africa was tuning up: unpromising sounds rose from roofs of corrugated iron, and even from the Plexiglas civic centers where it had been hoped that air-conditioning would lead to compromise. The situation was deteriorating.

He contrived to meet Cordelia Ware at lunchtime during the second week, in a pub rather far from the office. Although he was prompt, she was already there when he came; and if she had had the sense she was born with would not have looked so hang-dog. The weather had changed. The very mornings were now crepuscular. Everywhere there were signals of autumn, even of winter: dark afternoons, spirals of petals and blown leaves, and the miners threatening strike.

Christian put the newspaper in his raincoat pocket and sat be-side Cordelia Ware. "The whole world," he cautioned her, "is going up in smoke." If only this would give her a sense of pro-portion. If only the tinderbox condition of the globe would ob-scure, minimize, or even make irrelevant his own dilemma.

"It will be a bitter winter," he announced; and she looked, looked. "If the miners go out." He could not now say whether that stare was steadfast or implacable—neither being entirely desirable. "No one can deny, of course, that a miner's life is intol-erable." *If we lose our humanity.*

She said, "People are on their side. There is that." Tepid shan-dies were handed over the counter, and he paid. "I mean, they are heroes. What with the risk and the pit. We all know it is frightful. In an office there is not even that."

He did not like this. "Aren't you dramatizing?"

She leant back against the Edwardian effect of quilted plastic leather, her head frankly reclining. A young man at the bar looked at her white throat. Christian put his hand on hers, on her knee beneath the table. *Forgive me, Cordelia; and you have some cause.* Her eyes at once met his: *no cause, no cause.* He did not understand his own irresolution—wanting now this, now that. Still less could he see why vacillation should seem at pres-ent his only virtue.

He had handled it badly from the word go. *And if that word have not quite kil'd thee.*

In books and films The Girl brought matters to a head. *We must not meet again; this is goodbye, Mr. Christian.* Like most banality, the formula was now seen to originate in fundamentals. Cordelia Ware was evidently not about to avail herself of her unbearable and commendable prerogative.

She took up a parched sandwich whose lifting corners bared a scaled sardine. She left the tough crusts with the half-gherkin on her plate. When they went out the man at the bar looked at her openly, tenderly, ignoring Christian's claim or seeing through it.

In the street Christian said, "You had an admirer in there." He did not mean himself.

"Yes."

Having drawn the man to her attention, he was displeased to find she had seen him. In no time obviously she will take up with someone else. You iron your hair, you nickname God's creatures, go thy ways.

In the taxi she sat straight in a corner with her fingers laced on her knee. So many fingers—there must have been the right number, but it seemed a veritable lattice of fingers, fingers. Beside her the window was pitted with sudden rain. The cab darkened. She was almost facing him from her corner, her hair the only bright thing and her eyes the color of rain.

The window clouded like a spoilt mirror. Christian said, "My word, it's close." He was wondering how to make his necessary separate exit from the cab in the sudden downfall; or downpour. He was wondering if after all he did not love this incomparable girl.

When she got back to the pool, the supervisor was saying, "There are not enough long carriages to go round." They might have been preparing for a state procession. Scrolls of lined paper were distributed like proclamations: "If you roll it in reverse it goes flat."

Cordelia Ware sat before her long-carriage typewriter with head bowed, as if saying Grace.

Christian, coming out of a discreetly later lift, looked about him with alertly upward head, like a hound that has lost the scent. From the region of the pool there came the sound of typewriters ticking in measured desperation, like last messages from the bridge. He remembered her bitter speech: the risk and the pit.

"Back to the salt mines." It was Elphinstone, himself late from a root-canal job. They loitered. The news was ominous. Could not have come at a worse time either, what with Barger still on Mykonos and Talbot-Sims on antibiotics. Elphinstone had the latest about the Secretary of State.

"Dropped a brick and lost his marbles. The Emperor

Augustus, what?" Reaching the end of a corridor, they wheeled and walked slowly back, like a palace guard. "I happened to have the opportunity of observing him at close quarters." Elphinstone had once briefly sat in the front seat of a car in which Cabinet members were rear passengers. "There is, quite frankly, no discretion. None whatever."

They were at Christian's door; yet Elphinstone detained, Elphinstone deplored. There was earnestness in it. "Take it from me, Thrale. I cannot claim to have achieved much in my life. I must say. But whatever I have achieved has been by observing the rules. We cannot be too scrupulous."

Whether these words were intended for Christian was debatable. The debate engaged him throughout that afternoon. Culpability, unfelt for Grace or Cordelia, was, in regard to the office, deeply stirred. And what of the rising cake of Christian Thrale? Perhaps Armand meant well, no friend like an old friend, a word to the wise. A stitch in time. Or was worse to follow?—Christian literally on the carpet, called into a room quiet with authority, a door closing, a chief saying, "Your private life, Thrale, is of course your own business," and meaning of course it was not.

> And they cross'd themselves for fear,
> All the knights at Camelot.

But he was letting imagination run away with him. Run, in fact, riot.

Reasonable speculations commuted madly, repudiated at the frontiers of belief. The most innocuous appointment became a summons to social and professional doom. He completed the day's tasks with attention wrackingly divided. Hanging like a dead weight from a strap in the Underground, he thought, This cannot go on; I am behaving like—well, like Raskolnikov.

The risk and the pit. That evening he was distraught, though he did not show it, throughout a benefit performance for which Grace had bought expensive tickets months beforehand.

Next morning there was an appalling development: Cordelia Ware appeared in his office. She stood in the doorway—he later fancied she had leant against the lintel but this grotesque embellishment merely reflected the dread the incident inspired.

(He imagined, too, for example, that her look had been challenging; whereas at the time its most awful element had been
abjection.)

Through a stroke of immense good fortune, Miss Mellish was
not in sight. Christian got up from his desk—and it seemed that
year he was ever sinking down or rising up at that desk, as if at
some anchorage or place of prayer. "Cordelia," he said urgently,
coming over to prevent her approach, "I cannot possibly. This is
not the place for. The last thing either of us wants is."

It was hideous. From her expression, she might have done
anything: wailed, wept, made havoc of his draft report. He took
her elbow—the sensation charged with almost clinical imper-
sonality, as if she had been a patient in a hospital—and steered
her for departure. Her very submissiveness alarmed. He was
talking, talking: "We mustn't lose our. Let things get out of. This
serves no useful. Cordelia do be." She had not said a word.

She went. The terrible receded, with labored breaths, into the
highly regrettable. A time and place for everything. She does not
know her place. The position had already been filled.

Under existing conditions there was in fact no time or place
for Cordelia Ware.

The girl was obviously neurotic. All things considered he
could congratulate himself on a narrow squeak. There was no
telling what she might or might not. It would be appalling if—
but that was out of the question. Only in plays. Ophelia. The
awful apparition in his doorway was in retrospect suggestive of a
Mad Scene.

Everything in disarray. The trees shredding, the shrubbery
tousled with rain; the sails of Dulwich furled and the wind whistling in the shrouds. It was time to call a halt, there and then.
With some difficulty, Christian arranged to meet Cordelia Ware
after work. He telephoned Grace, blaming Africa. Rising, at six,
from the launching pad of his desk, he could only remind himself, like a child, that at this time tomorrow it would all be over.

To make a long story short—which was the way Christian put
it to himself in later years, in the synopsis of remembrance—he
made himself clear, once and for all. There was nothing for it
but the clean break. It was, as he told her, the hardest thing he
had ever had to do. I blame myself. If I have hurt you, Cordelia.

IF, she said; and in such a voice. If, as I say, I have hurt you. Harrowing. He had never seen anyone cry in a restaurant—not even at another table. It was bizarre to think he had originally been attracted by her reserve.

He said, "I think I have learnt my lesson."

She leaned her elbow on the table and her brow on her hand. Strands of hair stuck along her cheek, and trailed over her ear. In his heart, as the unconscious used to be called, he knew he had asked for this; but loathed every second of it.

Thank God he did not have the car. He took her to the train. Inevitably they had just missed one. People glanced in their direction, and away. She said, "Please go. Please go." But he stuck it out to the bitter end. He had been young once himself, and felt her suffering as if it were his own. After all, he was not made of wood.

There is no question here of defending his conduct, which was inexcusable from beginning to end. If, however, he had not felt a colossal release when that train at last pulled out, he would scarcely have been human.

Shadows on the Water

ANDREW FETLER

ANDREW FETLER teaches in the MFA Program in Creative Writing at
the University of Massachusetts, Amherst. His fiction has won an
Atlantic Monthly "First" prize, the *Northwest Review* Fiction Award,
and an NEA grant for creative writing. His work includes a novel,
The Travelers, published by Houghton Mifflin, and a collection of
stories, *To Byzantium,* published by the University of Illinois Press.

I

M Y BROTHER DIED a suicide in Newhall Hospital, California. He was forty-nine, seven years my senior. At
sundown, as I carried his phonograph and a cardboard box of his
effects to the parking lot, a man detached himself from a group
of inmates on the lawn and joined me. His name was Robert
Sladick, but everybody at Newhall called him Doc. Before his
commitment Mr. Sladick had taught philosophy at the California
State College at Morley. Talkative as a janitor, helpful and kind,

Originally appeared in *American Review 24.* Copyright © 1976 by Bantam
Books, Inc. Reprinted in *To Byzantium,* copyright © 1976 by Andrew
Fetler. By permission of the University of Illinois Press.

he ran errands for the nurses, expressed opinions about books, and had perhaps spent more time with my brother than anybody else at Newhall.

"I see you got Tom's stuff," he said. "How are you feeling?"

"Fine. How are you, Mr. Sladick?"

"Here, let me help you." He took the phonograph. It was a cheap portable model intended for the teen-age market, its case decorated with red white and blue stripes, its cover picturing a dancing girl in a bikini. Tom had bought the phonograph when he went to the hospital. Mr. Sladick peered in the cardboard box. "You got his records?" he asked.

"I got them." The cardboard box contained books, mostly, and three phonograph recordings: Nazi marching songs, Red Army songs, and gospel songs.

"All Tom cared about was this Carlyle book and the Nazi songs," said Mr. Sladick, trudging along beside me. "I'm getting a pass for his funeral."

I thanked him. Tom had hardly known anybody the last few years.

"They say he did it with Veronal?" asked Mr. Sladick.

"That's right."

"I'm really sorry," he said. "I wish he could have waited a year. Reforms take time. In a year, Tom might have been active again."

"Doing what?"

"He could have been a professor of mystical literature."

We passed two ambulances at Emergency. The parking lot ended at a high wire fence. A guard sat in the guardhouse by the gates.

"If you want to bury yourself," said Mr. Sladick, "bury your talents. That's what Tom did. He had it all at his fingertips— demons, devils, witches. But he did nothing with it."

"He was a priest for a while," I said.

"No, he wasn't," said Mr. Sladick. "Your father was a real Russian priest, trained and ordained. Tom's license from that crazy outfit didn't make him anything."

The cardboard box felt heavy in my arms. Except for a fitful nap on the 727, I had not slept since leaving Boston. I wanted my bed at the Sheraton Arms in Hollywood. I put the cardboard box and the phonograph in the Hertz car and got in behind the wheel.

"Look," said Mr. Sladick, "why don't you come see me tomorrow? I know a lot about Tom. How about lunch? I'll give you a good debriefing."

I had to bury Tom, settle matters with our lawyer, and fly back to Boston. "I'm fine, Doc. Thanks just the same."

"You don't look fine. Is that hill in Los Feliz all yours now?"

"Yes."

"Get rid of it," he said. "Tom figured you could get two hundred fifty thousand dollars for it. Somebody wants to build a posh dining place up there."

"They'd have to tear down the church."

"I know all about that church," said Mr. Sladick. "Give it to Disneyland. That's what Tom would have done, next time around."

"I have to go now, Mr. Sladick. Thanks for the talk. I appreciate it."

"Wait a minute," he said. He walked around the car and got in beside me.

I should have locked the door. The guard, I saw, sat in the guardhouse, watching us.

Mr. Sladick said, "You have a brother who killed himself, and you have the same blood. I should think you'd want to know why he killed himself?"

"Why did he kill himself?"

"I don't know. I'm only saying you'll want to think about it. While you're at it, think about Los Angeles. You know how Tom hated Los Angeles. I understand you can see much of Los Angeles from that hill of yours?"

"Mr. Sladick, I've got to get some sleep. I'll call you tomorrow, if I can. I'll know then what my schedule will be. All right?"

"You won't call," he said. "Let me tell you something, as long as you're here. People live in Los Angeles. How do you think they get by? They are adjusted to little systems like the I-Thou Temple or The Church of the Open Door, or The First Church of the Divine Mushroom. And not just churches. Neighborhood clubs, VFW posts, local taverns, political parties, motorcycle gangs, marriages. I was telling Tom last week: suppose you made a catalog of these institutions and listed their members, who would not be accounted for? Even the bum on his last leg has his daily haunts. All part of Los Angeles. And Los Angeles is part of America, and America is part of the world, and the world is part of the galaxies. Do you know what keeps this house of cards from coming down?"

I didn't.

"We bang around enough in it to bring it down," he said. "When your father died, Tom could play with that cute church and invent his own religion, if I can believe him. He loved metaphysical panic. But when your mother died he had no system left, just himself."

"Did he ever talk about me?"

"He didn't need you," said Mr. Sladick. "He had his Carlyle and his Nazis."

The sun had set and gusts blew sand over the parking lot.

"What about you, now?" said Mr. Sladick. "Are you still teaching Russian in Boston?"

"Yes."

"Crummy job. Professors have to write books nobody wants to write and nobody wants to read."

"That's true."

"All right, but don't quit. What would your next institution be? Do you know what Tom's last institution was, when his goofy religion folded? The Piggery on La Cienega."

The Piggery, an architectural fantasy squeezed in between The Tahitian Hut and The Roaring Twenties on La Cienega Boulevard's Restaurant Row, was built to resemble a pig with a pork chop in its mouth. It was a dark hangout for young people, bodies writhing to deafening rock, pinball machines, shrieks. At the exit in the rear, you stepped on a rubber mat that activated an electronic fart. Tom had been attracted for a season to noisy amusements. He visited roller coasters and tilt-a-whirls, and reported that the pleasures of youth are the torments of age.

"Tom used to eat hamburgers there," said Mr. Sladick. "He'd pick up girls at the I-Thou Temple just to take them to The Piggery. That was his last institution."

I closed my eyes for a moment, and when I opened them the

lights atop the hospital fence were lit. I could not decide whether the lights were functional or decorative.

"That's what happened to me, in a way," said Mr. Sladick. "You must know the risk of losing your wits if you step outside the institution. It's mad enough inside."

One day, Mr. Sladick went on to relate, when he was teaching at Morley College, he walked into his classroom and saw himself, or thought he saw himself, writing incomprehensible cryptography on the blackboard. To his amazement the students seemed familiar with it: they copied, read, discussed. Mr. Sladick stood at the lectern paralyzed, but another self within him held forth. Thereafter, he was habitually inspired in class and absent-minded out of class. He had always cultivated dullness to save energy, and sighed gratefully when the cretins avoided him, but that year he got the Distinguished Teacher's Award and was elected chairman of the Philosophy Department's Long-Range Planning Committee. Beside himself, he sensed mortal danger. At the award party he caught himself making indecent proposals to the dean's wife. He also flattered a colleague for publishing an unreadable book. Appalled, he quit teaching in a reckless moment of self-confidence. "And here I am."

Mr. Sladick got out of the car. "See you at the funeral," he said. "You'd better get some sleep. You look terrible."

I DROVE to Los Angeles. Gently rocking on the freeway at night, the lights of small towns passed on the right or on the left. In my somnolence I could feel, as did schoolmen of the Middle Ages, that time is an illusion and we exist in an abiding present. "*Alle Menschen müssen sterben,*" sings Bach. All people must die. The day before, I had been reading an encyclopedic punster sparkling with transitive verbs (a sign of genius) who recommended total rejection of all religions ever dreamt up by man, and total composure in the face of total death. If we knew why people lose their heads, total composure would be totally admirable. But I did not know why my brother lost his head, and why I might keep or lose mine.

After dinner once, at the home of a backsliding Unitarian, Tom and I argued into the small hours whether our hunger was moral or aesthetic. Believer and unbeliever, Tom and I went at it with some heat, perversely lighting the way for each other. Tom explained why women tempted him. When he understood himself best, he said, the devil tempted him most. The devil had reason to tempt, considering the prize, and over the years the devil had increased the temptations in pitch and frequency until Tom found his happiness on the threshold to the Nothing of All, and expected an illumination. Doubts? "The more I doubt, the more I believe," said Tom. What with the wine and the Unitarian's sloppy grinning—"That's the divine *nihil*, right?"—the mystery deepened and we began to lose our threads. Then our host's five-year-old daughter entered the room clad in Snoopy pajamas. She had been awakened by our shouts and derisive laughter, and came to kiss us all good-night. Which she did. Who made the lamb? I wondered, hoping she would blow away our verbal smoke with an angelic utterance. It was not to be. If God spoke through the child, He spoke only through her warm cheek on mine. But I did not trust my intention to read a message, or God's to send one. Truth is the death of intention, I have seen, and the mere consciousness of belief corrupts the affirmation. Please send me useless things.

II

IN HIS YOUTH my father had been a monk at the Zagorsk monastery near Moscow. He had knelt with other monks around fourteenth-century manuscripts, sung responses, blessed the candles, cleaned the icons, shed tears over the corpse of his Elder. He had lain prostrate on icy flagstones for his sins, swept paths in the snow with a twig broom, sat in the chapel vestibule with cripples and widows, gossiping and chewing his ration of sausage and dill pickle. He had kissed three corners of a golden reliquary as priest and choir winged their spirits into ancient beliefs.

For some years after the Revolution he served as Auxiliary of the Patriarch of Riga. In those days we dressed for dinner, my mother in flowing green with a high lace collar, my father in a

fresh cassock smelling of soap and winter air, I still in my
Fauntleroy, and Tom in his first long pants and tie, his buttocks
on the chair mashing his student cap for rakish effect, putting
the ceremony of dinner to some use.

The sun flooding the dining room tinted one and another crys-
tal pendant in the chandelier, and in the shadowed corner
glowed the grandfather clock, its face composing the spheres of
sun and moon, the stars and all the planets in inlaid mother-of-
pearl. Beside the clock arched a Romanesque window with a
border of stylized flowers in stained glass, red roses and white
lilies, eternally stiff and fresh. The white lace curtains tied with
yellow tasseled cords formed a theatrical curtain for the show in
the window. Slow taxis and droshkies in the wintry street, the
frozen canal winding through the park past the Opera white
with snow. Afar, behind a line of trees, stretched the parade
grounds. A clear, freezing day for military exercises. Companies
of brown horses bearing uniformed riders, and one white horse,
pranced and galloped toylike, pennants fluttering and trumpets
flashing in the sun.

When the finger bowls of perfumed water were served, my father opened the gilded Scripture and saw reflected in his memory of Zagorsk, as in a mirror, Isaiah's Zion, city of solemnities.
This city, he would read to my fidgeting brother and me, is a
quiet habitation, a tabernacle that shall not be taken down; not
one of the stakes thereof shall ever be removed, neither shall any
of the cords thereof be broken. "For here we have no continuing
city, but we seek one to come."

In the Byzantine cathedral on holy days, I would see him in
gold and lace, a smoking censer in his hand, his pectoral cross set
with rubies. I held my breath when he bowed low to the great
altar and the martyrs in heaven. Row on row the painted saints
stood ranged in proper order, above and below, long bodies and
small heads, their faces showing neither joy nor sorrow as they
witnessed the Terrible Judgment in the vast fresco over the main
portals. Christ, enthroned, seemed indifferent to the snake writhing up from torture chambers, where sinners, their faces also ex-
pressionless, were speared, quartered, and eaten by demons, in
truth and justice.

In our world we preferred art to science. We would have been

dismayed, when coming upon an astonishing circle of mush-
rooms in the forest, to learn that they marked the periphery of
underground mycelial growth. Give us the work of mild terror
and joy, a ring of dancing fairies, such as eventually blossomed
in Tom's familiarity with the devil, his taste, as Mr. Sladick had
put it, for metaphysical panic. A streak in the family. And all it
needed to go haywire was a Southern California free of the past
and the future.

After the loss of Zagorsk and the loss of Riga, their ancient
stakes removed and their cords broken, my father promptly restored the promise to himself by building his own little Zagorsk
in California, which he called Old Russia, on a 40-acre hilltop in
Los Feliz with a grand view of Los Angeles. A priest's house, a
quaint little Russian church of plaster and paint, and a graveyard. In Southern California nothing seemed more natural than a
gilded Russian church between a ghostly Taj Mahal and a coy
Swiss chalet on adjoining hills. And behold, wonder of the country, film companies offered money for location work, and when
the first film crew clattered into our garden with cables and
reflectors, he realized that he had succeeded and failed.

His brain could not comprehend the distance he had traveled
from Zagorsk to Hollywood. "Beware the chains of gold!" But
who could resist money in 1932, 1933, 1934, the country crashing
and people running to the movies, my mother learning to peel
potatoes and not touch the vacuum cleaner during rare thunder-
storms. "What a wild country!" she said happily, digging a hole
by the path to the church to plant a lemon tree, while my father
sat on a bench nearby, reading a journal from Berlin.

In time everything he built collapsed, and my brother could
thank him for his interest in the devil. Everybody knows something about the devil, but those who are puzzled by their
successes and failures can sometimes recognize the shapes he assumes. His works are many. Consider the spells he casts, the
dreams he sends, the vanities he insinuates, the illusion he spins,
the victories he grants, the defeats he disguises, the prayers he
teaches, the talents he strengthens, and the manner of his teasing
and tormenting and delighting body and soul, as he walks about
seeking whom he may devour.

Father and mother dead, I removed myself as far as I could, to Boston's stone houses and real gutters.

My brother alone remained to play with the church he inherited, the vestments, the jewelry and holy pictures, licensed to his own notion of the priesthood by the I-Thou Temple in Hollywood.

III

FOR SOME YEARS Tom rode the heady currents of spiritual fashion, mingling with truth-finders on inexpressible mental trips. He opened his doors to emissaries of maharishis, perfect masters, God, and the Mushroom, one slack-jawed anarchist bringing glad tidings of the atomic holocaust, and ate rice and sat with them in a circle on the floor of the church, holding hands for fellowship and purification.

The Balaban & Katz theater chairs that he had installed for an earlier wave of existentialists were pushed to the walls to make room for religious body language, Christ present now in new contexts, drums and electric guitars. Resplendent in our father's priestly robes and jewels, he intoned from the Secret Gospel According to Mark the sweet news that Jesus was a bisexual troilist. And one fine night during the expressive dance-testimony of a 62-year-old stripper wearing a purple wig, naked to offer her dugs humbly to the Lord, her last mite, two scouts from the Hell's Angels roared up to check out the I-Thou Russian Church, having heard good things. They came to scoff and stayed to cavort, their iron crosses and swastikas inspiring Tom to sing a Wehrmacht song, German words, for which they swore their love, kissed him, promised to castrate all who did him bodily harm, and thundered off whooping and hollering through the graveyard and a neighbor's putting green, their exploding bikes plowing the grave mounds and chewing up the nice turf.

All this was correct, Tom said to me when I visited him after his second nervous breakdown. He was by then a gaunt recluse in Old Russia, shambling to our graveyard in slippers and a tattered robe, to pay respects to Father and Mother in their graves. It was correct to sniff the rank creative pit between the death of one religion and the birth of another worthy of the name. Everything was going back to the great steaming pit, he said, the gurus and the messengers, the astrologers and calcified Christians, the oblivious youth worshipping the kingdom within —all bubbles in the ooze, and the fun may simmer a thousand years before another shape emerges true as Byzantium. For his part, boredom had set in. And fear.

He had found a little waitress near UCLA, a Peggy who resented working nights until two, serving drinks, getting goosed, sick of people making off with her tips. In a Howard Johnson's motel (free TV) he did the act of darkness with her and loved to hear her talk: "Sometimes you can really acquire a warped perspective of people, being a waitress? Catering to the public? Most of them are college students, only enough money to pay for drinks. You begin to look at people only how they are going to benefit you. Like, a source of income, not personalities with something more valuable. Kissing ass for a lousy dime is a rotten thing to have to do." Peggy could have done ITT measurable good, and Tom had listened to her with the interest he would have accorded a talking cat.

Nothing came of it, thank God. The church padlocked now and the graveyard and garden gone to weeds, Tom remained alone in the priest's house, ignoring creditors and studying ways to purge himself of a madness inflicted by girls in short dresses. He found women to be nymphs, monsters, demons in the classical dictionaries of Lemprière, Quicherat, and Grimal, and debated whether to commit himself to Newhall.

The place was expensive but comfortably appointed, and the service, he had heard from a connoisseur, matched that of a European hotel of the old school. Go back a bit, if you can't go forward a thousand years. A little custom and ceremony. Here in Old Russia he had relieved himself utterly of social duties. The house needed repairs and was going to hell. He had neglected to hire a gardener to mow the lawns and prune the bushes. The sight of the neighbor's gardener stepping on slimy snails moved him to tears of boredom. He needed an asylum to structure his days and concentrate his recalcitrant intelligence.

"Well, if you think . . ." I said tentatively, careful not to discourage him with my approval.

On the other hand, he said, he could not ignore the advantages of remaining in Old Russia to pursue his investigations.

I thought: a poor little waitress with a cute ass. Tom the Hippie courting spiritual suffering. *Difficult is the descent to God.* As he speculated, I could see in the window, stretching away to the horizon, the lights of Los Angeles beginning to glimmer, steaming with the luminous chemical secrets of a vast garbage dump. Pursue what investigations? Of his soul? As children, Tom and I had walked in the rain because we had been forbidden to run. What idea ruled us now? What was our law, and who were our prophets? I could try to emulate a German who found the true gospel of Christ nowhere, except once and irresistibly in "The St. Matthew Passion." Tom, unfortunately, wanted God. Perhaps only mystics pull through. Perhaps Tom's mystical talent, by some mystical definition, was unrecognizable as mystical. If I could trust my intuition, there was not a mystical spark in him. Yet his suffering was real. There are many people in the world who conceive an idea of themselves and must practice it. Was it not remotely possible that if such people set out on a fool's errand, some of them may not after all end on one?

IV

I SAT in our unventilated old parlor wondering how to get him to a doctor, or at least drag him to a restaurant if he would dress. Recently his daily fare, I had learned, consisted of three tacos and two Twinkies from a perambulating Mexican in the valley, nothing else. All right, he said, we'd go to The Piggery (a two-hour drive for hamburgers and French fries), but first he wanted to play three recordings for me. "You teach your students to babble in Russian," he said. "What then? What are they going to babble, or isn't that your field? How can you live such an idiotic life! Now sit and listen. I'm throwing you the lifeline."

He produced for my salvation what appeared to be his dearest treasure, the three phonograph recordings which he eventually took with him to Newhall: Nazi marching songs, the album cover showing goose-stepping storm troopers and swastikas; a Red Army chorus; and a gaggle of gospel singers. So his taste had degenerated to bombast. But why such a muddle of doctrines? Are Fascists, Communists, Christians all God's children? —or was it that they deserved each other?

I said, "Why the Nazis?"

The loudspeaker thundered as he scraped the stylus to make certain that the electrons were flowing properly through the wires. "Did you expect something more modern?" he said, giving me a sarcastic look. "Something innovative, you ass?"

"Something artistic, at least."

"Artistic!" he cried. "By God, I'll make you listen!"

Tom liked to share his discoveries, literary, musical, theological, as correctives of error. He could not go through life without making straight the way where he found it crooked. "Shut up now and listen. Listen and think." And putting the three recordings into his antiquated machine, he lay down on the dusty couch and closed his eyes.

He had turned the volume on full blast. Evening had come and our darkened parlor filled with the crash of barking Nazis. Coarse and unrelenting, cymbals clashed and a contrabass tuba, *das grosse Bombardon,* drove home the beat like a sledgehammer. Tom's pleasure in the raucous music surprised me. Lying on the couch in that insolent noise, he appeared to drift off into a sweet slumber, as to the sighs of flutes, his face relaxed, faintly smiling.

When he had not stirred for some moments, I retreated softly to the kitchen to make sandwiches, and found the sink full of dirty dishes and garbage. Garbage lay on the floor under the sink, spilt from an overturned paper bag. Cockroaches scattered. Crap on the windowsill: a black banana, two rotten tomatoes, a smear of margarine under a rusted knife. In the bread box a loaf of bread bristled with fungus in its unopened cellophane wrapper. In the refrigerator a broken egg had oozed over bacon spotted with mold, beside a filthy skillet with a spatula buried in hard grease. A carton of sour milk, a jar of dill pickles, a small hard sausage called Landjaeger bearing teeth marks, nine cans of sardines, a bowl of yellowish clabber whose chemistry I could not guess, fermenting in its corruption. In the freezer, a carton of popsicles in four flavors, and a cracked bottle of Pepsi-Cola. The Nazis finished singing in the parlor.

From the kitchen doorway I stood looking at him in the silence between the first recording and the second. He had opened his eyes and lay gazing at the ceiling, studying the darkest plane of the room. The phonograph clicked. He muttered something, appreciatively, and closed his eyes again as the Red Army marched in.

He would go to Newhall when he wanted to go, I thought, searching the kitchen for paper bags to put the garbage in—and stopped, lest I disturb him. Twenty pounds of junk mail lay on the kitchen table, as well as some unopened letters, bills. A window-envelope from the Internal Revenue Service appeared to be a tax refund, dated the month before, also unopened. I returned to my chair in the parlor and sat through the Red Army and then the gospel singers. Tom seemed asleep.

When at last the noise ended he pulled himself up and sat heavily on the couch. Behind him, the sky in the window held the twilight, but darkness had fully possessed the garden. It was the moment in the day when you can smell the faint bitterness of eternity. The room itself had grown dark. I could see Tom's face only in outline, feeling his eyes upon me. His distant air conveyed an awful solitariness and the question of what to do with it, nudging me into my own isolation. I cast about for something to divert the threatening uncertainty, the more so as Tom did not light the lamp and seemed content to sit in the dark.

"You weren't listening," he said.

"Of course I listened. How could I avoid listening?"

"You took your anal compulsions to the kitchen. Fussing."

"Tom, you can't go on like this."

"Like what?"

The spirit sees, the mind argues. Instead of trying to hold the moment, which might have revealed something rich and strange, I said what I would have said in the common stir of life: "Living in a garbage can."

When he spoke again it was in a voice so cold, so hard and alien to me, that I regretted my visit. "I am not," he said, "living in a garbage can, you damned fool." And he rose to his feet with weary disgust, as if by my inattention to his concert I had declined his offer of a priceless gift.

V

HE COMMITTED himself to Newhall half a year later, and flying out again I found him comfortably settled in a private room, clean and tidy. The three recordings lay on the floor beside a cheap portable phonograph decorated with red white and blue stripes and the picture of a dancing girl in a bikini.

Apart from the hated medicines that clouded his brain, he liked Newhall well enough and was left in peace to read Carlyle's *Sartor Resartus,* which holds that the Christian church is worn out and must be discarded, like old clothes, but that the underlying religious spirit must be kept alive at all costs.

"Really, you're looking very well," I said.

"You can face anything with stupidity and sound digestion."

Dr. Rogers said he ought to stay in the hospital a while.

Mr. Sladick, whom I then met for the first time, said, "He's marvelous! Absolutely marvelous!"

I had our old house in Los Feliz cleaned, fumigated, and locked.

TOM LEFT Newhall once, in his fourth month there, and went to Los Angeles to seek out Peggy. She had moved as such people do, nobody knew where. In The Piggery he smiled and danced with Sandra at a distance of three feet, aping her gyrations as best he could, jerking his hips and flapping his elbows, from step to step unable to find his center of gravity. Sandra wore dirty jeans with red and yellow patches on the buttocks, and her breath smelled of burnt rubber. She would not dance the slow dances, not liking to be touched, and between beers sat in a telephone booth talking to her sister, she said when she came back, thanking him for the dime. What mattered most to him as a man, Tom said to Sandra, was her personality. If she liked, they could talk at Howard Johnson's? Sandra said, "Fuck off, Buster!"

He said at my third visit, which proved to be the last, "You can't imagine the miles I walked for no reason."

"You must have had something in mind."

"My good passivity."

I could not get him to dress and walk in the hospital's park. He kept to his room, in pajamas. The three recordings lay on his dresser, Nazi, Communist, Christian. Two books lay on his nightstand, C. S. Lewis's *The Problem of Pain* and John Donne's *Biathanatos,* the latter subtitled (I did not trouble to look then) *That Self-homicide is not so naturally Sin that it may never be otherwise.*

He had left Newhall on a Saturday and walked the city till Tuesday morning, for three days and nights, and called Dr. Rogers from a businessmen's convention at the Wilshire East to take him back. At night the demons had come out and the dead rode in cars frothing at the mouth. Worst of all were the Christian churches all day Sunday, truckloads of too-stupid sermons, orthodox and heretical, cesspools of blather.

"And otherwise . . . how are you?" I asked him.

"I'll be going home in a month or two."

"Did Dr. Rogers say so?"

"You don't ask an accountant for an opinion about the soul. We've got to do something about Old Russia. I want to restore the church. Two bastards are waiting to build a restaurant in the graveyard. New thrill. Dine with your loved ones."

The year before, the residents below our hilltop, whose elegant houses of glass and redwood surrounded our acres, had filed a civil suit to deactivate our graveyard, or, as a co-plaintiff demanded, put the graveyard in mothballs. The value of our land having appreciated incredibly over the years, real-estate sharks with two-way radios joined the plaintiffs in disputing the sanctity of our burial grounds. An equal contest between piety and greed, enriching the lawyers. In court, counsel for the plaintiff argued that Tom's religious circus made the graveyard an illegal private operation. (His Honor held his head: since when did you object to private operations, and what makes a religion invalid, or valid?) Moreover, although our water was piped in from Lake Tahoe, some neighbors complained that their sinks emitted unwholesome exudations from the stagnant pond in the graveyard, and one matron in black silk pants and silver slippers deposed that on certain nights her kitchen faucets broke out in a cold sweat. Chemical analysis of the water revealed tolerable amounts of putrescence, but the defense showed that the decomposing organic matter came from the gambling casinos in Nevada, or could. Four months after Tom went to Newhall, on the very weekend of his mad walk through Los Angeles, the graveyard was finally closed to fresh corpses, but not ordered removed to a state cemetery.

Tom's debts had piled up. He owed property taxes and court costs, his lawyer had never been paid, shopkeepers and credit companies demanded satisfaction, and I-Thou Temple in Hollywood, the most imaginative of the gang, had filed a claim against Tom for six years of unpaid dues, printing costs, advertising costs, "service costs," missionary pledges, 18 percent interest, and consulting fees, all documented. I would have liked to hear some of those consultations, Tom fishing for the spirit in contaminated shallows.

"We have to sell something," I said to Tom.

"Don't sell the church," he said. "You can cut the garden into twenty lots."

Whatever our father's church had been, whatever it might be, Tom felt responsible because its possibilities existed now only in his mind. Perhaps the destruction of the church would let loose upon the air an evil influence to trouble his dreams. He wanted the church restored.

"What will you do with it when it's restored?" I asked.

"Why do anything? I'll sit and look."

"An expensive toy," I said.

"Not a toy. A revelation was always imminent there, even in Father's day."

"It did not happen," I said. "That's why I left."

"It did not happen," he agreed. "But it was always imminent. That's why I stayed."

If he still hoped to experience an idea greater than himself, his expectations had grown smaller. He no longer spoke of the church as an enterprise that might succeed. He merely wanted to restore it as one might a picture.

VI

THE DAY before Tom's funeral I drove up into the mountains of Los Feliz, parked the Hertz car by our old wooden gates, and entered into a silence I had long forgotten. From our desolate avenue of shaggy poplars a bird rose and flapped heavily toward the graveyard, where the trees grew close and dark. Half the vines in the arbor were still putting out leaves, and the lattice-work trellis, leaning askew, showed streaks of whitewash not yet erased. Passing the priest's house with its carved doors and small square windows designed for Russian winters, I took the path winding through the trees to the church. Here and there tangled bushes and weeds had obliterated the path altogether. At the turn by the dead lemon tree I felt a small stab in my chest, as I saw again the white and the gold of that sad wreck.

Again, as in my childhood, before me rose the large golden onion sprinkled with blue stars, and the smaller asymmetrical domes, one half concealed by the vestry gable, the other near the steps, and the high narrow windows decorated like Christmas cookies and Easter cakes, and the pillars twisted into colorful candy sticks—all teasing me to guess the one thing in life that is real and not an illusion, and saying fairy tales, fairy tales.

Everybody wanted to buy Old Russia, it seemed. Tom had had offers from neighbors, land speculators, transcendental med-itators, I-Am-ites, ashramites, nudists, turnip eaters. The faded old church (old for plaster and paint) could easily be rented to some sect or society in search of holy ground in Nixon's Orange County. But by now I had concluded that in a time of God's eclipse, nothing so traduces the religious spirit as religious insti-tutions. Believers are unbelievers now, and unbelievers are believers. Between my father's birth in Moscow and my brother's death in Greater Los Angeles, the church had fallen and could continue only as a parody of itself. Rather than letting it revert to a place of worship, whether of God or flowered gurus with pink lips, I would sell the land and see the church bulldozed. Paint blistered and peeling, foliage pressing in upon the windows, tough little bushes splitting the flagstones by the door, the whole structure seemed to be sinking into the high grass and nettles. Let the wreckers have it, I thought, and let the builders build, tidy up the grounds and put them to some good use.

But that night in my room at the Sheraton Arms I hesitated still. If not a sentimental scruple, a moral one? The dereliction perhaps of something of value? Would it matter if I returned someday and found the church gone, replaced by Sam's Cuisine, itself fated to crumble? Or found the church restored with hammered gold, a golden cockerel upon the gable, and by the door a tattered beggar dreaming of Byzantium? Church or theater, immortal wreck, what was I to do with it?

Tom would have derided my poetic impulse, pointing out a fallacy in "immortal wreck," *contradictio in adjecto,* which attributes a restorative predicate to a destructive subject. Perhaps in the end he did not care what the place had been, or was, or was to be. *Vocatus atque non vocatus Deus aderit.* Summoned or not summoned God will be there.

What do you do with the imminence of a revelation that does not occur?

VII

I BURIED HIM on a sunny Tuesday in Forest Lawn, near the memorial stones of Seventh Day Adventists and a colony of Shintoists. Tom had been so reclusive in his last years that only five people came to the funeral, all strangers to me except Mr. Sladick.

"I wanted to read Tom's motto," he said. "You don't happen to have it?"

"What motto?"

"I don't know it by heart. It's from Carlyle. He kept it with his Nazi record."

I did not engage a preacher to say a few suitable words. Mr.

Sladick rode with me to the reception at the Sheraton Arms. A buffet had been set out in the Hawaiian Room. The reception lasted a decent interval, 40 minutes.

"A shame to waste such a buffet," said Mr. Sladick. "Look at that cantaloupe with sugared fisheyes. If I were you, I'd go into the street and call in the lame and the halt."

Instead we carried gin and tonic and a bucket of ice up to my room. Mr. Sladick was taking the 6:05 Greyhound back to Newhall, time enough to talk about the training of psychiatrists and hospital reforms and the spirit of Napoleon in the work of Léon Bloy. In the jacket of the Nazi recording I found a sheet of typing paper, and unfolded it. Tom had written with careful calligraphy: "The Universe is not dead and demoniacal, a charnel-house with spectres; but godlike, and my Father's!"

"That's the one," said Mr. Sladick.

I took from the cardboard box the two other recordings, Red Army songs and gospel songs.

"Mr. Sladick," I said, "Tom must have told you something about all these songs. I mean, why did he have such a thing about them?"

"They're all heroic songs. Tom believed in heroes."

Perhaps I had hoped for something better. His explanation irked me and I realized that I would have to make my peace with Tom as best I could. When Mr. Sladick was gone, I plugged in Tom's phonograph and played the three recordings, one after another.

A SPIRITED male choir sang a marching song. *"O, du schöner Westerwald."*

Well, a case could be made: there was something about these songs that went beyond colonels and Gauleiters. Think of Socrates, when he retreated with Laches after the battle of Delium. Think of the flutes piping in his ears when he drank the hemlock. Xanthus heard them in the only memory he brought home with him from the wars, when he recalled that at the storming of Samos, "in the heat of the battle, Pericles smiled on me, and passed on to another detachment."

What can you do with the Red Army Chorus? The Russians marched smartly. They ran, they danced and wailed and dreamed a melancholy tale about somebody's kerchief. They huddled around fires in the bitter snow, ate cats and dogs in Leningrad, killed those same Nazis on the ice of Lake Peipsi, froze to death by the Volga, sitting on their horses. They held the line. And in their last song whole armies of them were returning from Stalingrad, good Bolsheviks all and more coming over the horizon in disordered ranks, carrying red banners and dragging their katyushas, whistling and shouting, having saved Mother Russia for the police state.

But by the time the Christians came on (Burl Ives in gospel songs with a choir of happy believers), I awakened as from a dull sleep to a lucid perplexity. Heads held high and eyes fixed heavenward, smiling through tears at silver linings, Burl Ives and his choir sang and clapped their hands. Could a case also be made for American Protestants, in whose hearts was born the language of automobile insurance policies? In Hartford, Atlanta, and Chicago, see how they rejoice in the imminent destruction of Magog Russia, as promised by God in holy writ. And here are Mormons chased by Presbyterians and Baptists, pulling their covered wagons over the Great Divide and heading for Salt Lake City, where in peace and freedom they can exclude niggers from their priesthood. "Come, come, ye saints."

Yet here too the spirit in their songs soared unperturbed, indifferent to the moralist's certitude and the aesthete's tight nervousness. When all had been disputed and defined, asserted, persecuted, contested, lost, won, vindicated, trivialized, something remained for song to transcend the limits of person, sect, nation, and language itself. To all but the faithful remnant in these last days of scoffers, the usefulness of these Protestant songs had long since been burned away by time and unbelief. These songs were as useless now as the songs the Wehrmacht sang, and the Red Army. Like holy ground, which may not be used for anything, neither for planting nor harvesting, whether of crops or billboards, these songs could at last be called religious. They had become art.

Tom had wanted to serve a Philosopher King, if one could be found among our porkish senators and Texas barracudas. But he scarcely pulled himself through the day and through the night, and for that alone needed metaphysical perspectives, Thomas

Carlyle at his elbow. Carlyle gave him a taste of blood and dust, and rattled his brain with the alarm and shock of battle—and it all came to this: the mad primeval discord seeking to be hushed in the hour of spiritual enfranchisement, when the ideal world becomes revealed, God-announcing.

In England, a wise man tells us, where every garden has a brick wall, it is unethical to traffic in abstractions, as the Germans do.

Yet the English, too, have songs.

So I buried my brother and was content to leave him. May it be so. Let him vanish in the Idea, but let its perfection endure.

Perpetual Care

SHEILA BALLANTYNE

SHEILA BALLANTYNE has published short stories in *American Review* and *Aphra*. Her novel *Norma Jean the Termite Queen* was published by Doubleday. She now lives in Berkeley.

December 18

I N ANSWER to your query of December 3, the law permits the placement of cremated remains in an occupied grave, if the family so desires. In our cemetery we require that the cremains be placed in a small concrete vault. It is sealed when the cremains are placed.

Part of our charge of $152.54 is $75.00 for a permit to place another body in an occupied grave.

The only marking on your mother's grave is a small cement locator. This was put on at our expense to identify the grave, and it has the initials of the deceased and the grave location. A double inscription marker in your choice of gray, mahogany, or pink granite, size 32″×20″, complete with installation in the ceme-

Originally appeared in *American Review* 24. Copyright © 1976 by Bantam Books, Inc.

tery and inscribed with both names and dates, would be $250.00 plus state sales tax of $13.25.

We are enclosing the interment order showing the breakdown of expense. This form should be completed and returned to us in toto.

> Cordially
> V. O. Vernon, Vice President
> Mt. Vernon Memorial Park
> Seattle, Washington

> February 20

We have not received a reply to our letter of December 18, regarding placement of the cremains of your father in the grave now occupied by your mother.

We will appreciate hearing from you as to your decision in this matter so that we may close our file.

> Cordially,
> V. O. Vernon, Vice President
> Mt. Vernon Memorial Park
> Seattle, Washington

> February 22

Hang in there, V. O. My father's ashes (or, as you people call them, *cremains*) are still in the humidifier up in the Reno crematorium. Your letters have been so—how shall I describe them? cordially obscene?—that I've been forced to consider Reno as the place of final burial. Actually, it's not just your letters, V. O.; the additional factor hanging over my head is the delicate matter of the mutual *couchette*. In addition to the oedipal considerations, what if I were to change my mind years later? I couldn't just dig them up and interrupt a thing like that. It would offend the average person's sensibilities, to say nothing of theirs, if indeed (admittedly, we're still in the larval stage of research on this) they have sensibilities. I can guess your position on this already, so I won't pursue it.

What I have to do before I can respond to your letter of De-

cember 18 is go to Reno to investigate the burial possibilities
there. I have already made one abortive trip for that purpose (a
week ago today). If it hadn't been for "the worst blizzard in
twenty years" (why do they always say that every time it
snows?) I might have made it. However, as things turned out, I
spun off the road in my MG, nearly totaling myself as well as the
car. It was a traumatic experience. I am very fond of my MG. If
it had turned out tragically, would you have considered interring
me in your cemetery with my car? In the grave now occupied by
my mother? And perhaps also my father? The thought of it raises
a host of interesting possibilities. You don't mind, do you, if I
take a few minutes to describe my feelings? Actually, I'm kind of
lonely, my husband and children are no help at all—no fault of
theirs, you understand—but the fact is, I have this decision to
make alone, and it's not easy, as you can see by my failure to respond to your letter of December 18.

Where shall I start? It goes so far back (I can hear you sighing; I know you run a business, but with your prices surely you
can afford to take a few minutes to listen to my explanation of
why I cannot as yet reply. Do you have an adequate supply of
cigars handy? Watch the ashes on your pinstripe). To get back,
the principal reason why the decision of *where to inter* is difficult
lies with my ambivalent feelings toward him. Her, she's pretty
much a blur after twenty-seven years; but him, more freshly
dead, you know, bits and pieces still linger, still adhere to the
mind. He did a lot of rotten things in his life, not the least of
which were done to her; but still and all, isn't it true? what they
say about death being the great equalizer? For this reason, it's
going to take a little more time, and another trip to Reno (there
was no damage to the MG; just a huge mass of snow impacted in
the radiator which froze solid and made the motor heat up and
scared the shit out of me as I still had another 30 miles to drive
in the blizzard, and it was getting dark). Funny, but lying there
in the embankment, becoming gradually obscured by falling
snow, came pretty close to the way he himself met his end. Now
some would see this as sheer coincidence; some (my analyst, for
instance), symbolic reenactment. How do *you* see it, V. O.?
(What does the V. O. stand for? Victor Osborne? Vernon
Oscar?) If you can just sit back, I'll attempt to be brief, although

it goes against my nature. You see, I'm doing this mainly because I didn't like your phrase about wanting to close your file. It had an abrupt ring to it, made me feel about to be closed out. Explaining things to you this way buys me a little time, makes me feel still "active"—if you know what I mean. File-wise.

They weren't what you'd call the ideal couple. (But then who is?) I have the strongest urge to say that both tried their best, but—in addition to the fact that they're both dead and can no longer be studied—there are as yet no scientific means by which to define what "best," in fact, really is. Therefore, I won't say it. Rather, he gambled and drank and she cried, I'm sure you know the syndrome. In addition (there are a lot of additionals in this account; I wouldn't be offended in the least if you wished to take a break for lunch at this point. Matters of reconstruction are always delicate and difficult. As an embalmer, you'll understand.)

On the way up (I'm referring to the first trip to Reno, the one I made in an attempt to settle this issue once and for all. You know what they say: if you don't bury the dead, they hang around and can affect you in various undesirable ways) I was stopped for speeding by the Highway Patrol. It was my first ticket; I've been driving for twenty years and had a perfect record. As you can imagine, I had a lot on my mind at the time; it's not the most pleasant way to spend a weekend, driving 400 miles round trip just to check out a cemetery. I imagine you, sitting at your desk, thinking I'm some kind of creep because I live in Berkeley and talk about inner meanings, but don't be alarmed, because if the Reno thing doesn't work out, I definitely have not written off your cemetery as a possible place for my father's *cremains*.

To get back: I was traveling fast, but not without reason. The road report had warned of blizzard conditions up ahead and I was two hours behind schedule due to the gas lines. Imagine my surprise when I saw the red light in the rear-view mirror! He appeared out of nowhere, like a bat out of hell (as the saying goes). I had been very careful, looking to the left, right, and rear, as usual. The only possibility could have been a row of dense shrubbery about ten miles south of Vacaville, California.

When you're going 85 miles an hour it's hard to keep your eye on every shrub—you've got the car to manage, and the road, in addition to all those maniacs who drive the freeway. This is what raced through my mind at that moment: 20 years down the drain, a perfect record blown to hell. But then the strangest thing happened. I received a mental image: a rough gray slab, it had all the usual on it—Here Lies, name, date, RIP—but what really caught my inner eye was the inscription: A Perfect Driving Record. I was collapsed over the wheel by the time he reached the window. He thought I was crying, as usual, what else are they to think when they flag down a woman? He assumed a compassionate face.

But, as it turned out, it wasn't a facade. Would you believe it possible for a Highway Patrolman to be capable of empathy? Not only that, he was proud of me. He scratched his forehead, pushing back his hat. He said, "You're really something! You were leaving them all *way* behind. I've never seen anyone like you!" I accepted it as a compliment, as I'm sure some small, uncorrupted part of him intended it. That tiny repressed aspect of his self that was born to delinquency reached out to that slightly larger part of my self that was born to same at that moment.

No longer wishing that epitaph for myself, I was free of striving for that particular perfection, and thus had that much more libidinal energy at my disposal. Hence my ability to refrain from crying, pleading, and so forth. I did have to answer honestly when he asked why I might have been going 85 miles an hour ("I'm on my way to Reno to bury my father"). I know what you're thinking, it's the same as crying, but it happened to be true. For once, I was grateful to the truth for coming to my aid. He spent ten minutes over the hood trying to arrive at a fair reduction. He settled for going 65 in a 55 mph zone. I thought it very fair. He was like the father I never had. He even cautioned me, not in an authoritarian way, but with what appeared to be real concern: "Please try to stay somewhere within a reasonable limit." It was touching, I was grateful. Compassionate limit-setting, just what I always needed and never got.

Do you have children, V. O.? Do you give them the attention they require? or are you down in the vaults most of the time? I won't bore you with the details of what happened after that:

stuck on Donner Pass for three hours; iced windshield wipers; broken chains. After the spinout, it was clear I wasn't going to make it to Reno; I spent the night in a friend's cabin, skiied a little the following day, and took Compazine. I'm all set to go again this coming weekend, the weather report looks good, and believe me, V. O., if this doesn't do it, I give up. They can keep his *cremains,* makes no difference to me any longer, this has been the longest funeral in history, five and a half years; don't you think that's enough time to have something like this on your mind? You're wondering about the five years. It was in all the Reno papers, but you probably missed it in Seattle; I would have missed it in Berkeley if the authorities hadn't called. He disappeared in the mountains in 1968 and they didn't find his bones until last Halloween. No, I'm not putting you on, V. O. Some hunter found the skeleton on Halloween. They couldn't find him at the time it happened because a blizzard came up (worst in twenty years), and the Civil Air Patrol couldn't get its planes up, and the sheriff's posse couldn't see where it was going. Three months passed before I stopped seeing him in my sleep. Now you understand my reference to the car in the snowdrift. Actually, the idea to keep (him) his *cremains* in Reno came to me on a chairlift; it was moving slowly past a stand of pines when I suddenly received the phrase about "Where the tree falls, let it lie." Know that one? and I thought, why not? Please don't be offended, V. O., I know yours is a much classier cemetery. I've given this matter serious and prolonged consideration. That's why I'm paralyzed at the moment. I'm counting on this weekend's trip to break that up and resolve this thing once and for all.

In order to know exactly what to do, what would be the "right" thing (you still believe in absolutes?), I'd have to make another trip, a major one, the one to my past, which I'm unwilling to do at this time, as my analyst can verify. It's funny, though, how you find yourself places, having arrived there by avenues which were not on the map. For instance, speaking just now of cars and mass burials reminded me of when we were all together, I was five, and he drove an old Ford, he and she would sit up front and I would be in the back. So if I had died in the spinout, and you had been good enough to inter me and the

MG along with him in the grave now occupied by her, it would
have brought everything back full cycle. It may not be possible
to go home again in exactly the same way as when you left, but
there are symbolic reunions still within our reach, don't you think
that's true, V. O.? The three of us together again, in the car, it
would have been so quiet down there, not like it was when she
used to scream at him back in 1942. He was a real terror on the
road, I know what you're thinking, but it isn't true. I have
worked diligently for over twenty years to be unlike him in every
way possible.

Well, V. O., it's been a pleasure talking to you, but I must
close now. I'll get back to you after my trip to Reno, and let you
know my decision. And listen, you are not to worry; *nothing*
could persuade me to go 85 again in that speed trap. In the
meantime, keep your frigging hands off my file; I am definitely
not ready to be closed out.

Yours truly

March 5

V. O.—Here I am again.

How are you? I'm sorry I let Monday go by without writing,
but I needed the extra day to recover from the weekend. As a
man in a sensitive position, you'll understand. And then again, as
a man who deals with death on an everyday basis (do you work
on Sundays, too?), maybe you won't. After getting the children
off to school I just sat and stared out the window, it was all I
could do. The tulips are up here in California; how is the
weather treating you there in Seattle? Rain, as usual? I planted
three colors this year: red, orange, and yellow, but for some
reason they bloomed consecutively, instead of together. (The
reds first, then they died; and just as they were fading the
oranges opened up, and so on.) It affected me in a strange
way, as though I should have known it would happen like that,
but didn't, and then was surprised.

To get back to the business at hand, I know you're anxious to
hear how things went. A lot happened, but not in terms of
straight linear action, so if you'd prefer to save this until later,

take it home with you where you can read at your leisure, please feel free.

Where should I start? The sunlight on the Truckee River at 11:30 in the morning? With just enough snow in its color to contrast with the green underneath? It held such promise, it began to feel like the most natural thing in the world to be laying a ghost to rest. There was none of the fear which usually attaches to these things. Entering Reno, I began searching for the cemetery straight off. I guess it's safe to confess I felt a mild pull in the direction of the casinos; I thought, why not throw one in the slot, for him. He gambled away all of his, and most of other people's. It seemed only fitting to make a gesture of that kind, now that I was there. But you know how it is, V.: first things first.

The Masonic Memorial Gardens is on the top of a hill overlooking the city of Reno. The dirt road leading up there nearly ruined my exhaust system. To the west the mountains shone in the midday light. Cattle grazed the length of the Truckee River. In my purse was a letter containing the name of the man I was supposed to see. It was a strange feeling driving through the gates, one of getting closer and closer to something you had put off as long as possible. What a place: everything spread out, disconnected, with little roads leading in all directions, then coming to a dead end. There were two mausoleum-columbariums, two offices, a garage-incinerator, and a trailer. I didn't know where to begin, so I went into the first columbarium and asked the caretaker where I could find Roy Granger's office. He was kneeling with his dustcloth at the foot of the niches, the glass-enclosed ones containing the copper urns in the shape of books with the deceased's name as title: a dark, dwarfed little man. He saw my camera and smiled. He had two front teeth missing. He said, "You take good pictures?" I became aware of a strange sound and, turning, noticed the 12-foot water fountain cascading at the far end of the hall. It had orange spotlights playing on it. There were also six or eight gigantic tanks of tropical fish. Do you have anything like that in your columbarium? Well, you haven't heard the half of it, V. O. There were carpets, ramps, and (are you ready?) Muzak. But that isn't what knocked me out, the columbarium in Oakland has that—organ-music Muzak. My first visit there I went crazy looking for the man playing the organ. It wasn't until I'd covered the entire place that I realized it was coming out of the ceiling. No, it wasn't that the *trend* is undoubtedly toward Muzak in mausoleums. It was that here, in this isolated, architect-designed death house on a windswept hill, dead center of the Far West, they were playing "You and the Night and the Music." I couldn't help myself, V. O., I started dancing. The caretaker was in the washroom filling the water vases, I wouldn't have done it with him around. I danced up the ramp, past the colored fountain, to the upper level. By this time the tune on the tape was "It Had to Be You." I couldn't help slowing down, I was on the verge of tears.

Why do they keep columbariums humidified? Everyone's sealed in the walls. Except for the humidity and those file cabinets, it was just like a hotel. They had very nice furniture, pale oyster velvet chairs, placed in strategic little groupings, lots of plants, miles of red carpets. I was the only one there. I stared at the marble walls, glowing in the humid orange light. One niche had fresh flowers and a note, one of those little florist cards. The message was handwritten, it read: Frank, I miss you and am always with you Day and Night we will never part your Wife, Rose Giannini. I found the caretaker and asked for directions to Roy Granger's office just as "The Blue Tango" started snowing softly down from the ceiling.

Now don't have a fit, I imagine you people aren't immune to class prejudices, but you mustn't make snap judgments. If you've never been to Reno, it's hard to appreciate that, in spite of innovations such as the mausoleum I've just described, basic values still hold sway there. Roy Granger's "office" was a little room in the garage, off to the side of the incinerator where they do the cremations. The trailer next door is his home. It was way over on the other side of the cemetery. As I learned later, the place I stopped first was the Catholic side, they've got more money, that's why the colored fountain and the Muzak. Over on the Masonic side things are very simple. The grass was unwatered. As I pulled up to the garage it came to me for the first time that my father was in there. It was one of those things which you knew was impossible but true nonetheless.

It was hard walking in, but I forged on; I'd come 200 miles for this. Incinerator dust glowed on the concrete floor. The only sound was the wind in the grass outside. I didn't shut the door after me, call it superstition if you like. Mr. Granger must have heard the car because this very large man came into the building right away. I said, "I'm looking for Roy Granger," and he replied, "I'm guilty." That's what I meant earlier about the straight-forward simplicity which obtains in Reno. I extended my hand and he removed his hat. He was wearing khaki work clothes. He was maybe sixty-five or seventy. Did you know they still refer to people in his position here as sextons? It said so on the death certificate, which I received later. It was reassuring, the term sexton; it took me back to the early seventeenth century, the graveyard scene in *Hamlet,* to be exact, know that one?

Well, V. O., I know you're a busy man, and I said I'd try to be brief. Funny, I had expected Mr. Granger would be someone like you—with the pinstripe and a plush office; I had tried before-hand to prepare myself for it, I even considered dressing prop-erly but, in the end, its being Reno, common sense prevailed and I was relieved that I'd decided on my denims, because here was Roy Granger in his khakis. It made what followed much easier. It would be stretching things to say I was relaxed, but I was straightforward. I said, "I've come to inquire about arrangements for placement of my father's remains." I couldn't bring myself to say *cremains.* In this atmosphere it seemed contrived. I knew that Roy Granger would have given me a funny look, as though to say, "That's the way they talk in the front office."

"Have a seat," he said. His desk was basic government issue, circa 1945. "I have a letter here," I said, fumbling in my Berkeley oriental rug bag for the letter, "which states two choices: 'Inter-ment in the columbarium niche, $100' or, 'Interment in the Masonic Memorial Urn Garden, $175.00 (approx.).' I'd appreci-ate seeing the two alternatives before I make my final decision." Roy Granger smiled. He lifted himself from his chair and fetched the "urn marker" ($150.00, plus tax). I've never seen anything more disgusting, I'm telling it to you straight, V. O. He said the cost of copper had skyrocketed, something I already knew, I read the papers. Just a lousy $8'' \times 12''$ plaque for the name, date, and one-line sentiment, with a copper bucket underneath to hold the *cremains.* It gets inserted in the ground in the urn

garden. I asked to see the urn garden, as well as the columbarium where the $100 niches were. He was very obliging. We
went out into the spring sun for our tour.

The Masonic columbarium is very simple. It is not architect-
designed. Its interior is basic marble, with folding chairs, bare
floors, and aqua altar accessories. There is, needless to say, no
Muzak. The $100 niches were at the ceiling; they resembled
post-office boxes. I said, "Show me the urn garden." It would
have been an act of pure hostility to put him in a p.o. box next to
the ceiling. I'm not saying he might not have deserved it, just
that I couldn't do it.

The urn garden: imagine an Olympic-size swimming pool.
Now imagine it filled, not with water, but with dry grass. (Excuse me, V. O. I have to refresh my vermouth before I can finish
this account. I don't care what your personal attitudes are with
regard to drinking, but speaking purely for myself, I've found—
somewhat late in life—it helps.) Thanks for waiting. There were
six or seven copper "urn markers" inserted in the dry grass in the
urn garden. They looked so lost there, it's hard to describe, as
though there was no other "natural" setting in which to place the
beloved's *cremains*, so the survivors, out of desperation, settled
on the urn garden. The rest was vacant. It took less than two
minutes for me to decide that my father wasn't going in there. I
thought of him, a loner all his life: he would say, some time after
placement, probably the middle of the night when everything
was quiet, What the hell did she put me here for? Who are all
these assholes next to me? What in the name of Jesus am I doing
in an Olympic-size urn garden?

On the way back to the garage Roy Granger opened up. He
told me his personal philosophy. I think he sensed my thoughts,
and, having satisfied his obligation toward impartiality and pro-
fessionalism, felt free to speak. "You know, when you've been
here as long as I have," he said, "you get philosophical." I
prepared myself to endure his philosophy. It came as a surprise
when his philosophy touched something very deep in me. He
said, "I had a heart attack last year, my third, and my wife and I,
we've got a will. It states: whichever one goes first, the other
scatters. If both of us go together, the eldest child scatters. It's

the only way." We continued walking. I listened. The wind stirred the dry grass. He was so tall, Roy was. He walked in a heavy, lilting way which was perfectly attuned to the natural surroundings. I had a brief flash that it was just like walking beside a father, but repressed it. He told me of a woman in Reno who had her husband cremated and then asked him to sculpt a box in the shape of a dice and paint the little dots on it; then she put her husband's *cremains* in it and put it on her mantle. Roy is a very respectful person, he didn't derogate her, but he mentioned it as an example of individual inclinations, bordering on the bizarre. Needless to say, he complied with her request. Another one, he was asked to cremate in an $800 coffin. I forget if it was rosewood or walnut. I think the body was in it for about an hour and a half, however long it took for the ceremony. Now you have to understand Roy is a tolerant person, but also practical. His blood pressure rose some describing this. It was clear he considered it a waste. It was also clear he considered it an individual right to make such a request, and his individual responsibility to honor it. As we walked, I felt very warm toward Roy Granger. I wish you could have seen the mountains in the distance that day, V. O.

Back at the incinerator, Roy walked over to a shelf against the wall. I knew immediately what was in there, and what he was going to do. He opened the door and ran his fingers down the row of $8 \times 8 \times 8$ aluminum cans. His hand stopped when he came to the can with my father's name on it. My heart jumped. Does that surprise you? Don't think just because you do these things every day that others can adapt just like that. I thought, *There he is—so small, reduced to that.* "Here it is," he said, lifting the can from the shelf. He shook it lightly. I was shocked to hear the sound of bones against the aluminum. Why do you people persist in referring to what's left as *cremains* or ashes? when all the time it's fragments of bone? At this point, I wanted to turn and run. My throat was very dry. Roy Granger started to remove the masking tape around the top of the aluminum box. "Please don't do that," I heard myself saying, "I haven't been here as long as you have, I am not 'philosophical.'"

"Oh, it's just bones, they're all the same," he smiled. "Come over here, I'll show you someone I 'did' yesterday." He led me toward the incinerator. I had averted my eyes from it from the start. There was a trough leading from the main body of the incinerator. I forced myself to keep my eyes open. In the trough were bones. Hip bones. Shoulder bones. Sockets, joints, even a partial skull. "He was a large man," Roy said. I confess my shock. Expecting ashes, then seeing the dry, pocked surface of a partial skull. However, I looked. I looked a long time. If I could absorb this "large man"—yesterday's *cremains*—maybe I could look at my father, it was within the realm of possibility.

We returned to the office. I said, "I have to think things over. I'll be back in an hour." Roy said, "I'll be here until four-thirty." I got back in the MG and headed for town. I went into Harrah's Club. It was so hot in there, breathing was difficult. I tried to make my way to the bar but it was wall-to-wall people, as they say here in California. I stood outside the circle of people crowded around the bar. On my right was a man, somewhere around sixty-five or seventy. He turned and put his arm around me and said, "You're so thin, I think we can squeeze you in here." I didn't recoil, not at all, in Reno things are very loose, basic, and simple. He had a sweet, defeated smile. Finally I caught the bartender's eye. As I paid for the drink I realized that the man's arm was still around my waist. He was so lonely, there was nothing sexual about it; didn't you know, V. O., that in casinos sex is unheard of? it's all money and despair. So I lingered a few minutes, he was speaking of Bill Harrah, the owner, and how he was a "dear personal friend" of his. He sounded so much like my father, what else could I do but let him go on, about how people like us spend all our money here so that Bill Harrah can come walking into his casino with some wonderful thin girl on his arm. You don't have to be a certified psychologist to realize that he was thinking of me, for the space of that five minutes, as his wonderful thin girl, and during that time he was Bill Harrah and his grief lessened. I thanked him for helping me squeeze in and get my drink, wished him luck, told him not to give it all away to Bill; he laughed and I went to a phone booth and took a Librium and an aspirin, in that order, washing them down with the vodka and tonic. I stayed in the phone booth for a half hour, thinking.

The drinks there aren't strong, but it was stifling in the phone

booth. I leaned against the wall, inviting visions. What came to
me were mountains. When I was a child, he was always going up
to the mountains, staking imaginary claims, some were even in
my name. When he was sent to jail for doing it with other people's money it caused me deep shame that it had been done in
my name—my name stamped there on the complaint, and on the
form in the recording office, on the mountain itself. (When you
stake a claim, is there really a stake? Is it driven into actual
ground? Does it bear a name the way a tombstone does?) It
wasn't just the heat, some resolutions materialize with unexpected ease. Still, I wanted it to sink in before returning to Roy,
so I made my way back through the crowds, the ringing bells, all
that burning currency greased with sweat. The MG was parked
in front of the Salvation Army, two blocks away. Tourists
skimmed the sidewalks with their drinks in hand. I drove west
along the Truckee River, wondering if I could do it.

I headed back to Masonic Memorial, up on the hill. To the
west the mountains simmered in late afternoon light. Mt. Rose
was still covered with snow. Mt. Rose dominates the Reno valley, to the southwest. It is where, according to Roy Granger,
many choose to "scatter." They still use that term which, to most
people's minds, applies to ashes. Don't fade out on me, V. O. You
aren't going to like what I have to say, but I didn't like your letters either, so fair is fair. Roy Granger was in his office. I smiled.
He knew what I was going to say. I said, "You're a lousy urn
salesman, Mr. Granger. I've come to claim my father." He understood it as a compliment meant for him. He brought the box into
the office and put it on the desk. I knew this part was going to be
hard, but claim means the same as commitment. "Have a seat,"
he said, withdrawing the papers from the drawer. I accepted his
pen and put my name on them. My father witnessed from the
southwest corner of the desk. *Is it really you?* I whispered. Roy
was so cool, he didn't say anything asinine like, You made the
right decision. He just smiled. V. O., I want to take this opportunity to thank you for your chilling cordiality, without which it is
entirely possible that I would be, at this very moment, interring
those *cremains* in the grave now occupied by my mother, in a
small concrete vault, and watching the double inscription marker

in my choice of pink granite being firmly fixed in place. I might be shaking your pink granite hand. Roy Granger put the papers in an envelope. I stared at the box. *Will he hand it to me?* was my next thought, which was immediately canceled by the knowledge that I was no longer a child; I had staked my claim. There is no other way to be rendered adult. I reach for the 8×8×8 aluminum box. I was unprepared for the weight. I thanked Roy Granger and walked to the car. I cradled the box/my father in my arm, it's the only way you can carry something that heavy. I put it/the bones/him in the trunk. The sound of the lid slamming shut had a jarring effect.

It was important to keep moving, I got behind the wheel and started back down the dirt road. I'm sure something in the exhaust system was ruined by one of those loose rocks. I wondered how I would explain having my father in the trunk if I were stopped for speeding. I was torn between ignoring the fact that he was in there, or playing with it. It was still daylight, so I played with it a while, I said, Hi, Daddy. I hope you weren't jolted too much back there. Don't criticize my driving, I'm in the driver's seat now. This is your last ride. We've all got to stop giving the orders, and renounce our supremacy, eventually, that's what death is all about. I am not unaware of the things you did in your life, I never was. I am not claiming you in spite of them, any more than I could refuse to claim you because of them. I claim you because I am honoring something in myself, don't ask me what it is, this whole business is new to me. I am taking you somewhere special, I think you'll approve. I'm not sure I can go through with it, but I've amazed myself this far. Don't do anything unexpected. Help me.

Heading out of town, V. O., there was an old man sitting on a bench by the side of the Truckee River. His head was bent, he was reading a book. From the back he looked so much like . . . I thought there had been a mistake. The road up Mt. Rose curved and twisted. The snow level was somewhere around 7,000 feet. At 8,000 feet, just below the summit, I parked the car. I lifted the box from the trunk and held it close. I told myself that was because I was afraid of dropping it, but there was a strange intimacy to it which was closer to the truth. I began walking through the snow, looking for a good spot. That was when I realized I had no shovel. I wasn't sure I could do this in the first place; now I panicked. What am I doing on the top of this fucking mountain with a box of bones and no shovel? I closed my eyes. It was freezing up there. Well, what did they do in the old days? I asked myself. Before shovels? I instinctively headed for a down-slope on the Reno side. When they found the skeleton, it had been lying under a tree. The reason I didn't want your concrete vault is because I believe organic matter should be returned to earth, where it can do some good, however remote. In this case, it should be allowed to nourish something; they put bone meal on roses for that purpose, don't they? I looked around for a tree. They were all over the place, pine, fir; I began to go nuts: which tree? Don't obsess, I told myself, if you hang around up here looking for the perfect place you'll end up being discovered on Halloween, too. I settled on a fir, part way down the slope, overlooking the valley. It had a large rock at its base. I thought: it will serve as a *natural* marker. As I bent down, an inscription went through my mind. It's really amazing, V. O., the things the unconscious serves up in moments of crisis. This one originated in the seventeenth century, too, Shakespeare again, from *Julius Caesar:*

> The evil that men do lives after them;
> The good is oft interred with their bones.

I broke off a small branch from the tree and poked it in the ground. The earth was soft and porous from all the melting snow. There was just enough of it at the base of the tree for the grave. I began to dig with the stick, it was very easy. Toward the end, I scooped the rest out with my hands. I stared into the dark space. *"I do not lie in't, and yet it is mine."* Now the really impossible part: picking off the masking tape from around the lid of the can. It had been sitting on the shelf since last November; it was stiff. I was glad to be a woman, that happens sometimes, because my nails came in handy. I thought: will I be able to look at the bones? I felt another surge of gratitude for Roy Granger, the second or third that day. I pulled at the lid. It wouldn't come off. It was just like what always occurs in the movies, in the middle of a perfect crime: something totally unexpected, and utterly trivial, happens at the last minute to render worthless everything that's gone before. I tore off a fingernail halfway to the quick before I realized the lid didn't lift up, it slid sideways. My finger was bleeding all over the can. *This is the last drop of blood you get from me,* I said to my father. Well, don't be so rigid, V. O., you don't really believe there's such a thing as unambivalence toward the dead, do you? Under the lid was a paper towel. Jesus, all these obstacles, how much longer do you think I can hold out with regard to viewing the bones? You think you can prepare yourself for these things, but if too much time elapses the whole thing can be shot in a minute, the nervous system was designed to handle just so much. Placed on top of the paper towel was a little card bearing my father's name and the information that this package contained his cremated remains, and a statement to the effect that he was F.D. in rural Gerlach, Washoe County, Nevada, on 10/31/73. I put the card in my pocket. There was blood all over the snow. This is utterly ridiculous, I didn't bargain for melodrama. The voice which reasons with me at times like this said, This is an important moment; if you don't assume a reflective manner the whole gesture will be without meaning. I lifted the paper towel. *You* might be immune, V. O., but there was nothing in my history which prepared me for this. There was a brief flash of exhilaration, followed swiftly by a feeling of profound shame, followed by the awesomeness of viewing some aspect of a person which that person himself had never viewed. I did not, I could not, dwell. I blamed it on the fact that a cold wind was blowing, but that was not the whole truth. I began to empty the contents of the can into the grave with as much respect as was possible under the circumstances. They tumbled out in slow motion, as in a dream. It seemed that bones would continue flowing forever, the can would never empty itself. At this writing, I remember only the shape of one round end of bone, probably elbow, something which once had fit into a socket. That was the last thing I saw as I folded the earth over my father and pressed it down. My eyes were tearing, I don't know if it was the wind, or if it came from within, does it matter? I broke off a small piece of fir and laid it on top. I scattered some snow over that, it fell through my fingers like white petals from a flower. I imagine all people have automatic gestures at times like this which bear a marked similarity the world over. I stood there a short time, thinking that this was the way people had buried their dead from the beginning of time. It was overwhelming to have become an adult, and also a link with the history of humanity, all in one day. This letter is a small token of my thanks to you, V. O., and to let you know it's OK to close your file on me.

Sincerely

A Passion for History

STEPHEN MINOT

STEPHEN MINOT is the author of *Chill of Dusk*, a novel, and *Crossings*, a collection of short stories. His work has appeared in many periodicals, including the *Atlantic Monthly, Harper's Magazine, Playboy, Virginia Quarterly Review* and *Sewanee Review*. He is at present an Associate Professor at Trinity College in Hartford, where he has taught since 1959. He is working on a second novel, called *Ghost Images*.

P
ICTURE: On the shore where the river joins the sea, a lobsterman's boathouse-home, gray-shingled and trim, morning dew drifting in vapor from the roof, a column of smoke rising from the chimney, flower boxes with petunias.

It's enough to turn the stomach.

He is not naive. He will not be trapped by sentimentality. He will not be seduced by those Currier and Ives virtues—thrift, honesty, piety, and hard work. These are slogans devised by the rich, by landholders and factory owners. There is no beauty in poverty.

First published in the *Sewanee Review*. Copyright © 1976 by the University of the South. Reprinted by permission of the editor.

Picture: On the ledge next to the lobsterman's home stands a couple. She wears a dress only a country girl would buy. Tall, long-boned, graceful, she would be beautiful if she had any notion of style. Beauty is there, hidden.

He has rumpled white pants and a blue polo shirt, the costume of a man consciously trying to be informal but not quite succeeding. He is older than she. But they are not father and daughter or brother and sister. As they look out on the glisten of the river which blends into the sea beyond, his right hand rests ever so gently on her right buttock.

They are mismatched, these two. It is more than her mail-order dress and his rumpled elegance, though that is a part of it. There is some deeper aberration here. Like a parent, he can sense something wrong without being able to describe it. But he is not the man's parent. He is the man himself.

It is Kraft himself who is standing there. The woman beside him is Thea. The cottage where she lives is to their left. He is conscious now where his right hand is and can, in fact, feel the warmth of her body.

This kind of thing has been happening to Kraft lately. He can't be sure whether some microcircuit in his brain is loose, blacking out certain periods of time, allowing him to stand on a bank *planning* to take a walk with someone and then skipping ahead to the actual event, or whether it works the other way around—being in the middle of an experience and suddenly viewing it from a distance, with historical perspective, as it were.

"Brooding?" she asks.

"Me? No. I don't brood. That's an indulgence. Thinking, maybe. Sorry. I was just thinking."

"Perhaps you miss teaching. Miss students and all that."

"No, not in the least. I'm not that kind of teacher, you know. A course here, a lecture series there. Not regular teaching. Not in my field."

He always underrates his academic work, he being a radical and teaching being a bourgeois profession and history departments generally being elitist and unenlightened. He prefers to think of himself as a political organizer, though he has done little of that since the 1960s. He hopes that, now in his forties, he is better known for his articles and his recent volume on the radical

movement in America. But Thea, his lovely Thea, has read nothing, heard nothing. She has lived her life here in rural Nova Scotia, and as everyone knows, rural Nova Scotia is nowhere. She
has never heard of him. He is for her just what he tells her about
himself. No less and no more.

"I'd love to learn history," she says.

"Never mind that," he says. "You've got history in you. That's
enough."

"No, I really would."

"Not the way *they* teach it you wouldn't. All dates and kings."

"And you?"

"Me? I teach about people. History is people. Little people.
The way they live. Know how one person lives and you know a
whole period. Not kings. People. Do you understand?"

"Of course," she says, taking half a step back and turning just
slightly to the right as if to search the treetops, checking to see if
an osprey nest had been built during the night, and incidentally,
innocently, pressing ever so gently against the palm of his hand
with the curve of her bottom.

Picture: On the smooth gray ledge which forms the bank of
the Worwich River at the point where it flows into the sea, a
man in white pants embraces a long limber girl, kissing her and
now beginning to undo the first of one hundred and two tiny,
cloth-covered buttons which run down the back of her dress, she
laughing, the sound drifting up like a loon's call.

From this height one can see not only the little boathouse-
home but the marshy estuaries formed by the meeting of river
and sea and farther, on the sea side, a great gray rectangle of a
house surrounded by tall grass, ledge outcroppings, and a scat-
tering of overturned tombstones.

This large rectangle is the house Kraft has bought for himself
and his family as a summer home—house and barn and outhouse
and woodsheds and 953 acres of land. This is what he has
bought with the royalties from his book on the radical movement
in America.

Like a mistress it is an embarrassment and a pleasure. He
makes a point of keeping it out of the press. His name *is* mentioned in the press from time to time since he is known to
liberals as "the guru of radicals" and to hard radicals as "a

running-dog revisionist." Thus he has no following whatever but he is read.

When interviewers press him, he refers to his property as his "rural retreat" or his "wilderness camp." Once a Maoist sheet—a sloppy mimeographed affair—reported scathingly that he had bought up a thousand acres of land in Nova Scotia. This, of course, he brands as a total fabrication. They have exaggerated by forty-seven acres.

His house up on the high land is in a permanent state of disrepair. He has not allowed one can of paint to be used inside or out. It is a weathered gray. There is no electricity and water must be lifted bucketful by bucketful from an open well. The plaster was half gone when he bought it, so they removed the other half, leaving the horizontal laths as semi-partitions between the rooms. It is, he reminds his family from time to time, their rural slum.

But this spring there is no family. He came up alone in mid-April, leaving his wife and three children in New Haven by mutual agreement. He was to have two and a half absolutely clear months to type the final draft of his most recent book, this one on the *liberal* tradition.

It was a perfect arrangement. No meetings to attend, no speeches to present, no teaching, no family to sap his energies. So of course he has done no writing.

There are times when he can't stand the clutter and filth of his own house—clutter, filth, and whispering deadlines. Those are the times when he comes here to the neat little boathouse-home on the river, the little Currier-and-Ives home Thea shares with her father.

Right now he is walking beside Thea, walking back to that perfect little place, his arm around her and hers around him. Seven of the one hundred and two tiny cloth-covered buttons down her back are undone. Ninety-five to go.

Kraft is not entirely certain that this is right. His wife, a sure and competent and rational woman with a law degree and a practice of her own, would consider this a serious malady. Worse than the flu. Akin to income tax evasion. And of course she would be right.

With these thoughts passing through his mind he sees in the far distance, inland, just coming out of the woods and beginning to cross the rocky field, approaching the boathouse-home, old Mr. McKnight.

"Oh," Kraft says, noticing for the first time that the barrow which the old man pushes has a wooden wheel. Involuntarily Kraft's mind provides a parenthetical notation. (*Hand-fashioned oak wheels disappeared from each county at the point when mail-order houses reached that district.*)

"Oh," Thea says, not hearing his unspoken observation. "It's father."

Kraft likes the old man—his courtly, country way. But he has mixed feelings about delaying what he and Thea had been heading toward.

"Well," she says, "no matter. He'll stay for a while and we'll talk. But then it'll be time for his scavenging."

Every day at low tide the old man scours the beaches for usable items—timbers, orange crates, even nails which can be pried out and ground smooth on the whetstone. (*Recycling has been an economic necessity until the last half of the twentieth century.*) Clearly old McKnight lives in the previous century.

"I don't mind," Kraft says. Actually he does and he doesn't mind. Both. But that is too complicated to explain. Even to himself. "I don't mind," he says again. They are on the front stoop—a simple porch with no roof. She sits in the big rocker and he is perched on a nail keg old Mr. McKnight has salvaged from the sea. It would be a time before the old man put the wood in the shed and came around to suggest a cup of coffee. Nothing whatever moves rapidly in rural Nova Scotia. Especially time.

"I don't mind," Kraft says, thinking that the last time he said it to himself in his own head. "It's good talking with the old man. Just this morning I wrote in my journal, 'I hope I see old Mr. McKnight today. He is my link with the region. I like hearing his voice. I learn a lot from him.'"

"Are you perhaps spending too much time with that journal of yours?" It is exactly the question his wife asked by letter the week before. Unsettling.

"I've kept that going ever since I was ten. I'm not going to stop now." He is, though, spending too much time writing in his journal and she knows it just as clearly as he does, so it is essential that he defend himself. "It's an act of survival, writing that journal."

"Survival?"

"Did you know that shipwrecked sailors rowing a lifeboat are taught to study their own wake? Otherwise they turn in great circles. Did you know that?" She shakes her head. "I wrote about that last week, as a matter of fact. 'Sheepherders,' I pointed out, 'talk to themselves and address their members with obscene endearments.' Well, I mean, here I am living in an ark of a house up there without electricity or running water miles from anywhere, adrift for two months with only a rough draft and a set of correction notes to work with and a publisher's deadline for navigation. Did you know that mermaids are an optical illusion caused by solitude and malnutrition?"

"I didn't know you believed in mermaids."

"I don't. You don't have to believe in them to know that they exist. I've got an entry about that too."

"Those entries," she says, shaking her head. He notices that she is shelling lima beans. Where did they come from? "You spend too much time with them," she says.

"It's just a trail of where my thoughts have been."

She shrugs. She is no lawyer and never argues. She makes commentary on his thoughts, but she never presses her point. "All that looking back," she says gently. "It'll turn you to salt." She smiles and a loon laughs. Either that or a loon smiles and she laughs. "Time to do up the dishes," she says. "He'll be coming in and he'll want a cup of coffee right soon. Come sit with me while I fix up."

Picture in sepia: A woman stands by the soapstone sink, her hand on the pump. There is little light in the room because the windows are small. (*Large windows were avoided not only because of expense but because of a strong sense of nocturnal dangers. Except in cities police protection was practically unknown.*) There is no view of the river or the sea.

The kitchen walls are made of the narrow tongue-in-groove boarding, a poor man's substitute for plaster. Open shelves rather than cupboards—the price of a hinge saved. Kitchen table bare pine, unvarnished, scrubbed with salt—to be replaced in the 1920s with white enamel. Kraft can glance at a photograph of an American kitchen and date it within a decade and can lecture without notes on its impact on the status of women, the institution of marriage, and the hierarchy within the family. Here in Worwich he has found a lost valley. Time has moved on like a great flock of geese, leaving a strange silence and sepia prints.

"He's been cutting wood," Thea says, pumping cold water into the dishpan and adding hot from the aluminum teakettle. Kraft's mind flashes a notation. (*The shift from the heavy cast-iron kettle to the aluminum was as significant for women as the replacement of the wood range by gas.*) "I imagine on your land."

"He's welcome to it. I've got enough problems without clearing my own woodlots." He has a quick vision of his study, the upper room in the big house on the bluff, his papers scattered about like leaves after a storm. His manuscript, the one on the American liberal movement, in cluttered piles; and in addition to his own journals there are his *father's* journals which he has foolishly brought. One more distraction. One more bit of clutter. So if old Mr. McKnight wants to poach, wants to clear land, he is welcome to it. Perhaps Kraft can persuade the old man to steal unfinished manuscripts as well.

Simplicity. Order. He looks at Thea there at the sink. She is both. Her cottage, her life is harmony. His own place is a shambles. How can a man, he wonders, pick a summer home so far from the complexities of contemporary society, so painstakingly distant, and work so hard to keep the place unimproved, simple, true to Thoreau, and still end up with such an enormous rubbish heap in his own study?

Thea has finished washing. She rinses the plates and mugs with one more spurt from the pump, dries each item, places each on open shelves, each in the correct place. He feels a great wave of envy for her life, a passionate and agonized longing which he mistakes for healthy sexual desire.

"It is madness to romanticize the nineteenth-century rural life," he has written in his journal only that morning. "Even a cursory examination of the McKnight family reveals a history of backbreaking work, sickness, and early death."

He silently recites his observation verbatim, cursed with total recall. No, blessed. Without some kind of historical sense of reality this recent affair with Thea will turn into a nightmare of complications.

There is nothing to envy in Thea's life, he tells himself, and the affair is only a passing sexual fancy, a mildly comic sample of male menopause.

The evidence of brutish living is all around him, after all. Abandoned houses, cellar holes where families were burned out in midwinter; private cemetery plots grown over with chokecherry, no one left to tend them. One such is right on the rocky scrub grass he calls his front lawn. McKnights. Half of them children. A family shattered by the brutality of what they had hoped would be their New Scotland.

They came from Scotland, looking for the good life, and they hung on for more than two hundred years. But now as a clan they are broken and scattered, beaten by isolation, by madness, by sudden death, the younger ones fleeing to Montreal, to Toronto, to the States, the survivors selling the last remaining house and most of the land to this American historian and his family who come north as summer residents, looking for the good life.

"Find it?" she asks.

"What?"

"Find it?" For an instant he thinks she has a witch's ability to read minds. (*Statements made about witches in the eighteenth century closely resemble fantasies of present-day patients described as paranoid; thus our diagnosis of mental illness depends from the outset on our current view of reality.*) But she has asked him for a pitcher of milk she has left on the window sill to keep cool.

He sees it, hands it to her. She smiles. "If you don't want him cutting your wood," she says, "you should tell him."

Kraft shakes his head. "I'll never get around to clearing up those woodlots," he says. "There was a time when all the fixing up around the place went well. We really got a lot done. The boys and me working outside clearing fields and cutting back chokecherry. Good, honest work. And Tammy and my daughter working inside, making the place livable. Like a bunch of colonists."

"But then . . ." His voice fades out. Why tell her all that? The second and the third summer, complaints from the children about the isolation; excuses to avoid the work; wry jokes about the lack of plumbing, the lack of electricity, the enforced intimacy, wisecracks growing sharper, less funny each summer. He finds this embarrassing. It is not the way he likes to think of his family. There is no need to share this with Thea.

She has finished the dishes and dries her hands on the roller towel, looking at him. Just the touch of a smile.

"They don't understand," she says. He wonders whether he has just voiced some of his disappointments or whether, again, she is reading his mind. "They don't understand, but I do."

"I don't know what I'd do without you," he says. Actually he does know. It is unutterable. Everything would fall to pieces without her around to listen, to be his lover. It is not just sexual; it is human contact. He depends on both her and her father. Their presence. Both of them.

And there, suddenly, is old Mr. McKnight. He is standing at the kitchen door. Gray-bearded but with no mustache—a tintype. No smile but not unfriendly. (*It is a significant comment on the impact of the industrial revolution that from the introduction of the camera in the mid-nineteenth century until after the first world war it was not customary to smile when having one's picture taken.*) Old Mr. McKnight gives just the ghost of a nod of recognition and extends his hand in an old-world handshake.

"I couldn't seem to get any work done this morning," Kraft says. He doesn't want to seem like a summer resident. He *isn't* a summer resident.

"All that work with your head," Mr. McKnight says. "It can't be good."

"Right."

"Come look at this," the old man says. Kraft follows him into the workroom where there is a skeleton of ribs fashioned to a backbone. It is the beginnings of a rowboat upside down, raised on two sawhorses. Mr. McKnight builds one a year, shaping the oak ribs in a crude boiler out back.

"Here," Mr. McKnight says, seizing Kraft's wrist. The old man's fingers are armored, rough plates joined. He takes Kraft's hand as if it were a plane and slides the palm along the oak keel.

Kraft winces, expecting splinters from any unpainted surface. But of course it is perfectly sanded. Needlessly sanded.

"A filly's ass," the old man says.

"She's beautiful," Kraft says. "Like everything of yours."

"Ha!" Mr. McKnight smiles for the first time. The two men share their chauvinistic joke like a brotherhood—the younger one uneasily. "Time for a cup of coffee," the old one says just loud enough for it to become an order for Thea. "Tide's not about to wait for me or you."

Kraft nods, thinking: When the tide's out for you it will be high for Thea and me. He smiles to himself but Mr. McKnight casts a quick questioning look. Does the old man read thoughts too?

Thea has placed three mugs of coffee on the kitchen table and beside each a cloth napkin and a spoon. They sit down. (*Informal eating was considered bad taste well into the 1920s and still is frowned on in rural Ireland and Scotland. The eating of food even under picnic circumstances was invested with ritual significance and required sitting correctly at a table.*)

"That skiff," old Mr. McKnight says, "is as fine as you can find here to Boston." (Boston *became a Nova Scotian term for all of New England by the 1780s.*) "Not one bit of metal in her, you know. No nails. All pegged. Even the cleat is cedar heart. Hard as brass and it won't tarnish." He nods to himself in full agreement with himself. "Gives pleasure twice, it does—once in the building and again in the owning."

"In Halifax," Thea says, "they make them out of plywood."

They all three smile. "Imagine that," the old man says. Kraft does not mention fiberglass. For the McKnights it doesn't exist yet. "Halifax skiffs are nailed too. Full of nails. Rust out on you sooner or later. Ten, fifteen years they'll rust out on you. Drown you sooner or later. Like putting a metal wheel on a barrow. Takes me a winter to shape a wooden wheel. Eight pieces glued and pegged. It's work, but it'll last a lifetime. Two, with luck. Same for lobster traps. Pegged and laced. You can't find a better trap."

Kraft nods, letting the old man continue, though he knows that in the States they are using a plastic lobster trap which is in every way superior. Ugly and indestructible as the aluminum beer can. "I build the best traps around here," the old man says. "The very best." They all nod, a part of the ritual. "Well, can't sit here all day. Tide's calling me," he says and abruptly he is gone. Quick as that.

And now, oddly, when the two of them are free, Kraft is hesitant. The room seems small, airless. Enclosing. Warily he looks to the window, to the door. He hears again the old man's proclamation—"I build the best traps."

He looks at her sitting there opposite him. For an instant she is in sepia again, posed there, a tall woman, high cheekboned. She is an image which would startle young readers browsing through an old photo album. "Who was that?"—the patronizing surprise of moderns who cannot imagine passion cloaked in formality. A sepia print. Colorless. How does such a lovely person stand a colorless life? How does she exist?

"What's wrong?" she asks. "You're having dark thoughts again."

"You're the one who should be having dark thoughts," he says.

"Why?"

"Cooped up here, trapped."

"I'm not trapped."

"With nothing to read."

"I'm not much for reading."

"No profession."

"I keep the place neat. I mend. Grow things."

"The monotony—it must be suffocating. I should think the isolation would drive you crazy."

"I'm not alone now."

"Now." She has no conception of future time. "*Now.*" He stands up. He needs motion. "You know, don't you, that Tammy is coming up in ten days. Tammy and the children. And the dog. The whole bit. Did you forget that?"

"That's in a week. Now is now."

She floats in an eternal present. He can't imagine how that would be. He feels rage and envy. For him the present is the peak of a slippery hummock; he is forever sliding down one side or the other—either counting the days to something out there ahead of him or slithering back into the past.

He is standing behind her, his hands on her shoulders. She

reaches up and takes both his hands and draws them down and around to her breasts. There is only the cotton fabric between his palms and the softness of her flesh. He feels her nipples. He stops thinking for an instant about past and future. I am holding the present in my hands, he thinks.

He is undoing the buttons down the back of her dress. She has leaned her head back so that it is against him, rocking gently.

"You're right," he says softly in her ear. "I'm not even going to think about Tammy."

Mistake! Mistake! The very word *Tammy* jars the mood, breaks his hold on the present. What is he doing? Somehow the action goes on, but he has floated up. The overview, the damned overview.

Picture: A man embraces a woman in an old-fashioned kitchen, her dress is loosened at the back, is down over one shoulder. The man is not at ease; he is harried by his passion, planning the next move, thinking ahead. He leads her up the stairs and into a simple, unadorned room: walls of vertical boarding, varnished dark. An iron bed, a rocking chair, a bureau with a wavy mirror attached, and a commode on which stand a kerosene lamp and a wash basin. Two books, a Bible and a copy of *Pilgrim's Progress,* both old. Perfect neatness. Perfect order.

Ninety-five tiny buttons open in a ripple and she stands barebreasted in her petticoat. She shakes her hair down and it is long. Her petticoat slips to the floor at her feet. He has seen this image somewhere before, standing this way in the palm of an enormous seashell. But this is no time for art. She is with him on the bed. Her skin radiates warmth.

"Fast," he says. "Quickly." He is on an anxious schedule, racing to meet a sudden departure. The bed cries out like a flock of frantic gulls.

Then, silence. Perfect silence.

That, one might imagine, was the climax of the day for him. But it was only the first of two. The second came after leaving.

He headed up the path toward his own house, not looking forward to returning, and he made the terrible mistake of looking back. A part of him knew that he shouldn't. But he had been living in the present and was careless. "Don't," he said to himself just as he turned, but it was too late.

There was the McKnight boathouse, the one he had just left, chimney smokeless, cracked, and leaning; the roof rotted through, sagging beams exposed, skeletal; windows all broken, flower boxes gone, holes black as empty eye sockets. Even the porch was gone, wrenched off by the grinding ice of winter storms years ago. Dead. All dead and gone. All history.

The Autumn Dog

PAUL THEROUX

PAUL THEROUX was born in 1941 in Medford, Massachusetts, and has lived abroad since 1963. Houghton Mifflin will publish a collection of his short stories in the spring of 1977.

M INE USED TO SWEAT in his sleep," said the woman in the white dress, a bit drunkenly. "It literally poured off him! During the day he'd be dry as a bone, but as soon as he closed his eyes—bingo!—he'd start percolating."

Her name was Maxine Stanhope and practically the first thing she had said to the woman who sat opposite was, "Please call me Max; all my friends do." They sat on the veranda of a hotel outside Denpasar, in Bali, in the sun the other tourists avoided. They had dark reptilian tans and slouched languorously in the comfortable chairs like lizards sunning themselves on a rock. Lunch was over, the wine was gone, their voices were raised in emphatic friendliness. They had known each other for only three hours.

"Mine didn't sweat that much, but he made the most fantastic noises," said Milly Strang. "He carried on these mumbling monologs, using different voices, and groaning feeling affectionate. He was really quite strong. He left bruises! I suppose he thought he was—what's the expression?—turning me on."

"They always think that," said Maxine. She held the empty wine bottle over the other's glass until a drop fell out. "Let's have another—wine makes me honest."

"I've had quite enough," said Milly.

"You're the boss," said Maxine. Then she said, "Mine weighed two hundred pounds."

"Well, mine was at least that. I'm not exaggerating. When I think of him on top of me—it's ludicrous."

"It's obscene. Mine kept gaining weight, and finally I said to him, 'Look, if this goes on any more, we won't be able to make love.' Not that *that* worried me. By then, I'd already taken a lover—not so much a lover as a new way of life. But Erwin said it didn't matter whether you were fat or thin. If you were fat, you'd just find a new position."

"The fat man's position!"

"Exactly. And he got this—this manual. All the positions were listed, with little diagrams and arrows. Arrows! It was like fitting a plug, an electrical manual for beginners. 'Here,' he said, 'I think that one would suit us.' They all had names—I forget what that one was, but it was the fat man's position. Can you imagine?"

"Mine had manuals. Well, he called them manuals. They were Swedish, I think. You must have seen them. Interesting and disgusting at the same time. He didn't want me to see them—I mean, he hid them from me. Then I found them and he caught me going through them. Honestly, I think I gave him quite a shock. He looked over my shoulder. 'Ever see anything like it?' he said. I could hear him breathing heavily. He was getting quite a thrill!"

"Did yours make a fuss over the divorce?"

"No," said Milly. "What about yours?"

"*He* divorced *me*. Nothing in particular—just a whole series of things. But, God, what a messy business. It dragged on for months and months."

"Mine was over before I knew it."

"Lucky," said Maxine.

"Up till then, we'd been fairly happy."

"Happy marriages, so called, turn into really messy divorces," said Maxine.

"I think not," said Milly. "The best marriages end quickly."

Theirs, the Strangs', had gone on serenely for years, filling us with envious contempt. It fell to pieces in an afternoon of astonishing abuse. They had pretended politeness for so long only an afternoon was necessary. Then we were friendlier toward the couple, no longer a couple, but Milly alone in the house and Lloyd at the club. The marriages in Ayer Hitam were no frailer than anywhere else, but we expatriates knew one another well and enjoyed a kind of kinship. A divorce was like a death in the family. Threatened with gloom, we became thoughtful. The joking was nervous: Milly had burned the toast; Lloyd had made a pass at the amah. Afterward, Lloyd clung to the town. He was overrehearsed. One of his lines went, "It was our ages. Out of the horse latitudes and into the roaring forties." He was no sailor; he was taking it badly.

Milly, unexpectedly cheerful, packed her bags and left the compound. Within a week, she was in Indonesia. Before she left, she had said to Angela Miller, "I always wanted to go to Bali. Lloyd wouldn't let me." She went, Lloyd stayed, and it looked as if he expected her back: Her early return to Ayer Hitam would have absolved him of all blame.

It did not happen that way. Before long, we all knew her story. Milly saw friends in Djakarta. The friends were uneasy with this divorced woman in their house. They sent their children out to play and treated her the way they might have treated a widow, with a mixture of somberness and high spirits, fearing the whole time that she'd drink too much and burst into tears. Milly found their hospitality exhausting and went to Djokjakarta, for the temples. Though tourists (seeing her eating alone) asked her to join them, she politely refused. How could she explain that she liked eating alone and reading in bed and waking whenever she wished and doing nothing? Life was so simple and marriage only a complication. Marriage also implied a place: You were married and lived in a particular house; un-

married, you lived in the world and there were no answers
required of you. Milly changed her status slowly, regaining an
earlier state of girlishness from the widowhood of divorce. Ten
years was returned to her and, more than that, she saw herself
granted a valuable enlightenment, she was wiser and unencum-
bered, she was free.

The hotel in Bali, which would have been unthinkably expensive for a couple with a land surveyor's income, was really very
cheap for one person. She told the manager (Swiss; married—
she could tell at a glance) she would stay a month. There was a
column in the hotel register headed "Destination." She left it
blank. The desk clerk indicated this. "I haven't got one," she
said, and she surprised the man with her natural laugh.

The tourists, the three-day guests at the hotel, the ones with
planes to catch, were middle-aged; some were elderly, some
infirm, making this trip at the end of their lives. But there were
other visitors in Bali and they were mostly young. They looked
to Milly like innocent witches and princelings. They slept on the
beach, cooked over fires, played guitars; she saw them strolling
barefoot or eating mountains of food or lazing in the sand. There
was not a sign of damage on them. She envied them their youth.
For a week, Milly swam in the hotel's pool, had a nap after
lunch, took her first drink at six and went to bed early: It was
like a spell of convalescence, and when she saw she had established this routine, she was annoyed. One night, drinking in
the bar, she was joined by an Australian. He talked about his
children in the hurt, remote way of a divorced man. At midnight,
Milly stood up and snapped her handbag shut. The man said,
"You're not going, are you?"

"I've paid for my share of the drinks," she said. "Was there
something you wanted?"

But she knew, and she smiled at the fumbling man, almost pit-
ying him.

"Perhaps I'll see you tomorrow," she said, and was gone.

She left the hotel, crossed by the pool to the beach and walked
toward a fire. It was the makeshift camp of the young people
and there they sat, around the fire, singing. She hesitated to go
near and she believed that she could not be seen standing in that

darkness, listening to the music. But a voice said, "Hey! Come over here, stranger!"

She went over and, seating herself in the sand, saw the strumming boy. But her joining the group was not acknowledged. The youths sat cross-legged, like monks at prayer, facing the fire and the music. How many times, on a beach or by a roadside, had she seen groups like this and, almost alarmed, looked away! Even now she felt like an impostor. Someone might ask her age and laugh when she disclosed it. She wished she was not wearing such expensive slacks; she wished she looked like these people—and she hoped they would not remind her of her difference. She was glad for the dark.

Someone moved behind her. She started to rise, but he reached out and steadied her with his arm and hugged her. She relaxed and let him hold her. In the firelight, she saw his face: twenty years old! She put her head against his shoulder and he adjusted his grip to hold her closer. And she trembled—for the first time since leaving Ayer Hitam—and wondered how she could stop herself from rolling him over on the sand and devouring him. Feeling that hunger, she grew afraid and said she had to go: She didn't want to startle the boy.

"I'll walk you back to the hotel," he said.

"I can find the way." Her voice was insistent; she didn't want to lose control.

The boy tagged along, she heard him trampling the sand; she wanted him to act—but how? Throw her down, fling off her clothes, make love to her? It was mad. Then it was too late, the hotel lights illuminated the beach; and she was relieved it had not happened. *I must be careful*—she almost spoke it.

"Will I see you again?"

"Perhaps," she said. She was on her own ground: The white hotel loomed behind the palms. Now—here—it was the boy who was the stranger.

"I want to sleep with you." It was not arrogant but imploring.

"Not now."

NOT NOW. It should have been *no*. But marriage taught you how to be perfunctory, and Milly had, as a single woman, regained a lazy sense of hope. *No* was the prudent answer; *Not now* was what she had wanted to say—so she had said it. And the next day, the boy was back, peering from the beach at Milly, who lounged by the pool. In the sunlight, he looked even younger, with a shyness that might have been an effect of the sun's brightness, making him hunch and avert his eyes. He did not know where to begin, she saw that.

Milly waved to him. He signaled back and, like an obedient pet responding to a mistress' nod, came forward, vaulted the hibiscus hedge, smiling. Instead of taking the chair next to her, he crouched at her feet, seeming to hide himself.

"They won't send you away," said Milly. "You can say you're my guest."

The boy shrugged. "At night—after everyone clears out—we come here swimming." He was silent, then he said, "Naked."

"How exciting," said Milly, frowning.

Seeing that it was mockery, the boy did not reply. He got to his feet. For a moment, Milly thought he was going to bound over the hedge and leave her. But in a series of athletic motions, he strode to the edge of the pool and, without pausing, tipped himself into it. He swam under water and Milly followed his blue shorts to the far end of the pool, where he surfaced like a hound, gasping and tossing his head. He returned, swimming powerfully, flinging his arms into the water. But he did not climb out of the pool; he rested his forearms on the tiles and said, "Come in. I'll teach you how to swim."

"I was swimming before you were born." She wished she had not said it, she wished it were not true. She picked up a magazine from her lap and plucked at a page.

The boy was beside her, dripping.

"Take this," she said, and handed him a towel. He buried his face in it with an energy that aroused her, then he wiped his arms and threw it aside.

"Time for lunch," said Milly.

"Let me treat you," said the boy.

"That's very thoughtful of you," said Milly, "but I'm afraid they won't let you in the dining room like that."

"They have room service. We can have it sent up—eat on the balcony."

"You seem to be inviting yourself to my room," said Milly.

"No," said the boy, "I'm inviting you to mine."

Milly almost laughed. She said, *"Here?"*

"Sure. I've been here for about six weeks."

"I've never seen you at breakfast."

"I never eat breakfast," said the boy. "And I've only used my room a few times in the past week or so. I met a girl over on the beach—they have a house there. But my stuff is still in my room. My money, camera, passport, watch—the rest of it. I don't want it stolen."

"It must be fearfully expensive."

"My mother pays."

"How very American."

"She's on a tour—in Hong Kong," said the boy. "I thought we were talking about lunch."

"If you're a guest at this hotel, then you must have other clothes here. I suggest you dress properly, and if there's an empty chair at my table, I have no objection to your joining me." Her voice, that fastidious tone, surprised and appalled her.

The boy's name was Mark. He told her that over lunch, but he said very little else. He was so young there was practically nothing he could say about himself beyond his name, and it was for Milly to keep the conversation going. It was not easy in her new voice. She described her trip through Indonesia, everything that had happened to her since leaving Ayer Hitam, but after that, she was stumped. She would not speak about Lloyd or the divorce, and it angered her that it was impossible to speak about her life without discussing her marriage. Nearly twenty years had to be suppressed, and it seemed as if nothing had happened in those years that could matter to this young boy.

To his timid questions, she said, "You wouldn't understand." She was hard on him. She knew why: She wanted him in the simplest way and she resented wanting him. She objected to that desire in herself that would not allow her to go on alone. She did not want to look foolish—the age difference was ridicule enough —and wondered if in shrinking from an involvement she would reject him. She feared having him, she feared losing him. He told her he was nineteen and eagerly added the date of his next birthday.

Milly said, "Time for my nap."

"See you later, then," said Mark. He shook her hand.

In her room, she cursed herself. It had not occurred to her that he might not be interested. But perhaps this was so. He had a girl, one of the innocent witches; but her fate was the Australian who, late at night, rattled the change in his pocket and drawled for a persuasive way to interest her. She pulled the curtains, shutting out the hot sun, and for the first time since she arrived, lay down on her bed wondering not if she should go but where.

She closed her eyes and heard a knock on the door. She got out of bed, sighed and opened the door a crack. "What is it?"

"Let me come in," said Mark. "Please."

She stared and said nothing. Then she moved aside and let the boy swing the door open. He did this with unnecessary force, as if he had expected her to resist.

MILLY HAD NOT written any letters. A few postcards, a message about the weather. Letters were an effort, because letters required either candor or wit, and her solitary existence had hardened her to both. What Milly had done, almost since the hour she had left Ayer Hitam, was rehearse conversations with an imaginary friend, a woman, for whom in anecdote she would describe the pleasure of divorce. Flying alone. The looks you got in hotels. The Australian. A room of one's own. The witches and princelings on the beach. Misunderstandings. The suspicious eyes of other men's wives. The mystery and the aroma of sexuality a single woman carried past mute strangers.

Listen, she imagined herself saying; then she reported, assessed, justified. It was a solitary traveler's habit, one enforced by her separation from Lloyd. She saw herself leaning over a large menu, in the racket of a restaurant—flowers on the table, two napkin cones, a dish of olives—and she heard her own voice: *I think a nineteen-year-old boy and a woman of—let's be frank—forty-one—I think they're perfectly matched, sexually speaking. Yes, I really do. They're at some kind of peak. That boy can have four or five orgasms in a row, but so can a middle-aged woman—given the chance. It's the middle-aged man, with all his routines and apologies, who makes the woman feel inadequate. Sex for a boy, granted, is usually a letdown, because he's always trying himself out on a girl his age, and what could be*

*duller? "It hurts, Jim," and "Hurry up," and "What if my parents
find out?" What I'm saying, and I don't think it's anything to be
ashamed of, is Mark and I were well matched, not in spite of our
ages but on the contrary, on the contrary. It was like coaching a
champion. I know I was old enough to be his mother, but that's
just the point. The age ratio isn't insignificant. Don't laugh—the
boy of a certain age and his mother would make the best of
lovers—*

But lovers was all they'd make. Conversation with Mark was
impossible. He would say, "I know a guy who has a fantastic
yacht in Baltimore."

A yacht. At the age of twenty-three, when Mark was one,
Milly had driven her own car to the south of France and stayed
with her uncle, a famous lawyer. That handsome man had taken
her on his yacht, poured her champagne and tried to seduce her.
He had failed and angrily steered the yacht close to the rocky
shore, to scare her. Later he bought her an expensive ring and in
London took her to wonderful restaurants, treating her like his
mistress. He renamed his yacht Milly. Lloyd knew part of the
story. To Mark, Milly said, "I was on a yacht once, but I was
much younger then."

For three weeks, in her room, in his and twice on the beach,
they made love. They kissed openly and made no secret of the
affair. The guests at the hotel might whisper, but they never
stayed longer than a few days and they took their disapproval
away with them. Milly herself wondered sometimes what would
happen to her when Mark left and she grew anxious when she
remembered that she would have to leave eventually. She had no
destination; she stayed another month: It was now November
and before Christmas she would exhaust herself of this boy. She
was not calculating, but she saw nothing further for him. The
affair, so complete on this bright island, would fail anywhere
else.

Mark spoke of college, of books he planned to read, of jobs
he'd like to have. It was all a hopeful itinerary she had traced
before: She'd made that trip years ago, she'd read the books and
known all the stops. She felt—listening to him telling her nothing
new—as if she'd returned from a long sojourn in the world, one
on which he, encumbered with ambition, was just setting out.

She smiled at his innocent plans and she gave him some encouragement; she would not disappoint him and tell him he would find nothing. He never asked for advice; he was too young to know the questions. She could tell him a great deal, but youth was ignorance in a splendid body: He wouldn't listen.

"I want to marry you," he said one day, and it sounded to Milly like the expression of a longing that could never be fulfilled, like saying, *If only I could marry you!*

"I want to marry you, too," she said in the same way.

He kissed her and said, "We could do it here, the way the Balinese do—with a feast, music, dancing."

"I'll wear flowers in my hair."

"Right," he said. "We'll go up to Ubud and——"

"Oh, God," she said, "you're serious."

His face fell. He said, "Aren't you?"

"I've been married," she said, without enthusiasm, as she had once said to him, "I've been to Monte Carlo," implying that the action could not possibly be repeated.

"I've got lots of money," he said.

"Spend it wisely." It was the closest she had ever come to giving him advice.

"It would make things easier for us."

"This is as easy as it can ever be," she said. "Anyway, it's your mother's money, so stop talking this way. We can't get married and that's that."

"You don't have to marry me," he said. "Come to the States—we'll live together."

"And then what?"

"We'll drive around."

"What about your college—all those plans of yours?"

"They don't matter."

"Drive around!" She laughed hard at the thought of them in a car, speeding down a road, not stopping. Could anything short of marriage itself be a more boring exertion than that? He looked quite excited by the prospect of driving in circles.

"What's wrong?"

"I'm a bit old for that sort of thing."

"We can do anything you want—anything," he said. "Just live with me. No strings. Look, we can't stay here forever. . . ."

It was true: She had nowhere to go. Milly was not fool enough to believe that it could work for any length of time, but for a month or two, it might be fun. Then somewhere else, alone, to make a real start.

"We'll see," she said.

"Smile," he said.

She did and said, "What would you tell your mother?"

"I've already told her."

"*No!* What did she say?"

"She wants to meet you."

"Perhaps—one day." But the very thought of it filled her with horror.

"Soon," he said. "I wrote to her in Hong Kong. She replied from Bangkok. She'll be here in a week or so."

"Mine was so pathetic when I left him," Milly was saying. "I almost felt sorry for him. Now I can't stand the thought of him."

"As time goes on," said Maxine, "you'll hate him more and more." Abstractedly, she said, "I can't bear them to touch me."

"No," said Milly, "I don't think I could ever hate——"

Maxine laughed. "I just thought of it!"

"What?"

"The position my husband suggested. It was called 'the Autumn Dog.' Chinese, I think. You do it backward. It was impossible, of course—and grotesque, like animals in the bushes. He accused me of not trying—and guess what he said?"

"Backward!"

"He said, 'Max, it might save our marriage'!"

It struck Milly that there were only a few years—seconds in the life of the world—when that futile sentence had meaning. The years had coincided with her own marriage, but she had endured them and, like Maxine, earned her freedom. She had borne marriage long enough to see it disproved.

"But it didn't save it—it couldn't," said Maxine. Her face darkened. She said, "He was evil. He wanted Mark. But Mark wouldn't have him—he was devoted to me."

"Mark is a nice boy."

Maxine said, "Mark is lovely."

"At first I was sorry he told you about me. I was afraid to meet you. I thought you'd dislike me."

"But you're not marrying him, are you?"

"I couldn't," said Milly. "Anyway, I'm through with marriage."

"Good," said Maxine. "The Autumn Dog."

"And Max," said Milly, using the woman's name for the first time, "I don't want you for a mother-in-law!"

"No—we'll be friends."

"What a pity I'm leaving here."

"Then we must leave together."

And the other woman's replies had come so quickly that Milly heard herself agreeing to a day, a flight, a destination.

"Poor Mark," said Milly at last.

"He's a lovely boy," said Maxine. "You have no idea. We go to plays together. He reads to me. I buy all his clothes. I like to be seen with him. Having a son like Mark is so much better than having a husband."

Milly felt the woman staring at her. She dropped her eyes.

"Or a friend like you," said Maxine. "That's much better. He told me all about you—he's very frank. He made me jealous, but that was silly, wasn't it? I think you're a very kind person."

She reached across the table. She took Milly's fingers and squeezed.

"If you're kind to me, we'll be such good friends."

Please stop! Milly wanted to say. The other woman was hurting her hand with the pressure of her rings and she seemed to smile at the panic on Milly's face. Finally, Milly said it, and another fear made the demand into a plea. Maxine relaxed her grip, but she held on, even after Mark appeared at the agreed time, to hear the verdict.

A Hundred Paths

HOLLIS SUMMERS

HOLLIS SUMMERS has written several books, including *How They Chose the Dead*, *Peddler & Other Domestic Stories* and *Start from Home*.

W E WERE OLD, not old, but not young. There were the four of us, my wife's college roommate, her husband, my wife, and I. We had known each other for almost thirty years. "My God," we said, laughing as if what we said were not true; "Not that long!" imagining somebody else's saying, "Not that long!" wanting to believe somebody else.

We had met when we were eighteen in a registration line at the University of Kentucky.

And then it is Labor Day, thirty years later, and Susan and I are visiting the Robinsons again. We were on our way home to Ohio from the Cape. Susan called Peg from Chatham. "Of course you'll stop for a visit, for a month or two," Peg shouted. Susan, smiling in the telephone booth, held the receiver toward me.

Originally appeared in *Epoch*. Copyright © 1976 by Cornell University Press.

Susan laughed loudly in the booth. "Two nights," she said. "I won't even check with Leonard." She raised her eyebrows, checking with me. I nodded. I felt good. There was sun, and the sound of traffic could have been the ocean. Susan said, "You'll have a marvelous dinner ready for us tonight, around seven?" Peg said, "Absolutely marvelous. You've never eaten such food. And tomorrow a picnic at the Park."

They were yelling at each other, as if they were eighteen in a registration line at the University of Kentucky.

For years we have visited each other on our ways to other places. Both the Robinsons and we have moved three times in twenty-odd years; from small towns, to cities, to the far edges of cities; from impossible little apartments, to suburbs where everybody's roses matched his neighbors', to rather handsome houses with high ceilings and long lawns. Now the Robinsons boast a tidy red barn at their Rochester place.

The Robinsons have a daughter, Jennifer. We are the parents of young Leonard. We grew up in a pre-pill period, but we were careful.

"We're parallel lines," Peg said after the marvelous dinner, as she has said for thirty years. We had eaten and drunk too much. We sat opposite each other, on the love seats Peg bought in Indianapolis twenty years ago.

"And we always say *we*, don't we?" Susan said, as I knew she was going to say. They could have been comparing lives over Coca-Colas at Dunn's Drug Store almost a third of a century ago.

Peg said, "Other people say, *I*. Cheryl Roethke—she's the woman down the road—you met her last time—Cheryl says *my* bedroom, and they sleep together. Harry's closet is in *her* bedroom."

Clarke said, "Come on, Peggy. You're not making sense." Clarke is a tall, thin, handsome man. I am always surprised at his handsomeness. I do not dwell on my height or my poundage.

"She's making absolute sense." Susan was sleepy. "Generally *two* people can't say *we*. We're *four* people, and we say *we!*"

"We, we, we," Clarke said. "We ought to go to bed. We've got to be alert for Peggy's fine picnic at the Park."

"It's going to be a perfectly fantastic picnic—we don't know how to have any other kind. Do you remember in Lexington when we . . ."

"And then we came back to our house and my aunts were there, all five of them, and we . . ."

"But you haven't told us nearly enough about Jennifer's job in New York, and . . ."

"And Leonardcito's really going to the Woodrow Wilson school? When I think about . . ."

"Whatever happened to that young man Jennifer was so crazy about, the one she met that summer in Vienna?"

"She's over that—him—a long time ago."

I suppose that through the years Clarke and I have been listeners. We are peripheral friends. We were not roommates. For a while Clarke "dated" Susan quite seriously. I "dated" Peg. The word "dated" sounds a very long time ago.

"There's somebody else now, named Paulsie, if you can imagine." Peg ran her tongue over her lips. "Honestly, sometimes I wonder . . ."

Mostly the girls talked about when Jennifer and the other Leonard were young.

Clarke said, "We're not old enough to spend an evening talking about our children."

But we talked about our children.

Susan said, "They're good kids. They've turned out well."

"We have so much to be thankful for. Finally—maybe finally." Peg had tears in her eyes.

"But we mustn't say that." Susan was crying. She leaned forward, her hands over her head, her fingers crossed.

"We *can* say," Peg said. "We can say it so far. They aren't in jail, and they aren't maniacs, and . . ."

Susan said, "Not so far as we know. But we don't know very far."

Peg said, "You make me sick, Susan. You're always negative. Forever you've been negative."

"Well, I beg your most humble pardon."

Clarke said, "Hear, hear."

It was not a quarrel. I cannot remember a real quarrel with the Robinsons.

Peg said, "I know what you mean. You know I know what you mean."

"I know, I know," Susan and Peg said together.

We had another drink before we went to bed.

I dreamed of all of us when we were young. I do not remember seeing our present faces or bodies in the dream. Five or six times I woke in the night, but it was a continued dream. I make nothing of it. I haven't been sleeping well these last few months, this last year, since I became Chairman of the Board of Amalgamated Enterprises, Susan's father's Enterprises. Once we were poor. Once I taught English in a high school.

In the dream Peg said, "We are well to do." In the dream I did not know what the words meant. I said, in the dream, "What does *well to do* mean, Peg Robinson?" Susan said, "Everyone knows what well to do means, Leonard Wayne!"

Twice in the night Susan woke me. "You're all right, honey. You're just having a bad dream."

We were late getting off to the picnic. Clarke and I walked their three dogs to the village, bought *The New York Times*. The day was hot; the day pretended it would never be autumn, but leaves fell from the ginkgo trees in the Robinsons' yard. Clarke said, "They look like butterflies, or warblers, falling."

I said, "Sure enough. You're a major poet." Clarke was in Public Relations before he became a university Vice-President in charge of Regional Branches.

Clarke laughed genuinely. "The University of Kentucky was a long time ago, wasn't it?"

We ate a slow breakfast. Peg said, "You weren't annoyed with me last night, Leonard? You don't think I'm a foolish woman, almost fifty years old? Susan wasn't annoyed last night. She promised me she wasn't annoyed. And she's not negative. She's the most positive thinker I have ever had the pleasure of meeting."

We laughed together.

THE PARK belongs to Clarke's University. There is a lake, and a little theatre, and paths, a hundred paths. Some alumnus willed a hundred paths to the University. Lately I am interested in the nature of wills, and human vanity. My estate, our estate, goes, of course, to Susan and Leonard. But I am pleased with the thought of a man who has written on a legal document: "One hundred paths." I would like for Susan and Leonard to remember me as capable of such a will.

The parking lot was full of small orange and yellow and red cars.

"Park there," Peg said. "There's a place. We look like a hearse, don't we? A hearse among the butterflies?" The Robinsons have always driven large dark cars.

We laughed.

Susan said, "I'm always proud to ride in your cars. Our next car will be large and dark."

"Careful, Susan. You musn't ruffle me." Peg was laughing louder than any of us.

"Yes, yes, Little Horse." It was a joke from thirty years ago whose significance I do not remember.

Clarke seemed to remember. Peg was convulsed. When she caught her breath she said, "If there are a lot of people at the picnic tables, I don't think I want to go. We'll go back home and eat. I think I don't want to be here."

Clarke said, "Don't be a goose." Susan said, "Really, Peg!"

There were dozens of places for us above the lake. A whole slope of tables waited under fine old maple and oak trees. Evidently the butterfly cars had brought only swimmers. Clarke, the Vice-President, explained, "After all, school's out. School hasn't started yet. These are the workers and the dregs. These are only the dregs. It's Labor Day."

Peg chose a middle table. "Marvelous. This is absolutely marvelous. Look, these grills, they're new, Clarke. And the tables are new. Look, just look."

"Absolutely. Marvelous," Susan said.

The girls' voices were young. I looked from Susan to Peg. Clarke was looking, too.

"We will take a walk." Peg plopped her fat handbag onto the table. "A man's place is at the grill; woman's place is taking a walk."

Clarke said, "Come off it, Peggy."

I was disappointed, too. I have inherited my friends from Susan. Perhaps, once, Susan and Clarke slept together. Our generation has not talked openly about such matters. I said, "Beware of rapists."

Clarke said, "And bears. There are bears in those woods."

Peg said, "We can handle them. We're liberated."

Susan placed her fat purse beside Peg's. She was giggling. I am grateful that Susan can still giggle. "You'll guard our luggage."

Peg tripped as she started up the slope. The girls laughed as if nothing in the wide world could have been funnier.

It was ridiculous to have worried over being left alone with Clarke. I genuinely enjoy Clarke. He talked about his work, the drop in enrollment, budget problems, his president's "thrusts." I traded business talk, about the energy crisis and strip mining.

Clarke started the fire. Slowly the charcoal briquettes oozed into flame.

For spaces of time we were quiet, looking down at the lake where very young men and women dived and shouted and pushed each other from platforms and floating logs.

Below us appeared a figure wearing a T shirt and blue and white striped shorts, waving to somebody in the water. The figure was thin, its hair wet, curling at its shoulders.

Idly I said, "Boy or girl? Young Leonard's hair is that long, even longer." I have tried not to worry over Leonard. I have pretended not to worry.

"Boy, I guess."

"I guess so."

The figure turned, moved toward one of the hundred paths. I nodded to her, feeling invisible.

"Hi," she said. She walked beautifully. "Oh, hello, Mr. Robinson. Hello." She smoothed her hands over her hair.

"Hello there. This is my friend, Leonard Wayne, a long-time friend."

"How do you do?" we asked each other. We assured each other that it was a lovely day.

When she disappeared down the path, I said, "She's very much a girl. I'm sorry. It's hard to tell about sex any more."

"What are you sorry for? She works in the Treasurer's Office. That's why she's here during vacation. I can't remember her name."

"She's pretty." I felt close to Clarke Robinson. I felt that he was my friend.

"Sure." Clarke was looking into the trees where the girl had disappeared. Perhaps he had slept with her. "She's going to the Meadow. Jennifer kept bees down there, when we first moved to Rochester. We had great honey for a couple of years. It was a Girl Scout project, 4-H, something."

"I probably wouldn't know Jennifer."

"That girl, that other girl, not Jennifer, she's probably meeting somebody. They'll probably make love, have sex, whatever you want to call it. In the bushes, or a car, maybe back in her room on campus. We have mixed dormitories, very mixed."

I said, "They've come a long way. We've come a long way." I wondered if Susan and Clarke had slept together.

"Sure." Clarke's eyes looked hard at me.

I said, "But we're lucky. Peg and Susan are right. We're lucky with our kids. Susan worries too much. She thinks Leonard is sleeping with somebody, a Chinese girl. I suppose he is."

Always before we had been people in a registration line, friends of a family, waiting in a queue.

"Paulsie," Clarke said, "the Paulsie Peg mentioned last night. Jennifer called day before yesterday. That's why it's good you are here. Jennifer is madly in love with him. I assume it's a him. They're living together. I try not to assume anything these days." Clarke did not lower his eyes.

I said, "I'll say. Young people will be young people." It is a foolish sentence I have often said to Susan. Perhaps I have never been young.

"Peg hasn't slept. Last night she kept saying, 'Should I tell them? Shouldn't I tell our best friends?' You're our best friends, Leonard. You're people we don't see much. What do you think of that, Leonard boy?"

I said, "Sure."

Clarke said, "I'm sorry we had children, a child."

I said, "A boy is easier, I guess. Less open. With me, at least. Susan has talked to him about the girl. Her name is Lois." For no reason that I can identify I wanted to exchange a confidence with this man who sat across from me at a picnic table in a park. I do not own many confidences. I have lived carefully, a good steward to the monies Susan has inherited. "Susan and Leonard had a terrible conversation. I listened from another room. I didn't join them. I was a coward."

Clarke looked down at his hands. His fingers were spread far apart. He said, "God damn you, Leonard. I wouldn't dream of talking to Jennifer." He seemed capable of crying. I felt as close to him as if we were strangers in a falling plane, determined to identify ourselves before we disappeared.

I said, "I hadn't any experience to speak of, when Susan and I were married. We were young."

Clarke closed his fingers. He wears a wedding ring. Susan did not give me a wedding ring. "I don't want Leonard to be branded," she said in Dunn's. Peg said, "Honestly, Susan, you are too dumb to listen to."

I have been faithful to Susan. I am a coward.

Clarke said, "I've tried to make up for it." I did not know exactly what he meant, but I heard the sound of the plane's falling. "It's, the whole business, I guess it's harder for women, wives, of our generation." Twice, according to Susan, Clarke and Peg were ready for a divorce. Clarke had a girl in Harrodsburg and another in Indianapolis.

I said, "Whatever that means." I was embarrassed. I am embarrassed to be forty-eight years old.

I did not mean to lower my eyes to look at my wristwatch. The girls had been gone for over half an hour.

"You're worried about them?"

"No. I guess so. Susan doesn't have any sense of time or direction. She gets lost easily."

Again Clarke spread his hands on the table. He pushed himself up. He stepped gracefully over the bench. "I'll go find them. Guard the fire. We could use a couple more briquettes."

We did not look at each other.

Clarke was gone for a long time.

I watched the young people in the water.

I picked up the fat purses and started up the slope.

I did not want to appear ridiculous, a man carrying two ladies' purses. I went back to the table.

I started the steaks. I was afraid I had started them too soon. I took off the grill and put them back. I was lucky with the steaks.

I was ready to take them off again when Clarke and the girls came scuffling down the hill. The girls were laughing so loudly that a man on a farther path stopped to look at them.

Clarke said, "I found them swinging on grapevines, with three bears and three rapists."

Peg said, "And we overcame them, everyone."

Susan said, "You weren't worried, were you, Worry-Box?"

I said, "Chow. Chow's on." I beat on the grill. I do not like a man who says such things as "Chow's on."

I received compliments.

Peg said, "There have never been such perfectly cooked steaks, not in the history of the world."

Susan said, "Peg makes the kind of potato salad they serve in heaven."

Clarke was as jolly as the girls. He said, "Leonard, old man, you missed your calling." He spoke as if we had never talked almost honestly to each other.

We have had such picnics before. We said, we, we, we. We said, "Do you remember?"

It was Peg's idea to take a walk. "We exercise, or burst. The Meadow. We haven't been to the Meadow forever, not since that silly project of Jennifer's."

We said words like, "Great," and, "Fine," and, "Sure."

IT WAS a long walk to the meadow. There was a kind of road at first, not big enough for a car, too wide for a path. We walked four together at first. There were little hills, up and down, and up again. Paths left the road, and returned. Some of the paths appeared to be shortcuts.

We walked in twos.

I walked by myself behind three people, behind two. My breath came hard. I tried to measure my breathing. We were all the same age. I was angry that my breathing was difficult.

The road was a cave of trees. The trees smelled like a cave. The cave was a tunnel. Relax, I told myself. I am enjoying the walk alone, behind three, two, one; I have no sense of urgency, alone.

Finally the three stood at the edge of the meadow.

Clarke turned to call to me. "I don't recognize anything."

The meadow was like a picture of a meadow. It had been recently mowed. The meadow was an oasis. It was a clean plate.

"They used this for a playing field, for a while," Clarke said. "Maybe they still do."

Susan and Peg are good tourists. "Beautiful," they said. "Glorious."

The sky had clouded. The meadow held an underwater light.

"I'm remembering." Clarke was a tourist guide. "There's an abandoned railroad bridge over there in front of us, on the other side of the meadow. Clarke pointed. His forefinger seemed larger than his hand.

Beyond the far trees stood the lattice of a railroad bridge.

Susan said, "Too bad about railroads."

Peg said, "Do you remember when we took the children to Cincinnati, to the Zoo, on the train?"

We remembered.

"Over there," Clarke said. "That's where Jennifer had her bees."

"It's marvelous," Peg said. "I can't wait to go home so we can come back again." Years ago Peg had first said the sentence, at Natural Bridge in Kentucky.

Clarke said, "It's a playing field all right. I can't keep up with everything that happens at the university."

Susan, standing in the center of the meadow, turned slowly. "I'm making a wish. But I mustn't tell the wish. When you make a wish in the center of a meadow, it always comes true." She smiled at Clarke as she turned.

I said, "Meadow or wish?" I wondered if all the paths led to the meadow.

Peg started to turn, too. "I am wishing, I am wishing."

The girls moved beautifully, like figures in a ballet. Clarke was watching them.

An engine sounded on the other side of the meadow.

Slowly Susan and Peg stopped turning.

The angry sound of a motor moved from right to left, from maples to willows.

Clarke said, "That can't be a car. There's no road over there."

"It's a motorcycle," Peg said. "It's twenty motorcycles."

"No. There's not any road. You remember when Jennifer had the bees, and we walked over there."

The sound stopped, and started again, and stopped.

"It's a motorcycle," Susan said. "I'm glad young Leonard never wanted a motorcycle." Her voice was loud.

We stood listening. I thought of reaching out for the hands beside me. We could have been a row of paper soldiers, cut from folded newspapers. I wondered what Susan had wished, turning in the meadow. I had not thought of making a wish. I do not know what I would have wished for.

The meadow was as quiet as a bowl of water, left long standing.

The sound returned.

The four of us started toward the sound. Paper soldiers can run quickly. I was tired. I remembered the face of Jennifer and young Leonard in the dream. I did not want to think about the dream.

I ran ahead of the others. I stumbled out of the other side of the meadow, to an embankment, pulling myself up by branches, dogwood and sassafras. Leaves fell from my hands. A branch snapped Clarke in the face. "Sorry, old man." The girls moved from the meadow behind us, mounting the bank.

Boards lay across the railroad tracks. A dirt road, a real dirt road, led up to the bridge.

Clarke said, "My God."

Two people on a throbbing motorcycle waited in the very center of the bridge. They leaned far to the right, looking down into the river. The person in front, the larger one, revved the motor. The couple wore blue jeans and checked shirts with long sleeves. They were surely a boy and a girl. They roared across the bridge to somewhere.

Clarke said, "God damn." Susan and Peg stood with us at the side of the dirt road. The girls and Clarke breathed heavily. I was pleased that they were breathing heavily.

We waited.

Susan spoke quietly. "There's a woman's shift hanging on a dogwood tree down there. And a pair of shorts, cut-off blue jeans. Did you notice?"

"And a white dress draped over a sassafras bush. And two necklaces, something gold." Peg was whispering.

Susan said, "And a ring. I saw a ring on top of the shorts, a high school ring, maybe. Leonard had one. Do you remember?" She was smiling as if she had wished a good wish in the meadow and received an answer.

I did not remember. I had not noticed anything.

Peg said, "And once we came to the meadow and Jennifer . . ."

Clarke said, "God damn it, shut up."

I suppose the four of us heard the car at the same time. We listened together, looking at each other. I felt very close to Susan and the Robinsons. Because we listened together I felt we were wearing the same face.

A car appeared. It was a tan two-door Chevrolet, four or five years old. It stopped at the edge of the bridge, not six feet from us.

A boy, no older than Leonard, opened the car door. He wore chinos, low slung, almost to his pelvis. His shirt was pink and white spring blossoms, opened but stuck into his trousers. He wore a ring on a chain around his neck.

He had a fine body, like Leonard's. His hair was long and yellow, neatly combed. I studied the comb marks in his hair.

A radio played softly in his car, rock music with a heavy beat. People sang. They said the same words over and over, but I could not distinguish the words.

The boy turned the radio volume high. Peg put her hands over her ears. Within, above the music, the boy got out of the car and closed his door. He did not look at us. We might have been trees watching. He walked around the front of the car to the other side. He opened the door on the other side. I cannot remember for how long he held the door open, looking into the car. It was as if he were letting something out, or letting something in.

He closed the door. He circled the car, returning to the bridge. He walked very slowly, as if he were counting his steps. He did not walk on to the roadbed of the bridge. He stopped at the very edge. He slanted his body against the right hand truss. The truss of the bridge was rusted. Susan whispered, "Careful." I have not asked her what she meant. Perhaps she was worried that the boy

would fall into the water. Perhaps she was afraid the rust would
stain the blossoms of his shirt.

He could have been a figure-head on a ship.

Clarke said, "Let's go." I am sure it was Clarke who spoke, but
we did not go.

After a while, perhaps after only a little while, the boy pushed
himself to a standing position. He lighted a cigarette. He stood
watching the water move under the bridge. The cigarette hung
from his lips. He held his arms straight beside him, his fists
clenched.

That evening at the Robinsons the girls could not talk enough
about the boy, stating the afternoon.

Susan said, "Pot. I know he was smoking pot, or something
worse."

Peg said, "Hostile. A sense of evil."

Susan said. "Those hands, those fists. He was about to explode."

Peg said, "A sense of orgy. Charged. The whole scene was
charged."

Susan said, "If we had met him on our beautiful walk, he
would have killed us."

Peg said, "One of us. He would have killed at least one of us."

I expected Clarke to say, "Come off it, Peggy." Instead he rose
from his chair, the Lazy-Boy they had bought in Harrodsburg.
"Refills," he said. "Refills all around."

"Why not?" Susan and Peg said together, lifting their empty
glasses as if to toast the world.

I suppose we were all looking at each other.

At the bridge we had looked at each other, not looking.

At the bridge Clarke said, "Let's get the hell out of here."

I know the boy was waiting for us to leave. I know we left because he was waiting for us to leave.

I was the last down the hill. I tried to look hard at the boy by
the side of the bridge. But I did not stay to see what was going
to happen.

I have never stayed to see what was going to happen.

But I felt close to the boy.

Rain spit at us across the meadow. Susan and Peg and Clarke
ran, as well as forty-eight-year-old people can run. Susan was

ahead, then Peg, then Clarke. Clarke stopped to grab the picnic basket from our table on the slope. The road back is always shorter than the road away.

"You're coming. You're all right?" Clarke called over his shoulder.

"Hurry, hurry," the girls, the women, called.

I held back, not, I think, because I was not in good shape. For a moment, for only a moment, I thought about returning to the boy on the bridge.

In the dark car the others were wringing wet, too. They were breathing heavily, too.

Susan said, "You're drowned. You're absolutely drowned."

Peg said, "Here's a towel. Dry off. You'll catch your death."

I assured them I was fine. I said, "It was a very exciting outing."

Susan said, "You're positive?"

I said, "Positive."

Peg said, "We'll look for the road then. Hurry, Clarke. We'll find the road that goes over the railroad bridge. It has two ends. Surely it has two ends."

I do not think that Clarke really tried to find the road. I was relieved that he did not find it. Perhaps the others were relieved, too.

The rain did not last long. We went to a "Museum of Machinery, 1820 Until Now." The sign was written in old English letters. I insisted on paying for all of us. The cost was three dollars each.

It is winter now. I do not know why I have written what I have written. I am not trying to force significance from a picnic, and a meadow, and a railroad bridge.

The Little Pub

PATRICIA ZELVER

PATRICIA ZELVER was born in California, and grew up in Medford, Oregon. She has an M.A. from Stanford, and now lives in Portola Valley, California, with her husband and two sons. She has published two novels, *The Honey Bunch* and *The Happy Family*, as well as numerous short stories. This is her fourth appearance in the O. Henry collection.

I T WAS January. Night fell abruptly, shrouding the oak-studded hills of Vista Verde in deep shadows. Only a few lights were visible from the picture window where Mrs. Jessup stood having her Happy Hour, her first—or was it her second?—vodka martini in her hand. She stood at the window in her house on La Floresta Lane, looking at the lights far below. They were the lights, she said to herself, of the Little Pub. The lights of the Little Pub twinkled cheerily in the darkness. Smoke would be curling out of its chimney in tidy loops like the chimney smoke in a child's drawing. Big Bill has lit a fire, she thought. Perhaps I should call Ruff and walk down there. But

would we be able to find our way in the dark? There were no
sidewalks and no street lights in Vista Verde, very different
from Chestnut Hill, where she and Mr. Jessup had lived before moving here. The lights were visible from the house, but
would they be, in the darkness, on the lane? Probably not visible,
she decided. Probably we would lose our way. And, anyhow,
I have the cards to finish. First things first, she told herself.
Sacrifices are always entailed whenever people put first things
first, as they must if they want to do things worthwhile.

That morning Mrs. Jessup had driven to the city to attend a
Seminar for Executive Wives at the Hyatt Regency, sponsored
by Mr. Jessup's corporation. It had been an extremely rewarding
session. A Social Anthropologist had spoken to them on "De-
veloping Inner Resources Through Creativity." Or was it a Social
Psychologist? She must try to remember to tell Mr. Jessup when
he returned. Distinctions of that sort were important to him, and
rightly so, though she was not absolutely sure why.

The Social Anthropologist or Social Psychologist had traced
the forces which made up the Modern World. The old-fashioned
sort of Community Life, which was extolled in magazines and
films and on TV, and about which so many people were foolishly
nostalgic, was archaic—a thing of the past. It was particularly a
thing of the past for dynamic men who set high goals for themselves. The world, not just their tiny community, was their
milieu; mobility their Life Style. It was important, he said, to
face facts. But this did not mean that their wives need lack
fulfillment. It was, he had pointed out, really up to them. There
were endless avenues open in which to be creative. He had
enumerated some of these open endless avenues—foreign language lessons; decorating and art and gourmet cooking courses;
working as a docent in a museum; volunteering to help the handicapped; entertaining graciously; bringing up children; graciously volunteering to entertain graciously; even, and perhaps
most important of all, providing a serene and loving atmosphere
for the executive husband. They—the executive wives—should
think of their jobs as a part of a Team Effort. Sacrifices were, of
course, entailed, but sacrifices were always entailed whenever
people did things worthwhile. The rewards would be their own
personal growth and their husbands' gratitude.

Mrs. Jessup had explored most of these avenues at one time or another, but she had not explored them lately. For the last six months, ever since they had moved into Vista Verde, she had really stopped exploring altogether. Almost the moment she had the furniture arranged and the new curtains up, Mr. Jessup had told her, in his proud, quiet way, that another Transfer was in the air, this time a very important one; the Chairman of the Board was about to retire, and he was in line for this position. It would be—now was—the culmination of his career. She had therefore done nothing in the way of exploring or making new acquaintances, and for this reason she was grateful to the Social Anthropologist-Psychologist for reminding her of what he called her "potential." As the wife of the Chairman of the Board, Inner Resources through Creativity would be more useful than ever.

AFTER THE SEMINAR, she had gone to the city's largest stationery store and searched through the cards, hoping to find a more original one than the ones she had sent so many times before. She had not succeeded, and had to hurry home in order to be there when Mr. Jessup, who was at a conference at the Airport Hilton —or was it the Airport Sheraton?—would phone her. There was three hours' difference, and with three hours' differences he always called at three o'clock to be present at the conference's Happy Hour before dinner. On the way, she had been struck by an idea. Perhaps she could make a card herself? During an art class she had taken once, in a past exploration of avenues, she had learned how to make a block print with a raw potato. Various designs and messages occurred to her. Cartoon figures? An old-fashioned script? Black and white? Colors? She had suggested the idea, somewhat shyly, to Mr. Jessup when he phoned.

"Make one?" said Mr. Jessup. "What did you have in mind?"

"I don't know yet. Something humorous, maybe. I thought it might be fun."

"Oh, let's keep it kosher," Mr. Jessup said.

"You mean, buy a card?"

"It seems to me you have enough to do, just addressing them," he said thoughtfully.

As soon as he hung up, Mrs. Jessup drove down to the Vista Verde Shopping Center, below their house, and bought the simplest card she could find. It was then almost four. She had called Ruff to feed him, but Ruff had crawled out from under the fence again, and was gone.

The nice young Vista Verde patrolman will bring him back, Mrs. Jessup said to herself.

Whenever Mr. Jessup was out of town, the private patrol car stopped by in the early evening, and the nice young man rang her doorbell and asked her if everything was all right. This was something Mr. Jessup insisted upon. Mrs. Jessup didn't mind because she liked the young man. He reminded her, somewhat, of her younger son, an engineer, now married and working in Saudi Arabia. She also liked the nice relationship the young man had with Ruff. He either brought Ruff back from the shopping center, where he liked to go, or, if Ruff came to the door with her, he would pat Ruff's gray fat back, while Ruff wriggled all over in ecstasy.

"I guess you can't be too lonely with old Ruff," the young man would say.

"Ruff is a good companion," Mrs. Jessup would tell the young man. "Of course, if a burglar came, he wouldn't be much help."

"Oh, we all know Ruff. He'd show the burglar around the house," the young man would say.

"Would you care to come in and have a drink?" Mrs. Jessup had said once.

"I'd sure like to, Ma'am, but we're not allowed to, when we're on duty."

"Of course, how silly of me," said Mrs. Jessup.

"Now, you take care of yourself, Ma'am. Just call us if you've any problems."

"Thank you, it's good just to know I can," Mrs. Jessup said.

THE VIEW from the picture window was of the wooded hills, now black shadows against the sky. Except for the lights of the Little Pub in the distance, you would never guess there were other homes around. The Vista Verde Neighborhood Association reviewed the plans of each house before it was built to be certain that no one's view was obstructed. The ad for the Jessup house, which was running in the Vista Verde *Crier* now, was

similar to the ads the real estate people had run the last six times
they had moved:

> Spanking new executive mansion in exclusive neigh-
> borhood. Secluded, three-acre, wooded retreat. AEK.
> Pool, three-car garage. Country Club.

Except for the lights of the Little Pub, one might think one
was stranded, alone, perhaps the last person alive in the whole
world. Mrs. Jessup had once read a book like that; the memory
of it still made her feel funny. She mixed herself another cocktail
at the wet bar, then she went into the kitchen and opened the
oven and looked at the frozen Stouffer cheese soufflé she had put
in before her first drink. Then she returned to the living room
window. If she did not have the other cards to do, she decided,
she would definitely call Ruff and walk down there; they would,
somehow, find their way in the dark. How pleasant it would be,
if she did not have the cards to do, to sit in her favorite chair beside the Little Pub's fireplace—the old, sprung, cracked leather
chair—or was it the old, sprung, chintz chair? It didn't matter.
The chair was not the important thing. What was important was
the general ambience.

The general ambience of the Little Pub was very agreeable.
The credit for this went to Bill. Big Bill, the regulars called him.
Mrs. Jessup was a bit too reserved for this; it was not her style.
She left off the "Big" and addressed him simply as "Bill." Bill
called her "Sugar."

"The usual, Sugar?" Big Bill would say to her, when she had
settled herself down in her favorite chair.

She would smile—a bit coquettishly—and nod. With anyone
else, she might have been offended, but not with Big Bill. Big
Bill, she thought, could call the Duchess of Windsor "Sugar" and
get away with it. He had such a nice, easy manner with the ladies, and everyone else, too, for that matter.

"One vodka martini on the rocks for my little Sugar," Big Bill
would sing out, as he mixed the drink himself. This was a little
joke they had together. He would then bring the drink on a tray
to Mrs. Jessup, and present it with a comical flourish. "And what
is Ruff's pleasure?" he would say, looking down at Ruff.

Mrs. Jessup would laugh. This was another joke she shared with Big Bill.

Mrs. Jessup sipped her cocktail and thought about the Little Pub. About her chair, the crackling fire, about Big Bill. About the general agreeable ambience.

"I'm leaving, Mr. Jessup is being transferred," she would tell him.

She could imagine Big Bill's regret at hearing this. "He's Chairman of the Board," she would say. "It's quite an honor, of course, but I shall miss the Little Pub."

Big Bill would, undoubtedly, present her with a drink on the house; perhaps he would even toast her and Mr. Jessup's future. Certainly he would ask about Ruff. "What about Ruff?" he would say. "How does he feel about this?"

"I'm afraid Ruff doesn't care much for Transfers," Mrs. Jessup would tell him. "The last one made him so upset I had to give him some of my tranquilizers."

Mrs. Jessup looked at her watch. It was five-thirty, almost time for the patrolman to bring Ruff home. In the meantime, it was pleasant to think about the Little Pub.

At the Little Pub you were surrounded by people of all ages and sexes. People of all sexes, including men. Yes, even though she was no longer nubile, as they said somewhere—perhaps in Japan—though she was of a "certain age," as they said in the Scandinavian countries—or was it France?—or "over the hill," as the common folk saying went, she still enjoyed a room with men, now and then, on a lonely evening during the Happy Hour.

She liked, she thought, the way men looked. The way their jackets scrunched up in back, and their trousers wrinkled at the crotch; the way they talked, sometimes in monosyllables or little grunts. Their laughs—their hearty men chuckles—she liked this, too. There were, of course, men in her life. The check-out clerk at the Vista Verde market, the pharmacist, her doctor, the hardware man, the nice young patrolman; Mr. Tanaguchi, the gardener. She had an especially warm relationship with Mr. Tanaguchi, who possessed an amazing understanding of plants. It would be resourceful—even creative—to go to the phone, right now, and call him up and invite him and Mrs. Tanaguchi over for a cocktail. But what if Mr. Tanaguchi didn't drink? Or, suppose he drank only sake? She had no sake in the house. Or—worst of all—suppose Mrs. Tanaguchi, whom she had never had the pleasure of meeting, misunderstood her warm relationship with Mr. Tanaguchi? No, this particular avenue was not open; she could not be the cause of any embarrassment to Mr. Tanaguchi.

THE DOORBELL rang. Mrs. Jessup went to answer it. The young patrolman was standing on the doorstep. Mrs. Jessup smiled at him. Just seeing him there gave her a nice feeling.

This time the young man did not smile back. His face, she noticed, was serious, actually quite pale. Could he be ill? Mrs. Jessup wondered.

"Ma'am, I have something to tell you," he said. His voice was not as hearty as usual, and he cleared his throat nervously. "Maybe you'd like me to come in, and you can sit down?"

Mrs. Jessup led him into the living room. She sat down, but the young man remained awkwardly standing.

He cleared his throat again. "It's about Ruff, Ma'am. I don't know exactly how to say it, but—we found him this evening. He was run over by a car on the road. I'm afraid there was nothing we could do. He was already—gone."

Mrs. Jessup's first thought was of the young man. How kind he was! How apologetic! But it was not his fault. Silly old Ruff was always digging out from under the fence and roaming around, which was against the Vista Verde leash law. Mrs. Jessup tried very hard to think of something to say to cheer him up.

"Dogs," she said after a moment, "are incapable of sacrifice."

The young man looked at her in an odd way. He seemed almost frightened, the way he stood there, clutching at his cap. Mrs. Jessup was determined to get her point over in order to reassure him.

"Dogs enjoy an old-fashioned community life, they are foolishly nostalgic," she said. "New neighborhoods—new and unusual odors and noises—fill them with a kind of frenzy. They forget their house-training, chew things up, dig under fences—and get run over! They lack inner resources and are not at all creative!"

"Mrs. Jessup, I have Ruff's body out there in the truck. I didn't know . . . Do you want us to take care of it, or would you prefer to?" He was stammering slightly, backing toward the door as he spoke.

Mrs. Jessup pretended not to notice his nervousness. Instead, she considered his words carefully. It would be nice, she thought, to bury Ruff in the back yard, with a little monument of some sort over his grave. "Ruff—A Good Dog." Something like that. But she could not expect the people who bought the house to keep up a grave. "It would be very kind of you—to dispose of it," she said.

The young man put out his hand, and Mrs. Jessup shook it. "Take care of yourself, now," he said, and left hurriedly.

Mrs. Jessup returned to the picture window. Should she go down to the Little Pub, she wondered, and tell Big Bill about Ruff? "Ruff is dead," she would say. It was important to face facts. It was important, too, to stop thinking about the Little Pub. There was no Little Pub. This was another fact that needed to be faced. No Little Pub existed in Vista Verde, and never would. Imagine the Neighborhood Association permitting such a thing! It would be against the zoning regulations, which did not allow Commercial Uses—only executive-style houses with proper setbacks and shake roofs on three acres. Worst of all, a Little Pub would attract Undesirable Elements. Undesirable Elements, sitting in old squashed leather—or chintz?—chairs (it did not matter), smiling coquettishly at Big Bill, letting Big Bill call them "Sugar."

One could not have that. She finished her drink and went into the kitchen and took out the soufflé and put it on the dining room table in its foil container. It was limp and sticky, but she managed to get most of it down. Then she went into the den and began, again, upon the cards.

"*Helen and Bill*," she wrote, filling out the blanks, "are moving to *4 Old County Lane, Greenwich, Connecticut*." There was a drawing of a doormat, and under that it said, "The Welcome Mat is Out."

She finished all of Mr. Jessup's list, which Mr. Jessup's secretary had sent her from his office. Tomorrow, she would begin the list of their friends. It was then ten-thirty. She made herself a nightcap and took it into the bedroom with her and flipped on the TV. She lay in bed, watching the middle of an old movie, sipping the drink, and thinking how surprised and grateful Mr. Jessup would be that she had accomplished so much in his absence.

Certain Changes

CHARLES SIMMONS

CHARLES SIMMONS is an editor of the New York *Times Book Review* and the author of two novels, *Powdered Eggs* and *An Old-fashioned Darling*.

C OTTON WAS FRIENDLY to him, wool was not. When he was a child the male bathing suit had a small skirt, shoulders, and was made of wool. The feel of wet wool drying against his body was uncomfortable, and he would have gone to his bungalow to shower and change if the custom was not to stay on the beach after swimming. Also, if he left he might miss a clamshell-scaling contest, the construction of a gravity sand-course for rubber balls, a couple necking behind a downed umbrella, or any of a number of chance pleasures of the beach. In winter, woolen trousers bothered him, and if he dribbled down the side of his leg after urinating they bothered him almost as much as a wet wool bathing suit. Since he got only one new suit of clothes a year, usually before Easter, it was important to

choose a smooth weave. Occasionally he would be seduced by
the manly look of a rough texture and suffer for it. One morning
when he was twelve he dressed before he was completely awake
and mistakenly pulled his pants over his pajama bottoms. He left
both garments on for the rest of the day and wore pajama bottoms for years after whenever his suits were rough. Once at a
party, when he was fifteen and the other guests were older, he
bunched his trouser legs around his thighs, exposing the pajamas; then he stuffed a pillow under his jacket, screwed up his
face, and bounded from room to room like a mad hunchback.
The act was a great hit, and because he would not explain the
presence of the pajamas he got a reputation as engagingly eccentric and thereby gained full admission to the group. Something
of the same thing happened in the army. The winter uniform
provided a rough wool shirt, which an undershirt only partially
protected him from. Out of desperation he cut the collar and
cuffs from a summer cotton shirt and wore it under the wool
shirt. This amused the other soldiers, and their amusement made
it easier for him to hide the fact that he did not like them. After
the army his father began wearing drip-dry shirts and gave him
his fifty white cotton shirts with French cuffs and detachable collars. The ritual of affixing cuff links and collar buttons pleased
him for a while, and occasionally he would reverse the detachable collar and imitate a clergyman, but one morning on his way
to work his collar rode away from the shirt. This had happened
before. He went into a clothing store, bought a drip-dry shirt,
and changed into it at his office. That evening he threw away all
his father's shirts and collars, clean and soiled. When the laundry
came back the following Saturday he threw away as well the
shirts that it contained. The collar buttons, although 14-carat
gold, he tossed from an open window. Each night he washed the
drip-dry shirt and wore it the next day. Eventually it turned yellow. He abandoned it and ordered two dozen ordinary button-
down cotton shirts, replacing them as they wore out. Of all his
clothes he most enjoyed a checked sports jacket he bought on
sale for $19 at the university shop of a stylish men's store. One
day an elegantly dressed man stopped him on the street and
asked him where he had gotten it. He later wondered if the man
was homosexual. He wore the jacket for twelve years, until the

armpits rotted. Now he takes most pleasure in his shoes, which he buys at sales in an expensive English shoe shop. As modes change he takes more pride in the old-fashioned wing-tipped style of his shoes. Shoemakers comment on their quality when he has them repaired. He wears double-ply black nylon stretch socks, which seem to last forever but eventually get horny in the nap. He will buy a modified double-breasted pin-striped suit, and it will bring him many compliments. You should wear nothing but double-breasted, he will be told; but before long he will put on weight and return to single-breasted styles and even pleated trousers. For a birthday in his fifties he will give himself the present of replacing all his ties. He will tell his older daughter what he did, and she will be offended because a month before she had given him one of the ties he throws away. In his fifties too he will again wear pajamas at night—in the army he had lost the habit—and they will be a comfort to him, reminding him of childhood. As his hair thins he will search for a comfortable hat, not to warm his head but to keep the longer hairs in place. No hat will be acceptable, however. In his sixties he will purchase his shoes two pairs at a time. His father had done the same thing in his sixties as a guarantee against death. Suits he will continue to buy singly, except on one occasion when he will buy two, a sporty herringbone ("The older the bird, the brighter the plumage," he will say to the salesman) and the other dark blue.

WHEN HE WAS two years old he moved to a new apartment house. He liked the new house, but he did not like leaving the old one. The new apartment house had twelve entrances, all facing a garden. In the center of the garden, under an arched bridge, was a pond. Goldfish swam there in the summer; in winter the pond was drained. He and his friends wondered where the goldfish were kept in the winter. Across the street from the front of the building, to the west, stood the Boy Scout Hall, a small wooden house on top of a hill, under a large tree. To the south was a large yellow-brick building in which yeast company chemists did experiments, also an empty lot where boys played baseball, football, sledded, or made fires, according to the season. To the east and rear was a train yard. And on the north was a rocky plateau where long weeds grew that could be pulled up and used as spears and where the ground broke into dry clumps that could be thrown or dropped and would burst on impact into clouds of dust. The window of his room opened onto the junior playground, which was filled with sand. The sand in the shady part stayed damp; with it he and his friends made runways for toy autos. When he was kept in for being bad or sick he talked to his friends from the window. Boys of ten and older could use the senior playground, on the opposite side of the building. It was made of brick and concrete and was good for playing handball, punchball, stickball, and catch. The windows of one of the stores in the rear of the building were painted dark green to a point above the eye. This store was the Men's Club, where men in the building played pool and cards. Members had to be twenty-one. His father played cards there one night a week and discussed the game with his mother at dinner the next evening. The building had many cellars. These were used for storing furniture, carriages, and sleds, and for housing dumbwaiters, boilers, and coal. Over the years he and his friends had obtained keys to the cellars and explored all of them but one, the deepest, reaching far under the garden. Lighting no matches for fear of being seen by the lantern-jawed, hook-nosed, German janitor who lived there, they worked their way along the rough walls. When they could go no farther he lit a match. Hundreds of water bugs, big as toys, scurried to and fro over the black floor. The boys bruised themselves in their panic to get out and never went back. When he was seven his family moved to a larger apartment in the building so that he and his brother could have separate rooms. He did not like sleeping alone and losing his view of the playground. Now his window opened onto the train yard, and at night the light from the switched tracks flashed on his ceiling. When he was thirteen his family moved again, to another building four blocks away. He went back every Sunday to the old house to visit a friend, thinking his parents thought he was in church. Later his mother told him they had known he was visiting his friend. Now that he was no longer a resident he realized he would never become a member of the Men's Club. Actually he went into the army when he was eighteen, and by the time he got out he had no use for organizations or all-male companionship. Also, because of the postwar business boom the clubroom was rented to a dry cleaner. Other changes occurred over the years. The Boy Scout Hall burned down, the hill on which it had stood was dug away, and a great white courthouse was erected. The yeast company moved out of the city, and a ten-story apartment house, the highest in the neighborhood, appeared on the site. The same sort of thing happened to the rocky plateau. The train yard remains, but before long the air space above it will be sold and a twenty-three-story apartment house will be built there and will be called "Skyline Spires." Although he will return by chance and intention every now and then he will not realize how shabby the building has become, until one autumn evening when, in his fifties, he will stroll into the garden and on the bridge begin to chat with the night watchman. He will see the boy in the face of the watchman, who is about his own age, and will ask him if by chance he grew up in the neighborhood. No, the watchman will say, he comes from Pennsylvania. And, yes, the place has changed. "There's a different element here now," the watchman will say. Garbage in the halls. A murder two months before. "People like yourself come in here and talk about how it used to be." Did the watchman know the names of any of these people? "No, but it must have been a nice place. There's a different element here now." The slate paths through the garden, for no reason that he can imagine, will have been cemented over. The building will be standing when he dies, but only because the neighborhood had fallen into decline.

His MOTHER taught him numbers before he went to school. First he learned the words, which he said as he unfolded, one by one, the fingers of his fists. Then he learned the numerical symbols for the digits. He had different feelings about each digit. One was perfect and friendly. Its appearance resembled its meaning. Two looked more complicated. However, if he drew it schematically, like the letter Z, and considered the middle line as a way to get from the top to bottom lines, it also resembled its meaning. Three was pleasing: its three points made it easy to understand and remember. He could add two threes by counting their six points. Four, if he wrote it with an open top, had four points. The system broke down with five, and five was hard to draw; but since it was half of ten quick and accurate things would be done with it. Six, although it was even, resembled an odd number because it was curved like three and five. Seven was the most difficult digit; it was hard to picture the number of units it represented: the best he could do was five units and two units next to them; it was deceptively simple to draw and somehow not to be trusted. He found eight appealing because it was paradoxical: it had the curves of an odd number, but because it was vertically symmetrical it was an appropriate symbol for an even number. The only way to deal with nine was as one less than ten, and, considering how high a digit it was, he did well with it: two tens were twenty; therefore two nines were two ones less than twenty, or eighteen. This worked all the way up to nine nines: that is, nine nines were nine ones less than nine tens, or eighty-one. Zero, like one, was perfect. He reasoned that since zero represented the absence of substantive numbers as darkness did the absence of light, perhaps zero also represented the sum of all numbers as black did the sum of all colors. One day when he was five and confined to bed with a cold, he recognized that the series zero to nine paralleled the series ten to nineteen, twenty to twenty-nine, and so on. He felt a great surge of power and wrote on a sheet of paper the numbers 1 to 151. Given time he knew he could continue creating numbers indefinitely. His mother checked the list for accuracy and showed it to his father that evening. His father was pleased and said that arithmetic had been his best subject in grammar school. Since his father had not gone beyond grammar school and since, as his mother said, his father was an extremely intelligent man, numbers must be a large part of his father's intelligence. Arithmetic became his own best subject in grammar school. His second-grade teacher announced at the beginning of the year that henceforth four was to be made with an open top. This suited him but disconcerted the other students: they had all been taught in the first grade to make four with a closed top. The thinking now was otherwise. He pictured a convention of grown-ups coming to this conclusion, probably during the previous summer. Because he had discovered the decimal system for himself he knew the relationships expressed in the multiplication tables, but the teachers insisted that he and the other students learn the tables by rote. As a result, when asked to multiply, he ran through the memorized tables and in time lost his feel for numerical architecture. In the first year of high school he was taught elementary algebra by a buck-toothed eccentric; the admixture of letters diluted the elegance of numbers, and mathematics became his poorest subject. By the time he entered the army he had forgotten parts of the multiplication tables—six times seven, seven times eight, eight times twelve—and he did poorly on the army intelligence test. He went to his commanding officer, explained the problem, and asked to be retested. The night before the test, he wrote down the tables, working out some of them by addition, and committed them all again to memory. Now his interest in numbers, beyond such practical uses as toting household budgets and checking bank balances, is mystical. He is struck by the recurrence of mid-eighties and mid-eight hundreds in his life. His house number when he was a child was 840; his high school was on Eighty-fourth Street; he got off at the Eighty-sixth Street subway station to visit his first serious girl friend; he now works on Forty-third Street, half of eighty-six; when the Dow-Jones average for industrial stocks is in the mid-eight hundreds, he feels he should buy or sell. He will buy an electronic calculator and play with it in periods of stress. The effortless answers it provides to arithmetic problems within its digital scope will relax him as sports did when he was younger. One day when he is haphazardly drawing square roots from the calculator and squaring them to determine the inadequacy of decimal approximations, he will realize that from childhood he had unconsciously thought he could be and then could have been a good mathematician, and he will now realize that he could not. This will be a relief to him. In his sixties he will wonder if the recurrence of numbers in the mid-eighties in his history will apply to the length of his life.

HIS PARENTS bought a summer place in the spring of 1929 for $1,700. He was five that summer and cut his foot badly on broken glass. Two years later his parents could have bought or sold the place for $250. Because of the Depression half of the thirty-two bungalows on the block remained empty through the '30s. He and his friends had access, with skeleton keys or through broken windows, to the unoccupied bungalows, most of which had a special character. Number seven, for instance, was sexy because one of the girls on the block was said to have undressed there for a boy from another block. Number one was haunted because its trim was black, and it was visited only in daylight. Thirteen was fit for abuse because a once-flung apple adhered, dried and discolored, summer after summer, to one of its plasterboard walls. When he and his friends wanted to break a man-made thing they went to thirteen. As war approached and the Depression eased, all the bungalows were finally sold. Thirteen was last, and it went to a childless undertaker and his wife. Jews and cars were not allowed in the community. Cars from the city were parked in lots outside, and Jews inquiring about bungalows were told they wouldn't be happy there. A majority of the inhabitants were Catholic, the rest Protestant, except for a small percentage said to be crypto-Jews. He tried to determine who these were but could not decide on anyone for sure. The father of a girl he went with one summer was said to be a Jew, but converted, and he did in fact seem to him to resemble his father's colleagues, most of whom were Jews. The swimming was excellent, particularly in his early years, when pools and sandbars formed at low tide. One boy broke his neck diving into a deceptively shallow pool. Sometimes he would scrape his nose diving off a sandbar. Once, before he could swim, he floated on a tube out beyond his depth, and the tube lost air. It was early in the morning, before the mothers had come to the beach. The only person present was an older girl from the block; she swam out to save him. In his panic he pushed his palms against her breasts and understood for the first time that breasts were boneless. A few years later he heard that she had developed breast cancer and wondered if there was a connection. In the beginning the boys and girls played together. Then for a few years they played separately. Finally they paired off, except for one boy, his best friend, who later went away to be a Jesuit, and one fat girl, who began going with an outsider. His day started with orange juice brought to him in bed by his mother. Afterward he rose, washed, dressed, had breakfast of a boiled egg and bacon strip, and went to the general store to shop for his mother. Then he was free for the rest of the day. He would join one or more of his friends; they would swim, play games, or go on adventures. They would walk say, the two miles to the end of the community called The Point, where they would find such ocean refuse as shark carcasses, tangles of fishhooks, sinkers, seaweed, line, and blood-streaked jellyfish. Sometimes they would walk to the other end, which abutted a coast artillery camp, sneak inside and examine the sixteen-inch guns, which had been there facing seaward since the First World War. When they were hot from the sun and had had enough of the water, they would sit in the shade of a bungalow and play word games. After lunch they would wait the hour prescribed by their mothers, swim, and begin again. His birthday falling in the summer, each year his mother threw a party and gave prizes of dimes for competitions: pushing a peanut with one's nose, walking on hands and knees with a potato on one's back. He won more than his share because he chose the games he was good at. Once a year they would go to a nearby amusement park and add the next more daring ride to their repertoires. One new girl in the community went on all the rides on her first trip and earned a reputation for bravery. During the war she served as a woman marine. When he went away to the service himself his parents sold the bungalow. He goes back there every now and then for old time's sake and once took his children along so they could see a favorite place of his childhood. They didn't like it. A great stone jetty has been built at The Point to protect the waterfront bungalows from erosion. The beach has deepened a quarter of a mile. The quick fall of the shore is gone, and the receding ocean, instead of cleaning the beach each winter, leaves debris. People drive cars directly to their bungalows, although there are still no Jews. The faces look suspicious now. He recognizes no one and feels as he walks down his own block that the inhabitants think he is a Jew. There will be apartment houses soon, built on great concrete pilings driven into the sand, and eventually the nearby city will condemn and buy the land for a public beach. Nowhere in his head will he be able to fault the change, not so in his heart.

HE WAS UNCIRCUMCISED, and the head of his penis was sensitive. He would pull back his foreskin but only so far. Once a doctor pulled it back all the way. This seemed to him a violation, and he made his mother promise not to let the doctor do it again.

Once in the bath when he was flicking his penis, small and soft, from side to side in play his mother told him he must not fool with it or he would get sick. At nine he became aware that his penis changed in size and firmness; this struck him as unnatural. On waking in the morning it was often large and hard and would not soften until he urinated. Urinating was difficult with a hard penis. The stream would shoot off to one side and miss the bowl, or perhaps split into two streams, one or both of which would miss the bowl. If the stream went singly—say, to a half-right—and he compensated by pointing his penis to the left, the stream might suddenly straighten and miss the bowl on the other side. A sure way to get all the urine into the bowl was to sit down on the toilet and force the hard penis under the rim of the seat. This would be painful if he didn't bend forward, and even then the urine would splash off the enamel, wetting his hand and the penis itself. The first time he saw a vagina he was walking along a neighborhood street in early summer. Children of seven or eight were jumping rope and playing potsy. Suddenly one little girl hiked up her short cotton dress, pulled her panties to one side and scratched herself. It was no more than a small hairless crack, but his face burned for a long time afterward. He didn't touch a cunt until he was twenty, in the army, and about to make love to a whore. After getting into bed with her, he felt around under the sheet for her cunt. He thought it would be in front, like a prick, but it wasn't. He was unwilling to ask the woman for help because he didn't want her to know he was a virgin. He remembered the saying that a nice girl is a girl who puts it in for you, and, propping himself over her, he placed her hand on his prick, and she guided it in. He was surprised that the cunt was between a woman's legs, and for some time considered this a fault in women. Through the first ten years of his marriage the only cunt he knew was his wife's. Although he thought about it a lot, was greatly attracted to it, invented fond jokes about it, his wife made it less and less accessible, and he was returned to a state of constant yearning, as in adolescence. He grew to feel that women tolerated rather than desired a prick in their cunts, so that when he had his first adulterous love affair, at thirty, he doubted that his mistress really enjoyed him. One night she convinced him that she did by telling him that he was a cautious fucker and that he should feel free to fuck her as hard as he wanted. His subsequent experiences with other women made him feel at home with cunts. He would examine them carefully, play with the lips and fatty mons veneris, lick the clitoris, and insert his tongue as far as he could into the vagina. Sometimes a cunt had a different character from its owner. Two women he slept with, although they were desirous, had cunts that seemed to narrow to a wedge and want him out. Another girl, who always looked angry when he fucked her, had a cunt that held his prick like a treasure. Occasionally a cunt was too large for friction. He solved the problem with one girl by squeezing the bottom of her ass with his hand when he made love to her. Now cunts are less important in themselves; he values them mainly as a means of attaching women to him. Through their cunts he makes women like and need him, and this does much to compensate for his growing coldness toward the world. Most of the cunts he knows now belong to women in their late thirties and early forties. As he ages, so will the women he sleeps with. In his fifties he will yearn for the cunt of a girl. He will try to imagine it—round, small, firm, with a full springy bush. Sometimes this will increase his pleasure when he is sleeping with older women and sometimes lessen it. He will pick up a young whore one night, the second and last whore of his life, but a Caesarian scar and her contemptuous manner will make copulation perfunctory. Near the end of his life he will develop a feeling for his penis akin to the faint fondness he felt for it when he was a child, that is, before the onset of the dilemmas and frustrations of adolescence. Except for odd, recollective moments and occasionally in dreams, he will lose his attraction for cunts, and when he makes love he will hardly think of them at all.

HE DIDN'T BREAK his thumb-sucking habit until he was eleven. His parents had been after him for a long time to give it up, but it was too great a source of consolation. His mother asked the help of the family doctor, a self-satisfied and all-knowing man who could tell a patient's condition from his stools ("To see the world in a grain of sand," he'd say). The doctor advised covering the thumbs with adhesive tape; later, painting them with iodine; still later, promising rewards. Nothing worked, although it must be said for the doctor that rewards were not tried. The doctor did not prescribe threats, but thumb-sucking had forced a space between his two front permanent teeth, and his father, projecting his own business concerns, explained how important personal appearance would be for him in the adult world. "Someone who makes a good appearance, a doorman opens the door for him immediately. Someone who doesn't make a good appearance, the doorman wants to know him first. The point I'm making," his father said, "is that for a good-looking person the doors fly open." Rather than give up thumb-sucking, however, he accepted the inevitability of ugliness and secretly planned to compensate by dressing splendidly: his father had also often commented on the importance of clothes. It was in the middle of the Depression that his twelfth Christmas approached. He went to his father and promised to quit thumb-sucking if he could have as a present the same model camera his brother had bought for himself with saved money. His father agreed immediately, recognizing that finally he wanted something more than thumb-sucking. Shortly afterward he started smoking cigarettes on the sly with friends. This sometimes gave him an erection; at the time he felt that the association of naughtiness with smoking and sex accounted for the erections. In later life an analyst reminded him that when he was very young and was taken occasionally into his parents' bed at night he would sleep on his father's side and hold his father's thumb, which smelled of tobacco. When he was fifteen he announced to his father that he had started smoking and intended to smoke at home. He didn't enjoy smoking in his father's presence and did it only in the cause of his independence. He also began biting his fingernails, not so much nervously as cosmetically, and instead of spitting out the severed parts he lovingly, with his tongue, passed them back and forth between his teeth. He went down on the second girl he slept with, intending it as a gesture of homage, and found that he enjoyed the taste and texture. The third girl he slept with disliked foreplay and did not allow cunnilingus. She said she was afraid he might expect her to do the same thing to him and she didn't want to. Then it was no privation, but now cunnilingus is an essential part of making love. Ideally he brings a girl to the point of climax with his tongue, enters her, and either comes with her or later at his leisure by himself. His taste for sucking breasts has diminished, so also his taste for kissing. When he is with a woman he thinks of his mouth as auxiliary genitals. The lips of beautiful girls remain attractive to him; he likes to look at them, touch them with his fingers; but the fitting place for his own mouth is in contact with their genitals. He will be drinking an Italian liqueur with a girl in bed and suggest that he pour some onto her cunt and taste it there. It will sting her so she will have to douche. When she returns to bed he will let her pour some on his penis. It will sting him too and finish their evening. In his fifties he will establish a liaison with a woman in her early forties who will enjoy this attention as much as he enjoys providing it. During one session there will be a sudden stinking discharge from her. They will disengage; she will hurry to the bathroom, dress, and leave in embarrassment. He will strip the bedclothes, seal them in a plastic bag, and leave them outside his door. In his sixties he will take up cigars, which he will smoke with increasing pleasure.

HIS EIGHT YEARS at St. Ursula's Grammar School coincided with the Depression. People could not afford to move from one neighborhood to another so that the student body did not change. One boy died from diphtheria in the sixth grade; and another boy, now a congressman, entered the school late and stayed only one year. The parents of this boy took him out when he continued to get perfect report cards even though he was skipped twice. The first grade was taught by Miss Thoma, who was pretty and young. She said to him one morning, "You always arrive with a smile," which made him understand that he enjoyed the school. The second grade was taught by Miss King. A breast fell out of her brassiere one day when she picked up chalk from the floor. She turned to the blackboard to put the breast back. The third grade was taught by Sister Noelita, whom everyone liked—boys and girls, bright and stupid, sassy and docile. One day she brought to class her twin brother, who was good-looking, amusing, and played the guitar. The class asked her to bring him back. She said she would, but he never came. The fourth grade was taught by Sister Ecclesiastica, the oldest nun in the school. She was brown and wrinkled and once whipped him and another boy with a cat-o'-nine-tails after ordering them to bare their calves by dropping their socks from the bottoms of their knickerbockers. His mother complained to the principal the following day, and there were no more beatings, even with a ruler. Sister Noelita, again, taught the fifth grade, and everyone thought this was great good luck. She left the order the next year, just before she was to take her final vows. One of his classmates said he would marry her when he grew up. In the sixth grade, boys and girls, who had studied together, were separated. The boys' class was taught by Sister Barnabas, a tall, handsome woman who said that she preferred teaching girls. The seventh grade was taught by Sister Clement, a pleasant and serious woman whose skirts he and some other boys tried to look up, through the grated landing of the rear exit, from which she oversaw play at recess. Sister Clement gave him a biography of a Catholic youth, dead twenty years, blessed but not canonized. She said the youth reminded her of him. He did not read the book; it made him feel like a fraud. The eighth grade was taught by Sister Immaculata, who held that all modern inventions and discoveries other than medical ones were bad. For instance, radio waves made street noises carry farther, and teaching was therefore more difficult. She also claimed that the classroom floors were getting harder year by year. She told how her uncle, an independently wealthy man, had developed from herbs a cure for cancer. However, he had taken the secret with him to the grave. "May God forgive him," she said. Following on this cue, one boy asked whether her uncle's refusal to share his discovery with mankind was a mortal sin. Her eyes glistened with tears as she said that it was not for her to judge. A couple, friends of Sister Immaculata, asked her to take their son, who had been expelled from a number of schools, into her class. She explained to the class that this boy came from a privileged background and was spoiled. The boy had a big head. The class rallied against the boy, and after three months he was put on trial. Sister Immaculata chose the prosecuting attorney, the defense attorney, and a jury; she was the judge. After two days of argument, the boy was found guilty of being a cheat, a coward, and a bully. In passing sentence, Sister Immaculata said that the trial had been punishment enough, that the boy had obviously been taught a lesson, and that she hoped he would turn over a new leaf. The church organist and his wife had an idiot son, who hobbled and slavered. Sister Immaculata confided to the class that the boy may have been God's punishment for past sins of one or both of the parents. Now he drives past the church and school every six months or so, always at night. Like so many landmarks of his childhood, they have become smaller. The once German and Irish neighborhood has turned black and brown. By happenstance one of the older boys in a family from his early summer community is pastor now. He hears through friends that this priest is bitter at having been assigned to a poor parish. The local candy store and the garages that served the nearby middle-class Jewish population remain. In a few years he will, on impulse, take a newspaper ad calling for a reunion of his St. Ursula classmates. Four, all male, will come to a downtown restaurant—a police lieutenant, the manager of a hardware store, the owner of a meat-distributing company, and an unemployed former boxer and stagehand. He will learn that the brightest boy of the class is an executive in a Maryland engineering firm, that the boys who ranked second and third at graduation are dead. He will wonder if there is meaning in this, since he was fourth.

HIS FATHER STOPPED boxing with him when he was five. Till then he had often stood between his father's knees, throwing punches, while his father, sitting on the edge of a chair, would feint and parry, occasionally taking one of his small fists in the face. When he asked his father why he didn't box with him anymore his father said he was getting too big. His father gave the same reason for not playing pickaback or lifting him upside down by the feet. He thought there was another reason, but he did not know what it was. He and his friends fought with their fists to settle grudges or respond to serious insults. Lesser differences were dealt with by wrestling. Wrestling established the fighting hierarchy of the group. His own position was high: no one younger than he could beat him, and he could beat a number of older boys. His greatest victory came at thirteen, over his brother, who was twenty. Chanting like a sideshow barker, his brother had called him a dog-face boy. In retaliation he fixed a cup of water on the frame of his bedroom transom in such a way that when the door was opened the cup would spill. He then went to his brother's room, where his brother was studying, and pounded on the door, a traditional act of incitement. He heard his brother rise; he noisily raced toward his room but hid in a nearby closet. His brother entered the room, and the cup tipped. He had never seen his brother so angry. They wrestled for a long time. Finally he pinned his brother to the floor. He later ascribed the victory to the fact that he had been wearing his Boy Scout uniform. During his first week of college the gym instructor, who was also the wrestling coach, chose him to demonstrate various holds. He resisted one of the holds, the instructor pressed, he still resisted, and soon they were wrestling. He threw the instructor in what the instructor later explained to the class was an unorthodox manner. After the class the instructor invited him to join the wrestling team. He won his three matches, although he had not mastered basic wrestling techniques. His fourth match was against a blind student. He had no will to win, was pinned in record time, and the next day quit the team. In the army he called a Southern soldier a cracker. The soldier challenged him to fight. The entire company gathered to watch, splitting into two factions, city boys and country boys. He wrestled while the soldier boxed. Bleeding at the nose and mouth, he established himself on the soldier's chest and was proclaimed the winner. The soldier got to his feet and challenged him to duel with mounted bayonets. He declined, and the soldier's faction proclaimed their man the moral victor. His distaste for army training rid him of any desire for physical contest for years afterward. However, now and then he arm-wrestles and feels a surge of pleasure at male contact. Before long an old friend who had wrestled with him in college will suggest at a party that they give an exhibition. He and the friend will be drunk, and although he will not want to wrestle he will agree because his friend's wife will be present and he will have been thinking of initiating an affair with her. At another party, given by an opera singer, a heavy basso some years younger than he, he will suddenly feel very strong and challenge the singer to Indian wrestle. The singer will grin, assume the proper position, and with wrist alone bring him to his knees. This will be the first indication that he is weakening with age. He will frequently have contests of strength with women in bed, usually trials of restraint and escape. One evening when he is in his mid-fifties he will be making love to a woman fifteen years younger than he; they will struggle to see who can mount the other. He will be startled and amused at her relative strength, and although he will win he will wonder if other women had falsified their strength in order to please him. One day when parking his car he will pull in front of a Cadillac that had been there before him. The Cadillac owner will blow his horn in protest, get out of his car, grasp him by the lapel, and raise a fist. He will be transfixed by a large gold ring on the Cadillac owner's little finger, then look at the man's face and see the anger change to shame because he is too old to be threatened.

AFTER SEEING a movie about entering the forbidden tomb of a pharaoh, he wanted to become an Egyptologist. Next he wanted to be an astronomer. Searching the sky for stars alone at night through a telescope was an activity he felt he could not fail at. His third ambition was chemistry. Each Christmas he received a progressively more elaborate and expensive chemistry set. Just before he was to get the most sophisticated set, which came in an attractive, hinged, wooden box and cost $25, he began collecting chemicals piecemeal from druggists. Because of his youth most druggists would not sell him poisons or corrosive acids, but he finally found one who sympathized with his need for these materials. From sulphur, charcoal, and potassium nitrate he made gunpowder, with which he lit bright fires on his windowsill and in the bathtub. He then made nitrocellulose, a relatively powerful explosive, which he packed into glass tubes and when his parents weren't home detonated with paper fuses. He bought a book on explosives, which explained how to make nitroglycerine, and although he had the necessary ingredients and equipment he lost his nerve because of a warning in the book that the liquid might explode by itself if it contained impurities. His favorite experiment, which he performed for friends, was a demonstration of spontaneous combustion. He would pour a few drops of glycerine onto a mound of potassium permanganate, and within a minute or two the mixture would smoke and burst into flames. One evening when his parents were sitting in the living room he put the glycerine and potassium permanganate into a small screw-top bottle, locked the bottle in a steel box, put the box close to his parents, warning them not to touch it, that it would soon explode. It did, the box hopping a few inches off the floor. His father was angry but said only not to pull that little trick again. Shortly afterward he put potassium permanganate and glycerine into a corked test tube and dropped the tube onto the awning of the grocery store two floors below his room. The awning caught fire. He was seen by the grocer trying to extinguish the fire by pouring pans of water from his window. The grocer told his parents and eventually billed them $18 for the damage. But that evening his father wrapped up all his chemicals to dispose of on the dumbwaiter next morning. He rose at dawn, undid his father's package, and salvaged his most prized chemical, a few ounces of mercury, which he liked to manipulate on a flat surface, watching it break into tiny balls and recombine into larger masses. In the last two years of grammar school he delivered oratorical pieces and performed in plays for the parents of students. He got so much credit for this he searched out collections of poems and prose passages intended for recitation. Learning and saying these gave him a sense of verbal harmony. In his third year of high school he wrote a realistic description of his fellow students, how they smelled bad, squeezed pimples, masturbated; it was a great success. Also, for a girl he had fallen in love with he wrote poems, which she said she treasured. By the end of high school he had decided to be a writer. When he told his father that this was his ambition his father said he would have to pick something more practical if he wanted to be sent to college. He lied and said in that case he would be a teacher. For a time he considered being a photographer but realized that his gratification came from unflattering portraits he took of relatives and friends (he even used special darkroom techniques to deform portraits that by themselves were pleasant). He had no success as a writer until he wrote comic stories about his marital difficulties. They seemed to be even-handed caricatures of his wife and himself; his wife, however, understood that she was being represented as an inadequate woman and he as her victim. While he was writing his first novel he suspected that for him the point of literary composition was vengeance and an extension of his childhood interest in explosives. Some years after the end of his marriage he will fall in love with a young woman. The experience will so loosen his feelings that he will hope to write warmly of people, but he will still have pity only for himself and a strong sense of grievance against others. Eventually he will understand that most people have as hard a time in life as he. He will try to make literature from this understanding, but he will not be able to.

FOR COMFORT he took certain objects with him to school. They had to be simple and impermeable. Ball bearings were almost perfect. The top of his school desk tipped toward him, so he would put the ball bearings into the pencil groove. When they were struck together they made a satisfying sound, but their movement in the groove and the simplicity of their relative positions restricted the ways he could think about them. When he was in the third grade his father gave him a magnifying glass used by textile merchants; it opened to form three sides of a cube and folded to a flat square. The hinged workings were smooth and tight, and the brushed surface of the stainless-steel frame offered a pleasant resistance to his passing thumb and finger pads. The glass was strong, and when a friend pointed out that, abandoned on a desert island, he could use it to concentrate sunlight and start a fire, the object took on special value. He liked well-made penknives. One day in class he was playing with a penknife that had a bone handle and a long blade. It closed on his left index finger. He could not open it with his free hand and had to take it to the teacher. She opened the knife and kept it, he felt unjustly. Sometimes he yearned to have a hunting knife in a leather case hidden under his arm or along his calf, but he never acted on the desire. In high school, after composing a poem, he would type it on a sheet of paper, fold the paper in four, and put it into the side pocket of his jacket to take out and read when observed, occasionally changing a word or phrase. He would keep the poem with him until he wrote a new one. He gave up knives in high school, and in the army all weapons became repugnant to him. But after his wedding he took a penknife on his honeymoon, along with a honing stone and a can of oil to slow the action of the stone. At leisure moments he honed the knife to an ever finer edge. When his marriage in its slow dissolution took temporary turns for the better he would buy a new knife to celebrate. When he began to have adulterous love affairs he sometimes marked them by buying new knives. Often he carried a book with him. At its most powerful the right book, he felt, would save him from death or see him through death without panic or despair. His favorites were small editions of Herrick, Catullus, Lucretius, and *Antony and Cleopatra*. From a copy of Marvell's poems he cut the page containing "To His Coy Mistress" and for years carried it with him, although he knew the poem by heart. During his long crisis, when he thought he was going to die, he was attracted to his wife's houseplants. He would study them before he left in the morning and when he returned in the evening. He made cuttings and distributed them to friends and neighbors so that something of the plants would be sure to survive. His wife in her separation complaint mentioned the knife on the honeymoon. Recently he understood that the stroking of a knife on a stone represented the thrust of his penis in a vagina; this pleases him because he had thought that his association of knives and women came from fear or hostility. Although he travels with personal equipment—pen, keys, wallet— nothing material has saving significance for him now. Soon he will feel that the quality of immutability, which once attracted him to certain objects, is worthless and that only certain ephemeral qualities, such as those present in the body of an athlete, are reassuring. He will treasure plant seeds for their intricate organization of information and keep them on his desk like talismans.

HIS MOTHER and father told him that children love their parents. His grammar school teachers told him the same thing, adding that the love of children for their parents is like the love of human beings for God. He did not love God or his parents and felt there was something wrong with him thereby. The first love he thought of as love was for certain girls. Some of these girls did not know he loved them. In the sixth grade he sent an unsigned declaration of love to a girl whose father was a prizefighter. She was quiet and gentle, and he considered these qualities all the more extraordinary in light of her father's occupation. In the seventh grade he fell in love with a girl whose mother had died; in the eighth grade with a girl named Helen, whom he kissed at graduation parties, took skating, and in the summer named a rowboat after. In the fall, however, she dropped him. He recognized love by the aura of pleasure that surrounded everything to do with the girl: her neighborhood, clothes, friends, books, pets; odd parts of the girl, like the nose and fingernails, struck him as perfect. In high school he was always in love with one girl or another, and when he was fourteen he fell in love with another girl named Helen. Eight years later he married her. This girl at first was passive and undemonstrative. He thought of her as a clean slate on which he could write his beliefs. She was so much in his mind that when traveling alone around the city he sometimes paid two fares by mistake. When his first child, a girl, was born he was not prepared for the responsibilities of fatherhood, and although she closely resembled him he resented her. But when she began to talk and he saw that her character too was like his he began to love her. His second child, also a girl, did not resemble him in any way, and he ignored her. There were so many difficulties in his marriage that after ten years he could not say to himself that he loved his wife. He had an affair with a woman who was also unhappily married. He did not know whether he loved her or not, although many times he told her he did, especially when they were making love. He enjoyed hearing her say that she loved him, but he did not feel the same concern for her that he remembered having felt for his wife. However, when the affair ended he was bereft and thought that perhaps he had loved her. After he and his wife were divorced his younger daughter phoned to ask if he loved her. They talked for an hour, wept, and he told her that he did; only then did he know that he did. After his father died he had a recurrent dream in which he tried to save his father from death; sometimes he succeeded and sometimes he failed; but the dreams were so intense that he came to believe that probably he had loved his father too. As a bachelor he has many affairs. The sudden release of emotion that accompanies them is gratifying; he wants to remain capable of it but also keep it under control. He will explain to a woman who wants him to love her: "If I love you you will have power over me. If I love you a little you will have a little power over me. If I love you a lot you might kill me." "But why would I kill you if you love me and I love you?" He will not know the answer. "You could love me secretly," she will say. "Maybe I do," he will say, but he will not, and, soon after, the affair will end. As he moves from woman to woman he will see that his first feelings about a new woman will have derived from his last feelings about the previous one. This knowledge will destroy the effect. Soon he will have a professional lunch at a restaurant with a young married woman. As he is shown to her table he will begin to fall in love with her. They will talk well, and his love will increase in surges, like blood filling an excited penis. During the next two weeks he will call her many times a day. He will meet her after work and drive her home. In the evenings he will write her long letters and have them delivered by messenger next morning. In his apartment he will drink and walk about, raising his hands to the ceiling and making sounds of pain. She will leave her husband, and they will live together. She will soon be unhappy and yearn for her former life. She will criticize everything he does and everything she considers him to be. She will fall in love with a young widower and leave him. His strongest feelings thereafter will be toward his daughters and toward young men who remind him of his past self.

His MOTHER kept an Irish nursemaid when he was a baby. The nursemaid stayed with the family for the first two years of his life. He remembers her boyfriend better than he remembers her. The boyfriend was a bus conductor with a red face. The boyfriend's job was to stand at the rear of the double-decker bus and collect fares. The nursemaid would wheel the baby carriage to the bus stop at a certain hour and wait for the boyfriend. The boyfriend had a ticket punch and a change maker. One day the boyfriend gave him a violet-flavored Life Saver. This pleased him and made him proud. Shortly afterward the family moved across the river to another apartment house, and the nursemaid left. She went back to Ireland to get married, his mother told him when he was old enough to ask. His mother also said that he began to talk only after the nursemaid had left. His first sentence, his mother said, was, "When are we going to the old home?" He would ask his mother, "What did she look like?" "She was pretty," his mother said. "Did she look like any*body*?" "No," his mother said. He didn't know whether that was good or bad. When he was seven he got his own ticket punch and made quarter-inch holes in many things. One day he looked for the punch, and it was gone. He searched through his possessions but could not find it. Every now and then he would yearn for the punch and go through his things again, certain that a really thorough search would turn it up, but it didn't. Once when he was ten and in a candy store he asked for violet-flavored Life Savers. The candy store man didn't have them and had never heard of them. On the way home from the candy store he went into a drugstore and asked the cashier, who seemed to specialize in Life Savers, for violet. "You mean grape," the cashier said. "No, violet." "Violet isn't a flavor, it's a color," the cashier said. But he knew exactly how it would taste if he could find it. Recently he visited a theatrical couple, who after dinner broke out some marijuana. He had never tried it, didn't believe it worked, had been drinking, and smoked both the pipe and cigarettes that were passed to him. Soon a plant against the wall, as in a movie trick, turned into a church palm. The space in the room divided itself into vertical and horizontal planes. He could focus his attention either deeply and narrowly or broadly and shallowly. Then the room changed into a long tiled path that led back to his birth. High tile walls stood on either side of the path. Above, the sky was clear and blue. The distant tiles, near his birth, were bright yellow and orange. The tiles near him were dirty and dark. The causes of the darkening, many and varied, stood like markers out of sight on the far sides of the walls. He could not see them, but he knew they were there. Suddenly at the far end of the path, near his birth, the figure of a woman ascended slowly into the sky. He strained to see her face, but either it was averted or had no features. He understood that her facelessness was due to a failure of memory and that the tile-darkening troubles in his life outside the walls were beyond the power of his mind to identify specifically. After the figure had disappeared into the sky a voice said, "It was bad to lose her when you were two, but it has been worse to love her more than your mother." This message struck him as so important and he thought it so

likely that he would forget it that he asked the host, who under
the influence of the marijuana was taking notes like a scientist,
to write it on a piece of paper and give the paper to him. Shortly
afterward he will lunch with a friend, a middle-aged college
teacher. He will tell him about the experience, show him the
paper, which he will be keeping in his wallet, and will say that
apparently there are more variations to the Oedipus complex
than Freud ever dreamed of in his philosophy. The friend will
study the paper and say that for the first time he realizes that he
married his wife because she resembled his own nursemaid.
Shortly before his mother dies he will tell her, too, about the experience. He will think that it will be an even more momentous
revelation to her than it was to him. "Oh," his mother will say, "I
knew that. She was a nice girl and *very* fond of you."

HIS BROTHER resembled his mother. He resembled his father. At
first he thought his father was handsome. Later he thought his
father was ugly and hoped he would grow up to look like someone else. He had a fat face and wished it were lean. He thought
his mouth was soft and, examining himself in the mirror, often
clenched his teeth and narrowed his lips. He wanted to look
hard, and outdoors he adopted a severe manner. In adolescence
he was pleased to hear that this or that girl liked his looks, but
he doubted the girl's taste. When he went into the army he was
told to get a short haircut; he had his head shaved instead and
felt very manly. When the army sent him far from home his face,
chest, and back broke out in lumps. An army doctor said that
nothing could be done about the condition because it was only
disfiguring, not disabling. After he returned from his first fur-
lough his company commander, a man with dark, smooth skin,
showed him a red-bordered letter from Eleanor Roosevelt. It
told how his mother had written to Mrs. Roosevelt complaining
that the army had not given him proper medical care. He was
sent to the camp dermatologist, who insisted, despite his denials,
that the lumps had been there since he was thirteen or fourteen.
At another camp he went to a dermatologist, who reassigned him
to limited service, which he afterward thought might have saved
his life. By the time he was discharged from the army his face

was scarred. He was grateful to his girl friend for still caring about him and a year later married her. Occasionally she caressed the scars, and although her touch was soothing it embarrassed him. For years he considered the scars not part of himself; in dreams his face was as smooth as when he was a boy. He envied men with good skin and was attracted only to women with good skin. However, once when getting off a ferry he offered to help a scarred young woman carry her heavy bag. She refused; he was relieved but thought that they both had lost a chance for comfort. He had his first adulterous affair with a woman who said his scars made him look dangerous, although later she said that his constant concern with his appearance was faggy. Later another woman he was sleeping with said that without scars he would have been too handsome for comfort. Because of his successes with women he now accepts the face he sees in the mirror as his own. As time goes on, the scars will be absorbed, even to the extent that unscarred skin on one side of his face will change as if to reestablish symmetry with scarred skin on the other side. For a while he will be amused by the signs of age: lines in his cheeks and between his eyebrows, ridges in his fingernails, spots on the backs of his hands, yellowing teeth, hair falling from his head and growing in his ears ("Just nature moving things around," he will say). But he will be put off by other, later signs: the boniness of knees and elbows, a breakdown of the orderly retreat of his hairline, the pendulousness of his earlobes, a whiteness to the skin of his inner arms, a looseness around the eyes so that they do not express his moods. He will have hoped to age into a rosy cragginess, but instead there will be a general slackness and grayness. When he understands that all future changes will be for the worse he will be struck by the fact that never in his life will he have been satisfied with his appearance. More and more he will remind himself of his father as he remembers his father before his father died. At night when he wakes and coughs or clears his throat he will hear his father's sounds. In unexpected reflections in shop windows he will see his father's late face: irritable, confused, and suspicious. Somewhere among his belongings he will know there are photographs of his father as an old man, which he will in-

tend to search out and study in order to discern how close the resemblance is. If the resemblance is an illusion it will mean to
him that his life span is not determined by the genes of his father, who died at seventy-two, but may be modified by those of
his mother, who will have lived longer.

Ladybug, Fly Away Home

MARY HEDIN

MARY HEDIN is a poet as well as a fiction writer. She earned a B.S.
degree at the University of Minnesota and an M.A. at San Francisco
State. She is now a teacher at the College of Marin, and lives in
California with her husband and four children.

1.

CONTEMPLATION. *The ablution has been made,*
But not yet the offering.
Full of trust they look up to him.

                                                    —I Ching

2.

I HAVE COME through the house, looking for Samuel. His
red hair. He is not here and has left no message. I am
extremely disappointed, but I am not at all sure why. What has
he to tell me anyway? What has he to do with my life?

Originally appeared as "Ladybird, Fly Away Home." In *Southwest Review*, Autumn 1975. Copyright © 1975 by Southern Methodist University Press. Reprinted by permission of the author and publisher.

Through cracks of the floorboards I see a red glowing. Is it fire? Yes, yes. I see small flames, yellow, now, and lapping. Someone must call the fire department. Who will call? Is there no one to help? Will the house burn down? Burn down?

3.

THERE SHE IS, sitting in the back of the room, apart from the others, asserting her difference, her superiority, by the islanding empty desks. Laura, her round face shining, glazed pink. An angelic look, as if she has transcended the earthly. Shawl over her shoulders covering new-sprouted wings. But I know better. Her eyes reveal: not ecstasy transforms her, nor vision. Suffering. She is suffering so that the heartbeats of her pain send rosiness to the skin. Yes, she looks quite beautiful. But that steady gaze is demanding, it is deep with hunger. What does she want of me? What?

Her need, her need.

Haven't I listened enough?

She is twenty-four. *I cannot cope with life,* she tells me. She had a miserable affair with a black man. *Everything that went wrong he blamed on my being white. But I loved him, I loved him.* Crazy then, she wandered. Went home to live with her father, who is, she reports, crazy himself. He tries to fit life to his idea of himself. He is idealistic, but cruel. He will not help her. He does not love her. *Yes,* she says, plucking long threads from the tattered dirty shawl, *he is mad.*

I've taken a job, she told me on Tuesday, *with this lawyer and his wife. I'm supposed to be a sort of companion to the children. Help them with their homework, help them be creative. I thought it would be a good job, I mean, I thought I would be part of the family. But the little boy, he's crazy.*

What do you mean, crazy? I ask. Yes, I try to understand.

I mean he runs around all the time, throws things. He can't sit still. He shouts things, Fuck you, Go to hell, you bitch. *I mean he's really terrible.*

There are three other children, five cats, two dogs, snakes.

They make her do dishes, wash clothes. She is only a slave there. They do not pay her.

You must talk to them, Laura.

Yes, she assents, head bowed, fingers working the gray strands. *If they are still unfair, you'll have to find another job.*

Yes, she assents. *I thought I'd be part of the family. At Shabbos dinner they didn't ask me to sit down. I had to stay in the kitchen.* She lifts her eyes, stares at me, tears rising.

Does she believe I am wise?

My psychiatrist says I'm paranoid. She watches me close as conscience.

Are you? I ask.

Maybe. The brown curls fall over a forehead like Athena's. *I have no place else to go.*

So now on Thursday at 11:50 her dark eyes fix on me, full of request. But the other students surround me, make appointments, plead for more time on their papers. And then Laura is gone. I tell myself she should have waited. I would have asked her to lunch.

4.

ARDYS IS SITTING at my desk, a thick stack of student papers at her elbow. She lifts the top paper, opens it, looks at the back page, writes on the grade sheet, places the paper to her left. Her face is pale and she looks very tired.

What happened? I ask.

They moved him to Sonoma County Jail. For his own good, they say. To keep him away from that prisoner who got him into the brawl. Now it will take hours to go visit. Her lips lift on one side, making the white face twist.

Nothing is ever his fault, she says. She keeps lifting papers, making immaculate marks on the squared sheet. *He complains: "Why did this happen to me?" And it's the third time. Drunk driving. A felony this time, he's eighteen. At least they're having him see a psychiatrist.*

The girl is lying in the hospital, a broken back. The column of grades lengthens under Ardys' efficient hands.

It is awful, she mutters, *how one's children work against one's happiness, one's marriage. By ourselves Cappy and I are fine. Something like this pulls us apart.*

Suddenly her head drops forward, as if its stalk had snapped. The fingers of both hands grasp the skull, the hair gray and tumbled over the knuckles. She weeps: *What right have children to do such things? What right have they to ruin their parents' lives?*

I put my arm around her narrow shoulders, I go out in the hall and get her a cup of coffee. Outside the dusty March window a scatter of starlings flicker across a pale sky, and by the library steps the crooked old plum tree holds up to the lemon light a great cluster of bloom.

How does one comfort? What is there to do?

5·

BECAUSE THE DOOR is open, I walk into Gerald's office. But Bridget is there. The silence is obvious: pause in argument. Bridget looks at me, and I see I am made judge. Tommy had to stay home from school, a fever. The babysitter has another job. Bridget has an appointment with her mother's lawyer. *I can't call him, now,* she insists. *He's a busy man.* She lifts a hand, pushes the red wayward curls from her cheek, pushing away anxiety.

Gerald is ruffled, he feels put upon.

I can't miss the Senate meeting, that whole business of English requirements comes up today.

Bridget believes her business over the estate and her mother's health is more important. Gerald looks at me, martyred. I understand. Ten years in the department, living hand in glove. Bridget will explode into one of her tantrums. Famous. Her absolute lack of restraint, her shouting. One sees it coming, the flush riding up the sides of her neck, the handsome mouth stretching.

Gerald tries bargaining, pink-cheeked, boyish with shame.

Could you stay home till two? I could get home by two.

Bridget sputters: *Gerald, you always expect . . .*

I leave; no arbiter, no judge.

Other boys of ten could be left alone an hour or two. But

Tommy on a calm morning in autumn dropped lit matches into the gasoline tanks of two parked cars. Astonished, Gerald and Bridget take on guilt.

What did I do wrong? Bridget plaintively queries, but expects reassurance.

Now Gerald steps into my office. He wants me to go to the Senate meeting, speak for the department. He gives me sheaves of papers. He stands then at the doorway and under the neon light his fine long nose makes a sharp knifelike shadow over his mouth and chin. The look he gives is tentative: should he flee? should he speak?

What can I do about Bridget? he quavers. *What can I do?*

Does he expect an answer? Does he believe I know? They are all seeing a therapist, all three. I look down at the page of poetry where light slides off the words: "Nothing is so beautiful as Spring/When weeds, in wheels, shoot long and lovely and lush;/ . . . What is all this juice and all this joy?/A strain of the earth's sweet being in the beginning/In Eden garden."

Oh, Bridget, I say. *Bridget is all right.*

6.

THE PHONE rings. A Mrs. Bradford: high anxious voice. *Can't you change his grade? He's just not a creative person. He's very sweet, but he's just not creative. He can't write essays. I mean, he's really upset about this. He has to pass this course, he's going into forestry. I mean, Randy is very hot tempered. I'm afraid what he'll do, getting an F like that.* Yes. A fierce violent young man. What will he do? Should I be afraid?

7.

a) The Academic Senate accepts the Curriculum Committee's recommendation: all English requirements will be dropped. The vote is 9 to 2.

b) The Academic Senate accepts recommendations of the Sabbatical Leave Committee. Gered Hallowitz is granted sab-

batical leave to explore alternative lifestyles. Aileen Weber is refused sabbatical leave for post-graduate studies at Cambridge.

c) Arnold Fell stands up and shouts: "When did balling in
communes become more valuable to higher education than academic studies? What the hell is this institution coming to?"

d) Arnold Fell is gaunt. Bags under his eyes. Six months ago
his daughter, fourteen, disappeared hitchhiking home from the
skating rink. Weekends he haunts hippie hangouts, bars. Puts up
posters, advertises. Is she alive? Is she dead?

8.

I LONG FOR ALONENESS, but there he is, lying on the davenport.
The blue light of the television flickers over the fleshy white face,
the dull eyes, incongruous audacious moustache. *Hello, Steve,* I
give out. How long has he been here? Only two weeks? But the
third time, uninvited. He arrives on the doorstep, all his belongings in his car. The car breaking down. His ears aching, his
throat raw. Hungry. He comes from the east, drives over plains
and Rockies, lands on the doorstep. He needs us, this classmate
of a son not home. Needs our food, our home, our ears.

He thinks he will work. He has registered at employment
agencies. He waits for the phone, for a job falling into his lap.
He sleeps till eleven, sits like that all day: staring at the blinking
screen. Eats yogurt and milk.

You should go to the firms, I tell him. *Apply at the banks in
person.*

He takes no advice. He wants to not rush, make the right
choice. Something will come along. Something is pending. He
will wait.

He follows me out to the kitchen. I begin to unload the gro-
cery bags. He watches, doleful, leaning elbows on counter top.

Did the agency call you about the job? I ask.

His hands droop together, a pair of doves. *It was gone,* he
mutters.

Have you been out today? I query, as if his warden.

Guilty, suffering, he shakes his head. *Nope, been in all day.
My throat's bad again. I think it's my tonsils.*

I give him a chore: out of some convention, not need for his assistance. He sets the table, goes to the piano. Last autumn, he has informed me, he tried to commit suicide. Camus's Caligula is his hero. I protest, he becomes angry. He used to paint, wild confused canvases. Now he composes, plays hours at a time, dissonant, fortissimo, passionate hymns of himself.

Suffering over student papers, tomorrow's reading assignment, I cover my ears, tortured. Sometimes I demand silence. He feels abused.

He has a camera, worth $600, he says. He shows me self-portraits—profiles: solemn stares under thick brows, nude shots: the heavy upper body hairy from head to waist. *I may be an artist, someday,* he says.

Art has no value, he also insists. *Art is not worthwhile.*

He denies a contradiction, prefers absurdity.

Can I not send him away? What is it I owe him?

The piano is silent. The little vegetables are simmering in their pots, the pink steaks ready for the grill. I hear his steps sounding through the dining room, stopping at the kitchen door. I turn, wait.

Can I borrow some more money? he asks.

9.

THE RING of the phone rides through the steamy kitchen air. It is Laura. Her words choke with weeping.

Can I come to live with you? She gasps. *Just for a while? Three or four weeks?*

I hold the phone away from my ear. On the stove the small pots beat their lids. Are they exploding? Is that fire flaring in the oven? The light fixture: sending out small sparks?

Is the house burning? Is the whole bright place closing about me? What is happening? Who will send help?

Flights

ALICE ADAMS

ALICE ADAMS was born in Fredericksburg, Virginia, and grew up in
North Carolina. Her novel *Families and Survivors* was nominated for
the National Book Critics Award. Her new novel, *Listening to Billie,*
will be published by Knopf this year. This is her seventh appearance
in the O. Henry collection.

O H YES, Valerie will like it *very much*," said the ener-
getic young man with blue-black hair and a sharply
cleft chin, in an accent that was vaguely "English." He and Jacob
Eisenman were standing in the large shabby room that overlooked the crashing Pacific, on Kauai, one of Hawaii's outer-
most and least populated islands.

Jacob later thought that the implications of his tone were a
sort of introduction to Valerie, although at the time he had not
entirely understood what was being implied. Jacob, the gaunt
German who was (incongruously) the owner of this resort. Then
he simply wondered why, why *very much?* The young man's

Originally appeared as "Flying" in *The Paris Review.* Copyright © 1976 by
The Paris Review, Inc.

clothes were pale, Italian, expensive-looking; it was unlikely that
he (or Valerie) would be drawn by the price, which was what
drew most of the other guests: older people, rather flabby and
initially pale, from places like North Dakota and Idaho and,
curiously, Alaska—and a few young couples, wan, tired families
with children. These people stayed but were not enthusiastic;
they would have preferred a more *modern* place (Jacob was
subject to radar intuitions). And so this young man's eagerness
to register for the room and to pay in advance, which was unnecessary (with a hundred-dollar bill) made Jacob apprehensive, as
though he were being invaded—a sense that he dismissed as par-
anoia, to which he was also subject. But before he could sort out
reactions the young man had swung out of the driveway in his
orange rented Datsun, presumably to fetch Valerie from the
nearby hotel, which he had said they did not like. "So loud, you
know?"

In fact for no reason Jacob found his heart beating in jolts, so
that quite out of character he went to the bar, unlocked it and
poured himself a shot of brandy.

The bar, a narrow slat-roofed structure, was ten winding steps
up from the pool, between the rental units and Jacob's own
office-apartment library. Curiously, it was almost never used by
the Alaskan-North Dakotans, nor the young couples. Nor was the
neat functional built-in barbecue, which was adjacent. Most of
the units had kitchenettes, but still wouldn't they sometimes
want to cook outside? The barbecue was the last "improvement"
that Jacob had given to his resort. He had spent most of his
earlier years in California, going up from Los Angeles to International House, at Berkeley; he later concluded that he had been
misled by that background. Only Californians liked barbecues,
and no one from California seemed to come his way.

Except for a disastrous visit from his best friend, fat Otto from
I. House days, and Otto's new wife—a visit which Jacob had determined not to think about.

THE DATSUN rushed back into the parking area, and "Valerie"
got out. At first and somewhat distant glance, filtered through
the bougainvillea that hung about the bar, she was a delicately
built young blonde, in dazzling white clothes. Huge dark glasses
on a small face. An arrogant walk.

Jacob took a too-large swallow of the rough brandy, which made him cough. So that both people turned to see him there at the bar, at eleven in the morning. ("You aroused such false expectations," Valerie said, later on.)

The young man, registered as Larry Cobb, waved, and Valerie smiled indefinitely. And, a few minutes later, all the way from the room that he had rented them, Jacob heard a loud harsh voice that boomed, "But darling, it's absolutely perfect."

Could that voice have come from such a delicate girl? He supposed it must. Jacob pulled on the large straw hat he always wore—he detested the sun—and hurried away from the bar.

THE PRACTICAL, or surface reason for Jacob's presence in this unlikely setting was that he had inherited it from his parents. However, as Otto had pointed out more than once, he could have sold it when they died, when the place was still in good shape. Now he'd have to spend God knows how much to fix it up—assuming, as Otto did assume, that he wanted to sell.

The Eisenmans had fled Berlin in the early thirties, with their young son and a few remnants of their once-thriving rare-book business; following one of the terrible and familiarly circuitous routes of the time (theirs had included Hong Kong), they finally reached Los Angeles, where they set up shop again and were (finally) successful enough to send their brilliant son to Berkeley. Later they were persuaded to invest in and retire to a warm island resort. It worked out well. They loved Kauai, where the sun warmed their tired bones and all around them magnificent flowers, flowers hitherto associated with expensive florists, effortlessly bloomed. Birds of paradise. Anthurium. Poinsettias, and of course everywhere the violent colors of bougainvillea and hibiscus. They tended their property lovingly, and, a loving couple, they died peacefully within a week of each other. Jacob flew out to settle the estate and quixotically decided to stay. Well, why not? His Berkeley landlady could, and did, ship his books; besides, he was tired of graduate school, instructorships. And, as he wrote to Otto, "You know I have a horror of airplane flights. This way I avoid the return trip."

He promoted Mrs. Wong who had been his parents' housekeeper to the position of manageress; he then instructed her to hire some local girls to help with the cleaning up. He was aware

—his radar told him—that some of the local islanders imagined Mrs. Wong to be his mistress. He didn't mind, actually he liked her very much, but nothing could have been further from the truth.

Mrs. Wong was plain, round-faced, fat, and slovenly in her dress, and Jacob was sexually fastidious to the point of preferring celibacy to compromise. In fact in his entire life—he was almost fifty—he had had only three love affairs, and none of long duration; he was drawn to women who were violent, brilliant and intense, who were more than a little crazy. Crazy and extremely thin. "Basically I have a strong distaste for flesh," he had once confided to Otto.

"Which would explain your affection for myself," ponderous Otto had chuckled. "Pure masochism, of course."

Their kind of joke, in the good old lost days.

THE NEXT AFTERNOON, late.

"It was like labor pains," Valerie loudly and accusingly said; she was speaking of the waves that had knocked her to the sandy bottom of the ocean, and from which the young man, Larry, had grabbed her out. "When Quentin was born, they kept coming back."

She spoke furiously: Why? From behind the bar where Jacob was making their drinks (he had never done this before but the bar girl was sick and Mrs. Wong was somewhere else) he pondered her rage. At being a woman, forced painfully to bear children—blaming Larry for Quentin? No, they were not married. Larry was certainly not the father of Quentin, and she was not that silly. Rage at Larry for having rescued her? No.

She was simply enraged at the sea for having knocked her down. It was an elemental rage, like Ahab's, which Jacob could admire—that was how he felt about the sun.

In the vine-filtered sunlight he could see that Valerie was older than he had thought, was somewhere in her thirties. All across her face, over the small nose, slight rise of cheekbones, were tiny white tracings. Tiny scars. An exquisitely repaired face: Jacob did not want to imagine the accident involved but then he did: driving too fast (in a convertible, it would have to have been a convertible) north of Boston, she had gone through a windshield.

Her eyes were large and very dark—at first glance black, then perceived as an extraordinary midnight blue. Her voice was rasping, a whiskey voice, the accent crisply Bostonian. She was wearing something made of stiff white lace, through which a very small brown bikini was visible.

She gulped at her drink: straight gin, with a twist of lime. "God," she said. "I'm all scratched."

Larry asked her, "Does it hurt?"

"No, it just looks funny." She turned to Jacob. "You're so pale. Don't you go swimming at all?"

"No, I hate to swim."

She stared at him for an instant, and then seemed to understand a great deal at once; Jacob could literally feel her comprehension, which reached him like an affectionate hand.

She burst out laughing, a raucous exhilarated laugh. "But that's absolutely marvelous!" she cried out. "I absolutely love it! You also hate the sun—right?"

Jacob nodded. But at the same time that he felt touched he also felt some part of his privacy invaded, which made him uneasy. He had been recognized.

"You must have a marvelous time here," said Larry, attempting a joke.

"I read a lot."

Larry did not like him.

"I need another drink," said Valerie, who probably had noted this too.

An impulse made Jacob say what he had not said before, to guests. "Look, I'm not always around. But if you want a drink that's where the key is." And he pointed to a spot at the top of a beam.

This was said to Larry (to make Larry like him better?) but it was Valerie who smiled and said, "That's really nice of you."

"We'll keep track," was what Larry said (and finally forgot to do).

Jacob left as soon as he could. He had decided to start rereading *Moby Dick*.

VALERIE LIKED his shabby place because she was rich, accustomed to grandeur. She was the opposite of upward ascendant—

downward descendant? Was she that? Quite possible. Larry was somewhat younger than she—and rich in a different way: he had earned a lot of money, recently, in something fashionable. A record company? TV? He resented Valerie's carelessness, her easy lack of ambitions.

AHAB SAID, "They think me mad, Starbuck does; but I'm demonic, I am madness maddened! that wild madness that's only calm to comprehend itself . . ."

VALERIE HAD (probably) been married several times. Perhaps a husband has been with her when she smashed up the car? A now-dead husband?

AT ABOUT eleven the next morning when Jacob approached the bar, Valerie was perched on a high stool, her long thin brown legs drawn up childishly. She had made herself a tall drink. "Won't you join me?"

"I don't drink much—no thanks." Then, to her raised eyebrows he added, "Yesterday was out of character."

"You aroused such false expectations." But she let that go, and then asked, as though it were what they had been talking about for some time, "How do you feel about flying?"

"I hate it; that's one reason I'm here."

In an instant she had taken that in, and her riotous laugh broke out. "God, that's terrific." Then she said, "But what do you do about it?"

"Obviously: I don't fly."

"If I could only understand why I'm so afraid. Larry has driven off to Koloa," she added, irrelevantly. "You'd think I'd be afraid to drive." And she told him about her accident, the crashed convertible in which her second husband had been killed—the crash that in some sense he had already seen.

Jacob grasped then that they were communicating on levels that he could not understand at all, that even made him somewhat uncomfortable. He could so vividly see and feel whatever she told him—apparently, in fact, even before she spoke.

"I have some idiot faith that if I could understand it, I

wouldn't be afraid any more. Of flying," Valerie said. "I think that's what's called shrink-conditioning. I've even tried to 'associate' to the fear, and I do remember something weird: myself, in a white wicker carriage, a *baby* carriage—how could I remember *that*? Anyway my nurse is pushing it, a young Irish girl, Molly. And we're at the top of a hill in Magnolia, near the shore, and some older kids tell her to let it go. . . ."

But she might as well have stopped talking, because Jacob could see it: a stone-fenced New England landscape, wild roses. A pretty dark maid with a tweed coat pulled over a white uniform. "But she didn't let go," he gently said.

"Of course not. But what in hell does that have to do with being afraid to fly?"

LARRY ARRANGED to go deep-sea fishing, near Lihue. Valerie sat by the pool, in a white bikini, with a stack of books. Seeing her there from above, as he conferred with Mrs. Wong about the necessity for a second visit from the plumber, Jacob was aware that he could go down to her and pull up a chair, they could talk all day. But that prospect was too much for him; it made his heart race. Instead he went back to the dim seclusion of his library; he went from *Moby Dick* to Nerval, "Je suis le veuf, le ténébreux . . ." He went out into the sunlight.

He and Valerie had a brief conversation about Jane Austen, whom she was rereading. "I read her to regain some balance," said Valerie.

"You might try reading her on planes."

She gave him a long speculative look. "What a good idea."

Pretending busyness, Jacob went back to his office.

In fact all that day was punctuated with such brief conversations. Her non-demanding cool friendliness, her independence made this possible—it matched, or supplemented his vast diffidence.

SHE ASKED, "How is it up around Hanalei, the northern coast?"

"I don't know. I've never been there."

"God, you're absolutely marvelous."

"DO YOU THINK it's a fear that someone will throw you out of the sky? maybe God?"

"Alas, poor Icarus."

"Yes, that's sort of it. As though you shouldn't be up there, so high."

SOMETIME in the middle of the afternoon he found her at the bar with a drink.

"You know what I really like about this place?" she asked. "The whales. God, they're terrific, spouting out there."

"Yes." Her tan intensified the whiteness of her scars, making a sort of jigsaw of her face. Her eyes were dark and wild, and after a little while Jacob realized that she was drunk, or nearly so: like most people, he had trouble recognizing conditions foreign to himself. It had taken him a long time to see that Otto's wife, Joanne, was very stupid; at first he had thought her crazy, which was something he knew more about. In fact she was both.

He said, "A long time ago a woman came here who hated the whales, she was terrified of them."

"*Really?*" Valerie leaned forward, toward his face, so that he caught a whiff of exotic perfume. Of musk.

"It finally turned out that she had them confused with sharks, and thought they would swim in and bite her."

"*God.*"

"She was exceptionally stupid. My best friend's wife."

The first surprise had been Otto's extreme prosperity, as evinced by a casual mention of the purchase of several condominiums, on the peninsula south of San Francisco. "Well, I have to have them for tax shelters." In fact he had come to Hawaii to talk to a group of businessmen in Honolulu who were interested in some California coastal property. Not to see Jacob. The second surprise, probably not wholly unconnected with the first, was Joanne. Joanne from San Antonio, with her raven hair and milk-white skin, her rosebud mouth. (Otto's taste in women had never been original.) Big girlish breasts. A tiny well-focused mind. ("Oh, I just think you're so *smart* not to waste your money on paint and fixing things up—I mean, who'd care?" And, "Oh, I just love all these darling yellow-brown people, they don't look a bit like darkies.") Over her head Jacob had at first sought Otto's eyes, but Otto wasn't listening; in fact (Jacob remembered too late) he had never enjoyed talking or listening to women—he probably didn't hear a word she said. But Jacob heard it all, each abrasive idiocy, delivered in that nasal soprano. "Those are really whales out there? But how does anybody dare to go in swimming?"

One curious—in fact to Jacob incomprehensible—facet of Joanne's character was her imperviousness to coldness on another's part, to slights. Not that Jacob really slighted her, but surely his politeness came across coldly? Actually he couldn't stand her, and he found it hard to pretend otherwise. But she continued her bubbling smiles and winks (Christ, *winks!*) at him; on any pretext at all she stood so close that her glossy head touched his shoulder—she would introduce a sentence by touching his arm. Incredible! Jacob considered (and instantly dismissed) the insane possibility that she was sexually drawn to him, but, modesty aside, he found that unlikely. He had none of the qualities that would have drawn her to Otto, for example: he was not rich or ebullient or pleasure-loving (God knows, not that). Also he was bony, his dry skin deeply lined, whereas Otto was sleek and fat. No, he decided, she was simply behaving as she always did with men.

Such was his estimate of Joanne, and of their situation up to the final terrible night of which he would not think: the knock at his door (he had somehow known that it was Joanne, had frighteningly thought that Otto must be sick). But, "You can't imagine how sound your old friend sleeps," she had said, pushing past him in her frilly thigh-length gown, beneath which unleashed fat breasts bounced. "I thought we could have a tiny drinkie together," she said. "I just feel as though I hardly know you at all." Her young face shone with joyous self-adulation.

Jacob couldn't believe it, not then or later (now) remembering. How had he got rid of her? He had muttered something about a strep throat, clutching at his neck. An insane impulse that had worked: Joanne was terrified of germs.

Most men of course would not have sent her away, and so friendship dictated that Jacob inform Otto. "You are married to a submoron nymphomaniac. Even if you don't listen to her conversation. She is a bad person. She will do you harm." Of course the next day he said nothing of the sort, and for all Jacob knew Otto and Joanne were still what is known as "happily married." Otto rarely mentioned her in letters.

"ONE ENCOURAGING THING I recently read," said Valerie, beginning to slur a little, "is that if you fall from more than six thousand feet—or was it sixty thousand—you die of a heart attack before you hit the ground. If you call that encouraging."

"I suppose you could."

"Well, I do. Christ, I'm sleepy. I'm going in for a nap."

She walked off unsteadily, between the clamorously brilliant blooms. Jacob heard the slam of her screen door.

THAT NIGHT, as he restlessly re-began *The Wanderer* (he was slipping from book to book, a familiar bad sign) Jacob could hear them at the barbecue (its first use); in fact he could smell their steak. Valerie and Larry. Her rowdy laugh, his neat clipped voice.

Then it turned into a quarrel; Jacob caught the tone but not the words. Very quietly he got up and opened his door. Without a sound he went out, walking away from them through the dark until he could hear nothing at all. Down the small road, past all the oversized blooming plants he walked, toward the small arc of beach, the surfers' beach, now coldly gray-white in the dark. There he stood on the mound of black lava rock, regarding the shining waves, their wicked curl before breaking, until one huge wave—as large, he imagined, as a giant whale—crashed near his rock and drove him back and he started home. As he reached his door everything was still, no voices from the bar or anywhere. Only the surf.

HE DIDN'T SEE Valerie (or Larry) all the next day until late afternoon when together they approached the bar, where Jacob had been talking to his liquor supplier, Mr. Mederious; he needed to order more gin. Valerie and Larry were merry, friendly with each other, holding hands. Sand dried in their uncombed hair, his so dark, hers pale.

"We found the most fabulous beach . . ."

". . . absolutely private, no one there at all."

". . . really beautiful."

They had made love on the beach.

"I could stay here forever," said Valerie dreamily.

"Baby, some of us have to work," Larry said, with a kind of affection. But of course this was an issue between them. Also, Larry would have liked to marry her, and she didn't want to get married, having done it so often before.

Jacob knew everything.

RE-EMBARKED on his own Jane Austen, he found that at last he was able to concentrate. He spent the next few days with *Emma*, *Persuasion, Northanger Abbey*—pure delight, a shining impeccable world, like Mozart, or Flemish painting.

When next he saw Valerie, in still another bikini, she was even browner. She was beside the pool; Larry had gone fishing again. She looked clear-eyed, younger. And Jacob heard himself think (ridiculously): she should stay here, it agrees with her.

Beginning out of context (a way she had) she told Jacob, "When we were in Honolulu we saw the most amazing man on the sidewalk. Dressed in red-white-and-blue-striped clothes, with an Uncle Sam hat. And sandwich boards with really crazy things written on them. Peace signs that were labeled 'Chicken Tracks Of A Coward.' Something about abortion and murder. Really extraordinary—the superpatriot. I could not figure out what he was about."

Of course Jacob could see the man. Hunched over, lost.

"You know," she said, "I've got to get into some kind of work." Her harsh laugh. "I might even try to finish school. Last time around I got married instead."

"I think you should."

She laughed again. "God, Larry will die."

"He will?"

"He's not strong on intellectual women."

ONE NIGHT, as Jacob lay half asleep on his narrow hard bed (his monk's bed, as he thought of it) he heard what he imagined to be a knock on his door. At first he thought: Good Christ— Joanne? But of course Joanne was nowhere near, and then his heart leapt up as he reached for the ancient canvas trenchcoat that served him as a robe, and he went to open the door.

No one there. (But had there been?)

He stood still in the starry flowering night, listening for any sound.

Someone was at the bar, and he walked in that direction.

Valerie. And at the instant that he saw her he also saw and heard the orange Datsun start up and swing out of the driveway, into the sleeping night.

Valerie, in a tailored red silk robe, was applying ice cubes to one eye, the cubes neatly wrapped in a paper napkin—her gesture was practiced, expert. She said, "You catch me at a disadvantage. I seem to have walked into the proverbial door."

"Can I . . . ?" He was not sure what he had meant to offer.

"No, I'll be all right. Care for a drink?"

She had one already, something dark on ice.

Jacob poured himself a shot of brandy.

She said, "You know, it's too bad that children are brought up with so many globes for toys. They see the world as a small ball full of oceans, with those insecure patches of land."

She spoke with great intensity, her visible dark eye huge. She was not drunk but Jacob sensed that earlier she had been. He wanted to ask her if she had, in fact, knocked on his door, but he did not.

She said, "Tonight I was thinking about those old globes, and how these islands look on them, and I thought we might fall off into space. Do you think I'm going crazy?"

"No."

"God, I may never get back on a plane."

Jacob wanted to say, "Don't. Don't go anywhere, stay with me. Read all my books, and I'll send for more. Talk to me when you feel like talking. Stay."

Valerie stood up, stretching. She still kept the side of her face that by now must be swollen and discolored turned away. She said, "I think I can sleep now. See you in the morning."

In the morning he could say to her that she must stay.

Jacob went off to bed and while he was still reading (impossible then to sleep) he heard the Datsun return. Stop. Slam.

IN THE MORNING Valerie and Larry came to Jacob's office together, both dressed for travel—she in dark blue linen, huge glasses covering whatever had happened to her eye, Larry in pale gray.

They had simply and suddenly decided to leave. They felt that they had to get back. Larry's new TV show, "Quentin."

Jacob and Valerie shook hands (their only touch). Her hand was small and hard and strong, and she wore a lot of rings. "God, I'm absolutely terrified," she said, with a beautiful quick smile. "All those flights."

Jacob said, "You'll be all right," and he smiled too. Goodby.

But he was not at all sure of what he said. All that day he was terrified of her flights.

Autobiography of My Mother

JOANNA RUSS

JOANNA RUSS teaches creative writing and science fiction at the University of Colorado at Boulder. She has written several novels, among them *The Female Man* and *We Who Are About To,* which will be published this fall.

I'm an I.
Sometimes I'm a she.
Sometimes I'm even a he.
Sometimes I'm veryvery I.
Sometimes I'm my mother.

I WAS VISITING FRIENDS in Woodstock; you may find it surprising that I met my mother there for the first time. I certainly do. She was two years old. My mother and I live on different ends of a balance; thus it's not surprising to find that when I'm thirty-five she's just a little tot. She sat on the living room rug and stared at me, with her legs bent under her in a position impossible to anyone but a baby. Babies might be lobsters or some other strange form of life, considering what positions they take up. A little light tug at the ornamental tassel of my shoe—not apologetic or tentative, she feels both modest and confident, but she has small hands. "What's that?" she says.

"That's a tassel." She decamped and settled her attention on the other shoe. "And what's *that?*"

"Another tassel." This baby has flossy black hair, a pinched little chin, and round pale-green eyes. Even at the age of two her upper lip is distinctive: long, obstinate, almost a chimp's. I think she thinks that every object has its own proper name and so—without intending to—I made her commit her first error. She said: "That's *a tassel.* That's *another tassel.*" I nodded, bored. She's of the age at which they always take off their clothes; patiently, with her own understanding of what she likes and what's necessary to her, she took off all of hers: her little sailor dress, her patent leather shoes, her draggy black cotton stockings. It's only history that gave her these instead of a ruff and stomacher. She practiced talking in the corner of the living room for half an hour; then she came over to me, nude, without her underwear, and remarked:

"That's a tassel. That's another tassel."

"Uh-huh," I said. Pleased at having learned something, she pondered for a moment and then switched them around, declaring:

"That's *another tassel* and that's *a tassel.*"

"No, no," I said. "They're both tassels. This is a tassel and that's a tassel."

She backed away from me. I don't think she likes me now. Later that night I saw her scream with excitement when her father came home; he held the tail of her nightshirt in one hand and her brother's in the other; they both played the great game of trying to scramble away from him on all fours. My mother shrieked and laughed. Even at the age of two she's addicted to pleasure.

It'll ruin her.

You GET STUCK IN TIME, not when you're born exactly, but when you "sit up and take notice," as they say, when you become aware that you have an individuality and there's something out there that either likes you or doesn't like you. This happens at about eighteen months. It isn't that you really prefer some other time, you don't know anything about that; you just back off (still crawling, perhaps), not shaking your head (for you don't know about that, either) just wary and knowing you don't like *that staircase* or *those visitors* or *this parent*. But what can be done about it? You're stuck. It would be the same if you could travel through time but not through space.

Like this story.

AT A CHINESE RESTAURANT: that is, a big room with a high ceiling and dun walls, like a converted gymnasium. Sepia-colored screens in front of the Men's and Ladies'. There is a fan of crimson coral over my mother's head and the chairs are high-backed and plain, the ultimate in chic for 1925. My mother is nineteen. When I was that age I discovered her diary and some poems she had written; they didn't mention the restaurant but here she is anyway, having dinner with her best friend. I've looked everywhere in them to find any evidence that she was abnormal, but there's none. Nobody hugs anybody or says anything they shouldn't, and if there's any morbidity, that's gone too. My mother's written remains are perfect. At that time I wasn't born yet. I'm not even a ghost in her thought because she's not going to get married or even have children; she's going to be a famous poet. It was known then that you had to have children. It was a fact, like the Empire State Building I saw every morning out of the corner of my eye at breakfast (through the kitchen window). When you looked at childlessness in those days you didn't even realize that you had made a judgment, an inference from one set of conditions to another, you just *knew*.

I sat down imprudently at my mother's table.

Now I'm not as pretty as she is (I don't look a bit like her with my big behind and my buck teeth) but I'm much better dressed, and having been able to arrange my entry to suit myself, I can turn on to the full that bullying, leering, ironical boldness I adopt so easily with women; I place my well-cut suede coat, my smart gloves, my modernique pearl earrings and Dior scarf directly in the track of my mother's green, beautiful, puzzled, nearsighted eyes. My mother didn't want me to sit next to her—she wanted her friend to come back. Strangers alarm her. When my mother is not with a good friend her spirits flag, she becomes vague, she loses control of herself and stares around the room, not because she wants to look at things but because she's diffused and anxious; it's a way of not meeting anyone's eye. She ducks her head and mutters (mannerisms that won't look so cute at fifty-nine). I want to protect her. Years later I'll hold her elbow when she crosses the street, suffer with her when she can't breathe in a crowd, but this is before she's perfected any such tricks, so I can only bare my teeth at her in a way that makes her uncomfortable. She essays a smile.

"Do you come here often?" I say and she draws on her gloves; that is, she wanted to draw on her gloves, began to move her hands as if she would do so, then didn't. She looked guilty. Mother has been taught to be nice to everybody but she doesn't want to be nice to me. Last week she wrote a romantic love story about a girl whose mouth was like a slow flame. When I'm eleven I will get felt up on my rear end in a crowd and will be too ashamed to run away. It may occur to you that the context between us is sexual. I think it is parental.

"Would you care to step outside?" I said politely. Mother demurred. Sitting there—I mean us sitting there—well, you might have taken us for cousins. I picked up the check and she suffered because she didn't know what to do. Her friend, who will never get here in time, forms in my mother's memory a little bright door. I dropped two anachronistic quarters on the table-cloth and then put my French purse back in my navy-blue suede bag, an easy forty-five dollars which she has never seen, no, not even in dreams.

"Do you mind if we chat?" I said; "Shall we have coffee?" and went on to explain: that I was a stranger in town, that I was new here, that I was going to catch a train in a few hours, I told her that I was her daughter, that she was going to marry eventually and after two spontaneous abortions bear me, that I didn't usually ask for favors but this was different.

"Consider what you gain by not marrying," I said. We walked out onto Columbus Avenue. "All this can be yours." (Be the first one on your block; astonish your friends.) I told her that the most sacred female function was motherhood, that by her expression I knew that she knew it too, that nobody would dream of interfering with an already-accomplished pregnancy (and that she knew that) and that life was the greatest gift anybody could give, although only a woman could understand that or believe it. I said:

"And I want you to take it back."

WE WERE BOTH ELEVEN, on roller skates, skating towards Bronx Park with our braids flying behind us, but my mother was a little younger and a little slower, like my younger sister. I called her "Stupid."

IN THE FIRST PLACE I never borrowed it, in the second place it hasn't got a hole in it now, and in the third place it already had a hole in it when I borrowed it. I was going to show her all the kingdoms of the world. I wanted to protect my mother. Walking down Columbus Avenue in this expansive and generous mood— well, my mother didn't know what to make of me; like so many people she's puzzled by a woman who isn't beautiful, who doesn't make any pretense of being beautiful, and who yet flaunts herself. That's me. I asked my mother to tell me her daydreams, daydreams of meeting The Right Man, of being kept by an Older Woman, of inheriting money. Money means blood in dreams and blood means money. The autumn foliage in the park, for example, because the sun hadn't quite set. My mother was wearing a shapeless brown cloth coat that concealed her figure. It's very odd to think that this is 1921. Overheard: I thought it would be different.

I told my mother that when women first meet they dislike each other (because it's expected of them) but that's all right; that soon gives way to a feeling of mutual weakness and worthlessness and the feeling of being one species leads in turn to plotting, scheming, and shared conspiracies. I said that if we were going to be mother and daughter we ought to get to know each other. As we walked on the stone-flagged park paths my

mother's soul flew out from under my fingers at every turn, to
every man who passed, a terrible yearning, an awful lack, a
down-on-your-knees appeal to anybody in the passing scene. She
didn't like my company at all.

"Do you know what I want you to do?" I said. "Well, do you?"

"Well, do you?" my mother echoed earnestly, looking up at me
with her nymph's green eyes.

"Look here—" I said.

("Look here—")

I suppose you expect me to say that I listened to her artlessly
simple chatter, that I confided in her, or that next she will be a
big girl and I the little one, but if you expect me to risk her
being older than me, you're crazy. I remember what that was
like from last time. I told her all of it—the blood, the sweat, the
nastiness, the invasion of personality, the utter indecency (except in middle age, except with money) and she only looked up
at me as if she knew things, that girl. She didn't like me. The pal-
isade looking out over the river. The mild October air. We stood
arm in arm, like chums, watching the wakes of the boats in the
water. She said I couldn't understand. She said with complete
conviction:

"You were never young."

MY MOTHER, a matron of fifty but for some reason shrunk to the
size of an infant and wrapped in baby clothes, is lying in her cradle. Swaddled, her arms at her sides, furious. Frowning—this is
no way to treat a grown woman! She is about to wawl. I could
leave her there and she'd die—dirty herself, starve, become mute
and apathetic—she's just a baby. Maternally I take into my arms
my fifty-year-old mother because you can't leave a baby, can
you? and cradling her tenderly to my breast I start dancing
around the room. She hates it. Screaming and red-faced. Maybe
she wants a different dance. I change into a waltz, rocking her
softly, and right away, my goodness, the little baby is rocked
into quiet, she's straightening her corrugated little brows,
unwrapping the snaky moist curls that come finely from under
her cap, smoothing her sulky little mouth. I guess she likes waltzing. If I didn't take care of her, how would she ever grow up to
be my mother? It would be infanti-suicide, to say the least (if

not something worse). When she stops crying I'll put her back into the cradle and sneak off, but there is command in that steely little face, those snapping little eyes, she stares up at me like a snapping turtle making plans, telling me with her expression all the terrible things she's going to do to me when I'm the baby and she's the mother and I know she did them because I was there. *You keep on rocking me!* she says.

So we keep on waltzing around the room.

WHEN I WAS a child—
  a child—
  When I was a chidden child—
  I came into my right mind at a certain age, I think I inherited it, so to speak, although they didn't allow me to use it until I was already fairly cracked. Coming home from the dentist at sixteen on winter evenings with the sky hot-pink and amber in the west and the wind going right through your coat; it's discouraging to find automata in the living room. Cars shooting by to cheery dinners, homey lights from the windows above the stoop. Mirages. Inside, a steamy kitchen, something horrible like an abstract sort of Frankenstein's monster made up of old furniture, plates, windows misted over. My mother, who is with us tonight, is also sixteen, and going this time under the name of Harriet (I think) which is a false name and no kin to the beautiful, imaginary playmate I had when I was four, who could fly and would write me letters with hand-painted stamps on them (canceled). After coming all the way in the cold, to be in a room with no living persons in it. To be distressed. To feel superior. To hold myself in good and hard, to know what's possible and what's good for me. Little Harriet Shelley watches wide-eyed the intercourse of a real human family.

AUNT LUCY: No one would tell you the truth about yourself, Harriet, unless they loved you very much. I love you and that's why you can trust me when I tell you the truth about yourself. The truth is that you are bad all through. There isn't a thing about you that's good. You are thoroughly unlovable. And only a person who loves you very much could tell you this.

UNCLE GEORGE: Tell me all your troubles, but don't say a word against your aunt. Your aunt is a saint.

MY MOTHER SITS listening to the radio, learning how to sew. She's making a patchwork quilt. Does she dislike her family? She denies it. She's not really going to grow up to be a poet. My mother has a mind like a bog; contraries meet in it and everything becomes instantly rotted away. Or her mind is a peat bog that preserves whole corpses. The truth is that I haven't the right to say what's going on in her mind because I know nothing about it.

She goes on sewing, gentle, placid, and serene, everything she should be. I told her that she could have any color car she wanted as long as it was black but even this failed to shake my soundless mother; One's Personal History Is Bunk, she might have answered me but didn't; she didn't even move away down the couch because my mother is not even mildly stubborn. Perhaps if she were not so polite she would say, "I don't know what you're talking about," but no, she's perfect, and when she raises her great, wondering, credulous, tear-filled gaze, it's not for me but on account of bad Mr. X in the kitchen, who is telling stories to Uncle George about the women who have jobs with him, for example, that their asses stick out:

MR. X: ---- ---- ----- ------ ----- ass.

UNCLE GEORGE: Mr. X is only joking, dear.

MR. X: That's right. Don't be so sensitive. How can you go out and get a job someday if you're so sensitive? I don't have anything against the ladies who work with me. I think they're fine. I think you're fine, even though you're so sensitive.

AUNT LUCY: See? Mr. X thinks you're fine.

MR. X: I think your aunt is fine, too.

UNCLE GEORGE: He thinks your aunt is fine, too, because he *likes* ladies.

AUNT LUCY: See? Mr. X is generous.

UNCLE GEORGE: Even though your aunt Lucy is a fool.

To cut out those noises people emit from time to time. To be hard and old. To retreat finally. To be free.

"My parents love each other," says my mother, shaking out her work, malignancy in its every fold. She's a wonder. She really believes. I used to think I knew the form of the ultimate relation between my mother and myself but now I'm not so sure; there's

that unbreakable steel spring in her accepting head, no longer
can I come clattering up the King's highway on my centaur/cen-
turion's hindquarters (half Irish hunter, half plough horse, gray,
fat, lazy, name: Mr. Ed) and I no longer look down from my
wild, crazy, hero-assassin's eminence at the innkeeper's little
daughter in her chaste yet svelte gingham (with its décolletage)
and her beautiful, spiritual, dumb eyes and her crumby soul.

"Do you," I said, "do you—tell me!—oh do you—believe me!
—*do you*—DO YOU—BELIEVE ALL THAT?"

"Yes," she says.

Oh if you only knew! says her face. Her hands, resting on their
sewing, change their import: Life is so hard, hard, hard. An
unspoken rule between us has been that I can hate her but she
can't hate me; this breaks. (A day in the longed-for life: for once
when my mother is carried across the crumbling battlements on
the screen the audience laughs, they hoot when she wrings her
hands, when she obeys her father's prohibition they howl, when
she is seduced they screech, when it starts to snow and the hero
walks on her face with his lovely black boots it's all over, and by
the time she commits suicide, *there is nobody there*.)

"I think," says my mother thoughtfully, biting a thread, "that
I'm going to get married." She looks at me, shrewdly and with
considerable hatred.

"*That way*," she says in a low, controlled voice, "*I will be able
to get away from you!*"

(When she was little my mother used to scare her relatives by
asking them if they were happy; they would always answer, "*Of
course* I'm happy." When I was little I once asked her if she was
happy and she said "Of course I'm happy.")

SOMETHING that will never happen: my mother and I, chums,
sharing secrets, giggling at the dinner table, writing in each
other's slambooks, going to the movies together. Doing up each
other's hair. It's not dreadful that she doesn't want me, just embarrassing, considering that I made the proposal first. She would
beam, saying sentimental things about her motherhood, anxiously reaching for my hand across the table. She was not
wicked, ever, or cruel, or unkind. We'll never go skating together, never make cocoa in the kitchen at midnight, snurfing in

our cups and whooping it up behind the stove. I was never eight.
I was never eleven. I was never thirteen. The mind I am in now
came to me some time after puberty, not the initiation into sex
(which is supposed to be the important thing) but the understanding that everything I had suffered from as a child, all my
queerness, all my neuroses, the awful stiffnesses, the things people scorned in me, that all these would be all right when I was
an adult because when I was an adult I would have power.

And I do. I do.

Power gave me life. I like it. Here's something else I like:
when I was twenty-nine and my mother—flustered and in-
genuous—told me that she'd had an embarrassing dream about
me. Did she expect to be hit? It was embarrassing (she said) because it was incestuous. She dreamed we had eloped and were
making love.

Don't laugh. I told it for years against her. I said all sorts of
awful things. But what matters still matters, i.e. my mother's
kicking a wastebasket the length of the living room in a rage (as
she once bragged to me she did) or striking her breast, crying
melodramatically, "Me Martian! Me good! You Jupiterian! You
bad!" (as she also did). Bless you! do you think she married to
get away from me, the Lesbian love-object? I wasn't born yet.

It's immensely sweet of her to offer to marry me, but what I
want to know is: do you think we're suited?

Don José, the Brazilian heiress—wait a minute, I'm getting them
muddled up, that was the other one where I was the Brazilian
heiress, this one's Don José and he's *Argentinian* and an *Heir*—
anyway, his cruel smile undressed her with his eyes, I don't think
I can go on writing like this, she said. Are you not woman
enough to know? And the unfortunate sadist tossed his typewriter out the window. That is what they called working girls in
those days. My mother will never forgive me. For what? cried
the incautious maid with the almond-blue eyes. Thank you, sir, I
shall make the bed, she sobbed. Only do not lay me in it; that
will crease the counterpane and I will be fired. And your children, his mustache twitching, I have sworn to have them, have
me first, no, have a shashlik; there is blood on my dress.

Blood!

I have murdered the butler.

(A lively game of bed-to-bed trash filled the evening air as the charming little summer-camp maedchen disemboweled the myth and passed it gigglingly from hand to hand. Salugi! Gesundheit. Thank you very much.)

What Every Woman Knows.

It is quite possible that none of this happened or has value; still I wish life could have been different for my mother. But we're all in Tiamat's lap, so there's no use complaining. In the daytime we stand on Her knees, looking up at Her face, and at night She hides Her face so we get uneasy. Our Father Witch (in whom I used to believe) is very jealous of his name or it's a secret or it's too ugly (or maybe he hasn't got any) but you can call Her Nyame and Tanit, call Her 'Anat, Atea, Tabiti, Tibirra. over the place and She doesn't mind kiddies pulling at Her skirt; call her Nyame and Tanit, call Her 'Anat, Atea, Tabiti, Tibirra. This is what comes of re-meeting one's mother when she was only two—how willful she was! how charming, and how strong. I wish she had not grown up to be a doormat, but all the same what a blessing it is not to have been made by somebody's hands like a piece of clay, and then he breathed a spirit in you, etc. so you are clay and not-clay, your ingredients fighting each other like the irritable vitamin pill in the ad—what a joy and a pleasure to have been born, just ordinary born, you know, out of dirt and flesh, all of one piece and of the same stuff She is. To be my mother's child. (Your pleasures and pains are your bellybutton-cord to the Great Mother; they prove you were once part of Her.)

I asked, Why couldn't my mother have been more like You? But She didn't answer. I felt something coming from Her. Times She doesn't like me—I don't always like myself—but we're still the same stuff.

Change my life! I said.

Sorry, won't. Her fog veiled Her face (that is one of Her moods) and Her towns (which are the rings on Her fingers) grew ugly. Tiamat is talking. She spoke through me as in the Bible, that is I spoke, knowing the answer:

Am I my mother's mother?

ON WINTER NIGHTS, when my mother and I were twelve, we
would go out together with chocolate cigarettes and pose under
street lights like little prostitutes, pretending that we were smoking. It was very glamorous. Now we do it in our cheap dresses,
our tight shoes; my mother has waited for The Man all her life,
that's why she had no time for me. In the beauty parlor, on the
street, in the nursing home, waiting for The Man. We lean on
each other, very tired, in our make-up, a sad friendship between
us. We even hold hands.

Will you be my best friend? she says.

I say yes.

Will you live with me?

I say yes.

Will you sleep with me and wake with me?"

I say yes.

Will you marry me?

I say yes.

ALL YOU NEED IS LOVE.

How's Your Vacuum
Cleaner Working?

EMILY ARNOLD McCULLY

EMILY ARNOLD McCULLY was born in 1939 in Galesburg, Illinois.
She has illustrated fifty books for children and has received citations
for excellence from the Children's Book Council and the American
Library Association. She has two sons and lives in New York City. This
is her first published story.

S HE SITS at the kitchen table, scrawling a note with the
stub of a pencil found, finally, on a windowsill under
cobwebs that link potted geraniums to the glass. A stray Vitamin
E capsule rolls away from her elbow.

Her handwriting is an awkward, uneven effort, forming
stanzas that slant down the page, as if the ruled lines of the legal
pad were insufficient to support their weight. This writing is
gauche, in both senses: she is left-handed, and the product so
clumsy as to appear childish, except for the speed with which
she proceeds. The page is quickly filled.

She is writing her last note, in the style of many composed and stored, over the years, in a box. This one is addressed to her friend Miriam, but it will not be delivered. The pretense is necessary for her to order, even to examine, her thoughts. She does not write to her husband although it would be traditional and certainly considerate to do so. She plans to leave a set of instructions, however, regarding the children, the dinner she has planned, even partially prepared, the whereabouts (if she can find it) of the pink slip required to get her winter coat from the cleaners (and to whom the coat might be passed on). Her husband's incisive mind, sharpened in courtrooms and libraries and conference rooms, has long made her feel small and futile in company, where his words are attended and she is frequently ignored or interrupted. But she doesn't trust him to handle these matters alone because she knows he finds them trivial and is unpracticed in domestic management.

"Dearest Miriam," she has written. "James said last night that he sympathized but disagreed with my attitude. Disagreed. In his overbearing tone. I am so tired of this that the thought of not seeing the children again doesn't dismay me so. It's the only way I can avoid seeing James, so certain he can take care of me, so suffocating with what remains of his love. Oh, I have thought of this before, in states of high emotion, but when it comes to mind, mid-morning, cold-sober, it seems a soothing inevitability: I will kill myself."

There have been dreams, lately, billowing, airborne, inflated sighs of dreams, in which she gives up the struggle and submits, thoroughly, deliciously, to something that feels like love used to but seems not to involve another person, unless it is possibly a woman, more mother than lover—a bosomy expression of pure approval.

Death seems, this morning, to offer some of that: fear of dying has been the pit of her existence—she imagines a peach pit, the flesh around it ripening prematurely and invisibly until it rots before the surface has reddened. Perhaps an embrace of her enemy, without its predictable dialectic (symptoms, suffering, treatment, suffering, interment) will bring the same easeful release from combat her dreams suggest.

There will be no one for lunch. James is at his office in the city and the children stay late at school. She selects one of the juice glasses by the sink, shakes a drop or two out, and fills it with vodka. A few sips suggest further observations she might make to Miriam, but more urgently they arouse her appetite. With the children gone, there is no reason she can't have an outrageously self-indulgent last meal, composed of ingredients she has forbidden them in her zeal to nurture their lives while her own withers. Today it's not too much trouble carefully to slice a half dozen potatoes, for example, just for herself, to fry them in fat, make a monstrous sandwich of bits of various moldy cheeses, tomato from the garden, her homemade mayonnaise (what a waste that is), some leftover chicken . . . a pickle. While she works she reviews her note:

"I never could relate well to girls, yet here I am, writing my last note to a woman, as if it were the only way I could give my gesture significance. Intercourse with James is collaboration with the enemy. I feel fragile as glass, the victim of masculine good health that threatens to sliver my flesh, crack my spirit. Nowhere the sweet descent into mutuality I experience in my dreams. How I do long for a sacrifice, the twin to mine."

Potatoes sizzle in the pan; her nerves are mildly anaesthetized. Orchestrating this little banquet, selfishly designed, and therefore totally absorbing, she doesn't notice the arrival of a car in the drive. The sun has burned off an early fog, and this vehicle—finned, exhausted, chromed, puced, and unmuffled—gleams evilly in the bright light. As an apparition, it might inspire her to reflect on her sexual awakening in the fifties, but it is real; someone has descended and now knocks loudly at the door.

Caught in the act! Implicit in the preparations had been plans to obliterate all traces of the orgy before her body was discovered. On second thought, though, it is the interruption she resents. Everything is just ready to eat, and much of it can't wait —for instance this quart of French fries, already going limp on their towel.

But someone has come to her—an enormous challenge—and it won't do to depart life with a final failure to confront her fellow man. Her husband's authority and enthusiasm for commingling have made her hesitant and defensive, so today she will make the supreme effort: be charming.

Lately, she has spent some time before the mirror, lamenting the changes in her face, the fatigue and lack of spirit stamped there; but now a quick check in the smoky glass hung near the ill-lit doorway is reassuring. She opens the door.

A young man stands on the step below her, his hair wetly combed back, generous sideburns flanking a lean, uncertain expression. She looks at him, breathless with the effort it took to expose herself, swaying slightly in the aftermath of confrontation. For her, anything that follows will be anticlimax.

He asks, in an artificial tone, "Do you need any vacuum cleaner bags?"

She doesn't know the answer to that one. He waits, longer than he'd planned to, and then, to fill the silence, recaptures a rehearsed rhythm, "Always smart to keep extras in the house."

"Well, yes, I suppose so. I'm not sure I have any money." This is all very strange. She is suspicious. Can he be genuine? He produces his next line:

"Well, how's your vacuum cleaner working? I could look it over for you. I could test your machine, if you have a minute."

This seems practical, and she doesn't feel compromised by the suggestion. "OK, have a look." But, to be businesslike, to demonstrate that he can't take her for a fool, she adds, "The motor sounds sluggish. It doesn't purr to a stop, you know? And it drags on, so. I think it must be the fan belt; it doesn't perform at all the way it used to. And the suction has been affected. Not strong any more."

The young man sets a foot on the doorsill and she backs into the entry, but he hesitates and says, "Do you mind if my partner comes in? I'm kinda new at this . . ."

Well, he looks feckless enough, taking into account up-to-date styles in that department. Bring him in then. Do the job right. While this message is carried to the huge sedan, she scurries to the kitchen, wets her whistle.

There is a scuffling at the door while the young man and his much older colleague enter and she attempts to welcome them in the confined space without giving ground. They manage to approach the kitchen, which smells of burnt fat and potatoes, and harbors, she remembers, a most intimate document, not to mention the vodka bottle. It's inadvisable to leave them there, so she beckons them into the living room and goes to locate the vacuum cleaner. The young man now defers altogether to his partner, a pink and pleasant fellow in a flawlessly ironed short-sleeved shirt, with thinning gray hair and a sincere manner she can't help aping a little. When she hauls the machine up to them, this senior adviser grabs it and begins his routine.

The pair comes, it seems, from a local repair/distributorship and the older one is training his successor. From all appearances, they are on their maiden run. With a certain respect she respects, the dad examines the vacuum, observes that it is fifteen years old, and, as if to read her mind, explains that he can spot all models—he's worked for the company since 1939. Ah, she nearly cries—the year I was born. And this, the day I am to— Well.

She does feel jolly, though, and alert to coincidence. The machine he's peering at belonged once to a deceased, though conscientious mother, had been rebuilt and well maintained until it fell into her own hands. Fitting it is that now, when it fails, such a *médecin* appears to handle the case.

"The fan belt (AHA!) is slackening here. Not giving you the suction you need."

He speaks calmly, melodically, and she finds herself, the obedient flower, bending to the sound. Turning gallantly to her on his knees, he says, "You're not getting the efficiency you deserve from this machine. It's an old one, and they made them right in those days, but . . . Let's test this out, and I'll show you what I mean. Do you have the chromium balls?"

Assistant dives into gear for same. As he hands the gleaming things to his boss, he glances at her, and she sees his teeth for an instant, gleaming too.

"Now, watch." And suddenly, here is the music man, an early W. C. Fields on the road, can't stoop too low nor rise too high to make his point. Can these guys be *real?* He pours the balls into a translucent tube and applies the vacuum nozzle to its mouth. One ball makes a feeble leap upward, but the others lie low. For her it is a shocking demonstration of frailty, of deterioration nobly endured. She is moved, her earlier glib diagnosis notwithstanding. It brings to mind the Oriental rugs she also inherited. (What a burden this second-hand life is.) She hasn't paid much attention to them, having relied, of course, on the old gray mare of a vacuum cleaner to keep them tidy.

"You see?" he asks the younger man (for he is a teacher, after all, not a shill). "This is operating at something less than one-third capacity." The young man rocks back on what she notices are platform shoes, high-heeled beneath flared trousers. There is a sulky style here, and he is unimpressed by the ball trick.

The older man turns to her: "We can talk a bit about the attachments that will make it perform even better after it's been overhauled. You'll be patient with us, I hope. I'm showing my young friend here the ropes. You've lived here less than a year, haven't you? I thought so. I came around last year just about this time. Always took care of their machine."

Well, that's a relief! The suspicion had lingered that this was an elaborate con operation, but the old guy seems genuine now and committed to a certain faded excellence besides. He patiently explains the workings of the motor to his sidekick, but so simplistically she has trouble believing either of them knows more about it than she does. The boss observes that this suction problem may have escaped her attention because she had grown accustomed to it. She glances to the carpet to see if he has found a turd there, or something that she failed, in her mooning adjustments, to suck up. But he is nice. He is nice to pretend it isn't entirely her fault the house is less than clean. She warms to him.

Yet, the buck has been passed. Time to muster a little skepticism. So she says, "We have Oriental rugs, and I worry sometimes that a tube model doesn't clean them thoroughly. Isn't it true that an upright is recommended?"

He says nothing for a moment but gives her an almost conspiratorial smile. "We've anticipated your needs, missus. Of course the lady of the house doesn't want to vacuum her rugs without being sure they're really clean after all that work. Just like she doesn't want to launder the clothes if they're going to come out gray. What's the use, I want to know?" She nods seriously at him. "Your rugs are valuable. They need the best care you can give them. And we have just the machine. Get the 20040." The young man exits. "We'll do a simple little demonstration, if you have ten minutes. You have ten minutes?" She nods again. "I'll give your rugs a real cleaning. You can make up your own mind.

I'm not pressuring you at all. You see for yourself. This is the machine designed for the job."

It seems a good bet. She assents. But really, his tricks have become more than vaudevillian. After gathering up the chromium balls, he actually produces a bag of dirt and strews it on the floor. The subordinate re-enters and is directed to unpack the wonder machine; the boss is an artist working up to his act. He chats with her, a critical eye on the young man's labored progress with the box. He seems quite unable to manage the staples, the glue, and the cardboard at all. Testy, he rejects offers of assistance. Finally the machine is unboxed and hefted in the direction of the dirt. She regards it with relief, after a detour, meanwhile, to the kitchen and her glass.

"Well!" she says, and they both look at her.

Work is resumed: the old man assembles the deluxe model and they bend to their task. It is apparent—she is getting sleepy —that this will take longer than ten minutes. The thing is ready to go. They've gone to a lot of trouble for her so she sits on the couch, clasps her hands about her knees, and attends.

"Now, then," he says, "You'll observe that the suction is far stronger than it is on your model. The optional attachment alone could improve your old machine once it's fixed up." He turns it on and glops up the sand and dirt. He empties the dirt bag into a sack. She is beginning to feel vaguely disoriented, as if she were in someone else's house.

"Now, I want to show you what's still in your rugs, ma'am. When did you last vacuum them, recently? Good. So, the dirt bag is empty now, and I'll just give this rug a once-over . . ." Wh-r-r-r.

He empties the bag again onto a sheet of newspaper, and sure enough, it was full of unrecognizable grit—an indictment of herself and her old machine. The master addresses himself to his apprentice:

"You see? There's a dramatic illustration of what this 20040 can do. It tells the story at a glance. You don't want to bother a customer with a lot of detail. No hard sell, you know what I mean?" And, to her, "Am I right?" To underscore his point, he begins to gather up the equipment. He asks her to save the dirt on the newspaper and show it to her husband—that's all—he'll be convinced.

Unable to endure the getaway preparations, she returns to the kitchen and stands, leaning against the sink, holding the last finger of vodka, and gazing out the window at the big old car. She switches off her brain and rests. Boy, does she need a rest.

A voice just behind her says, "Man, that's some number he does, isn't it?"

She whirls, spilling most of her drink.

"Sorry. Say, I didn't mean to scare you. Just thought I'd come on in and chat for a minute." He gestures to her glass. "You want to spread that around a little? Sure could use a shot of something after tooling around all morning with him." He grins. "Pre-historic, you know what I mean?"

"I'm not sure I should . . ."

"Aw, come on. Be friendly. It won't hurt you. You know," and he leans against the counter, eyes narrowed, "I've been watching you very closely. You didn't know that, did you? I have a way of doing that, and people don't know it. I think you and I have a lot in common."

Amused, now, she takes another glass, rinses it this time, and pours him a shot. He accepts it with a deliberately intimate air, an air of communion.

"Hey," he bursts, post-swallow, "you don't think I'm just some vacuum cleaner salesman, do you?"

"Well, I really hadn't give any thought . . ."

"Well, if you *did* think about it, you'd guess right away what I really am. But I'm going to tell you." He pauses, sips, looks hard at her. "I sing. I'm a rock singer. I'm just doing this for the bread, until my buddy and I can start a group. We're going to call it *The Energy Crisis*. Far out, huh? Don't you love it?" He leans toward her and she nods her head.

"My friend thought it up."

The front door opens and they both turn to look out the window at the old man lugging his boxed 20040 and her vacuum cleaner to the car.

"Listen," says the young man, very near, close to her ear, "I really like you. I can talk to you, you know? Are you free tonight?"

She laughs, too startled to reply for a moment. A crisp,

sweetish odor blossoms between them. It triggers an abrupt, sensory recollection she cannot translate—not pot, no. Chewing gum, it must be. Breath freshener for the salesman, release for the youth. She discourages her children from chewing and abstains herself. But back in the days when dental bills were the last thing either of them thought of, the swagger of a boy rhythmically elevating the tension between them by pressing a piece of gum between his teeth was as memorable as the kiss that followed, as the first feel.

In the pause the young man smooths his hair—it's not quite as fifties hair-do as she'd thought at first, but there's blind nod to nostalgia that endears him and is even vaguely stirring.

He says, "I mean, I don't want to make you do something you don't want to." And brightens: "But, you know, sometimes people don't know what they really want, and it takes someone else to tell them." When she remains silent, he frowns, glancing about the room as if to seek escape. "Is it me? Is it something about me you don't like? Look, a lotta women . . ."

"No. No. Surely you understand . . ." She finds herself actually putting a hand on his sleeve, soothingly. How old must he be?

"Well then. You'll be here tonight?"

"Look, I couldn't possibly—I have a husband. I'll be home with him tonight."

"Get rid of him. You won't regret it. Listen," he lowers his voice still further, whispers through a slick smile. "I'll bet your old man isn't as hot in the sack as he used to be, is he? You'll think of something. You'll get rid of him." He looks back over his shoulder, then presses his face close to hers. "You need it. I can tell."

The door opened and he says, loudly, "Well then, ma'am, I'll be in touch with you . . . about your vacuum cleaner. I think you can have confidence in our workmanship. We're specialists, if you know what I mean."

The boss appears in the doorway, anxious to get a move on. "It's been a pleasure, missus. I'm sure my young friend here will look after you very well." His young friend winks covertly and they go out of the door, settle into the huge sedan. They drive off in a puff of smoke.

She sits for a while at the kitchen table, trying to recapture something of what had been in the air before they came. It's no good, though; she's been defeated, become somnolent, irresolute. The potatoes are tossed into a paper sack, along with her note, which proves more absorbent than absorbing, and she lies down in the living room for a nap.

THE TELEPHONE RINGS. Feeling thick, uncertain, and guilty, she answers.

"Hello?"

"Hi, dear." Oh, the self-assurance in his voice. *He* knows who's going to answer. "How are you doing?" She has encouraged clinical concern and decides not to counterfeit a response, even though today hasn't been half-bad so far, has in fact been unusually lively.

"As usual. I was asleep. I felt depressed."

Irresistible is his need to possess the flawed her. "Well, try to do something." His impatience shows: "Get out of the house, call someone . . . call Miriam . . . go for a walk . . . weed the garden."

"I did, the day before yesterday."

"Well, go get out your bicycle. Don't you like it?" A recent birthday gift, she does like it very much for its associations with flight, gaiety, abandon, and honest effort. But the roads nearby are without interest after all the monotonous automobile rides she has taken over them on unvarying errands. She has discovered, from the more intimate vantage point of the bicycle seat, that weeds grow alongside them, and they bore her too.

"I'll take a ride," she concedes flatly.

"Good, good." Cheerful now, he gets to the point. "Look, I've got a meeting in ten minutes and I can leave as soon as it's over. I'll pick up the boys on the way home." There is a pause. "Let's have a nice evening. Let's relax. What's for dinner?"

Christ, what a question. Doesn't he think about anything else? Doesn't she, for that matter?

"I'll do something nice. I have to hang up."

"OK, I'll see—" but she does hang up, exhausted by resentments it's too troublesome to acknowledge. She sinks to the couch, pulls a pillow to her breast, grips it hard, slowly relaxes, is asleep.

CHILDREN APPROACH. They belong to her, in a way. They are hers. The day has come to that, already. Her brain harbors a kernel of heavy, insistent pain, but she struggles awake.

"Michael, wipe your feet. Where have you been?"

"A-h-h-h-." Michael crumples, gets the staggers, indicates he is too tired to take direction.

"Please don't wreck dinner because you're exhausted, Mike. I want you to rest for a while."

It is generous of him to signal his mother that he is out of control, but she has absorbed too much and, like a saturated sponge, begins to ooze when pressed.

"Motherrrr. I'm not tired, I wanna watch TV."

"No."

"Why not?"

"Because you watch it too much." Clever.

"I don't watch it enough." Apt pupil.

"Don't be a smart aleck. Leave me alone for a while, at least. I have to think about getting some food down you that won't be rejected, like everything else. Go rest, and no more argument." Tyrant, bully. Her vacancies fill with the power she has over these children.

But Michael ignores her and crouches to tie his shoelaces, throwing grown-up curses into the air when they unravel. Both boys give up too easily, a trait she credits to her own genes. On the other hand, she identifies warmly with the impulse that led him to try something new when he felt inadequate.

"I repeat: Rest, before dinner, in your rooms!" Timmy grabs a hunk of his irritable brother's hair. They both scream and run noisily off to the kitchen, discover cold potatoes in a sack. By the time she arrives, they have fought over them and spilled the lot about the room.

They are all raging when James saunters in. Carefully avoiding the collaborative effort that is their only hope at this hour, she declines to greet him. But her final command to the boys, as futile as any of them are, is directed as much at him:

"Out of the kitchen! Out, out!"

He hears it and herds them away.

"Mommy, Mommy," Michael shouts over the din. She turns to him with a sigh. "Oh, God, Michael, what *is* it?"

He pauses and grins at her, his mouth and his eyes helpless.

"I forget."

JAMES RETURNS, picks up the newspaper from the floor and asks, "Would you like a drink?"

She drinks alone. "No, thank you."

He makes one for himself and disappears. She wants to cry, she feels so messed up.

Presently, Michael trots in and says, "Mommy, I made a picture of you in school today but I forgot it. It was of an ambulance. I'm hungry. Give me something to eat."

"Please," she adds absently. Timmy runs in and cries, "I wanna, I wanna." James comes back, opens the cupboard, and gives them each a cracker.

"James," she spits at him, "Why did you do that? It's dinnertime."

"Which do you want? That racket, or peace and quiet? Relax," he says back sternly. "Don't worry about it."

"I've worked so hard, trying to plan meals, to give them the best foods I can and teach them to value them. Nutrition matters a lot to me. Why in hell do you have to come along and sabotage it?"

"I don't sabotage anything, sweetheart. I just think you overdo it. It turns them against what you do. You're the saboteur." Sweet reason.

"I thought I just heard *you* doing it. Without my help."

"Why is this so important to you?"

"Should I feel foolish? Should I feel that making the most of my limited opportunities, of trying to nurture where I can when I'm so handicapped is somehow bad? And besides, it *does* matter what they eat. We're surrounded by poisons."

"Oh, hell. I grew up eating all kinds of crap and I still love it. I'm healthier than you've ever been."

"So, nothing I do makes any difference?"

"Well, of course it makes some difference. Just don't get so hotheaded over it. You frustrate your own efforts. You'll make them hate what you want them to like."

"'OK, OK, James. But they wouldn't hate anything if they didn't hear you denigrating it.'"

"Let's lay this to rest. Let's have a nice family dinner. I have to read a brief tonight and I'd like everything to wind down a little."

A brief? Read a brief? She seems to have mislaid something. Good God, the vacuum cleaner man . . . boy. She composes herself.

"James. I thought you might like to get out tonight and relax. Can't the brief wait? I was going to suggest you go to a movie. You can't really relax here."

"Why can't I relax here? What do I want to go to a movie alone for?"

"You resent it when I do. You feel left out. Here's your chance to make up for it. I'll baby-sit."

"I can't do it. Why don't you go?"

"That's not what I'm suggesting. I'm not asking you to concede more to me." She assumes an air of judicious generosity. The idea of the salesman arriving to find James makes her panic. "Why don't you break loose for once?"

"What is this?"

"Nothing, nothing. I'd just like to be alone tonight, that's all, and I want you to have a good time."

"You can stay upstairs and I'll stay downstairs. No problem."

She watches him open the refrigerator, take out some cheese, carefully sliver off a piece, and pad toward the door, leaving the round on the counter.

"Why didn't you put that away?" she asks.

"Why don't you shut up?" he replies.

Stricken, she tracks him back across the room, her body rigid.

"Shaddap!" pipes Timmy, and adds, "Don't talk to me that way."

"It's none of your business," continues his father, "how I do things."

"None of my business? I slave away here—all day, alone. You come home too high and mighty to help out, but you can get in the way any time. This place is a wreck and what do you do about it?"

"Look, what do *you* do here all day? Why the hell can't you keep order? I can come into my own kitchen, for God's sake. This isn't some Victorian upstairs/downstairs scene."

The older boy had disappeared and now returns with a book. James sits, opens it, and helps him sound out the words. Timmy climbs into his father's lap and, feeling censured, she returns to her recipe, stiff with the realization that no one here will offer charity. She and James, living so competitively, in a death struggle, have clipped the feelers of their emotions until they can perceive nothing but one another's wounds. She feels caricatured by the husbandly concern he showed on the telephone. Excluded now, there is nothing to do but what she does best, perhaps: feed them.

Attending to her Chinese cookbook, she does not notice their departure, but it is quiet in the house. She glances out the back window and sees, in the descending fields below their house, the tiny and tinier figures of father and sons, winningly blowy and engrossed as they pull on a kite string sharing energy and release. Wind rips their hair and their clothes, and they run and run while she watches from the window, helpless to influence their experience or to encompass them as the window does, or to be free of them as distance separates them from her, slows their movement. While she watches, they all collapse in a breathless, giddy heap, pick themselves up and start back to the house.

But there are fifty steps to be memorized; no time to check the book after the wok is hot. The kitchen din suddenly crescendos: here is James drinking orange juice from the refrigerator container and both boys have spotted him, insist on having some too.

"James!"

"OK, boys, out of the kitchen. Mommy needs peace and quiet."

They go, and she ponders her options. It was so foolish not to have told the vacuum salesman to stay away. Why on earth didn't she? But it's too late now. She wonders if he is smart enough to check before he blunders up to a door or a window— surely he is. And if James should see him, won't he automatically assume he's a prowler? He wears the masterly, protective mantle so effortlessly he'll never suspect. But she is uneasy. She has violated too many rules already, and it hurts.

Her recipe calls for Chinese cabbage. The seventy days maturation have finally expired. She grows things with pleasure, and in contradiction of her general impression that life is ebbing. While she went downhill all summer the little plants grew greener, more vigorous, and now, finally, useful.

The garden is laid behind the garage, and behind it is woods. She rounds the bend with her basket and only gradually comprehends what has happened. Disaster! The obedient little rows she remembers laying with such exasperation over the seeds, the stooping, the heat, and the bugs are gone—the whole crop must have been devoured by woodchucks. She edges closer. God! It *is* that bad! A few sprouts left here and there, but almost everything above the base of each plant has been nibbled off.

She leans against the side of the garage, trying to figure why everything seems to go wrong, why her innocent sloppiness becomes so malicious. She'd wanted only to feed her children, give them healthy bones, muscles, teeth—the works. She wants to love them, even set an example, most of the time. Tomorrow the fall peas will be gone.

She runs to the house, already laying a little blame on James, who wasn't vigilant, won't care as much as she does. But she needs him, nevertheless, and gives an agitated account at the door.

He says, "Let's have dinner. Let's think about it for a while. It's never so bad as it seems at first." And he draws his hand gently across her cheek.

Dinner is completed without Chinese cabbage, and they all sit. The boys, sensing something is up, have no complaints, either about the exotic food or the chopsticks she has provided for tools. Everyone is silent for a while, until James says, "Why don't I just borrow Dave's gun and have done with it?"

For a moment she thinks, confusing her thoughts with his, that he means to shoot her—to put her, finally, out of all their miseries. But no, he means the woodchucks. Like most strong resolutions to the problems she continually presents, it is not im-

mediately persuasive. She has to scrape away his authority to appreciate what he says.

"Why don't I get the gun and just spend the night in the garage loft?" He looks thoughtfully over their heads into the dark.
"Woodchucks usually come around pretty early in the morning—
before dawn." He looks at her. "So, instead of running the risk of
missing them, I'll just go out there, read my brief, get a little
sleep, and be ready for them whenever they come."

"I think it's a good idea." She can hardly believe it. She feels
suspended, out of focus. So it will happen, after all.

James goes off, then, like any pioneer, and she hurries to get
the children out of the way, in bed. Michael detains her, wondering gravely if he will remember to take craft materials they've
requested at school.

"Mommy, please remind me. I know I'll forget. I always do."
She feels a terrible pang, watching worry sprout in that face that
is just his own—not hers, not James'. These first few days of
school are as terrifying for her now as when she was a child. The
most painful ingredient of Michael's emerging self-awareness is
the conscience that has attached itself like a leech to his carefree
little body.

"Brush my teeth, Mommy."

"We'll do that in the morning. Please. Be a good boy. Say good
night."

"Good night. Mommy, mommy, mommy."

Oh, she melts, runs remorse. But there is much to be done.

Downstairs, she slumps in a chair for a moment, considering a
choice of lingerie. Should she put on a nightgown? First she
should have a touch of brandy.

Carrying her glass, she goes upstairs, changes into a sheer
nightgown never before worn (a gift, my God, from the Mother-
in-Law), and dabs a little cologne behind her ears and at her
throat. Just what she used to do, before dancing with an adolescent, one full of himself, with big ideas, and eager for her. Tonight, if he shows, he'll be as if newly thawed for her.

James interrupts these thoughts by shouting upstairs that he's
got the gun. "I'll be OK," he adds. "OK," she says back. "Well,
good night."

He must be hurt. She suspects he wanted her to reject his solution, to protest that it was more important they be together to-night, patch up their differences, than to shoot woodchucks. She returns to the living room to wait. Today has been a profound failure, in a way others have not, but there is no cause for de-spair. Opportunities to make amends are as abundant as the days ahead. She feels a kind of itch and attributes it to his being propped up a hundred yards away with a .22. She imagines tak-ing him a conciliatory cup of coffee and being shot dead, while he'd never have to answer to charges. So she stays put, more anx-ious than she'd like to admit, wondering if that kid will come.

There is a sound at the back door? Would he go there? He might be seen from the garage, so she races to the kitchen to let him in. In the dining room she collides with James.

"Where are you going in such a hurry?"

"Nowhere. Why aren't you in the garage?"

"I forgot my brief." He passes her and peers about the living room, where the lights have been dimmed. "Where's my brief-case, do you know?"

"I think it's at the foot of the stairs, isn't it?" He looks.

"Oh, yeah." He takes a sheaf of papers and shuts the briefcase.

"Well, back to the bunker." He grins, stops, and examines her. "Say, you look great." Comes to her side. "And you smell great. You haven't worn perfume in years. Ummmm." He puts an arm around her, his lips to the nape of her neck. "Well, you'll never cease to amaze me. I thought you were sending me out into the gloom without a thought. I'm sorry about today, too." He pulls her with him to the couch, sits, and pats his knees. "Come here. Sit down. I've got time. Let's forget the brief and forget the woodchucks for a while."

She hesitates, confused. It isn't often she commits herself to a plan—risks she is used to, but they are arbitrary. She can't aban-don her first purposeful activity in ages.

"I'm sorry, James. I really didn't expect you. I was feeling ter-rible all day—that's why I wanted to be alone tonight, and still do. But I had to raise my morale a little. Please try to under-stand."

His face goes slack for a moment, then hardens in an expres-sion of severe injury. He stands, picks up the sheaf of papers, and goes back to the kitchen door without a word. She follows him, almost calls him back; waits, instead, to be certain he has gone to the loft. She sees the flashlight switched on.

IN THE LIVING ROOM she sprawls, feeling rotten. It's getting late and she's certain now that he won't come; that, at best, a familiar guilt will waken her at four. Just her cavalier treatment of her husband. Only recklessness she can't afford.

But someone is tapping at the window; she makes out a grin on a face out there. He gestures at her, she puts a finger to her lips and points in the direction of the garage. He pantomimes bewilderment, she tries to respond, and they give it up. She opens the front door very carefully and he slips inside. They whisper.

"Is he gone?"

"Yes."

"How'd you get rid of him? Where is he?"

"He's out in the garage."

"In the garage? Jesus. What's he doing out there?"

"He has a gun. He's waiting to shoot woodchucks."

"He has a what?" The boy falls away from her, gives her a look of pure wonderment and heads for the door.

"Wait, wait. It's all right. He'll be there all night."

"You're one crazy lady. How can you be sure of that?"

"He made a bet with someone. He has to bag two more tonight or he loses everything. You don't have to worry."

"I can't make you out at all."

"Stay."

"You're not afraid?"

"Not any more. We'll be alone. Where did you leave your car? I don't want any of the neighbors to see it."

"I'm not that dumb, baby. I left it in the next block. I'm like a cat. No one saw me. You sure we're safe? I don't want my ass shot off."

"Yes, yes."

So he embraces her. "Oh, baby, this is good." Premature, she thinks. He leads her to the couch, his hand on her buttocks. "Should we go upstairs?"

"No. The children. Stay here, it's all right."

They recline. He unzips his fancy-pants. Everything is proceeding apace. She feels wholly detached. Earlier today she had written Miriam that this sort of thing is anathema to her, but now she does not protest. Suddenly she is so tired. It's a fitting end, surely, to a miserable day. She'd like to share the irony with her new lover but doesn't trust his intelligence. He wouldn't appreciate it.

"Are you on the pill?" he inquires.

"No. They gave me hot flashes."

"Okeydoke." He takes out his wallet and extracts a condom. She goes limp, amazed that this aspect of the encounter had slipped her mind entirely. How responsible this young man is, compared to herself. She feels faint.

"Help me, baby," he whispers, and she obliges until he can insert himself into his stocking, and then into her.

And he digs away while she thinks things over. Where is the expert who dwelt, earlier today, in this youth? All talk, it seems, all talk. He looms above her, his face in a grimace that shuts his eyes to her. She mustn't pull rank, the way the older man had while examining the vacuum, but she tries to offer some guidance. Tries to shift his weight, get a little purchase herself, wondering at the sudden appeal of *la petite mort* instead of the real thing. But he is stubborn, or too bulky to realize, or as innocent as his years, and he insists on his own technique, driving himself heavily into her again and again, holding his breath, as alone as he can be, straining for all he knows of this. He has made her sore with this peremptory stuff by the time he comes and falls on her with a groan. Finally she stirs; he is hurting her.

"Sooooo good, baby," he mumbles drowsily.

"Hey! Don't go to sleep. You can't stay here." She is desperately uncomfortable now, tries to push him off.

"Come on, baby, just a minute. Come on," and his voice trails off.

She lies listening, fearful and full of distaste. There is a thud upstairs and Timmy begins to cry. She stiffens and the body imprisoning her is suddenly rigid too. "What's that?" "My son. He must have fallen out of bed. I'll have to go." There is a chance Timmy will come to find her, but more likely he'll lie on the floor and screech until Michael wakes up.

The salesman springs to his feet, pulls on his trousers, and looks about the room until he spots a mirror. He combs his hair hastily before it.

"Well," he says, "I guess I better get going. Mind-blowing, him out there with a gun. Or were you kidding?"

"I was kidding."

"Whew! Well, so long. And thanks."

She remains draped along the couch as he salutes her, clatters off into the vestibule, carefully opens and shuts the door.

Then she climbs the stairs, thinking how surprising it is that she can put James entirely out of her mind. He might as well not exist, yet there he is, out there with his rifle and probably long past caring.

She'll have to do something nice for him. Have to make amends, somehow, if only to appease her own demons. Will it be enterprising enough, she wonders, to fix eggs Benedict, instead of cereal, for breakfast?

The Lone Pilgrim

LAURIE COLWIN

LAURIE COLWIN was born in New York and grew up in Philadelphia and Chicago. She attended Bard College and Columbia University. Viking Press has published a collection of her stories, *Passion and Affect*, and her novel, *Shine On Bright and Dangerous Object*. Her stories have appeared in *The New Yorker*, *Mademoiselle*, *Redbook*, *Cosmopolitan* and *Antaeus*. She now lives in New York.

I HAVE BEEN the house pet to several families: friendly, cheerful, good with children, and, most important, I have an acute sensitivity to the individual rhythms of family life. I blend in perfectly, without losing myself. A good houseguest is like an entertainer: Judy Garland, Georgette Heyer, Noël Coward. You know what a specific public wants—in my case, groups of two, with children.

For example, Paul and Vera Martens and their children, Ben and Violet. Paul and Vera are lawyers. Paul spends rainy Sundays fishing, and although Vera is a real cook, she is not fond of cleaning fish, so Paul's grandfather's knife is entrusted to me. I do the neat job of a surgeon. Vera, who likes precision, was so impressed by my initial performance that she allowed me into her kitchen, and we have been cooking together ever since. I knew by instinct where she would keep her pots, her baking dishes, her mixing bowls, her silverware. If you are interested in people, their domestic arrangements are of interest, too. That's the sort of student of human conduct I am.

In Maine, I visit Christopher and Jean Goodison and their little son Jean Luc. The Goodisons are haphazard housekeepers, but I have their routine down pat. Their baby and I get along famously. We have had a few moments together: a hailstorm he observed from my lap; learning to crawl; an afternoon with a kitten. The best way with babies, I have come to know, is quietude. Never approach first. Be casual. Pay minimal tactile attention, and never try to make them love you. You can sit on the same sofa with a child and do nothing more than clutch its little foot from time to time, and before long you will have that child on your lap.

The Goodisons will leave Jean Luc with me when they go shopping, although ordinarily—with ordinary mortals, that is— they are very protective of their son. When they return, I surprise them with a Lady Baltimore cake. Alone in their house, I admire their Shaker table, the fancy-back spoons I find mixed in with their spatulas, the dried-flower arrangements in their lus-treware pitchers.

And there are others: the Hartwells in Boston, who live in a spartan apartment decorated with city-planning charts. The rigorous Mazzinas, who take me camping. The elegant Jerricks, who dress for dinner and bring you a breakfast tray on Sunday morning: coffee, toast, and a small vase with a single flower in it. My friends admire my charm, my sagacity, my propriety, and my positive talent for fitting in with the daily life of others while holding my own.

The adhesive tape on my mailbox reads: "P. Rice." Paula Rice, that is; known to all as Polly. I am the charming girl illustrator. I did the pictures for "Hector the Hero," "The Pig Who Said Pneu," "Fish with Feathers," "Snow White and Rose Red," and "The I Don't Care Papers"—all children's books. Five feet four, reddish hair, brown eyes, long legs. At college, I studied medieval French, but kept a sketchbook with me at all times. During the summers, I studied calligraphy, papermaking, and bookbinding, and worked as an apprentice at the Lafayette Publishing Company, printers of fine editions. I make a living illustrating children's books, but to please myself I do etchings and ink drawings, which I often present to friends on special occasions—marriages, anniversaries, birthdays.

On the side, I am a perfect houseguest. I have the temperament for it. Being a designer teaches you the habit of neatness, and an appreciation for a sense of order not your own. Being a houseguest allows you to fantasize with no one crowding you. After all, you are but a guest, an adornment. Your object is to give pleasure to your hosts. Lolling around in other people's houses allows your mind to drift. Inspired by my surroundings, I indulge myself in this lazy, scene-setting kind of thought. For example: a big yellow moon; the kitchen of an old house in an academic community. On the window ledge a jar of homemade jam, a pot of chives, a cutting of grape ivy in a cracked mug. A big dog sleeps in front of the stove. If you open the window, you feel the crisp October air. An apple pie or a loaf of bread is in the oven, and the house is warm with the scent of it. You wonder if it is time to deal with the last pumpkin, or to pickle the basket of green tomatoes. In the study, your husband is drowsing over an elevating book, a university-press book in blue wrappers. You are wearing a corduroy skirt, a chic blouse, and a sweater of your husband's is tied around your shoulders. You are a woman contemplating seasonal change.

Or you go to the Martenses' on a rainy night. They occupy two floors of a Victorian brownstone, and as you contemplate the polished moldings and watch the rain through the leaded windows, you feel you are in England in the spring—in a little house in Devizes, say, or Bexhill-on-Sea. Your children have just been put to bed. You have finished reading a book on the life of Joseph Wright of Derby. There is a knock on the door. You start up. Your husband is away, and it is foggy outside. At the door is an old lover, someone who broke your heart, who is in England on business and has tracked you down.

Of course, the fact of the matter is that you live in a flat in New York. Your work is done at an oak drawing table, sur-

rounded by pots of brushes and pens. In other people's houses
your perspective widens. You contemplate the Martenses' old
Spode platter. You know the burn on their dining-room table—
the only flaw in its walnut surface—is from Paul's cigar, placed
there the night before Ben was born. These details feed the
imagination.

Oh, domesticity! The wonder of dinner plates and cream
pitchers. You know your friends by their ornaments. You want
everything. If Mrs. A. has her mama's old jelly mold, you want
one, too, and everything that goes with it—the family, the tradition, the years of having jelly molded in it. We domestic sensu-
alists live in a state of longing, no matter how comfortable our
own places are.

You cannot be a good houseguest and be married. Single, you
carry only the uncluttered luggage of your own personality,
selected and packed by only one pair of hands. Marriage is two-
dimensional to the unmarried. No matter how close they get to a
couple, they view the situation without any depth perception. If
companionship is what you want, and you don't have it, any part
of it looks good, including complaints, squabbles, misunderstanding. If only, you feel, you had someone close enough to
misunderstand. Intimate enough to squabble with. Well known
enough to complain about. Marriage is a condition, like neatness,
or order. It is as safe as the wedding silver on the sideboard. To
the unmarried, marriage is a sort of trapping, right down to the
thin, unobtrusive gold bands.

That's romanticism for you. No one fantasizes about dreary afternoons, despair, unreasonableness, chaos, and boredom. Not
the unmarried, that is—especially if they contemplate marriage
from a perch of well-savored solitude. Solitude provides you the
luxury of thinking about the closed, graceful shapes of other people's lives. My friends are steady, just like me. But, steady as I
am, why am I so solitary? No matter how orderly, measured, and
careful my arrangements are, they are only a distillation of me,
not a fusion of myself and someone else. I have my domestic
comforts, except that mine are only mine.

MY LIFE changed with the appearance into it of Gilbert Seigh. It
was for Gilbert that I produced my best work: illustrations for
"The Art of Courtly Love" and "The Poems of Marie de France."

Gilbert's father, grandfather, and great grandfather had been publishers of fine editions. After practicing law for five years, Gilbert took over the business when his father's eyesight began to fail. Gilbert was born into the business, and was infected with it. His great-grandfather did editions of the Book of Common Prayer, of James Fenimore Cooper, Thackeray, and Mrs. Scott Courrier-Maynard, a now unknown poet of Connecticut. His grandfather went in for U. S. Grant's memoirs, Washington Irving, and Speeches of American Presidents. Gilbert's father did the poets of his day, edited and published a little magazine called *Lampfire,* and produced double-language volumes of Rimbaud, Rilke, and Christian Morgenstern. Gilbert goes in for the classics, for naturalist works, and for Melville. Three thousand dollars will get you the Seigh Press edition of "Billy Budd." Six will get you his two volumes of "Wild Flowers of the North American Continent."

Gilbert does not look like a man of books. He looks like a young auto magnate: large, ruddy, and enthusiastic. His glasses fog over from sheer enjoyment. He has a hot temper and a big, loud laugh. I often picture him in his leather chair at his office, laughing and wiping his glasses on the vest of his woolly suit. I like to watch him go up against his master binder, a fiery Italian named Antonio Nello, fighting about the ornaments for a spine. This clash of hard-headed perfectionists brings forth stubborn shouting from Gilbert and operatic flights of invective from Antonio, after which the correct solution is reached.

Several months after I met Gilbert, I fell in love with him. I was sent to him by Paul Martens. Gilbert, at dinner with Paul and Vera, had said he was looking for an illustrator and couldn't find one whose work he liked. He had been to dozens of galleries, museums, and agents. He had looked through hundreds of illustrated books. Then Paul showed him a drawing I had done to celebrate the birth of Violet; it shows a homely little girl sitting in a field of lavender and purple flowers. Gilbert asked if the artist was still alive. It was the best thing he had seen since Arthur Rackham, he said. Vera produced copies of "Fish with Feathers" and "Snow White and Rose Red." Thus the girl illustrator met Gilbert Seigh one rainy midmorning. He skimmed through my portfolio, and since there was nothing at stake, I felt free to dislike him. I felt he was cavalier with my work. I felt I had been set up by the Martenses to meet an available man whose tastes were similar to my own. He closed the portfolio and began to hum happily, at which point I figured him for a moron.

" 'My heart is like a singing bird,' " he sang.

My reactions were coming thick and fast now. I thought he was arrogant, insolent, pretentious, and dopily eccentric. I picked up the portfolio and tied its ribbons.

I said, "Thank you for seeing me." And began to leave.

"Oh, wait," he said. "I've put you off. I'm terribly sorry. You think I haven't paid proper attention to your work, but I already know your work. Vera showed me your books and the picture you did for Violet. I was behaving like a fool because it's so good. I'm too mono-minded to have told you. You're the illustrator I've been looking for. Please sit down."

I sat. I thought he was cuckoo. Then he described the project he had in mind: an edition of Andreas Capellanus' "The Art of Courtly Love." I told him I had studied medieval literature. He glowed with delight, and wiped his glasses. He still seemed a little batty to me, but he certainly knew what beautiful books were all about.

That's how it began. I went home, finished my last assignment, and began doing my best work for Gilbert Seigh.

We worked elegantly together. It was a perfect match. He took me out to lunch often, and never so much as brushed my arm with his sleeve. It was said he had been keeping company with a lady lawyer, who had been more or less a fixture in his life since his divorce. So it was to Gilbert that I dedicated my heart. I brooded about him constantly. Being in love with him brought me all the things in life I counted on: a sense of longing, something to turn over and over in my mind, and that clear, slightly manic vision you get with unrequited love. Each line I drew was a dedication of sorts. Going over proofs with him, choosing type, browsing through books of paper samples, planning and designing gave me an extreme sense of heady pleasure. If that wasn't love, what was?

WELL, I'll tell you what was. I had suffered in love three years before, and it had not stopped haunting me. The man in question was an astronomer by the name of Jacob Bailey. Somewhere in the heavens is a galaxy named for him: the Bailey galaxy. It can only be seen through an observatory telescope—he showed it to me once at an observatory in Vermont. I will probably never see it again. I met Jacob in the line of work—the way I felt it was proper to meet those with whom you will have a profound connection. I was doing the drawings for a children's book on Kepler, and Jacob was checking the text and pictures for accuracy. It was love at once—hot, intense, brilliant, and doomed to fail. When it did, and we parted, it was with much puzzlement and despair. Jacob wanted a grand event—something you would never forget but not something to live with. I wanted something to live with. A love affair conducted with the same thrilling rev-up that starts a Grand Prix race usually runs its course and stops. When the Rice & Bailey show was over, I went into a form of mourning. My friends knew I had suffered. I felt that being crossed in love had changed me, and it had, but my life stayed the same. I worked with what I felt was new depth, and carried Jacob around as a secret in my heart.

When you fall in love like that, it strikes like a disease, and you can understand why nineteenth-century poets felt they were either sick with love or dying of it. Divorced people sometimes remember the joys of married life as strains, but in a love affair just the reverse is true. Since marriages are final and love affairs are open-ended, you tend to think about what might have been instead of what was. So I recalled Jacob's gorgeous smile but not his cruel streak. I remembered the resemblance I thought he bore to an angel but not his frequent nastiness and its effect. But what difference does it make? I remembered. My life—my inner life—became a kind of reverie, and it would not have shocked me had I found that in some dreamlike state I had created a little shrine to Jacob Bailey: his photograph, my book on Kepler, a parking ticket from the Bronx Zoo, the little pearl earrings he gave me. The idea of committed, settled love is as remote to a romantic as lunar soil.

GILBERT'S TASTE in music is that of a tin-eared highbrow. He goes to the opera. He likes Mozart. He listens, abstractedly, but music is just another taste to him, and not his primary taste by a long shot. To him it is a sort of cultivated white noise, like glasses tinkling in the background during an expensive meal at a restaurant. Well, I can hum along with the best of them, but my reactions are hardly cultivated. Music is not a taste to me but a craving—something I must have. If I find something I love to hear, I play it over and over again. Then I am able to sit on a bus and play a Brahms quartet in my mind from memory, or any of a million rock-and-roll songs I love. Music becomes foreground then, or landscape gardening. It alters or complements my mood. On windy nights, I like to go home, light a fire, and flip on a little Boccherini, just to warm up. By the time I sit down to work, another mood overtakes me. My best drawing for "The Art of Courtly Love" was done listening to the Everly Brothers singing "Sleepless Nights." When that palled, I started on Jerry Lee Lewis singing "Another Place, Another Time." After a few hours of work, I like a good weep, to the Harp Quartet.

The thing about music is it's all your own. It puts you into a complex frame of mind without your even leaving the house. I can relive long moments with Jacob Bailey by playing what I listened to when he was around or what I wept to when he wasn't. It makes your past come back to you, and if you must pinpoint a moment in your life you can say, "That was in 1962, when 'He's a Rebel,' by the Crystals, was a hit," or "1969, after the Dietrich Fischer-Dieskau concert." This kind of music worship is a form of privacy, and a great aid to highly emotional people who live in a hermetic state—a door key to the past, an inspiration.

Gilbert and I worked on "Courtly Love" for a year, and after it was sent to the printer we began on the poems of Marie de France. The poems, since they are about love in vain, made me think of Jacob Bailey. I would break from work to stick my head out the window in an unsuccessful attempt to locate the Bailey galaxy. I worked accompanied by a record of country hymns. My favorite was called "Lone Pilgrim." A man comes to the place where the Lone Pilgrim is buried, and hears someone calling to him. It is the Pilgrim, who tells his story. Away from home, far from his loved ones, he sickened and died. I played one stanza over and over again:

> O tell my companion and children
> most dear

To weep not for me now I'm gone.
The same hand that led me
    through scenes most severe
Has kindly assisted me home.

Since I was thinking about Jacob Bailey anyway, this song
made me long for him. I knew he was on an expedition in
Greenland, all alone. I thought of the scenes most severe he
might be passing through and the kind hand that might lead him
home: mine.

There were days when I thought I saw him on the street. My
heart jumped: I thought he had come back. But it never was
Jacob. I wanted to go up to the man I thought was Jacob and
shake him for not being, to shake him until he was. There were
times when I could not believe our connection had been broken.
That was love, wasn't it?

ALL THIS TIME, of course, I continued to be in love with Gilbert.
What I thought might be a crush had turned into true affection.
The year we spent working on "The Art of Courtly Love" had
given me ample time to judge his character.

The worst you could say of him was that he was prone to fits
of abstraction. In these states, when spoken to he took a long
time to answer, and you felt he was being rude. When he was
concentrating, papers littered his desk, causing his secretary to
wonder if he was messy at home. At home he was messy when
abstracted. His bed went unmade. Clothing piled up on his bed
in the shape of an African termite nest. Mail, newspapers, books,
and catalogues were scattered on his desk, his coffee table, in the
kitchen.

But the result of his abstraction was perfection. Gilbert's books
were more than handsome; they were noble. His energy was
bountiful and steady, and he gave people the same attention to
detail he gave to books. Gilbert got to know me, too. He knew
when I was tired out, or when I had faded on a drawing and
couldn't see what form it was taking. He knew how to make me
laugh, what sort of food I liked. He learned to have a cup of hot
tea waiting for me at the end of a day, and he remembered
things I told him. When we first started working, I described to

him a plate that I had seen in an antique shop and that I wanted with all my heart. This was by way of illustrating a point: we were talking about impatience, and the wisdom of holding off from obtainable pleasures as a test of will. The day, one year later, that "Courtly Love" went to press, the second cousin to the plate I wanted was presented to me by Gilbert: dark-blue Staffordshire, with flowers all around.

In short, he was just like me. When he was not abstracted, his quarters were immaculate, and arranged for sheer domestic pleasure. He bought flowers when people came to dinner. He liked to take a long time over a meal. I in turn knew how to cheer him when he became cranky and dispirited. I knew he loved rhubarb pie, so the first of the season's rhubarb went to him. But best of all we were perfect workmates.

The night we saw the finished edition of "Courtly Love" we went out to dinner to celebrate, and drank two bottles of champagne. Gilbert walked me home, and on the way he stopped, and astonished me by taking me into his arms and kissing me. I was giddy and drunk, but not so drunk as not to know what my reactions were. He had never so much as brushed my sleeve, and here we were locked in an embrace on an empty street.

When he released me, I said, "Aren't you going to kiss me again?"

"Sometimes if you work very closely with someone, you get used to working, and don't know how to gauge what they feel," Gilbert said.

In my apartment, he told me what he felt, and I told him. Then we celebrated our first night together.

THE SOLITARY MIND likes to reflect on the pain of past love. If you are all alone, it gives you something to react to, a sort of exercise to keep the muscles flexed.

I knew that Gilbert was falling in love with me. I watched it happen. And Gilbert knew that I was falling in love with him. We thought we had been fated for one another, but actually we were only getting used to good romantic luck. It is not so often that well-matched people meet. My being in love with Gilbert was accompanied by a sense of rightness I had never felt before, and we decided that we would marry within a year.

But when I worked alone in my apartment I was consumed with a desire to see Jacob Bailey. This desire was sharp as actual pain. I wasted many sheets of stationery beginning letters to him, which I tore up. When your heart's desire is right within your reach, what else is there to do but balk?

I pictured my oak secretary next to Gilbert's Chinese lamp, my books next to his, my clothing beside his in the closet. All my friends live in pairs, except me. I had only fallen in love—love being what you one day wept over in private. What did you do with love that didn't end? That ceased to be sheer romance and moved on to something more serious?

You get used to a condition of longing. Live with it over time and it becomes part of your household—the cat you don't take much notice of that slinks up against you at mealtime or creeps onto the foot of your bed at night. You cannot fantasize being married if you are married. Married to Gilbert, what would I long for? I would not even be able to long for him.

Woe to those who get what they desire. Fulfillment leaves an empty space where your old self used to be, the self that pines and broods and reflects. You furnish a dream house in your imagination, but how startling and final when that dream house is your own address. What is left to you? Surrounded by what you wanted, you feel a sense of amputation. The feelings you were used to abiding with are useless. The conditions you established for your happiness are met. That youthful light-headed feeling whose sharp side is much like hunger is of no more use to you.

You long for someone to love. You find him. You pine for him. Suddenly, you discover you are loved in return. You marry. Before you do, you count up the days you spent in the homes of others, in kitchens, at dinner tables, putting other people's children to bed. You have basked in a sense of domesticity you have not created but enjoy. The Lone Pilgrim sits at the dinner parties of others, partakes, savors, and goes home in a taxi alone.

Those days were spent in quest—the quest to settle your own life, and now the search has ended. Your imagined happiness is yours. Therefore, you lose your old bearings. On the one side is your happiness and on the other is your past—the self you were used to, going through life alone, heir to your own experience.

Once you commit yourself, everything changes and the rest of your life seems to you like a dark forest on the property you have recently acquired. It is yours, but still you are afraid to enter it, wondering what you might find: a little chapel, a stand of birches, wolves, snakes, the worst you can imagine, or the best. You take one timid step forward, but then you realize you are not alone. You take someone's hand—Gilbert Seigh's—and strain through the darkness to see ahead.

Breed

JOHN SAYLES

JOHN SAYLES was born and raised in Schenectady, New York. His first novel, *Pride of the Bimbos,* was published in 1975. *Union Dues,* his second, will be published this year.

B RIAN WOKE on the lee side of a hill with a buffalo licking his face. At first he was only aware of the tongue, sticky and thick as a baby's arm, lapping down to sample his ears and cheeks. He had laid his sleeping bag out in the dark, snuggling it at the foot of what he took to be a drift fence, to have at least some shelter from the grit-blasting Wyoming wind. If it *was* still Wyoming; he hadn't been awake enough during the last part of the ride to look out for signs.

As he squirmed away from whatever the big thing mopping at his face was, he glimpsed through half-sleep that each of the posts in the fence was painted a different color. Cherry-red, lime-green, lemon-yellow. He was in a carny-colored corral with a live bull bison.

No.

He tried to go back under, thinking it was only the effects of
the three-day power-hitch across the country from New Jersey,
all that coffee and all those miles talking with strangers. But then
the rich brown smell dawned on him and he knew. He knew. He
had never seen a live buffalo before but he was sure this was
what they smelled like. It smelled like The West.

The buffalo retreated a few steps when Brian sat up, fixing
him with swimming brown walleyes. There were bare patches
worn in the wool of its flanks and hump, shiny black leather
showing through. Its beard was sugared with dust and meal of
some kind, and Brian could hear the flop of its tail chasing flies.

"Morning, Buffalo."

The animal snorted through its flat nose for an answer, made
munching quivers with its jaw. Brian fingered matter from his
eyes and peered out over the fence to where he remembered the
road. There were cut-out letters hung from a crossbar like the
ranches he'd seen in southern Wyoming had. Brian read them
backward. CODY SPRAGUE'S WILD WEST BUCKIN' BISON RIDE, it
said, FOOD—GAS—SOUVENIRS. Brian didn't understand how he
could have missed the sign and the flapping pennants strung
from it, even in the dark. The buffalo licked its nose.

Brian pulled on his sweat-funky road clothes and packed his
sleeping bag away. The buffalo had lowered its eyelids to half-
mast, no longer interested. Brian stood and walked around it. A
shifting cloud of tiny black flies shadowed its ass, an ass cracked
and black as old inner-tube rubber. There was something not
quite real about the thing, Brian felt as if stuffing or springs
would pop out of the seams any moment. He eased his hands
into the hump wool. Coarse and greasy, like a mat for scuffing
your feet clean on. The buffalo didn't move but for the twitching
of its rump skin as insects lit on it. Brian gave it a couple of gentle, open-palmed thumps on the side, feeling the solid weight
like a great warm tree stump.

"Reach for the sky!"

Brian nearly jumped on the animal's back as a cold cylinder
pressed the base of his neck.

"Take your mitts off my buffalo and turn around."

Brian turned himself around slowly and there was a little

chicken-necked man pointing an empty Coke bottle level with his heart. "One false move and I'll fizz you to pieces." The little man cackled, showing chipped brown teeth and goosing Brian with the bottle. "Scared the piss outa *you,* young fella. I seen you there this morning, laid out. Didn't figure I should bother to wake you till you woke yourself, but Ishmael, he thought you was a bag a meal. He's kind of slow, Ishmael."

The buffalo swung its head around to give the man a tentative whiff, then swung back. The man was wearing a fringed buckskin jacket so stained it looked freshly ripped off the buck. He had a wrinkle-ring every other inch of his long neck, a crooked beak of a nose, and dirty white hair that shot out in little clumps. Of the three of them the buffalo seemed to have had the best sleep.

Brian introduced himself and stated his business, which was to make his way to whatever passed for a major highway out here on the lone prairie. Thumbing from East Orange to the West Coast. He had gotten a bum steer from a drunken oil-rigger the other night and was dumped out here.

"Cody Sprague," said the little man, extending his hand. "I offer my condolences and the use of my privy. Usually don't open till nine or ten," he said, "but it don't seem to make a difference either whichway."

He led Brian across the road to where there was a metal outhouse and an orange-and-black painted shack about the size of a Tastee-Freeze.

"People don't want to come," he said, "they don't want to come. Just blow by on that Interstate. That's what you'll be wantin to get to, isn't but five miles or so down the way. They finished that last stretch a couple years back and made me obsolete. That's what they want me. Obsolete."

Sprague clucked away at Brian's elbow, trotting a little to stay close as if his visitor would bolt for freedom any second. He called through the door of the little Sani-Port as Brian went in to wash and change to fresh clothes.

"You got any idee what it costs to keep a full-grown American bison in top running condition? Not just a matter of set im loose to graze, oh no, not when you've got a herd of one. Got to protect your investment, the same with any small businessman.

Dropping like flies they are. That's an endangered species, the small businessman. Anyhow, you don't let him out there to graze. Don't know *what* he might pick up. You got five hundred head, you can afford to lose a few to poisnin, a few to varmint holes, a few to snakes and whatnot. Don't make a dent. But me, I got everything I own riding on Ishmael. He don't dine on nothin but the highest-protein feed. He's eaten up all my savings and most of the last bank loan I'm likely to get. You ever ridden a buffalo?"

"No," said Brian over the running water inside, "I've never even been on a horse."

"Then you got a treat coming, free a charge. You'll be my ice-breaker for the weekend, bring me luck. I'd offer you breakfast, but confidentially speakin, the grill over here is out of commission. They turned off my lectricity. You might of noticed the lamp in there don't work. How they expect a buffalo to keep up its health without lectricity I'll never understand. It's that kind of thinking put the species on the brink of extinction."

BRIAN CAME OUT with fresh clothes and his teeth finger-brushed, and Cody Sprague hustled him back into the corral with Ishmael.

"Is there a saddle or anything? Or do I just get on?"

"Well, I got a blanket I use for the little girls with bare legs if it makes them nervous, but no, you don't need a thing. Like sitting on a rug. Just don't climb up too high on the hump is all, kind of unsteady there. Attaboy, hop aboard."

The buffalo didn't seem to mind, didn't seem to notice Brian crawling up on its back. Instead it lifted its head toward a bucket nailed to a post on the far side of the corral.

"How do I make him go?" asked Brian. There was no natural seat on a buffalo's back, he dug his fingers deep in the wool and pressed his knees to its flanks.

"That's my job, making him go, you just sit tight." Sprague scooted out of the corral, then returned with a half-empty sack of meal. He poured some in the far bucket, then clanged it with a stone. Ishmael began to move. He was in no hurry.

"Ridem cowboy!" yelled Sprague.

Brian felt some movement under him, distantly, a vague roll of muscle and bone. He tried to imagine himself as an eight-year-old kid instead of seventeen, and that helped a little. He tried to look pleased as the animal reached the bucket and buried its nose in the feed.

"This part of the ride," said Cody apologetically, "is where I usually give them my little educational spiel about the history of the buffalo and how the Indians depended on it and all. Got it from the library up to Rapid. Got to have something to keep them entertained at the halfway point while he's cleaning out that bucket. You know the Indian used every part of the beast. Meat for food, hide for clothes and blankets, bone for tools, even the waste product, dried into buffalo chips, they used that for fuel. There was a real—real *affinity* between the buffalo and the Plains Indian. Their souls were tied together." He looked to Brian and waited.

"He sure is big." Brian threw a little extra enthusiasm into it. "I didn't realize they were this big."

Sprague spat on the ground, sighing, then looked up to see what was left in the bucket. "Pretty sorry attraction, that's what you mean, isn't it?"

"Well, I wouldn't say—"

"I mean *isn't* it? If he don't eat he don't move." Cody shook his head. "The kids, well, they pick up on it right away. Least they used to before that Interstate swept them all off. What kind of ride is it where the animal stops and chows down for five minutes at a time? Got so bad he'd commence to drool every time he seen a human under twelve years of age. Feed, that's all they understand. Won't mind kindness and he won't mind cruelty but you talk straight to his belly and oh Lord will he listen. That's how they got extincted in the first place, they seen their colleagues droppin all around them but they were too involved with feeding their faces to put two and two together. They'd rather be shot and scalped than miss the next mouthful. Plain stupid is all." He gave Ishmael a thump in the side. "You'd just as soon name a rock or a lump of clay as give a title to this old pile of gristle." He squatted slightly to look the buffalo in the face. "A damn sorry attraction, aren't you? A damn sorry fleabag of an attraction."

He straightened and hefted the meal. "Might as well be stuffed, I figure. Put him on wheels. The few people I get anymore all want to snip a tuft of wool offen him for a souvenir. I had to put a stop to it, wouldn't of been a thing left. Cody Sprague's Bald Buckin' Bison."

Ishmael lifted his head and flapped his tongue in the air a couple of times.

"Got to fill the other bucket now. He expects it. Took me the longest time to figure the right distance, long enough so it's two bits' worth of ride but not so long that the thoroughbred here thinks it's not worth the hike. The kids can tell though. I never been able to fool them. They feel left out of it, feel gypped. Um, if you don't mind, would you stay on him for the rest of the ride?" Cody was hustling across the corral toward another hanging bucket, with Ishmael swinging a liquid eye after him. "He needs the exercise."

Brian sat out the slow plod across the corral and slid off when it reached the bucket. He brushed his pants and got a stick to scrape his sneakers clean of the buffalo stool he'd stepped in. The rich brown smell was losing its charm.

"You'll be going now, I suppose," said Sprague coming up behind him.

"Uh, yeah. Guess so." It was a little creepy, the multicolored corral in the middle of all that open range. "Thanks for the ride, though."

"Nothing to keep you here, Lord knows." He was forcing a smile. "S'almost nine now, business should pick up. Ought to build a fire, case anybody stops for a hot dog." He gave a weak cackle. "I could use it for part of my pitch—frankfurters cowboy style. Call em prairie dogs."

"Yuh."

"You'll be wantin that Interstate I suppose, get you out of here. Five miles or so north on the road and you'll smack right into it."

"Thanks." Brian shouldered his duffel bag. "Hope the trade improves for you."

"Oh, no worry, no worry. I'll make out. Oh, and here, take one of these." He fished an aluminum star from his pocket and presented it to Brian. "Souvenir for you and good advertising for me."

"Deputy Sheriff," said the badge, "Issued at Cody Sprague's

Wild West Buckin' Bison Ride." There was a picture of a cowboy tossed high off the back of an angrily kicking buffalo. Brian
pinned it on his shirt and Cody brightened a bit.

"Who knows," he said, "maybe today's the day. Maybe we'll
get discovered by the tourist office today and be written up. You
get your attraction in one of those guidebooks and you got a
gold mine. Wall-to-wall customers, turn em away at the gate. I
could save up an maybe afford an opposite number for Ishmael.
Don't know if or what buffalo feel but I suppose everything gets
lonely for its own kind, don't you?"

"I suppose."

"Say, I wasn't kidding about that fire. If you're hungry I could
whip us up a late breakfast in no time. There's stock I got to use
before it goes bad so it'd be on the house."

"I really got to get going. Sorry."

"Well, maybe you brought me luck. Yessir, maybe today will
be the day."

Brian left him waving from the middle of the corral, buckskin
fringes blowing in the quickening breeze. When he was out of
sight around the bend he unpinned the aluminum star and
tossed it away, it dug into his chest too much. Then the signs appeared, the backs of them first, then the messages as he passed
by and looked behind. Every thousand yards there was another,
starting with WHOA! HERE IT IS! and progressing to more distant
warnings. When Brian got to FOR THE RIDE OF YOUR LIFE, STOP
AT CODY SPRAGUE'S he couldn't hold out anymore, he dropped his
bag and trotted back to where he'd chucked the star. He found it
without too much trouble and put it in his back pocket.

HE WENT through the land of blue-green sage clumps, leaning
into the wind whipping over low hills, walking alone. There
weren't any cars or people. More sage, more hills, more wind, but
no human trace but the road beneath him like a main street of
some vanished civilization. Open range, there were no fences or
water tanks. He looked at his Road Atlas and guessed that he was
a little ways up into South Dakota, a little below the Bear in
the Lodge River with the Rosebud Indian Reservation to the east
and the Pine Ridge to the north. He tried to remember who it
was he'd seen in the same situation. Randolph Scott? Audie

Murphy? Brian checked the sun's position to reassure himself that he was heading in the right direction. There was nothing else to tell by. A patch of hill suddenly broke free into a butternut cluster of high-rumped antelope, springing away from him. He was in The West.

He had been walking on the road for over an hour when an old Ford pickup clattered to a halt next to him. A swarthy, smooth-faced man wearing a green John Deere cap stuck his head out.

"Who you workin for?" he called.

"Huh?"

"Who you workin for? Whose place you headed?"

"I'm not working for anybody," said Brian. "I'm trying to hitch west."

"Oh. I thought you were a hand. S'gonna give you a ride over to whatever outfit you're headed for."

Brian tried not to look too pleased. Thought he was a hand. "No, I'm just hitching. I was walking up to the Interstate."

"You got a hell of a walk. That's twenty miles up."

"But the guy said it was only five."

"What guy?"

"The old guy back there. He's got a buffalo."

"Sprague? You can't listen to him, son. A nice fella, but he's a little bit touched. Got a sign up on 90, says it's only five miles to his place. Figured nobody's gonna bother, they know the real story, and he's right. Guess he's started to believe his own publicity."

"Oh."

"But you hop in anyway. I'm goin up that area in a while." Brian tossed his duffel bag in the back and got in with the man. "J. C. Shangreau," he said, offering his hand. "I'll get you north surer than most anything else you're likely to catch on this road. If you don't mind a few side trips."

Brian had to kick a shotgun wrapped in burlap under the seat to make room for his legs. "Don't mind at all."

"Got to pick up some hands to help me work my horses." Shangreau had quite a few gold teeth in his mouth and very bloodshot eyes. "Got me a couple sections up there. I run seventy-five head. Gonna have ourselves a cuttin bee if I can roust out enough of these boys."

They turned off left on one of the access roads and began to pass clusters of small trailer houses propped on cinder block. Shangreau stopped at one, went to the door and talked a bit, then came back alone.

"Hasn't recovered from last night yet. Can't say as I have either. There was nothin to celebrate, cept it being another Friday, but I did a job of it. You know when your teeth feel rubbery in the morning?"

Brian wasn't used to adults asking him hangover questions. "Yeah."

"That's the kind of bag I got on. Rubber-toothed."

He stopped at another trailer with no luck. This one hadn't come home overnight.

"Hope he's feelin good now, cause there's an ambush waitin at home for him. I had a big one like that in the kitchen I'd think twice about carryin on. She'll just squeeze all the good time right out of that man."

"Many of these people around here Indian?" Brian asked it noncommittally, fishing. The drill-rigger the night before had gone on and on about how the Indians and the coyotes should have been wiped out long ago.

"Oh sure," said Shangreau, "most of em. Not many purebred though, things being what they are. Most of these boys I'm after is at least half or more Indian. You got your Ogalala around here, your Hunkpapa and the rest. I'm a good quarter Sioux myself. Old Jim Crow who we're headin after now is maybe seven-eighths, fifteen-sixteenths, something like that. It's hard to keep count. Jim has got three or four tribes to start with, his mother was part Flathead as I recall, and then he's got white and I wouldn't be surprised if one of them buffalo soldiers didn't slip in a little black blood way back when. But you won't see too many purebred, less we catch Bad Heart at home, and he's another story altogether. What are you?"

"Irish."

"Me too, a good quarter. Monaghans."

They came to a pair of trailer houses that had been butted up together. A dozen fat little children wearing glasses ran barefoot out front. An older fat boy with extra-thick glasses and a silver-sprayed cowboy hat chased them, tossing a lasso at their legs. Brian got out of the pickup with Shangreau and a round, sad-looking man met them at the door to the first trailer.

"I see you're bright-eyed an bushy-tailed as everone else is this mornin," said J.C. "Them horses don't have much competition today, it looks like. Jim Crow, this here's Brian."

"Hey."

Jim Crow nodded. He was wearing nothing but flannel pajama bottoms and his belly hung over. His slant eyes and mournful expression made him kind of Mongoloid-looking.

"You know anyone else could join us? Couple of my possibilities crapped out on me."

"My brother-law's here from over the Rosebud. Sam. I'll ask him. And Raymond could come along. Raymond!"

The boy in the silver cowboy hat turned from where he had just cut a little sister out from the herd.

"You're coming along with us to work J.C.'s horses. Go tell your ma."

Raymond left the little sister to untie herself and ran off looking happy.

Sam was a little older and a little heavier than Jim Crow and had blue eyes. Brian sat in front between J.C. and Crow while Raymond's hat blew off almost immediately and they had to stop for him to run get it. His father told him to sit on it till they got to J.C.'s.

They stopped next at a lone trailer still on its wheels to pick up a young man called Jackson Blackroot. All the men got out and went to the door to try and catch a glimpse of Blackroot's new wife, who was supposed to be a looker. She obliged by coming out to say Hello boys and offer to make coffee. They turned it down, suddenly shy. She was dark and thin and reasonably pretty though Brian didn't see anything outstanding. Jackson was a friendly young guy with a big white smile who looked like an Italian. He shook Brian's hand and said he was pleased to meet him.

Bad Heart's trailer was alone too, a little box of a thing sitting on a hill. J.C. stopped out front and honked once.

"Be surprised if he's there," whispered Crow.

"If he is I be surprised if he shows himself."

They waited for a few minutes with the motor running and Shangreau had the pickup in gear when a short, pock-scarred man emerged from the trailer and hopped in the rear without a greeting.

It was a long bumpy way up to Shangreau's ranch and he did most of what little talking went on. The other men seemed to know each other and about each other but weren't particularly comfortable riding together.

"Brian," asked J.C., "you in any big hurry to get up there?"

Brian shrugged.

"I mean if you're not you might's well stop for lunch with us, look on when we work the horses. Hell, you can join the party if you're careful, can always use an extra hand when we're cutting."

"Sure." Brian was willing to follow just about anything at this point if there was food in it. He hadn't eaten since yesterday morning. He wondered exactly what cutting was going to be.

THE J. C. RANCH wasn't much. A side-listing barn surrounded by a wood-and-wire corral and a medium-sized unpainted shack in a couple of thousand acres of dry-looking open range. The shack squatted on a wood platform, there was a gas tank and a hot water heater on the front porch. J.C. explained that this was the working house, they had another aluminum-sided place further west on the property. There were wide cracks in the floorboard inside, blankets hung to separate the rooms. Shangreau's broad-faced wife grunted a hello and went back to pouring cornstarch into her stewpot. She had the biggest arms Brian had ever seen on a woman.

The men took turns washing their hands in a pail and sat around the kitchen table. Lunch was a tasteless boiled beef and potato stew that the men loaded with salt and shoveled down. There was little talk at the table.

"Well now," said J.C., pushing back his chair when everyone seemed finished, "let's get at them horses."

The men broke free into work. They readied their ropes and other gear while Brian and Raymond collected wood, old shack boards, and dead scrub for the branding fire. They built up the fire in a far corner of the corral, Jim Crow nursing it with a scuffed old hand bellows. When there were bright orange coals at the bottom and the irons were all laid out, the men spread with ropes in hand, forming a rough circle around the narrow chute that led into the corral from the barn, what Shangreau called the squeezer.

"And now, pilgrim," he said waving Brian back a little, "you gonna see some *masc*ulatin."

Raymond went up and started the first horse out through the squeezer and things began to happen fast, Brian struggling to keep up. The horse was not so huge, its back about chin-high to Brian, but it was thick and barrel-chested, its mottled gray sides working fast with suspicion. Raymond flapped his hat and clucked along the chute rail beside it till it was in the open and the men were swinging rope at its hooves, not picture-book lassoing but dropping open nooses on the ground and jerking up when it stepped in or near them. It took a while, plenty of near misses and times when the horse kicked free or the rope just slipped away, and Bad Heart was closest to Brian cursing a constant chant low on his breath, fuckin horse, goddamn horse, hold im, bust the fucker, and Raymond was in the corral trying to get his rope untangled and join the fun and Brian was hustling not to be trampled or roped.

"Bust im! Bust im!" J.C. was yelling and the stocky horse wheeled and crow-hopped but was met in every direction by another snapping rope. Finally Sam forefooted him cleanly and Jim jumped in quick to slip one over the head and jumped back to be clear as they hauled the animal crashing down onto its side.

"Choke im down! Choke im down!" yelled J.C. and they held its head into the ground with the rope while Bad Heart, cursing louder now and grimacing, wrestled its hind legs bent, one at a time, and strapped them back against its belly. They held it on its back now, writhing and lathered, eyes bugged hugely and nostrils wide, the men adding a rope here and there to help them muscle it still. Shangreau motioned Brian up with his head and handed him a rope end.

"Choke im," he said, "don't let him jerk. You let him jerk he's gonna hurt himself."

J.C. went to where the tools were laid out on a tarp and returned with a long, mean-looking jackknifey thing. The horse rested between spurts of resistance now, its huge chest heaving, playing out in flurries like a hooked fish. The men used the pauses to dig in their heels and get a stronger grip. J.C. waved the blade through the branding fire a few times, then knelt between the stallion's pinioned legs.

"Hold him tight, boys, they're comin off!"

The horse farted and screamed and shot a wad of snot into the blanket Bad Heart held its head with all at once, its spine arched clear off the ground and whumped back down, but J.C. had them in his fist and wouldn't be shook. He aimed and he hacked and blood covered his wrists till they cut free in his hands, a loose, sticky mess that he heaved into the far corner of the corral. He wasn't through. The horse rested quivering and Brian shifted the rope from where it had scored its image in his palms and J.C. brought what he had pointed out before as the masculator, a pair of hedge clippers that gripped at the end instead of cut.

"Ready?" he called, and when they were straining against the horse he worked the masculator inside and grabbed it onto what he wanted and yanked. There was blood spurting then, flecking the horse and the men and staining solid one leg of J.C.'s work pants. The rest was relatively easy, the branding and the tail-bobbing, the horse too drained to do much more than try to wave its head under Bad Heart's knee. With the smell of burnt flesh and fear around them, the men shortened their holds, worked in toward the horse, quiet now, Bad Heart's stream of abuse almost soothing. Each man grabbed a rope at some strategic point on the horse, J.C. taking over for Brian, and when each nodded that he was ready, they unlooped and jumped back in one quick motion. The horse lay still on its back for a moment, as if it had fallen asleep or died, then slowly rolled to its side and worked its legs underneath. It stood woozily at first, snorted and shook its head a few times, groin dripping thinly into the dirt, and then Raymond opened the corral gate to the range beyond and hat-flapped it out. It trotted a hundred yards off and began to graze.

"Forget he ever had em in a couple minutes," said J.C. He thumped Brian on the back, his hand sticking for a moment. "Gonna make a cowboy out of you in no time."

THE MEN sat near each other, leaning on the corral slats, resting.

"What's it for?" Brian decided there was no cause to try to seem to know any more than he did. "Why can't you leave them like they are?"

"It's a matter of breed," J.C. was working a little piece of horse from the masculator jaws. "You leave them stallions be, they don't want a thing but fight and fuck all day long. You don't want your herd to inbreed. Let them inbreed and whatever it is strange in them comes to the surface, gets to be the rule rather than the exception."

Bad Heart sat alone across the corral from them, over by where the genitals had been thrown. Raymond tried to do tricks with his rope.

"Don't want em too wild," said Jackson Blackroot.

"Or too stunted and mean," said Sam. "Or too high-strung."

"And you don't want any candy-assed little lap ponies. Like I said, it's a matter of breed. We keep one, maybe two stallions isolated, and trade them between outfits to crossbreed. You stud my herd, I'll stud yours. What we want is what you call your hybrid vigor. Like all the different stock I've got in me. Irish and Indian and whatnot. Keeps one strain from takin over and going bad."

"But you do keep a stud horse?"

"Oh yeah. Now I know what you're thinking, these sod-pounders up here haven't heard of artificial insemination. We know all right, it's a matter of choice. I been up to county fairs and whatnot, seen the machines they got. The mechanical jack-off machine and the dock syringe and all that. If that's your modern rancher, well you can have him. If God meant beasts to fuck machines he would of given em batteries. It's like that ASPCA bunch, always on our backs about the modern rancher and the proper way to masculate. Now there isn't but one way to do it. Ours. Horses know they been *cut*."

Cutting and branding and bobbing took about a half-hour per horse. It was tense, hard work and Brian got numbed to where only the burnt-hair smell when the brand was seared on bothered him. He liked the shouting and sweating and the physical pull against the animals and supposed the rest, the cutting and all, was necessary. They didn't seem to mind much after it was done.

The men seemed to loosen and touch more often as they got deeper into work, breaks between cuttings grew longer and more frequent. They sat on a little rise to the side of the corral passing dripping ice-chest beers and a bottle of Johnnie Walker J.C. had provided, gazing over at the string of fresh-cut geldings. Gimme a hit a that coffin varnish, they would say, and the bottle would be passed down, bloody hand to bloody hand, all of them half-shot with liquor but soon to work it off on the next horse.

"Must be some connection with their minds," said Sam. "Once you lop their balls off, whatever part of their mind that takes care of thinkin on the fillies must turn off too. So they don't even remember, don't even think like a stallion anymore. They forget the old ways."

"They turn into cows, is what. Just strong and dumb."

"But you got to do it," said J.C. "Otherwise you might's well let them run wild, run and fuck whenever they want, tear down all the fences and keep territory all to themselves. Nosir, it's got to be done."

The afternoon wore on in tugs and whinnies. Raymond fore-footed a big roan all by himself and Brian caught a stray hoof in his thigh that spun him around. One of the horses, a little scab-colored animal, turned out to be a real bad one, kicking all red-eyed and salty, running at the men instead of away until Bad Heart up with a branding iron, swinging at its head and spitting oaths but only managing to herd it right on out of the half-open corral door. It scampered up the rise with the others, kicking its heels and snorting.

"Raymond, dammit!" yelled Jim Crow. "You sposed to latch that damn gate shut!"

"I *did!*" Raymond had the look of the falsely accused; he took his silver hat off to plead his innocence. "I closed it right after that last one."

"Then how'd it get open?"

"It wasn't me."

"Don't worry about it," said J.C. "We'll have to go catch him tomorra. He's a tricky sumbitch to bring in. Just a wrong-headed animal, is all. That's the one you give me," he said to Bad Heart, "pay back that loan."

Bad Heart grunted.

IT WAS TURNING to evening when they finished. A cloud of fat black flies gloated over the heap of testicles in the corner. Brian had a charley-horse limp where he'd been kicked. They sprawled on the rise and pulled their boots off, wiggled red, sick-looking toes in the air, and sucked down beer in gasping pulls. Still-warm sweat came tangy through their denim, they knocked shoulders and knees, compared injuries, and debated over who would be sorest in the morning. Bad Heart coiled the rope he had brought and lay down alone in the back of the pickup. They pondered on what they should do next.

"The way I see it," said Jim Crow, "it's a choice between more of Minnie's cooking and goin out for some serious drinking."

They were silent then, it was up to J.C. to pass the verdict on his wife's cooking.

"Sheeit," he said, "if that's all that's keepin us here let's roll. What's open?"

"Not much. Not much legal, anyways. There is that whatsis-name's place, up to Interior."

"Then let's get on the stick. Brian, you a drinkin man?"

"I suppose."

"Well you will be after tonight. Interior, what's that, fifty mile or so? Should be able to get there afore dark and then it's every man for himself. No need to change but we'll have to go round and tell the women. Let's ride, fellas."

In the pickup they talked about horses and farm machinery and who used to be a bad hat when they were young and who was still capable of some orneriness on a full tank and about drunks they'd had and horses they'd owned and about poor old Roger DuPree whose woman had the roving eye. They passed liquor front seat to truck-bed, taking careful, fair pulls of the remaining Johnnie Walker and the half-bottle of Mogen David J.C. had stashed under the barn floor. Brian closed one eye the way he did when he drank so they wouldn't cross and Bad Heart carefully wiped the neck when it was his turn. They banged over the yellow-brown land in the long plains twilight, holding the bottles below sight-line as they stopped at each trailer to say they wouldn't be out too late. Raymond started to protest when it was time for him to be left off, but Jim Crow said a few growling words and his mournful face darkened even sadder; it would just *kill* him if he had to smack the boy. Raymond didn't want a scene in front of the guys and scooted off flapping the rump of an imaginary mount with his silver hat. The liquor ran out and Sam's belly began to rumble so they turned out of their way to hunt some food.

They reached a little kitchen emporium just before it closed up and J.C. sprang for a loaf of Wonder Bread and some deviled ham spread. The old woman in the store wore a crucifix nearly half her size and wouldn't sell alcoholic beverages. For PEACE OF MIND, said a faded sign over the door, INVESTIGATE THE CATHOLIC FAITH.

"Sonsabitches damnwell ought to be investigated," said Jim Crow. "Gotten so I can't but give a little peep of colorful language around the house and she's off in the bedroom on her knees mumbling an hour's worth of nonsense to save my soul. What makes her think I'd trust that bunch with my soul escapes me."

"Now they mean well enough, Jim, it's just they don't understand Indian ways. Think they dealin with a bunch of savages up here that haven't ever heard of religion. Think that somebody's got to get theirselves nailed to a tree before you got a religion."

"Fuck religion!" shouted Bad Heart from the back, and that ended the conversation.

A sudden rain hit them with a loud furious slap, drenching the men in the back instantly and smearing the windshield so thick that J.C. lost sight and the pickup sloughed sideways into the shoulder ditch. It only added to their spirits, rain soothing them where the sweat had caked itchy, not cold enough to soak through their layer of alcohol. It gave them a chance to show they didn't give a fart in a windstorm how the weather blew, to pile out and hunker down in the mud and slog and heave and be splattered by the tires when the pickup finally scrambled up onto the road. The flash downpour cut dead almost the moment the truck was free, just to make its point clear. J.C. spread a blanket over the hood and the men stood together at the side of the road waiting for Jackson Blackroot to slap them down a sandwich with his brand-new Bowie knife. The ham spread was a bit watery but nobody kicked, they hurried to stuff a little wadding down to soak up more liquor. They pulled wet jeans away from their skin and stomped their boots free of mud on the road pavement. J.C. came over to Brian.

"Don't you worry about the delay, son. We'll show you a real cowboy drunk soon enough."

"No rush."

"Damn right there's no rush. Got time to burn out here. Time grows on trees. Well, bushes anyway, we're a little short on trees. There isn't a picture show or a place with live music in some hundred miles, the Roman Church is about the only organization has regular meetings and you can have that. Isn't much cause for people to get together. Workin horses like we done is something though. A little excitement, even if it is work. Hell, it's better that it is work, you feel good about it even after it's over, not like a drunk where it takes a couple years of selective memory to make it into something you like to talk about."

"Doesn't seem so bad."

"Oh, there's worse, I'm sure. But I see you're passing through, not staying. Nobody lives here unless they were born here and can't hack it anywhere else. It's why most of the land around here was made into reservation, nobody else wanted it. Oh, the Badlands, up by Interior, they're striking to look at so the Park Service took them for the tourists, but the rest—hell, even the migrating birds don't come back anymore."

"Where you traveling to, Brian?" It was old Sam that asked.

"California."

He frowned. "You best be careful. That California is wild. Had a brother was killed there."

"I'll watch myself."

"I'd steer clear of it if it was me. They say it's wild."

J.C. laughed. "When was this brother killed, Sam?"

"Just around the start of the war. Got himself caught in something called the Zoot Suit Riots and that was all she wrote. Just plain wild."

"You know where I found Brian?" said J.C. "He was walking up Six-Hat Road there by Petrie's, sayin he's gonna walk to the

Innerstate. Seems he got his directions from old Cody Sprague there."

The men laughed. "Be better off gettin em from the buffalo," said Jackson Blackroot, "at least he's a native."

"Sprague isn't from around here?"

"He come out from some city back east, what was it, Philadelphia—?"

"Pittsburgh."

"Right. He come out from Pittsburgh on his vacation one summer and he sees all these roadside attractions up there on 90, the prairie dog village, reptile farms, Wall Drug Store, all that, and he thinks he's found his calling. He worked in some factory all his life and always had something about bein his own boss, owning his own business. So he takes his savings, which couldn't of been much, and buys himself two acres down on Six-Hat, the most worthless two acres in the whole state probly, and somewhere he gets ahold of that animal. Gonna build a dude ranch with the money he makes selling rides. Well it's been six, seven years now and I don't know how the hell he survives but he still hasn't got but them two acres and that animal."

"He's a nice old guy though," said J.C. "Talk your ear off, a little crazy, but a nice old guy."

"He's a character all right," said Jackson.

"He's an asshole." Bad Heart climbed into the rear of the pickup.

THEY HAD EATEN all the bread and were talking about Sam's brother getting killed in Los Angeles when Jackson remembered something.

"Hey," he said, "what we gonna do about that wake they're having over there for Honda Joe? Suppose we ought to go?"

"Just slipped my mind," said J.C. "Live just five mile away from us, no way I can't make an appearance, and it slipped my mind. Listen, as long as there's all of us together and we got the truck—"

"I suppose we ought to go."

"Damn shame it is, young kid like that. Goes through all that Vietnam business with hardly a scratch, gets himself a Silver Star, then comes back to smash hisself up on a goddamn motor-sickle. Young kids like that seem bent on it. I remember I couldn't talk my brother out of his plan for all the world, nosir, he had to have his California."

"It wasn't this it would have been some other," said Jackson.

"If it wasn't the bike maybe he would of drunk himself to death like some others around here."

"No, I don't think so. Honda Joe was always in a hurry to get there."

"Well he got there all right. In a couple pieces maybe, but he got there."

"We ought to go look in on him, for his mother's sake. What say, fellas?"

"I never liked Honda Joe," said Bad Heart.

"Well then, dammit, you can stay in the truck."

"If there's one thing I can't stand," said Jim Crow very quietly when they were on their way to Honda Joe's wake, "it's a sulky Indian."

It was still twilight when they passed by the access road to J.C.'s place again. He didn't offer to drop Bad Heart home before they went on. They crossed Six-Hat Road, Brian was just able to make out one of Cody Sprague's signs to the right, and then a half-mile further along they were stopped by a horse standing in the middle of the road, facing them.

J.C. turned on the headlights and they saw it was the scab-colored one that had escaped in the afternoon.

"The hell's he doin out here?" said J.C. He turned the engine off and got out quietly. He left the door open and walked slowly toward the horse, talking soft. "Good horse," he said, "nice horse. Come to papa. Attaboy."

The horse stood for a moment, nostrils wide open, then bolted off the road and out of sight. J.C. slammed back into the truck. Only Bad Heart dared laugh.

The trailer was alone and far away from the blacktops, far even from the oiled road that serviced most of the other places around. It sat as if run aground next to the dry streambed that cut through a gently sloping basin. Young men's cars, Pintos and Mavericks, Mustangs and Broncos, surrounded it, parked every whichway. To the rear was an orderly block where the family men had pulled in their Jeeps and pickups. J.C. slipped in among these and the men eased out. They had sobered, what with the food and the surprise rain and the knowledge of the work cut out ahead of them. They shuffled and stuffed their hands in their pockets, waiting for J.C. to lead. The mud and blood had stiffened again on their clothes, they tried to get all their scratching done before they had to go in. Bad Heart stretched out in the rear, glaring out into space. J.C. sighed and fished under the seat, behind the shotgun, and came out with a pint of gin. "I was saving this for an emergency," he said, and tossed it to Bad Heart. "Entertain yourself."

They were met at the door by two dark old Indians wearing VFW hats. Evening, gentlemen, glad you could come. There was a visitor's book to sign and no place to sit, the trailer was crammed to its aluminum gills. There were nods and hullos from the men already inside, crop and stock and weather conversations to drift into, and woman-noise coming from back in the bedrooms. Drink was offered and declined, for the moment anyway. A knot of angry-looking young men leaned together against one wall, planning to make yet another wine run up to Interior and back. Suspicious eyes lingered on Brian, coming hardest and hairiest from the young men. Brian felt extra uncomfortable in his sun-lightened hair and three-day road stubble in the midst of all the smooth, dark people. He was glad for the stains of horse-cutting left on him, as if having shared that gave him some right of entry.

Mrs. Pierce was on them before they could get their bearings. She smelled of tears and Four Roses and clutched at their elbows like she was drowning.

"J.C.," she said, "you come, I knew you would. And Jim. Boys. I knew you'd all come, I knew everybody'd come for my Joey."

She closed one eye when she had to focus on somebody. She squinted up to Brian. "Do I know you?"

"This is Brian, Mrs. Pierce," said J.C. "He's been workin horses over to my place."

"Well Brian," she said sober-faced, talking slow as if explaining house rules to a new kid in the neighborhood, "you just make yourself at home. Joey had him a lot of white friends, he was in the Army."

The woman had straight black hair with streaks of iron-gray, she stood up to Brian's shoulders, her face flat and unwrinkled. She could have been anywhere from thirty-five to fifty. She was beautiful. Brian told her not to worry about him.

"You come to stay a while, J.C.? You have something to drink? We got plenty, everybody brang for my Joey. We'll go right through the night into tomorrow with him. Will you stay, J.C.?"

"Well, now, Mrs. Pierce, we'd really like to, we all thought high of young Joseph there, but like I said we been workin horses all day and these boys are just all *in*. I promised their women I'd get them home early and in one piece. You know how it is."

The woman gave a little laugh. "Oh, I do, I surely do. We'll get him home in one piece, that's what the recruiters said, come onto Rosebud when we were over there. Make a man of him and send him back in better shape than when he left. Well, he's back, I suppose. Least I know where he is, not like some that are missing or buried over there. Don't figure anyone'll want to borrow him anymore." She stopped a moment and turned something over in her mind with great effort, then looked to J.C. again. "We're havin a service Tuesday over to the Roman. Appreciate it if you all could be there."

"We'll make every effort, Ma'am. And if there's anything you need help with in the coming weeks—"

"Oh no, J.C., save your help. Won't need it. After the service I'll just hitch up and drive on out of here. Go up north. I got people. I put two husbands and four sons in this country now and I'll be damned if it gets a drop more outen me. No, I'm to go up north."

"It's hard livin up there, Mrs. Pierce."

"Well it aint no bed a goddamn roses down here neither, is it?"

THE MEN hung on in the main room a bit more for courtesy, swapping small talk and trying to remember which of the wild Pierce boys had been responsible for which piece of mischief, trying to keep out of the way of the women, who seemed to know what they were there for. Mrs. Pierce weaved her way through the somber crowd assuring and being assured that her poor Joey was a good boy and would be sorely missed by all.

Brian noticed she was wearing the boy's Silver Star on a chain around her neck.

It took a good hour to get through the crowd, the people didn't seem to see much of each other and there was a lot of catching up to do, but they were herded steadily, inevitably, toward the bedroom where they knew Honda Joe would be laid out. They shied and shuffled at the doorway a little, but there was no avoiding it. A steady, humming moan came from within, surrounded by other, soothing sounds. J.C. took a deep breath and led the way.

Whoever did the postmortem on Honda Joe must have learned the trade by mail. The corpse, tucked to the chin under an American flag, looked more like it should have been leaning against a stuffed pony at the Wall Drug Store than like something that had lived and breathed. The skin had a thick look to it and a sheen like new leather, and even under the flag you could tell everything hadn't been put back where it belonged. The men went past the Murphy bed on both sides, up on their toes as if someone was sleeping. They clasped their hands in front of them and tried to look properly mournful. Jackson Blackroot muttered a few words to the corpse. Brian took his turn and concentrated on a spot on the boy's hairline till he felt he'd put in his time. He was moving away when he heard the whooping from outside.

"Yee-haaaaa!" somebody was yelling. "Yipyip-yeeeeee!"

There was the sound of hooves then, and the whooping grew distant. The men emptied out into the night range to see what it was.

"Yeow! Yeow! Yeow!" called a voice over to the left. Someone was riding a horse out there in the pitch black, someone pretty loaded from the sound of him.

"Goddamn Indians," grumbled one of the old men wearing a VFW hat. "Got no sense a dignity."

"Yee-hahaaaaa!" called the rider as a gray shape galloped by on the right.

"Sounds a bit like Bad Heart," said J.C. "Sounds a whole lot like him."

They went to J.C.'s pickup and Bad Heart was gone. There was some gear missing too, some rope, a bridle. They checked in

the front. J.C.'s shotgun was still there but Jackson's Bowie knife
was gone.

"He loses it I'll wring his goddamn neck," said Jackson.

The men all got in their cars and pickups then and put their
headlights on. The beams crisscrossed out across the little basin,
making eerie pockets of dark and light.

"Yah-haaaaa!"

A horse and rider appeared at the far edge of the light, disappeared into shadow, then came into view again. It was Bad
Heart, bareback on the little scab-colored stallion. It strained
forward as if it were trying to race right out from under him.
There was something tied with rope to its tail, dragging and
flopping behind, kicking up dust that hung in the headlights' arc.
Bad Heart whacked its ribs and kneed it straight for the dry
streambed. It gathered and leaped, stretching out in the air, and
landed in perfect stride on the far bank.

"Fucker can ride," said Jim Crow.

"Fucker could always ride," said J.C. "Nobody ever denied
that. Like he's born on horseback."

Bad Heart lay close to the line of the stallion's back, seemed to
flow with its every muscle. With the day's blood staining his old
tan Levis and the scabby red-brown of the horse it was hard to
tell where one began and the other left off.

"Yee-yeeheeeeeeee!"

Bad Heart circled the trailer a few more times before a couple
of the young men commandeered Jeeps and lit out after him. It
was a good chase for a while, the Jeeps having more speed but
the little stallion being able to cut and turn quicker. They
honked and flicked their lights and kept Bad Heart pinned in
view of the trailer but couldn't land him till he tried to make the
horse jump the streambed one time too many. It just pulled up
short and ducked its head, sending him flying over, tumbling
through the air till he hit halfway up the opposite bank.

The horse trotted off out of all the lights and Bad Heart lay
wailing.

He was pretty scraped up when they got to him, one side of
his face all skinned and his left leg bent crooked from midway
up the thigh. He cursed as they made a splint from a rake han-

dle, cursed as they carried him in on a blanket, cursed when they
laid him out on the Murphy bed next to Honda Joe.

"Wait'll the fucker wakes up in the mornin," he kept saying
while they tried to calm him down. "Gonna have a big surprise.
Wait'll he wakes up. Big fuckin surprise."

Jackson found his Bowie knife tucked in Bad Heart's boot
when they pulled it off. The knife was bloody up to the hilt.

Brian went out with J.C. and Jackson to see about the horse.
Everyone had turned their headlights off so J.C. got his flashlight
from the pickup. They walked out in the dark a bit and then
they heard whuffing up ahead and J.C. shined at it.

The stallion held its head up high, eyes shining back amber in
the beam, bridle dangling, chest and sides lathered and heaving.
It stood and looked at them as Jackson whispered his way up
and took the bridle.

J.C. came up and took the Bowie knife from Jackson. He cut
the rope free from the stallion's tail. Brian went back with him to
see what had been dragging behind.

It was a blood-sticky hide. The hair coarse and greasy, like
something you'd scuff your feet clean on. It had a sad, lonely
smell. It smelled like The West.

J.C. played the light off away from it. "I suppose we best take
this thing over, break the news to old Sprague. You wanna come
along for the ride?"

"Sure."

"Spose we'll call it a night after that. Get you up to go in the
morning." He turned the flashlight on the stallion, limping a bit
as it followed Jackson toward the trailer. "There isn't all that
much to do in Interior anyways."

Mac in Love

STEPHEN DIXON

STEPHEN DIXON lives in New York City, and has published stories in
Paris Review, Iowa Review, StoryQuarterly, Harper's, Georgia Review and *Carolina Quarterly*. He was born in New York and graduated
from City College.

S HE SAID "You're crazy, Mac," and shut the door. I
knocked. She said "Leave me be?" I rang the bell. She
said "Please don't make a fuss." I kicked the door bottom. She
said "Mac, the neighbors. You'll get the police here and me
thrown out." I said "Then let me in." She said "Maybe some
other day." I said "Just for a minute to explain." She said
"There's nothing to explain. The incident's over. It never
should've begun. It began and now it's over. So go away. Now
don't get me evicted. It's a cheap sunny place. It took me a long
time to find. I like this apartment, building and neighborhood
and I don't want to leave. You leave. Please leave now? I know
you'll feel different in the morning."

First published in the *Antioch Review*. Copyright © 1976 by Stephen
Dixon.

I went downstairs and left the building. Coming up the stoop as I was going down it was Jane's closest friend. Ruth said "Hello, Mac, you just up to see Jane?" I said "Yes, and how are you, Ruth? Nice day out. Actually, the whole week's been grand. Some weather we're having. Just look at that sky. No I'm serious: really look at the sky." I pointed. She looked. I said "Blue as can be. And people talk about pollution. But then they also say most pollution can't be seen. The experts say that, I mean, and that what appears to be clean air because the sky looks clean doesn't necessarily have to be clean air but dirty, except it doesn't look dirty because most pollutants, because of something to do with particles and refraction, can't be seen by the average naked eye. Well it's nice having the illusion if we can't have the fact. What I mean is isn't it nice that even if the air's dirty it at least looks clean? Even though it isn't, I'm saying. Or rather they're saying —the experts."

"It's a nice day as you say. And I suppose Jane's in, so I'll be seeing you, Mac. Take care."

"You too, Ruth, and give my regards to Jane. Or rather my love. Here, give her my love," and I wrote on a memo book page "my love," tore the page out and gave it to Ruth and said "Give it to Jane. Tell her I give it to her with my deepest love," and I wrote on another page "deepest love" and gave it to Ruth. "Please tell her I give her these messages with all my love," and on a third page I wrote "all my love" and gave it to Ruth. "Have a good weekend," I said; she said "You too" and climbed the steps and I crossed the street. I looked up at Jane's third floor apartment. All the shades were raised high. The bedroom and bathroom windows were open a few inches, the livingroom window was closed. The ceiling light in the bedroom was on, the living and bathroom ceiling lights were off. Jane opened the livingroom window all the way and began watering her plants. She turned to look into her apartment. She set the yellow watering can between two plant boxes on the outside window ledge and left the window. She was probably answering the door. "Hi," she would say to Ruth as she let her in. Ruth would say "Hi" or "Hello" and they would briefly hug or kiss one another's cheek or the air beside the cheek but not hug and kiss both. Ruth would take off her coat and put it on the chair next to the door as she always did or at least did when I was there and Jane would pick the coat off the chair and hang it in the closet facing the front door as she almost always did when I was there when Ruth put her coat on the chair. Ruth would mention seeing me and show Jane the pages. Jane would read them, frown, say how these messages were indicative of what she considered my growing craziness regarding her or maybe just my growing craziness. How she was thoroughly tired of my insisting she see me when she doesn't want to. How she was disgusted with my saying how much I care for her when she hasn't any feeling left for me except pity, and maybe not even that. They would go on like that. Ruth would say I had acted kind of strange downstairs. Jane would say "How do you mean strange, outside of these notes?"

"His going on about pollution and refraction and the illusion of the blue sky and such and urging me to look at it though I've seen it a thousand times this week and can very well appreciate a sky without him telling me to and in fact appreciate it a lot less when people urge me to. I didn't know what to make of it all."

"What I make of it is that if he comes around here again I'm going to call the police. I don't know how many times I told him on the phone and in person and once even in a letter to leave me alone. A normally reasonable person would have understood by now. Mac doesn't. He doesn't want to understand. Like a child he's still got to get the thing he's been told countless times he can't have and which will even make him sick. That's one of the things that turned me off to him. Another is that I simply grew out of being fond of him."

"Well I never thought he was right for you from the start. He was just always so eager to please me. There was just something so specially peculiar about his style—and not that he tended to talk too much or was so jittery—that scared or repelled me sometimes."

"I felt the same way in the beginning, but after a couple of dates he didn't seem peculiar at all. He became natural and nice. What I mean is he lost his nervousness or peculiar nature or whatever it is you might call it—that a doctor might call it—and became sweet and calm and generous and we had a pleasant relationship for about a month till something happened in him.

He didn't snap. Not that. He simply returned to being peculiar
again though in a much worse way than before. Before he was
only silly peculiar around people, which we both occasionally
found amusing. But lately he became peculiar around people in
a way that embarrassed me both for him and myself, and peculiar when we were alone that at times frightened me with the
possibilities of where it might lead to. But I'm not making myself
clear, am I?"

"You're trying to be tactful, though I understand what you
mean. Like that time—"

"Oh let's forget him, because I've had him up to here. Today,
yesterday, the night before. Always calling up or dropping by
when the last person I want to see is him. Like an hour ago he
called to say he was in the neighborhood and I said 'Really, Mac,
I'm very busy. I'm busy all the coming weekdays with rehearsals
and tapings and in the evenings with acting classes and class exercises and this evening and all day tomorrow with a friend,'
though I didn't mention you by name."

"Why not? I wouldn't've minded."

"But it's me. He hasn't any right to any explanations anymore
or knowing anything more about my personal life. But he came
around anyway and got in the building by ringing a neighbor's
bell."

"Didn't the neighbor try and find out who she was letting in?"

"That's what Mac told her as he climbed the stairs. This Mrs.
Roy, on the second, she opened her door and yelled for him to
leave the delivery carton on her door mat as she didn't want any
supermarket roaches in her apartment, but Mac said 'Excuse me,
ma'am, but I must've rung your bell by mistake. You should always ask who it is before you tick back. Best way to get burglars
in the building,' he said—you know, conning her, as he walks
past her apartment apologizing some more for the inconvenience
he caused her. She immediately got all flustery with his good
manners or I don't know what and said it was a good thing the
person she let in by mistake this time was such a nice polite man.
Then I hear him coming up to my floor and first thing he says
when he gets here is that he wants us to go to bed."

"For what? I don't understand. Came out with it in the hall or
in here?"

"Right here. He—but what should I do with these notes?"

"They're your treasures, not mine."

"Dump them, that's what I'll do. Love love love love. But what do you say to some tea. Jasmine or—oh just let me put the water on first. So before—"

"I think you're going to need more water than that for two cups."

"Right. So before, I let him in here. I had to avoid the big scene he swore he'd make in the hall, and immediately he grabs my hand and says 'Jane, I've thought things over and decided the most perfect remedy to all our present difficulties is for us to forthrightly though very calmly go to bed.' I said 'Oh sure, oh thanks, oh anything you say, Mac,' but he still had my hand and when he clutched it even tighter and tried leading me into the bedroom, I told him 'You're crazy, Mac. You're absolutely insane.' I finally had to pull my hand out of his and go to the window and threaten to shout for help unless he left. He said he didn't believe my threat as he didn't think I'd want to cause trouble for myself with the landlord, but as a courtesy to me he'd leave. But once outside the door he knocks and rings and kicks the door to get back in. When I refused he started to cry. Crazy cries. I told him to cry downstairs, cry out of the building, cry anywhere but here, and he said he would. And next thing I know you're ringing my downstairs buzzer and I think it's him and that's why I didn't answer that fast. But when you spoke into the speaker when I turned it on to listen to some sign that it might or might not be him, I let you up. How did he ever give you these notes?"

"On the stoop where we met. Wrote them up one after another in a way that seemed almost logical and clever to me in the sequence and routine he used. But having someone around like him would really scare me, to tell the truth."

"He's essentially harmless, don't worry. He'd never hurt anyone—just bother them to death. But why can't he say as let's say most other men might say 'Well it's over, Jane, and it's been fun, blah-blah,'—but not like that, of course. To quietly accept it and disappear. Relationships can't be one-sided, I told him. I told him no matter what happened between us in the past, if I no longer have any romantic or affectionate or sexual feelings towards him, then I'm just not going to come around again. He's making me a total wreck."

"Jane?" I yelled from the street.

"There he is again," Jane said.

"Jane? You left your watering can on the window ledge."

"I didn't quite get that."

"Something about my watering can. I left it on the outside ledge."

"What are you going to do?"

"About the watering can?"

"About him. Yelling your name out there. About him still being there."

"Ruth?"

"Now he's yelling your name."

"Ruth? Will you please tell Jane she left her watering can on the window ledge."

"He's going on about something about the watering can again."

"He said you should tell me I left it on the window ledge."

"What I feel like telling you is to tell the police there's a maniac on the street screaming out our names."

"Mrs. Roy?"

"Who's that now?"

"The second floor tenant I spoke about."

"Mrs. Roy? Will you please tell Ruth, who's a visitor of your neighbor, Miss Room, to please tell Jane she left her watering can on the window ledge."

"Maybe Mrs. Roy will solve your problems by phoning the police."

"No such luck."

"Jane?"

"Good God, Ruth, what should I do?"

"Jane? Will you please tell Ruth to tell Mrs. Roy to tell Ruth to tell you you left your watering can on the window ledge."

"I'm going to call the police."

"Ruth?"

"Do it. Just tell them he's down there. I'll back you up."

"Ruth? Will you please tell Jane to tell Mrs. Roy to tell you to tell Jane she left her watering can on the window ledge."

"Police? My name is Jane Room, 31 East 13th, apartment 3B. There's a man outside my building by the name of Mac Salm who's constantly shouting out my name in a way to cause embarrassment to me and who's been annoying me for days to get into my apartment. . . . No, I know him. For about a month. . . . I've told him that for a week now, but he still comes around uninvited and causes commotions in my building's hallways and lobby till I'm forced to let him in. . . . No, but I can just as well be protected from his verbal abuse and the mental and emotional harm he's causing me, can't I?"

"Mrs. Roy?"

"Now he's shouting my second floor neighbor's name. Mrs. Roy. Ernestine. If you had any kind of amplifying device on your phone— Then I'll tell you."

"Mrs. Roy?"

"He repeated her last name."

"Will you please tell Ruth to tell Jane to tell you to tell Ruth to tell Jane she left her watering can on the window ledge."

"He said that Mrs. Roy should tell my friend to tell me to tell Mrs. Roy to tell this same friend to tell me that I left my watering can on the window ledge. . . . Because I was watering my outside plants when the doorbell rang. Not him this time but a friend at the door. I already said he's harmless that way. Well then I said it to my friend here but to you I remember saying I didn't think Mr. Salm would physically harm me. . . . Well I remember. . . . Ruth. I don't see why I have to give her last name to you. If you send someone over and she's still here, which she promised to be, then you can get her full name and address as a witness. . . . Excuse me, but are you going to send an officer over or not? . . . Yes, this is a complaint. . . . S-A-L-M. I—thank you.

"He said a patrol car will be right over."

"What was that argument about my last name?" Ruth said.

There she is. At the window looking down towards me. "There you are, Jane. I suppose Mrs. Roy finally told Ruth to tell you to tell Mrs. Roy to tell Ruth to tell you your watering can's on the window ledge."

She took the watering can. "I called the police, Mac." And closed the window, pulled down the shade.

Why don't I leave and not come back as she says? Because I think if I persist in telling her about my love for her she'll once more love me in return. Because she was in love with me once. She once told me that. She said "I was in love with you once but I'm not now." She never once said "I'm in love with you now." Just that she was in love with me once. When was she in love with me? Once when we were on a bus and she curled up in my arms because she was sleepy and cold and it was late and the bus was unheated and we were returning from a dinner party uptown. And another time when we wanted to get to the theater before the movie began and I suggested we run so we ran, she alongside me and running very good for a girl and that smile she gave me then. She was in love with me as we ran, if that's possible. And we held hands during the movie and from time to time looked deeply at one another and gently kissed. She was in love with me then: running, on the movie line when she hugged me, inside. She was in love with me another time when we were in the park. That first spring-like Sunday and we fell asleep on the grass just past the shade of a flowering dogwood in flower and just before she fell asleep she was lying on her back with her arms raised and I was leaning halfway over her and we looked at one another without smiling and I was so happy with her that a tear came and instead of wiping it I let it drop on her face because I thought to wipe it was as unimportant an act as to let it fall and then tears came from her and rolled past her ears and neck onto the grass and we kissed each other's eyes. She was in love with me then though she didn't say it. And other times but not now. I hear sirens. "I'm going, Jane. So long, Ruth." But the sirens are for someone else. People passing look at me. They think I'm crazy, drunk or both. I understand that. A man doesn't yell out on the street what I've been yelling without running the risk of people thinking him crazy, drunk, both or something else. But why did she stop loving me? That's what I should yell if I yell out anything else. But she already told me she doesn't quite understand why she stopped loving me. That feeling that allowed her to run along the street smiling lovingly at me went, she said last night when I recalled the incident for her, hoping to reawaken in her the same feeling. That feeling that allowed her to lie or sleep comfortably beside me went, she said before when

I half jokingly asked her to come to bed with me. That feeling for wanting to do anything with me went. For wanting to talk to me went. For wanting to even talk to me about why she can't talk to me went. It all went. She doesn't know why it didn't in me but did in her but it did and that is that, she said. All gone, she said. Don't cry, she said. She said she hates to see me cry and might even cry herself if I cry, she said. She said cry somewhere else then, she said. She said she knows how I feel because if this will be of any comfort to me she once loved a man very much who didn't love her anymore but once did and she felt something like what I must be feeling and she knows it's a terrible feeling but she got over it and I will too. She knows. "You're a person with a lot of love to give and I wish what we once had could have continued like it did and blossomed like it didn't but it didn't and love's the one thing in life that can't be forced," she said. "At least from me," she said. She meant for herself. A patrol car was coming down the block. "I won't be bothering you anymore," I yelled to Jane. "I'm sorry for all my ridiculousness about the watering can before and the trouble I've caused you and Ruth and Mrs. Roy and really you've been right all along because like you said when the feeling's gone it's gone and that's that so so long," and I walked to the corner.

Two policemen got out of the patrol car. One asked me to please stand still, lean against the car with my hands on the hood and legs spread wide behind me so I could be searched. He searched me. He said I was clean. He said a person named Jane Room issued a complaint against me. I said I know all about the complaint or at least the reasons for it and she's absolutely right. "I only now know how crazy and wrong I've been. I won't annoy her anymore. I don't know how I can make my feelings any more clear to you on this matter other than to say I'll do anything you want me to do. I'll go to the station house without any bother or leave this block peacefully and never walk on it again if you don't want me to or for as long as you don't want me to. I'll positively not phone or contact her in any way again. I swear."

"All right," one of them said. "No more trouble then."

"No more."

"If there is any, we'll be forced to arrest you. That is, if Miss

Room doesn't withdraw her complaint or if she or someone else complains to the police on this matter once more."

"I understand."

"I think he'll be all right, Herb," the other policeman said.

"Okay," Herb said.

"Okay," I said.

They got in the car but didn't drive away. I walked around the corner and along the avenue towards 12th Street. The patrol drove parallel though a little behind me till I crossed 12th and headed for 11th. Then it sped up down the avenue and made a right several blocks away.

As a joke I should walk back to Jane's and yell out her name or something one last time. Something to Jane to thank Mrs. Roy for telling Ruth to tell Jane to tell Mrs. Roy to tell Ruth to tell Jane her watering can's on the window ledge. After all, I could say, the can could have fallen off the ledge and hit someone on the head. I could yell out that in the combined act of our telling Jane about her watering can we possibly saved someone's life or at the least saved someone from getting hurt or at the very least saved Jane from losing or damaging her watering can. I bought her that can at a Japanese gift shop a week ago. But by the time I got through yelling out all this the police would be back, summoned by Jane or maybe Mrs. Roy. Surely Ruth would demand that Jane call the police or Ruth might call them herself over Jane's protests. I would be brought to the station house. I would spend the night in jail. It would be a change. I feel terrible. My stomach and head ache. I still can't accept not being with Jane anymore. I'll have a miserable night unless I'm with her or dead drunk or confined in a cell in a station house and I'll only get deathly sick if I get dead drunk again and Jane will never let me be with her again. "Once I'm turned off to someone I once loved I'm turned off to them for good," she told me today.

I ran along the avenue towards Jane's block. I stood across the street in front of her building. All her lights were on. The bathroom shade was up. The windows in the living and bedroom were partly open. The sky was no longer light blue but getting dark. "Jane," I yelled. "Will you thank Ruth for telling Mrs. Roy to tell Ruth to tell you to tell Mrs. Roy to tell Ruth to tell you your watering can's on the window ledge." The patrol car was coming down the street. The same two policemen got out. They looked angry. "Ruth? Will you thank Mrs. Roy for telling you to tell Jane—" but the police were on me before I could finish. One got me from behind. He pressed the middle of his club in my mouth in a way where I couldn't push it out or bite his hand. Then I was on the ground on my stomach. Herb had his knee in my back and my arms twisted behind me. I was handcuffed. I was told to stand when I thought I could stand like a peaceful quiet citizen and not before because if I stood before then I was going to get knocked to the ground but this time by a club. "We're not fooling around," Herb said. "We've got a job to do and you should know that by now."

I said I knew it and was ready to stand the way they wanted me to. "Peacefully and quietly?" Herb said, and I said yes and he took his knee out of my back and helped me up. I yelled "Jane?"

A Stay by the River

SUSAN ENGBERG

Susan Engberg was born in Dubuque, Iowa, and educated at Lawrence College in Wisconsin. Her stories have appeared in the *Kenyon Review*, the *Massachusetts Review*, *Ascent* and *Southern Review*. This is her second story to appear in the O. Henry collection. She is married and has two daughters.

I HAVE FLOWN a thousand miles to visit Melanie and Todd. A few minutes ago Melanie and I descended barefoot to the garden, and I watched while she selected the red and pale green lettuce leaves I am now rinsing one by one in a kitchen that is cut like a windowed cave into the slope on which the house was built—how many years ago, Melanie?

Almost a hundred, she says and opens the screen door to call out to Todd and the children in the gazebo, Shall we eat down there?

Tomorrow I will go to the garden and weed the vegetables; I saw tonight that I could go there regularly by myself and without asking directions find useful and ordinary work. Already I think I can feel my mind easing itself. I am glad for the river at the base of the bluff. From the kitchen window I can see the water glinting in late sun through the trees, but not the train whose wail I am hearing for the second time since my arrival. My room upstairs has a leaded casement window that I can crank open or shut while sitting in a flowered reading chair. Melanie cranked the window open for me this noon and said they haven't bothered to change the house much from the way Todd's parents had kept it. What else could you do with a house like this? she said. She laughed as if the house doesn't matter to her, or as if she scarcely believes the way she is living.

Alone, pausing at a mirror in the upstairs hallway, I pressed my forefingers beside my eyes and pulled taut the lines of fatigue. I looked from one eye to the other, and back again. Without hurry I saw how light entered my eyes and gave back color.

I came downstairs and found Melanie with the children in the sun room above the kitchen. In spite of myself I thought that if I want a child of my own, I have only a few years left. Melanie's oldest girl sat coloring on a long cushioned window seat. She was keeping her crayons in a matchbox that she slid open and shut each time she chose a new color.

Now Melanie wraps the wet washed lettuce in a towel and takes it out the door to the mossy terrace. I see the balloon of thin white towel circling in the air, spraying waterdrops, as she makes a windmill of her arm. Leaning my hand on the thick stone wall of the doorway, I think of how long these stones have been here, motionless.

Melanie cuts fresh dill and long green onions on a board. I wonder if she is aware of her hands. She is wearing an old white blouse, and I like her brown neck and her long brown switch of hair. I sit idly, luxuriously in the dark wood breakfast booth, listening to the chicken broiling and watching Melanie's hands. There is a band-aid on one of her fingers and on another a silver and turquoise ring.

She is talking about a cottage down the road. We'll walk down there tonight or tomorrow, she says.

Who did you say he is? I ask.

Burdock. Martin Burdock, she repeats patiently, and for a moment I feel as if I am one of Melanie's children. I wonder what it

would be like to be one of Melanie's children, sitting perma-
nently among window seat pillows, choosing colors from the sliding inside of a matchbox.

Melanie is deft. Already she has gotten up a tray with seeded
rolls and butter, plates and silverware. She takes wine from the
refrigerator. I wonder where she has learned this casual deftness.
Mostly I remember her earnestness, and her candor. One of the
children begins to cry from the yard, and I see a slight change in
Melanie's mouth and down the center of her forehead. Let's go
fast, she says, gathering things up, before they all get too tired.

Todd leads me down the steps to a wooden landing high in
the trees above the railroad tracks and the river. We are finishing
off the wine.

My Grandfather built this bench, he says.

A hundred years ago? I ask.

No, not that long, he laughs. We are sitting close and enjoying
each other's company. In the gazebo Melanie kissed us both and
then took the children up for their baths. You come for the tuck-
ing-in, she called back to Todd. The youngest of the three, a boy
of two, threw a rock down into the tree tops before he followed
his mother.

Did you hear it land? asked Todd through the lattice-work
and screens. That's for the train coming, Dad, said the boy.
Whatever that means, said Todd to me, winking. He picked up
the bottle and I took our glasses and followed his pale grey shirt
down the steps into the darker trees.

Why did your grandfather choose this place? I ask.

Lord knows, he answers. There's an Indian burial ground on
the property—did you know?

That's a treasure, I suppose?

Anna's gotten afraid of the ghosts. She's old enough to think
about those things.

I drink the light white wine and ask Todd when the next train
is due. If this is Saturday, then not until tomorrow morning, he
says, stretching out his legs. I like him immensely. He and
Melanie were already married twelve years ago when I met her.
I liked him then. It gives me pleasure to drink this wine and to
sit next to him in the dark trees, knowing we are both twelve
years older and still good friends. He leans his ruddy, bearded

head towards me and gives me the last few drops from a bottle that in the thick light I can only barely tell is green.

The boat yards are closing down—did Melanie tell you? he asks.

No. Is that bad for you?

Not so bad. If it hadn't been for Dad's death, I probably never would have come back here anyway. It's amazing, we intended to stay a few months to clean up his affairs, and here we are, four years later.

What will you do? I ask.

Oh, there are a few other interests—shipping and storage and so forth, if that's what I want.

Is that what you want?

I'm not much of a businessman, he says. It took months just to understand what my dad had going. He must have thought that he would live forever. His offices were still upstairs at the yards —you can picture it—outside staircase, wooden filing cabinets, dusty windows, dusty ship models, dusty sunshine, and God what a mess of papers. The place still smelled of his pipe. Todd leans forward and lays the empty bottle between his shoes.

I can see it, I say, the historian examining his origins.

Something like that.

And now?

Now that building has been sold and will be torn down this summer, and I've got to decide whether to keep on with the rest of it or sell out. What would you do?

This place is beautiful. When Melanie wrote that you were moving here, I couldn't quite imagine it, but it's beautiful, the river is marvelous.

I don't think Melanie has quite settled in.

Todd's body makes me think of my own. I see the lightness of his shirt sleeve and his almost invisible hand, and I think of the length of my legs within these soft, loosely fitting slacks.

Todd lets his voice speak on. Sometimes I think I could do nothing more than live off a garden and be with Melanie and the children, he says. We could sell the furniture piece by piece, and then our clothes, piece by piece.

I see Todd and Melanie lying on the carpet of an empty living room, naked in the moonlight of the open French doors.

The shrilling of insects and tree toads seems to be rising in false panic. I try to do nothing but empty my mind and understand those layers of sound, but instead I am thinking about the Indians who are dead and buried someplace on the property. I am thinking that I woke up this morning half-way across the continent. I make a sound, but forget what I had intended to say.

Are you tired? asks Todd. Do you want to come up and say goodnight to the children?

SYLVIE IS running up and down the broad, breezy hall in a blue summer nightgown patterned with white butterflies. Light opens out into the hall from the bathroom and bedrooms. My own room, I see, is luminous. Melanie must have come into my room, perhaps with Peter naked on her arm, to turn on the light beside my flowered chair. Sylvie follows me and stops at the foot of my bed, twisting the hem of her nightgown in one hand. She allows me to come to her and pick her up, but she is lighter than I supposed, so light that for a moment I feel we could take off from earth on the unused energy of my expectation. Tonight I am relieved to be tethered by a child. She giggles as I press my face against her belly, and I wonder how the vapors of wine must seem to her.

A net has been thrown around this house. It is made of tree branches and shadows and fretted layers of sound. We pass down the hall and through a lighted doorway. I try to think in a simple way about the net of love into which I have slipped for a brief visit. Anna is already asleep with her crayons beside her bed.

Sing to me, says Sylvie, reaching out for her blanket, and I hear myself singing a song I probably haven't thought about for thirty years.

Out in the darkened hallway I find Melanie leaning slackly against the couch, turned towards the puffing curtains of the open window.

I AM in the garden, working methodically up and down the rows with a triangular hoe. I have done the radishes, the red lettuce, the green lettuce, and now I bend between horizontal strings of peas in purple blossom. Someone has put collars of straw at the base of the staked tomatoes. When I straighten up again to rest, I see Todd, starting down the road.

He stretches across the front seat of the car and calls. I didn't know anyone else was up.

I don't think of anything to say. I stand with my hoe, smiling, thinking simply of the early heat of the sun. I wave and he drives away. I think how I would like to be responsible for this garden. I would like to have been the one who carried straw to the tomato plants and tied strings along the rows of peas. Last night Melanie seemed quick and indifferent as she gathered the lettuces and radishes. I marvel at that, now that I am in between the rows myself, slowed down to garden time, cultivating foot by foot and noticing each plant's signs of growth. I think how I could like an entire summer to be measured solely by a garden.

After four more rows Melanie calls me for breakfast. When I come up the slope to the terrace, I see a young woman with hunched, awkward shoulders talking to Melanie. Extra children shout on the swings and beneath the awnings of the sandbox. I look briefly to the river curving out below a point of land some distance along the bluff top, and when I reach the table and am introduced, I am thinking that land coming to a point high above a river would be a naturally chosen burial ground.

The young woman has brought strawberries in a flat pan, small ones that she explains are sweeter and larger ones that are not so sweet. Her voice trembles slightly and she listens solemnly as Melanie tosses off a gay incident of strawberries from her childhood. Melanie is in motion. Some time ago, when I was in the garden, her morning began, and now she is speaking with a force and swiftness that might be called impatience. She glances now and then at the children. Someone cries. She goes to pick up Peter and comes back still talking. She is forcing the world away from her with words. The young woman stares down into her coffee cup, tipping the dregs of it from side to side and looking as if she is holding back a helpless pain. I take toast and boiled eggs from a basket and sit quietly eating, stealing my hand out now and then for a strawberry and wondering when the real Melanie will return.

Oh, God, says Melanie, crumpling down full-length on the

grass when her visitor has left. That girl is in love with me and I have no idea what to do.

Is that what was going on? I say, while I am wondering how Melanie can read such love, how does she know?

I find it exhausting, she says, I'm afraid I do more damage than good. Go on, go on, she urges me, I wish you'd eat every last one of those strawberries. She calls the children over and tells them to eat strawberries, while she herself lies down in the grass alongside a bed of daisies and poppies. Peter spits the berries out.

Come here, Peter, she calls and catches hold of him, and together they go rolling over and over down the grass. Melanie's laugh is wild and fierce, and the children catch her mood and go rolling over and over. I run inside to get my camera, and as I pound up the stairs I barely hear the trailing sound of the train between their high, rolling cries. Halfway down the hall I stop. I see myself in my apartment, coming out of the darkroom at night, examining a proof sheet of Melanie's life, frame after frame of someone else's life. I turn instead into the bathroom where I lay a cold cloth over my face, pressing it to my eyes, and then I wipe the garden dirt from my arms and legs. Taking off my shoes and lifting my feet one and then the other to the basin, I wash them in cool water.

Today a dozen moths, some yellow-white like paper and others thicker and mottled brown, that were lured by last night's bathroom light are clinging, asleep or waiting for death, against the walls. I think of telling Melanie about the stillness of the moths in the growing heat and commotion of the morning, and I hear her saying, pushing back her hair, Todd has been meaning to fix that screen.

As I finish washing my feet, I watch a sluggish lightning bug crawl along the edge of the basin. His back is segmented, the small anterior part touched with red and the lower section long, black, halved, like a stiff frock coat. My own back is a single supple chain of bones; I can feel the nerved complexity of its beginnings at the nape of my skull and at its base the shielding bones of my pelvis and the strong sockets of my legs.

How does Melanie know? I thought last winter with Michael that I knew, now nothing seems to be left. I became critical and bewildered; I resumed my long walks alone. He did nothing to hold me. Why did he do nothing to hold me?

I go downstairs, and Melanie is at the kitchen sink. Peter presses into her bare legs, crying. Outside the door Anna shouts something bossily to Sylvie and then rides around the corner of the house on her new two-wheeled bicycle; Sylvie cries and throws a clump of dirt against the screen door.

Stop it, Peter. No one can stand to listen to that. Stop it! I wish you would tell me what you want, I don't want to listen to those tears.

Melanie's hands never stop lifting dishes from the soapy water. The announcer on the kitchen radio tells the news. Do you hear me, Peter? she says. You've got to stop these scenes and tell me what you need.

We ARE passing through unmown grasses at the end of the property. I am talking with Anna, holding her by the hand, while Melanie pushes ahead through the heat, straddling Peter on one hip. For some minutes Sylvie has been whining to be carried. She will have none of me today. Melanie reaches down finally for her middle child and then struggles on like a beast of burden.

The air is scented with purple clover. We are going to visit Martin Burdock. I brush at the gnats and listen to Anna, who says that fairies leave and reenter their underground homes at the base of trees, where the roots show. She asks me if I have ever been at the equator. She says it is possible to fry an egg on the equator. I ask her what she thinks the equator looks like, and she says it is probably flat, but not very thick. She asks me if I know that Sylvie wants a two-wheeler but can't have one because her legs aren't long enough. I look down at Anna's own gangling legs beneath her faded shorts, her thin chest and urgent face, and my next breath comes quickly, like an ache.

Martin Burdock has retired to a cottage with a garden and a view of the river. Melanie sits on the grass beside his chair with Peter asleep across her lap. The girls whisper in their make-believe beneath a flowering hedge. I am not sure what is happening. It seems to me as if Melanie has brought an offering to Martin Burdock, that she has brought herself and the children, even me, into his garden as gifts, as species of blooming flowers.

I do not feel like a flower. I am nondescript, my color sucked away. We drink English tea, and I notice that Martin Burdock and his garden are at the same time fastidious and disorderly. He pushes aside a pile of newspapers and fusses a bit at the angle of the sun, adjusting a dilapidated umbrella over the table. We must, it seems, be able to see each other without strain, in the proper light. I see violet and green shadows all along Melanie's skin; her face is flushed and her eyes are grey and yellow.

Martin Burdock is writing a book, and as Melanie sets down her cup and eases her legs beneath Peter, I know suddenly that she is using Martin Burdock's eyes. She sees Anna and Sylvie in the shadows, she sees the brilliant river, in a sliding glance she sees me, then the hot heavy head of Peter—all through the eyes of Martin Burdock, and then in the next moment as I look at Martin Burdock's ageing face, the way its lights and hollows of color incline themselves to Melanie, my breath presses hard in me and I seem to have lost a space of time. Here it is again, I think. Here it is: if I had been Melanie, would I have known? Could I have let it happen?

I AM losing track of days. This afternoon a storm brings in cooler air. My mail has been forwarded to me by Edward. My parents are well; they themselves will travel in two weeks. An insurance payment is due on the nineteenth. My brother Julien will stop to see me in August. Genevieve says they're saving most of the proofs for me and that three of the photographs for the catalogue had to be retaken. Edward says the city is unbearable, he says my cat mopes but manages a few mouthfuls, he says my avocado plant suffers from the heat, along with everyone else, he says he came across the hall and played my piano the other night, knowing I wouldn't mind, he says, How are you anyway?

I have turned my reading chair away from the room so that it faces squarely the window bleary with rain in its diamond-shaped panes. In my lap are the letters that verify my reasonable life. When I work, I work very well. I take the time to do my work well. But still, a momentum builds for which there seems no end; I go ahead deliberately, and yet I seem to myself to be racing. No one reaches out to stop me. Michael is a worker, too, and when we would come together, it would be because we could no longer work.

Downstairs I find Melanie lying on the living room rug, exercising slowly by the half-open French doors. The storm has subsided into an even rain. Melanie has created a space around herself by the concentrated positions of her body. She smiles at me, but I go away to the sun porch where I sit on Anna's window seat, just inside the rain. I try to think about nothing much but the rain, another summer storm, and about how everyone has to live somewhere, in some conditions or in others, everyone has a life. I pick up a magazine and read three recipes for blueberries, I think of Melanie's hands cutting green onions and a limp bouquet of feathery dill, I see Todd's shirted back descending through the trees, one hand holding up the wine bottle like a torch.

Melanie comes in and sits down in a wicker lounge, still in her leotard. Are you feeling more rested? she asks. You're beginning to look more rested.

Are the circles going away?

Either that, or they're melting into your tan.

This place is beautiful, I say.

You really think so? I notice a careful lightness to her voice.

I do, don't you?

Maybe it's too beautiful. I wake up in the morning and look out the window and I think God, this place. I look at Todd and the kids and I think my God, look what has happened. She gestures loosely with her hand, from the wrist, and I see nothing but the perfect repose of her exercised body. There's too much, I'm not equal to it, she says.

Melanie asks me again about my work. I am suddenly suffocated by my work, angry.

I envy you, she goes on.

There's nothing to envy, you don't know what you have.

My words make her stop and regard me. We are afraid we have hurt each other. After a time she nods and says, still cautious with her voice, That's what I meant, I don't understand what I have. And maybe you don't either, she adds.

She tips back her head and we are quiet. Where are the children? I ask.

Peter is asleep. The girls are somewhere, the gazebo, I think, I can trust Anna.

I am trying to remember Melanie as I knew her twelve years ago, six years ago.

Do you know what has been happening to me? she says. I have begun remembering all sorts of things. Some days I can barely keep my mind on the present time. Exhaustion, probably. God, but children are exhausting.

What do you remember?

You really want to know? Melanie laughs. All right, this one happened a couple of weeks ago. I was coming downstairs. It was an ordinary day—well, no, rather special because I had been over to talk to Martin the night before. I was coming downstairs and I remembered that when I was twenty-one I had a vision of Christ. Do you think that's possible? she asks without pausing. I was in love with Todd, he had gone away, I had agreed to go out and help at this church camp, and there he was one night, Jesus Christ, standing in his robes on the edge of a stream at vespers. I just looked, and he melted away, and I haven't thought about it for thirteen years.

What did you at the time?

Nothing. I told no one. I just buried it all. I wasn't even going to church at the time. I'm certainly not going to church now. What on earth do you do with something like that?

Melanie is trying to sound humorous, but I see her body is jerking slightly with tremors. She looks very much like Anna just now, six years old, only much older. I feel powerless.

Has anything like that ever happened to you?

No, but I don't think it sounds unlike you, I say.

What do you mean? Do you think I'm a dreamer?

I smile at Melanie, but my eyes are trying to see beyond her black-suited figure to the form of what she means. An experience like that seems to fit in with your intensity, I say.

Intensity! Melanie laughs sharply, and I see she is close to tears. She has tipped back her head once more and is staring at the ceiling, sucking in her lips.

Why are you wanting to cry? I ask, and in a rush I understand that this is the way Edward talks to me, I am almost hearing the inflections of his voice.

There's so much now, says Melanie finally, there's so much at stake now that I find it almost impossible to know the truth of what I'm feeling.

You mean Todd and the children?

All right, if you want to put it that way: Todd and the children. Her voice is abruptly dry, analytical. I don't do anything purely anymore, she says. She is looking at me steadily.

I meant what I said about intensity.

Gradually her face softens. Well then, I thank you, she breathes. You see how needy I am, I twist everything about just to get a few crumbs of assurance.

You're being very hard on yourself, I say.

No, you've got it wrong, she says quietly. I haven't been nearly hard enough.

WE ARE at one end of the living room watching a rerun of the day's hearings. Todd has bathed and put the children to bed, all but Sylvie, who sits stubbornly in his lap, eating graham crackers and letting herself be petted. The living room is airy and pleasant, carefully decorated by the previous generation. Todd wears a pair of threadbare jeans. Melanie is in a soiled robe, intending to bathe, but held, as we all are, by the sordid drama, difficult to understand as real. I am sitting on the floor, pulling the drying skin from hoeing blisters on the palms of my hands.

Todd holds the feet of his daughter in one hand, stroking her skin with his thumb. He rubs her back with his other hand. I glance up now and then and see her taking cracker after cracker from the box on her lap until Melanie says, Don't you want a glass of milk, Sylvie? You'll gag on all that dryness.

I want grape juice, says Sylvie contentedly, and I see Melanie and Todd open their eyes to each other above her head, above my head, above the shifting faces on the television.

I CAN'T GO to sleep. My head hurts above my eyes and the back of my neck is tight. My mind rushes repeatedly down a cataract of night and finds itself lodged against the same stones. The pain in my forehead is heavy, my tongue is thick and unwanted, and my heart refuses to lighten itself. I stare at a darkened window. Here is one stone: why should I not have a garden? I had one as a child. What is wrong with me that I don't go someplace where I can have a garden? Another stone, another and another: why can't I learn to read signs, why should I not be able to know the truth about myself, am I impoverished?

I SIT IN the kitchen booth. Melanie slides me a mug of camomile tea. Stop it, Peter, I'm trying to talk, and I don't want to listen to a little boy whining.

She throws up her hands. I'd like to fly away, she says. I could float. She twirls once, her arms above her head. Good-bye, good-bye.

She is talking quickly and laughing. Peter has thrown himself on the floor. He cries without conviction and kicks the edge of the booth monotonously with one bare heel.

You'll bruise yourself, Peter, says Melanie, and his tears renew themselves.

No, dummy Mama, he cries.

The tyranny of children, says Melanie, I don't know whether to laugh or cry, I'm inadequate.

I think you do fine, I say.

If I were smart, I'd think up something else for him to do besides cry, but my mind is empty, I'm ashamed of him, I'm ashamed of myself. Come here, Peter, will you sit on my lap? she says, but as she bends to lift him up, his kicking lands upon her chest. Stop it! she screams, her voice changing, and I sit dully with the settling flowers of my tea as she carries him from the room.

Sometime later she finds me in the garden. He fell asleep, she says as she works along with me, thinning the bean sprouts, some of which are still curled, head bent, while others are holding out new double leaves, like open palms. But he let me talk to him and read to him, she says, so I guess that's something, anyway. Lord! Do you ever want children? Do you mind my asking?

I think I'd like children very much. I just haven't been able to find the right set-up yet.

I wish you'd come here more often, she says, straightening up and shading her eyes. I wish a lot of people we've known could be here with us.

I smile. Now that I am bent under the sun, I feel better, the strain of sleeplessness has left my head and passed into a comfortable bone-tiredness. I like the rush of blood in my face as I stoop lower to pull a weed. From my night awake I feel on the edge of my life. The pleasure is intense of sight renewed simply by another day; I could shout aloud with what my eyes are seeing. I tease: I thought you were already suffering from a surfeit.

There's a difference! With enough of the right people around I think I might be freer to be more the way I want to be.

You'll have to enlarge your garden, I say.

You're not taking me seriously.

Actually, I am. I might have said the same thing myself. I stoop again, and the suppleness of my back, the nimbleness of my bony brown plucking fingers, my filthy toes gripping the dirt astound me with their exultant mortality.

THE PEA PODS are forming, and the spinach sends up an occasional spike of blossom. Lemon lilies and poppies bloom; an iris clump stands with moist collapsed flowers beside the gazebo, patterned inside with filtered light, littered now with the Sunday paper and the crumbs of our breakfast. Anna is picking clover at the edge of the grass, where the field takes over. Todd and I are in charge. He straddles a tree limb above me, tying a rope for a new swing. All right, there, try it, Sylvie. Two inches lower, I call up, helping Sylvie down.

Get on again, Sylvie, says Todd. Can you do it by yourself?

I want a turn, calls Anna. She comes running up and flings herself on Todd as he climbs down the tree. Take me on your back! She stuffs clover down his shirt and presses her hands over his eyes.

Sylvie hangs from his knees. Throw me around and around, she shrieks.

Don't you want to swing? I ask, but no one hears. Todd is blinded. He pulls them across the lawn, roaring like a monster.

I am the first to hear the screams. They have nothing to do with play. Someone is hurt. Peter. I run up to the terrace and around the corner of the house, slipping on the grass of the hill under the silver olive tree. He lies beneath his tricycle on the gravel, bloody on the elbow, inconsolable.

I carry him in through the cool front hall, rarely used, across carpet, past pictures and doors opening onto rooms with chairs, lamps, downstairs to the kitchen. I am thinking that I am simply making myself strong enough to contain his writhing. My ears don't care about the cries. I am thinking simply of running water, of blood diluted and grit washed away. I am more durable than I know. I am holding Melanie's child, and he is a stranger. Some day he will have legs like Todd's, the same thighs, and I will see him stride across a room to shake my hand, perhaps to kiss me, and I will be known as an old friend, from the very early days.

MELANIE HAS shed her shorts and shirt and thrown them in a corner of her bedroom. Now she comes in wearing a white halter dress that doesn't quite hide the dirt on her ankles. We are drinking iced wine and soda, companionably. Melanie and I have weeded all the flower beds. We have assembled salads and arranged platters of cheese and sliced meats for the party. I have scooped out too many melon balls to count.

All right? she asks. She holds her hair on the top of her head.

Jewelry, I say.

She rummages and finds an antique brooch of gold with turquoise beads that she clamps into the cotton between her breasts.

That will do, I say. Are you going to wash your feet?

Todd comes to lounge in the doorway. He has been swimming with the children.

Where is everyone? asks Melanie.

Eating watermelon outside, Todd answers.

I look at Todd, looking at Melanie. I look at Todd and think of Melanie coming towards him in a white halter dress.

Are the kids eating my melon balls? I ask.

No, they're not eating your melon balls, says Todd. He grins at me, and I am Todd, straddling a tree, tying a rope and looking out at the river and down at my three-year-old daughter and at a friend I like so much I don't even bother to entertain her. That friend is myself.

I settle deeper into the chair, enjoying the cold wine and the look of my own sun-burnt legs and dusty feet, enjoying this marriage of friends. We have been working in the sun so long that we talk with a burned-out, pleasant incoherence. Today my mind has emptied out, filled up. I told Melanie about the winter, about Michael, and suddenly she began to laugh, and then I laughed. Love: I still have my heart to use: I could lie with Melanie and Todd in this walnut bed inherited from his parents and laugh about love until there is no difference between us.

THE EVENING carries us along. We bathe, but the water cannot wash away the feel of sun. We let the children stick melon balls on their fingers and eat them off one by one. Todd is catching the first of the fireflies when the guests begin to arrive. The feast is simple, but as I lean back on the grass beside a thin man who looks like Zola in Manet's painting, I wonder when bread spread with butter has tasted so good. Speech seems unimportant beside this food. I think of telling my companion how much I am enjoying the pure sight of him, but the words are swallowed along with the last bite of this extraordinary bread and butter. We talk of mulberry trees. I see Melanie weaving among the guests in her white dress. We are talking of trees that attract the birds. My new friend says the mulberries should be ripe soon; he says when he was a child they used to spread old sheets under the trees and shake down ripe berries; he says their juice stains the teeth and hands a reddish blue. I see Melanie and Todd, the children, myself, these few amiable guests shaking down a mulberry tree and crouching around a sheet spotted with reddish blue stains. Have I ever eaten mulberries? Perhaps once as a child: I seem to remember the house of a friend, a side yard, a driveway of black cinders. Someone laughs from the gazebo, and a moment later the human sound is caught up in the whistle of the train passing below.

The night sweeps us along. We begin to become aware of the full moon. Are you having a good time? whispers Melanie. I have worried this week, she says, that maybe it wasn't worth your while to come all this way, we do so little, we're so dull here in this backwater.

We are standing beside a lounge chair where Anna, all legs and cradling arms, has been overtaken by sleep. What can I give to Melanie? Tonight my sight is perfectly clear; I have countless images to give away. I tell her that the fireflies, again ascending in a mating ritual from the field of clover between here and Martin Burdock's cottage, look to me like a million sparks under water, slower than fire, fluid, phosphorescent.

It's a good thing we looked them up in the encyclopedia, says Melanie, now we know the facts of life.

Todd is organizing an expedition. Roll up your trousers, hold up your dresses, he says, we're going to the point, who's going to the point?

Take Anna to bed first, says Melanie, she'll get chilled with the dew.

I see Todd carrying Anna past a window upstairs. On his way back he passes through the lighted living room to turn up the music—Vivaldi: an expanse of vertical sound that I feel in my spine. I think how all week the bones of my body have extended themselves into a garden hoe. Now I feel myself straightening up, sending up liquid sparks of sensation.

My eyes grow used to the night away from the terrace. We pass single file behind Todd through wet grass. The legs of the man ahead of me are white, with tight knots of muscle at their calves. Melanie has tied her dress around her hips, her bare arms free to pass along the tops of grasses. I try it and come away damp.

We leave the music behind and walk through waves of moonlight. Then the grass becomes thinner, rocks appear. We are walking on uneven, spongy ground, climbing higher than the trees growing in the shadow of the bluff below. Finally we are on a jut of land above the river, open to the sky, and we disperse ourselves to rest. The moon is magical.

Indians are buried here, says Todd's voice.

THE AIRPORT wind sock erratically fills, swivels, sags against a heavy sky. Peter and Sylvie beg for bubblegum from the clouded glass of a machine. Anna, too, hangs around, looking at the artificially colored balls, her legs twisted, knobby at the knees.

Oh, all right, says Melanie, opening her purse, I suppose it won't kill you.

Todd, in a business suit, paces the waiting room. He stops occasionally to look at the same headlines on the newspaper stand.

Melanie's hair is held up loosely with a barrette. She wears a raincoat over her bluejeans and smokes a rare cigarette.

What's the cigarette for? asks Todd on one of his turns.

Melanie gestures to the metal ashtray stand beside her. I'm responding to my environment, she says.

My plane comes in. We see it land, turn on the minimal runway and then taxi to the cyclone fence. A few people wait outside in billowing clothes.

Todd pries Peter and Sylvie from the window and we go out to the gate. Speaking loudly against the dusty wind, tasting bits of earth with our words, we seem unable to keep our minds upon this leave-taking. The children run in circles, veering with the gusts. Our good-byes are ordinary and quickly blown away. What I see finally are faces, set against a mesh of fence, a magnitude of sky and ploughed fields—ancient prairie: I am reminded of how far inland I have come.

The President of the
Argentine

JOHN CHEEVER

JOHN CHEEVER lives in Ossining, New York. Among his books are
The Wapshot Chronicle, *The Wapshot Scandal* and *Bullet Park*.

C OLDNESS FALLS from the air, she thought, as she carried
    the white roses up the stairs to the paneled library.
That, or: How like sandpipers were the children on the beach,
she thought, as she stood by the rusty screen door of their rented
house on Nantucket. Zap. Blam. Pow. Here endeth my stab at
yesterday's fiction. No one's been reading it for forty years. It
went out with easel painting, and by easel painting one means
the sort of painting that used to be displayed on easels. Two cu-
rates playing checkers by a cockatoo's roost. Painting has cast
off its frames, and yet one deeply misses these massive and
golden celebrations—fruit and angels—for their element of ultimate risk. By framing a painting the artist, of course, declared it

to be a distillate of his deepest feelings about love and death. By junking the frame he destroyed the risk of a declaration. He may, as he will claim, have opened doors, porticos, gates, and mountain passes onto an unframed infinity of comprehension; or he may merely have displayed his abysmal lack of vitality. The woman climbing the stairs with her white roses is in a sense a frame, a declaration, and my account of putting a hat on a statue is frameless and may indeed not deserve a frame at all.

The statue of Leif Erikson was wearing a necktie that day when I started to walk down Commonwealth Avenue from Kenmore Square to the Boston Public Garden. The statue's tie was a foulard, frayed and stained. It was a cold afternoon but I carried my vicuña over my arm because my father had taught me never to wear a coat unless it was absolutely necessary. If I wore a coat I might be mistaken for an Irishman. I think my knowledge of Boston to be comprehensive and vast but framed entirely in the language of a farewell. I claim to know the cheapness of good-byes—that boyish shrug sent up as a lure for some lover whose face I have never seen although I have seen and tasted everything else. I am not a Bostonian but my provincial credentials will get me over the border. I have no true nostalgia for the city because I remember the aristocracy in my youth as being tragic and cranky. Old C. F. Adams was still challenging anyone— anyone at all—to a sailboat race and Hester Pickman was translating Rilke, but I can remember Jack Wheelwright tossing the sandwiches for tea onto the fire because they were unsuitable. The maid cried. She was a pretty Irish girl. The painting over the mantle was a Tintoretto and Jack had been talking about Henry Adams, his favorite uncle, but when I walked home the night was dark and cold and I, having already read Proust, could recall nothing in his accounts of the fall of Paris that seemed to me so horrible as the smoking sandwiches and the weeping maid. My credentials seem to pass; indeed they take some true knowledge of the situation in order to be assessed. "Oh, do sit down," Mother exclaimed, "do sit down and let me tell you about the funeral of Phillips Brooks! On the day of his funeral there were *trumpets* in Copley Square. Oh so many *trumpets!* I don't remember the time of year but it seems to me that it was cold and brilliant although of course that may have been the loud music of the *trumpets*. Phillips Brooks was a big man, you know. He was a very big man. He used to go right down to the South End and drink beer with strange Irishmen! He was not the sort of skinny clergyman who drank sherry. And speaking of sherry, did I tell you about your father and the sherry last Thursday?"

I KNEW THE STORY although she counted so on innuendo that one would have had to know the facts in advance to understand what she was talking about. My father was a celebrated drinking companion. He had drunk Robert Ingersoll and James O'Neil under the table at the old Adams House when Frank Locke ran the bar. The story mother was about to hint at had taken place on Thursday morning. This was in the old house on the South Shore. It was eleven. Father wanted a drink. It was Thursday and S. S. Pierce would deliver his potables that afternoon but the delivery wouldn't be until after three. The sherry decanter on the sideboard was full. He unstopped the decanter and drank the sherry. Then, as a precaution—merely a precaution—he pissed the decanter full. The color was exactly right. Everything in the room was as he had found it except that the fireplace was smoking. He gave the logs a poke and, with his spirits greatly renewed, he went upstairs to read the Shakespeare sonnets to his cat as he so often did. Enter the rector, then. Enter Mother, taking off her apron. "Oh, do sit down, Father Frisbee," she said, "do sit down and join me in a glass of sherry and a biscuit." So the poor man of God, sitting in a Windsor chair with half its spokes broken, coughing in the smoke of a fireplace that wouldn't draw, ate moldy pilot crackers and sipped piss. No wonder none of us ever wanted to go to Harvard.

So I banged down Commonwealth Avenue in the cold. The statue of Wm. Lloyd Garrison was wearing a scarf. Statues in parks, I've always thought, have a therapeutic effect on one's posture. Walking among gods and heroes one always keeps one's head up. I saw two women walking dogs. One of the dogs was a Labrador, a line I've bred, but when I whistled to the dog and he pulled at his leash, the woman—a good-looking woman—pulled him in the other direction and hurried off to Beacon Street. She seemed in flight and I was hurt. A black man in a sleeping bag lay on a bench saying: "I din' do nothing wrong. I din' do nothing wrong." There were two couples hitchhiking on the avenue. They were ragged and looked dirty. I thought that I had never seen hitch-hikers in a city before, not ever in a city that counted so for its strength upon deeply rooted, concentric provincialism. Ahead of me I could see the statue of the President of the Argentine. The statue is vulgar and bulky and what in the world was he doing on Commonwealth Avenue? I decided to put my hat on his head. Why should I, a grown man, put a hat on a statue? Men have been putting hats on statues since the beginnings of time. My father read Shakespeare to the cat, my life is impetuous and unorthodox, and I cannot distinguish persiflage from profundity, which may be my undoing. There was a faded ribbon and a handful of wax flowers on the President's pedestal. I decided to make my ascent by his cosmic and Rodinesque tail-coat.

My hat was a Locke hat. My coat is a very, very rare vicuña, left to me by my fourth father-in-law, a Des Moines haber-dasher. My coat is thirty-five years old but I have discovered that there are only three clubs left in the world where the age of my coat is respected. Only that afternoon, when I threw it over an empty barstool in the Ritz, the man on the next stool fingered the material and I was pleased to think he admired the age, ra-diance, and beauty of the vicuña, but what he was admiring, it seems, were the numerous darns. This put him, in my eyes, into the lower classes and presented me, in his esteem, as a straight thrift-shop type; secondhand rose. I put my folded vicuña on the pedestal and started my ascent. The President is difficult to climb. I would sooner write about my mountain-climbing ex-periences—coldness, indeed, I thought, falls from the summit of the mountain—but that would be some other afternoon. I was struggling up the bronze surface when a man said: *"Ciao, bello."*

He was a good-looking young man who wore a serge middy blouse with three crimson chevrons sewn to the sleeve. No navy in the world, I knew, had ever issued such a costume, and I guessed he had mostly seen the ocean from the summit of some rollercoaster. *"Desiderai tu un'amico?"* he asked.

"You've got a terrible accent," I said. "Where did you learn Italian? Bergamo? Someplace like that?"

"From a friend," he said.

"Break it up," shouted a policeman. "You boys break it up." He came running down the walk from a cruise car that was parked on Exeter Street. "Break it up, break it up or I'll throw you both in the lockup. You spoil everything."

THE MAN in the middy blouse headed north, and the policeman's anger seemed so genuine and so despairing that I wanted to explain my purpose but I couldn't do this without sacrificing any chance to be taken seriously. "I'm very old," I said. "I'm really terribly old and I insist upon the prerogatives and eccentricities of my time of life. I can remember when there was an elevated train on Atlantic Avenue. I can remember the Boston Police strike! I can remember when every village, homestead, hill, and pasture in this great land was dominated by a tree called The Elm. There were the English Elms, the Portuguese Elms, the Wineglass and the Penumbra Elms. They were shaped like fountains, columns, and explosions of grace. They were both lachrymose and manly. They were everywhere and now there are none."

"Common's full of elms," he said.

"All right," I said, "then Chestnuts. My father told me he could remember when every hill in New England was crowned with the noble, native Chestnut. In the autumn their leaves turned a deep, rich brown and the nuts they bore were delicious. I've never seen one of these beautiful trees. Not one! My generation was left with the Chestnut Hill Country Club, the Chestnut Grove Tearoom, and quite a few undistinguished streets called Chestnut."

"Please go away," he said. "You spoil everything. Everything."

I went away. I went up to the Exeter Street Theatre and saw a few reels of a Bergman film in which a woman mutilated herself with broken glass. I do not choose to describe the scene but I couldn't anyhow because I shut my eyes. Then I returned to Commonwealth Avenue, determined to put my hat on the President. During my absence the light had changed. The light in Boston, on a good day, I've always thought, has the incandescence of a sea light. Only the alchemy of sea air could have turned the statue of George Washington into the fairest ver-

digris. So in this fading sea light I returned to the President of
the Argentine. A young girl was sitting on a bench near the
statue and I sat down beside her. "May I?" I asked.

"Certainly," she said.

"What's your name?"

"Pixie," she said. "That's what they call me. My name is Alice-
Mae."

She had marvelous legs and breasts. I don't mean at all that
they conformed to any measured beauty but that there was some
extraordinary congruence between their proportions and one's
desires. The legs were not showgirl legs, they had nothing thrilling, lengthy, or brilliant about them. Their gleam and their
shape were modest and youthful.

"Do you live around here?" I asked.

"I live in a dormitory," she said. "We're not allowed to have
men visitors."

"What's your university?"

"It's not a university. It's really a college. They call it an acad-
emy. It's where my parents wanted me to go."

"What does your father do?"

"He's a funeral director," she said.

Then I knew that she was a student at the embalming school
in Kenmore Square. This had happened to me once before. I
picked up a very good-looking girl in a hamburger place called
The Fatted Calf. At first she said she was studying anatomy but
then she came clean, or clean enough to say that her task, her
study and vocation, was to beautify death, to make death com-
prehensible to the cruelly bereaved.

"What do you study?" I asked.

"Well, we don't have regular courses," she said. "I mean we
don't study history or arithmetic or things like that."

"You are learning," I asked, "how to beautify death?"

"Oh yes, yes," she exclaimed. "However did you know?"

And so we will end as the movies do when, having exhausted
the kiss, the walk-off, the reconciliation, and the boundlessness of
faith, hope, and charity, they resort to a downward or falling
crawl title giving the facts in the case—usually to the fading
music of police sirens. The girl's real name is Alice-Mae Plumber
and she has flunked out of embalming school and is afraid to tell

her parents. The man in the middy blouse is named Lemuel Howe and he will be arrested three days later for possession of dangerous drugs and sentenced to five years in the Suffolk County Jail. The man who wanted to put his hat on the statue of the President is I.

MAGAZINES CONSULTED

American Review
Bantam Books, 666 Fifth Avenue, New York, N.Y. 10019

Antaeus
Ecco Press—1 West 30th Street, New York, N.Y. 10001

Antioch Review
P. O. Box 148, Yellow Springs, Ohio 45387

Aphra
Box 3551, Springtown, Pa. 18081

Applachian Journal
Box 536, Appalachian State University, Boone, N.C. 28607

Ararat
Armenian General Benevolent Union of America, 628 Second Avenue, New York, N.Y. 10016

Arizona Quarterly
University of Arizona, Tucson, Ariz. 85721

Ascent
English Department, University of Illinois, Urbana, Ill. 61801

Aspen Leaves
Box 3185, Aspen, Colo. 81611

Atlantic Monthly
    8 Arlington Street, Boston, Mass. 02116

Aura
    Box 348, NBSB, University Station, Birmingham, Ala. 35294

California Quarterly
    100 Sproul Hall, University of California, Davis, Calif. 95616

Canadian Fiction Magazine
    P. O. Box 46422, Station G, Vancouver, B.C., Canada V6R
    4G7

Carleton Miscellany
    Carleton College, Northfield, Minn. 55057

Carolina Quarterly
    Box 1117, Chapel Hill, N.C. 27515

The Chariton Review
    Division of Language & Literature, Northeast Missouri State
    University, Kirksville, Mo. 63501

Christopher Street
    60 West 13th Street, New York, N.Y. 10011

Colorado Quarterly
    Hellums 118, University of Colorado, Boulder, Colo. 80304

The Colorado State Review
    360 Liberal Arts, Colorado State University, Fort Collins,
    Colo. 80521

Confrontation
    English Department, Brooklyn Center of Long Island Uni-
    versity, Brooklyn, N.Y. 11201

Cosmopolitan
    224 West 57th Street, New York, N.Y. 10019

Cutbank
    c/o English Dept., University of Montana, Missoula, Mont.
    59801

December
    P. O. Box 274, Western Springs, Ill. 60558

The Denver Quarterly
Dept. of English, University of Denver, Denver, Colo. 80210

Descant
Dept. of English, TCU Station, Fort Worth, Tex. 76129

Epoch
159 Goldwyn Smith Hall, Cornell University, Ithaca, N.Y. 14850

Esquire
488 Madison Avenue, New York, N.Y. 10022

The Falcon
Mansfield State College, Mansfield, Pa. 16933

Fantasy and Science Fiction
Box 56, Cornwall, Conn. 06753

The Fault
41186 Alice Avenue, Fremont, Calif. 94538

Fiction
c/o Dept. of English, The City College of New York, N.Y. 10031

Fiction International
Dept. of English, St. Lawrence University, Canton, N.Y. 13617

The Fiddlehead
Dept. of English, University of New Brunswick, Fredericton, N.B., Canada

The Fisherman's Angle
St. John Fisher College, Rochester, N.Y. 14618

Forum
Ball State University, Muncie, Ind. 47306

Four Quarters
La Salle College, Philadelphia, Pa. 19141

Gay Literature
Daniel Curzon, English Dept., State University of California, Fresno, Calif. 93740

Georgia Review
 University of Georgia, Athens, Ga. 30601

Graffiti
 Box 418, Lenoir Rhyne College, Hickory, N.C. 28601

The Great Lakes Review
 Northeastern Illinois University, Chicago, Ill. 60625

Green River Review
 Box 56, University Center, Mich. 48710

The Greensboro Review
 University of North Carolina, Greensboro, N.C. 27412

Harper's Magazine
 2 Park Avenue, New York, N.Y. 10016

Hawaii Review
 Hemenway Hall, University of Hawaii, Honolulu, Haw. 96822

Hudson Review
 65 East 55th Street, New York, N.Y. 10022

Iowa Review
 EPB 453, University of Iowa, Iowa City, Iowa 52240

Kansas Quarterly
 Dept. of English, Kansas State University, Manhattan, Kan. 66502

Ladies' Home Journal
 641 Lexington Avenue, New York, N.Y. 10022

The Literary Review
 Fairleigh Dickinson University, Teaneck, N.J. 07666

The Little Magazine
 P. O. Box 207, Cathedral Station, New York, N.Y. 10025

Lotus
 Department of English, Ohio University, Athens, Ohio 45701

Mademoiselle
    350 Madison Avenue, New York, N.Y. 10017

Malahat Review
    University of Victoria, Victoria, B.C., Canada

The Massachusetts Review
    University of Massachusetts, Amherst, Mass. 01003

McCall's
    230 Park Avenue, New York, N.Y. 10017

The Mediterranean Review
    Orient, N.Y. 11957

Michigan Quarterly Review
    3032 Rackham Bldg., The University of Michigan, Ann Arbor, Mich. 48104

Midstream
    515 Park Avenue, New York, N.Y. 10022

Moment
    55 Chapel Street, Newton, Mass. 02160

Mother Jones
    607 Market Street, San Francisco, Calif. 94105

The Nantucket Review
    P.O. Box 1444, Nantucket, Mass. 02554

The National Jewish Monthly
    1640 Rhode Island Avenue, N.W., Washington, D.C. 20036

New Directions
    333 Sixth Avenue, New York, N.Y. 10014

New Letters
    University of Missouri–Kansas City, Kansas City, Mo. 64110

The New Renaissance
    9 Heath Road, Arlington, Mass. 02174

The New Yorker
    25 West 43rd Street, New York, N.Y. 10036

The North American Review
University of Northern Iowa, 1222 West 27th Street, Cedar
Falls, Iowa 50613

Northwest Review
129 French Hall, University of Oregon, Eugene, Ore. 97403

The Ohio Journal
164 West 17th Avenue, Columbus, Ohio 43210

Ohio Review
Ellis Hall, Ohio University, Athens, Ohio 45701

The Ontario Review
6000 Riverside Drive East, Windsor, Ont., Canada N8S 1B6

Paranthèse
59 East 73rd Street, New York, N.Y. 10021

The Paris Review
45-39–171st Place, Flushing, N.Y. 11358

Partisan Review
Rutgers University, New Brunswick, N.J. 08903

Perspective
Washington University, St. Louis, Mo. 63130

Phylon
223 Chestnut Street, S.W., Atlanta, Ga. 30314

Playboy
919 North Michigan Avenue, Chicago, Ill. 60611

Ploughshares
Box 529, Cambridge, Mass. 02139

Prairie Schooner
Andrews Hall, University of Nebraska, Lincoln, Nebr. 68508

Prism International
Dept. of Creative Writing, University of British Columbia,
Vancouver 8, B.C., Canada

Quarterly Review of Literature
26 Haslet Avenue, Princeton, N.J. 08540

Quartet
1119 Neal Pickett Drive, College Station, Tex. 77840

Redbook
230 Park Avenue, New York, N.Y. 10017

The Remington Review
505 Westfield Avenue, Elizabeth, N.J. 07208

Revista/Review Interamericana
305 Cesar Romon (altos), Hato Rey, Puerto Rico 00919

Rolling Stone
625 Third Street, San Francisco, Calif. 94107

Seneca Review
Box 115, Hobart & William Smith Colleges, Geneva, N.Y. 14456

Sequoia
Storke Student Publications Bldg., Stanford, Calif. 94305

The Sewanee Review
University of the South, Sewanee, Tenn. 37375

Shenandoah
Box 722, Lexington, Va. 24450

The Smith
5 Beekman Street, New York, N.Y. 10038

The South Carolina Review
Dept. of English, Clemson University, Clemson, S.C. 29631

The South Dakota Review
Box 111, University Exchange, Vermillion, S.D. 57069

Southern Humanities Review
Auburn University, Auburn, Ala. 36820

Southern Review
Drawer D, University Station, Baton Rouge, La. 70803

Southwest Review
Southern Methodist University Press, Dallas, Tex. 75222

StoryQuarterly
720 Central Avenue, Highland Park, Ill. 60035

Sun & Moon
4330 Hartwick Road, #418, College Park, Md. 20740

The Tamarack Review
Box 159, Postal Station K, Toronto, Ont., Canada M4P 2G5

Transatlantic Review
Box 3348, Grand Central P.O., New York, N.Y. 10017

Tri-Quarterly
University Hall 101, Northwestern University, Evanston, Ill. 60201

Twigs
Pikeville College, Pikeville, Ky. 41501

U. S. Catholic
221 West Madison Street, Chicago, Ill. 60606

Vagabond
P. O. Box 879, Ellensburg, Wash. 98926

The Virginia Quarterly Review
University of Virginia, 1 West Range, Charlottesville, Va. 22903

Vogue
350 Madison Avenue, New York, N.Y. 10017

Washington Review of the Arts
404 Tenth Street, S.E., Washington, D.C. 20003

West Coast Review
Simon Fraser University, Vancouver, B.C., Canada

Western Humanities Review
Bldg. 41, University of Utah, Salt Lake City, Utah 84112

Wind
RFD Route 1, Box 810, Pikeville, Ky. 41501

Woman's Day
515 Broadway, New York, N.Y. 10036

Works
    A.M.S., 56 East 13th Street, New York, N.Y. 10003

Yale Review
    250 Church Street, New Haven, Conn. 06520

Yankee
    Dublin, N.H. 03444